Strath

STRATH

BESS ROSS

CANONGATE

First published in Great Britain
in 1997 by Canongate Books Ltd,
14 High Street, Edinburgh EHI ITE

Copyright © Bess Ross, 1997

The moral rights of the author have been asserted

The publishers gratefully acknowledge subsidy
from the Scottish Arts Council towards
the publication of this volume

British Library Cataloguing-in-Publication Data
A catalogue record for this book is available on
request from the British Library

ISBN 0 86241 668 X

Typeset by Palimpsest Book Production Limited,
Polmont, Stirlingshire
Printed and bound in Finland by WSOY

For Dicky

Chapter One

Mairead Beaton was the wrong shape for a woman. Tall and rawboned, she appeared to have little to commend her physically. Her chest was flat, her hands and her feet large and coarsened by the life she lived. Her feet she was very conscious of. When in company of any kind she could push her hands below her apron, but there was nowhere for her to hide her feet. Mairead was not good with people and although some did come to her for help, she never grew accustomed to these interruptions. Confronted with visitors she'd dip her head, even when being addressed, fold her hands across her belly, beneath her apron, and try to make her feet disappear below the hem of her frock. She'd press her knees together and turn her toes inwards, as if by doing this she could somehow make herself smaller, neater. She had no near neighbours, her house was built away from the village, but she lived well enough within the boundaries she set for herself. They were the only security she knew.

At one time there had been her father, her mother, brothers and a sister, but now there was only Mairead, living among the animals she gathered about her. Broken birds, mangled cats and hares, all looking to her to mend them.

She'd talk to the wild things and they understood her words, for her words were more than words. Her voice was their home and they were healed as much by its sound as by her hands. So, although she was uneasy with her own kind, afraid even, there was none of this with the animals. With them she was free just to be and they were glad enough to receive the good that was in her. They saw what the world didn't and were grateful. In her words they heard the water running over the stones in the burn, they heard the whisper of the wind in the trees. And they looked into eyes as clear and as deep and as brown as the pool which the deer drank from.

That day in the wood Mairead thought that her heart would burst from her chest. The sound of it silenced the birds in the branches as she hacked at the roots of the wintergreen plant. On her knees she gathered, one-handed. Her apron was a bag. Into it she scooped what she dug from the earth, the other hand catching together the bottom corners. Up through the soles of her bare feet the earth's pulse beat, joining her own so that they became one. Fused together, she was of the earth more than from it. And the earth was her. No separation. By concentrating very hard on what she was doing she tried to squeeze the Minister from her mind but she could not. His image kept breaking in on her. She'd been gathering at the edge of the wood and had just stood up to move deeper in. Her eyes were on no place in particular. They saw everything, yet nothing, when a black moving shape cut across her vision making her forget to breathe. All she could do was stand there. She was useless, she had no sense. Her arms fell to her sides, her hands fell slack and open. The roots were at her feet. She tried to make her eyes, her lungs, work but she could not. It was the Minister. He was on his travels, taking the short-cut through the trees to the far country. The Minister. As thin and as dry as old paper. As white as bog-cotton. His face as white as his hair. But to herself this huge black force which haunted her whether she was sleeping or awake.

Gradually her breath came back, she felt her body relax. Her ears were picking up on sound. But she was disordered, disarranged. Although about half a mile lay between her and the Minister, her mind could make no sense of this. Her mind spread fear through her, making her blunder blindly through the trees. Her hands became her eyes. Outstretched, they led her on. The fear came from her mouth in a single broken note. The Minister was after her. Her breath was turning on her, it was strangling her. Like an animal she opened her throat and cried for air. She dropped to the ground again and began her hacking. She had no idea where she was, she had no idea what she was doing. Behind the thick knots of her hair the fear spilled from her eyes and trickled down her face. She dug up whatever her hand grabbed. The earth was a river and she was adrift on it.

She did not know a time when she did not have the fear, or if she did, it was so long ago that she had forgotten. It was a part of her that had always been. Like her face, there. Like her hands, like her feet, there. She trailed it about with her like an old torn sack. She didn't question its place in her. If she did, again she couldn't remember. Some days it would come on her what a wonderful place it must be where there wasn't fear in it. But in what way wonderful she couldn't imagine. Her mind wouldn't take her that far. All it would tell her was that it would be different and the days would be different. But she couldn't imagine different either. She didn't know different. So after a while she'd give up thinking and let the old feeling reclaim her.

A long time ago, when she had been strong, when her feelings had been sure, she had tried to go back to the place where she had been first aware. But even then she could not find it. It would be as well to say that one day she realised that she could talk, could sing, could walk. There was no tracing it. And the passing of time did nothing to lessen its intensity and the effect it had on her. Although she was about twenty-seven years she still carried about with her the confused child she had been.

If she was going to mark the fear by anything she would mark it by her mother's death. She knew it had been there then and there was as good a place as any to stick the marker. It was a place she didn't want to stay in for long. Her mother's struggle to live and latterly to die was a painful thing for her to look on.

She couldn't remember leaving her father's and mother's land and crossing the water in a boat to come to the part of

Scotland the people called Strath. Sometimes her mother talked about the journey and her people. Her mother buried her other children on the way. Her father never talked about the journey, even when there was only himself and herself left. The river took her father, the cattle had toppled the boat. The beasts had swum for the bank, a man found them and came to tell her. Her father couldn't swim. She screamed at the man for a long time when he told her, she couldn't stop. She was wild for a long time because of her father. She went to the river to look for him but he wasn't there. Her mother had died the winter before. So now there was just herself. She'd lost a lot of herself in the space of that year. That was when she cut herself off from the people around her.

Thrown off-course by the unexpected appearance of the Minister, she thought again of her mother. Her hands slowed in their tearing and tugging. Sitting back on her heels she allowed her head to fall forward and clasped her hands across her belly.

The memories always started from the same place, her mother trying to crawl from the mattress. Determined that she would go to the new Minister's church with herself and her father. Her mother's face as grey as the peat ash that breathed on the fire. Her mother's hands, swollen lumps of wax, as they tried to put her brooch into her shawl to hold it. Her mother's eyes, dead before the rest of her, dull, flat and marbled as they raked her father's face. Her mother's hair, dead like her eyes, like her hands. Colourless like her eyes, white where it had been brown. Dead hands trying to hold dead hair, trying to coil it into a plait. Dead hair falling from dead hands. Her mother's head swathed in the white linen. Not her mother then, a stranger mother, linked to that later time. The light gone from her mother, the light gone from her father. Gone too long the stout-hearted mother matching her father stride for stride going to the church. The light gone from her father.

The Sabbaths passing and her mother becoming less. In the beginning struggling to be what she had been. Her mother's last winter. Nothing left in her then. Not able to crawl from the mattress. Herself and her father going off to the church, both empty without her. Her father's emptiness so wild, her own so sorrowful. She cried. The both of them heaping every rug and skin they could find on top of her mother to keep the cold from her. Twenty-nine years, two years more than Mairead now. And then the Minister.

She wrapped her arms about herself, holding herself as she let everything come. The Minister in the church, bawling to the roof about the people who weren't there. His face a shining red skull. His finger an old bent bit of branch aimed at her father about her mother. Bawling up to God to strike the wicked among them. She was rattling on her stool and crying into her father's scratchy sleeve. Her father wearing the wild wolf's face, flames in her father's eyes, his mouth was missing, teeth where his mouth had been. Her father's voice broken ice as it told her to rise from her stool, his hand on her, broken ice as it pulled her from the church, past the shadow people.

Outside her father's anger taking his words from him, taking every word from him on the long walk home. Her father's anger making him walk fast, making him walk away from her, closing up his ears to her crying.

The Minister. Up at the house before the Sabbath was done. Bawling down at her mother on the mattress on the floor. Her mother knowing nothing, her hand a claw at her breast as she tried to rise up for him, her face had passed through life to death, was wearing death's colour. The Minister. Making nothing of her mother, turning on her father and herself, words which were not theirs spewing from his lipless mouth. Herself terrified into immobility, standing like a rock, with as much coming from her. Not one word from her when he demanded the catechism. Her father bursting like the river, catching the Minister's coat and pushing him from the house, the Minister's dancing feet tangling in their black silver-buckled shoes with her father's boots. Hearing her father's voice outside the house shouting at the Minister. Hearing it forever. Did it come from his mouth, that mouth that was made for songs and loving?

And that was the end of it. They waited two whole weeks for the Minister or the Men to come. But they didn't come.

They never came. Herself and her father put her mother into the ground and heaped stones on top of her to stop the beasts getting at her. Her father spoke, but not to the Minister's God. He asked the spirits to watch over her mother. Then they sang to her mother an island song. The two of them sat beside the stones and with the wind and the rain sang to her the songs she told Mairead long years ago. Herself still going, still singing.

The thought of her mother receded and the Minister present resurfaced. As a child she would run from things which frightened her. The wild wind, the river when it was angry, even the burn when it was upset. She still ran from the wolf, kilted her skirts and raced like a hare. As a child she thought that she could fly from her fear. But she could not, no matter how quick she was. She merely carried it with her faster. Chasing the birds it was there, chasing the hares, helping to carry the peats home. One day at the peat cutting she felt it very sharp, she could hardly bear it, it was sharper than ever it had been. She cried with it. She took the fear to the Wise One who was loading his peats into a basket. The Wise One put her right. There was a wide crack in her foot's sole, her blood was going onto the ground. The Wise One told her to go and see the Old Wife. The Old Wife bound up her foot in moss and green leaves and in time her foot was mended and after that time the fear was never quite so sharp. Since then she often went to the Old Wife's.

As she grew the thought of the Minister grew with her. In the harvest field he was there. Running along the bank of the burn with the primroses he was there. At the pool he was there. And later at the river.

She didn't know what to do, which way to move. Was he still out there, waiting? Had he moved away or had he moved in closer to her? She scooped her day's work into her apron, caught together its bottom corners. Once upright, she stood a while to listen. Her ears were tuned to the earth and what lived on it. They strained for any strange noise, her nose sniffed for any strange scent. Scenting nothing alarming, she waded through the undergrowth to the last band of trees. From behind one she lengthened her neck and poked her head forward. Her eyes swept the familiar country ahead of her. There was nothing that was different out there. Every bush, every hill, every rock was where it should have been. They all wore their familiar colours. Nothing had moved or changed its shape or multiplied. And there was no sign of any human. Had she made him up? She smacked her forehead with the heel of her hand. She knew she hadn't.

She waited no longer. She threw her head back and like a galloping horse she ran. Her legs were long so her strides were long. Her feet felt nothing as she raced. She moved for cover. From the trees to the green whins, from the shelter of the whins to the back of a rock, one hand bunching her apron, the other flapping by her side, her mother's brooch bouncing up and down like her breasts. Behind the rock she threw herself onto her back. Her breath came from her in lumps. She tried listening but now her breath was deafening her. Up on her feet again. A final burst and her house was lying before her. A quick look over her shoulder and still holding her apron, she plunged through its low doorway.

A jumble of turf and stones, Mairead's house gripped the side of the hill like a limpet gripping a rock. And neither was it unlimpetlike in appearance. Not tall enough for Mairead to stand upright in, bracken, heather and more turf, supported by branches, shaped its ill-balanced roof. It had no chimney and the smoke from the fire (a circle of stones in the centre of the floor) escaped by whatever means it could: through a hole in the roof, through holes in the walls. The soot covered whoever was inside. Grown people and big animals were layered in it, their eyes screaming from it, their hair, their skin, their clothes baked in it, reeking of its smell. Babies, crawling children and the small animals escaped it, coming as they did below the soot's level. The only daylight in the house came in through the door, when the doorway wasn't choked with branches and broom. It floated above and around the piles of animal dung which clarted the floor. Some light did its best to come in through the hole in the roof, fighting its way past the smoke rushing out.

In front of the fire Mairead let go of her apron, allowing what she had gathered to tumble on to the floor. A large black dog-shaped cat stood watching her. Water boiled into bubbles in a pot on the fire. She hooked the pot clear of the flames with a y-shaped bit of broken branch and lowered it to the floor, then went to the stack of peat piled just inside her door for a few peats. When she had put them on the fire she sank onto the large rectangular flat stone beside it and, hunching forward, lifted her skirt right up and spread her legs so that the fire could warm her. When she was warm enough, she scooped the pot back onto the fire and, picking up her plants one by one, dropped them into the water.

> Harder than rock
> Blacker than night
> Swift runs the river
> Life of life

Over and over she kept repeating the rhyme, her litany to the unknown. On her stone she rocked to its rhythm. The words came faster, she rocked faster to them. Stirring the pot, prodding the fire, chanting, rocking, no break in the words, the actions, the tempo. The big cat came and lay down beside her. His eyes were on the goose considering the contents of the water-jug. A smouldering piece of wood at last turned to ash in the fire, depositing its flaking remains in front of the cat. The cat opened his mouth wide and turned his eyes on Mairead. No sound came from him. Mairead stopped her rocking and poking and spoke to him.

'What now? What have you to tell me?'

The cat, his mouth now shut, continued to hold Mairead's eyes. Still no sounds from him, no purring, no miaowing.

'Yes, I know that,' she said. 'Between us we'll have to see to it.'

The cat squeezed his eyes shut at the sound of her. His face, with its curved mouth, looked as if it was smiling. Then he rose, easily, no stiffness about him, no muscle stretchings, one fluid movement, and walked around the fire and came back to where he started from. He did this three times, then he lay down in his place again.

'What you're saying is correct,' Mairead told him. 'Aren't you always?' and she reached out a long finger to stroke the cat's face. 'Chase that one from the water,' she told him, pointing her stick at the goose. 'Then come back to me. I'm needing to talk to you,' and she went back to her rocking and moaning.

The cat walked over to the goose and looked at it. Feeling in control he sat back on his haunches, bunched his neck and thrust his head forward, his eyes glued to it. He remained in that position for some minutes. And still the goose did not move. Then the cat lifted a heavy paw and swiped the goose across the head. Unflinchingly the goose took the blow. It knew the cat, it had lived long enough with its domineering ways. However brightly the twin green lamps in the cat's head burned, the goose didn't care. This time it put its head back and squawked loudly at the cat's face. For a few minutes both held their ground, their eyes locked on each other. Then something, known only to the goose, changed in the cat's expression. It sent the goose flying for the door, with wide wing flappings, making it reel like a drunken dancer, blowing flakes of white peat ash from the fire about Mairead's face and eyes as it scattered from what looked like turning nasty. The cat went back to Mairead, his rear end swaying with satisfaction, and lay down at her feet.

'I saw him,' she said. 'On my way to the wood.' The cat stretched his throat at the sounds she made. He rubbed his ball head against her bare ankle. Mairead's smile acknowledged the good feelings the cat's touch gave her. The cat closed his eyes and rolled his head along the length of her foot. His body grew slack, his limbs lay loose. 'You like that, now,' her voice poured down on him light, liquid, soothing. 'It's me that was the quick one, though. It'll be a sad day for you and me the day that one catches us.'

The soundless cat kept up his rubbing and rolling. Outwardly unchanged. But something in him spoke to her. It made her change her voice, made it quicken, become urgent. Sweet music turned to iced water. 'No killings,' she said. 'There'll be none of that now. Not while I'm still in it. Take that from me, now. I have spoken about it.'

Still no visible change in the cat. The change in Mairead, halting her in her stirrings, making her forget her rocking. 'I do feel safe with you, Master,' the words breaking. 'Believe that of me whatever else you'll believe on me. I'd never take another into this house before you.' A pleading tone now. 'Never. As you yourself say, you are the Master.'

The cat's head moved slowly along her foot.

Mairead jabbed fiercely at the boiling water with her stick.

'Do you remember when you came to me?' Her tone was easy again. The apprehension had left it. 'That was a long time ago. And you picked me for your own. The people came and said I would never be able to keep you with me. Who can keep what belongs to the wild? they said. But we knew, Master. We knew. We showed the same ones what wild is. Are they laughing at us now? Not that I hear.'

For a time no more passed between them. The smoke cast its dim net over the house and its occupiers, the water in the pot boiled up the roots with plopping sounds. The sick were quiet, grateful to the cat that in their sickness, for this night at least, they wouldn't have to face the goose. There was nothing ailing with the goose and his robust health threatened to crush them. A small squirrel trembled in his fur and put his hands over his eyes.

'Can you remember what you first said to me?' They heard her words for the cat. 'After I mended your poor leg?'

The cat paused in his rubbing once more and looked up into her broad flat face. What he saw there did not displease or discourage him. His head began to roll on her foot again. She opened her toes, spread them, and raked them the long length of his back. 'You wanted me, Master. From the start.'

The cat took her games for a while. He lay over onto his side so that her toes could get at his belly, twice warm now

with fire heat as well as body heat. When he'd had enough
he rolled his hard body clear of her, turned his back on her.

'You're tired. I know, you're tired.' Mairead sighed. 'Myself
is too.'

The cat lay away from her; a back paw pushed out and
kneaded the floor, making scratching marks in the packed
earth. 'I'll leave you to be,' she told him. 'You're not needing
those other ones about the place,' and she rose from her seat
and grabbed her long stick. 'Away with you.' She hobbled
through the mirk with her back bent, and chased what could
stand before her. 'This is Master's house.' Half-seen shapes
hurtled past her, making for the gap in the wall. The squirrel
took his hands from his eyes and tried to burrow beneath
the peats. 'You can come back in when it's morning,' her
tired, flat voice called through the door to the temporarily
dispossessed. Taking armfuls of broken branches and bundles
of whin bushes, which filled her house, she tried to block the
doorway, so that nothing could re-enter.

'I'm going to bed,' she said to the cat. He was back at the
fire, his belly now open to it. Using both hands to hold the
stick, she hooked the pot from the heat. 'If you go near to
that, you'll scald,' she told him and using her foot she nudged
the cat aside while she built up her fire with more peats and
peat dross, smoothing the peat dross down, caking it with her
hands so that the fire would sit and simmer until she rose in
the morning.

'I'm that tired,' she told the cat. 'I'm away to my bed,' and
her weary mouth could barely shape the words.

Although the day was still young enough, terror had taken its
toll on Mairead. She felt weak from it and at such times, only
her bed would do, just to put her head onto her pillow.

There was no pattern to her day. Mostly, though, she rose
with the sun and slept when the dark came or, like now, when
she was tired. She slept in the open when the weather was fine,
just rolled herself up in her blanket in the lea of a rock, in a
handy hollow or some place. Otherwise she used her house.
When something came to shake her she ran for the safety of

her house. She ate, if she had food, when she was hungry. Mostly she fed on what she found growing on the bushes and some of the trees. And her share of the village grain meant she had bread some of the time. For milk and butter and cheese she looked to her cows. But if her food ran out she went hungry like the rest of the people of Strath.

Under the skins which had once covered her mother and her father, lying on her mother's mattress, she made the words into the dark which would take her safely through the darker darkness of sleep and on into the morning. Her first words were whispered to the spirits of life, that they would watch over her and Master and all who depended on her, and all on whom she depended, and to keep them safe from harm. She felt better after saying these words, to say them brought some peace to her. Sometimes, she felt the spirits very near to her. At such times she didn't feel alone. She felt she could hold them close against her chest and sleep with them beside her. But the feeling didn't last, she couldn't hold on to it, it went from her. The fear too soon came back and took the feeling about the spirits from her. The fear made her say words to the Minister's God.

Chapter Two

After four days of incessant rain the day broke clear and clean. Colour came once more to the face of Strath. Across the Kyle the hills of Sutherland had put off their grey cloaks. Ben Kilibreck, Ben More, Ben Hope and Ben Stack danced in their frocks of purple and blue. Along the burn the purple heads of the Scottish primroses twirled with the purple-marked leaves of the pale butterwort, weaving a royal spread. Wild orchids and twinflowers roamed among the white heads of the bog-cotton. The yellow of the whins was everywhere, the green of the trees. A soft breeze, the first herald of summer played in the leaves of the oaks, the aspens, the pines and the tender birches. The sky was high and blue and far away. Colour was everywhere, in everything, scalding the eyes.

The Minister had left his house early, eager to catch the best of the good day. Already he had put many miles behind him but, with the sun climbing higher, the best part of his journey still lay before him. Having had nothing to eat or drink before he left home, he was by now hungry and very thirsty. His step slackened, it began to drag. Leaving the track he waded through the heather and made his way to the large round greyish white boulder. Gratefully, he slumped against it. His breathing was laboured. Beneath his hat's broad brim perspiration washed his brow. His face, normally pale, gleamed red from his exertions.

The Minister had come to Strath in 1638, after the changes in Scotland's Church which saw the beginning of the end of the English Church's influence in her pulpits. Although eleven years had passed since that time, he had never quite recovered from the shock he had received on his arrival. In his pride he had thought himself equal to whatever challenge God might send him. It was not long before he began to doubt this. Such a wild place. And remote. Worse than anything he could have imagined. And the people living in it, as fierce and untamed as their country. And that was to do them a kindness. Centuries of the previous Church seemed to have done little for them, had done nothing to teach them, to even begin to address their fears and their suspicions. Savage they were, degenerate in some cases, living among filth and squalor. Humans and animals living in the same house, lying sometimes in the same bed. And there were those who'd turn against their own as soon as against an enemy. To them ownership meant nothing. What belonged to a neighbour belonged to them, as of right. What they needed they took. They didn't look on their actions as right or wrong. They didn't know right from wrong and so the question was never asked.

He had learned too how a priesthood, with no competing religion, could do what it liked with the people. And what it liked was to keep them in ignorance. That way their Church could shape them to its way, could keep them fanatically loyal to that Church, but utterly deceived by it. And their clan chief? He gave them protection, they gave him their blind allegiance. To him, they were willing slaves and battle fodder. The Minister's heart ached for this poor Highlander, bred to confusion and chaos, still living in it.

He felt the rock's heat spreading through his clothes, warming his back and he was comforted. From its nest in the heather, he drew out a clay jar. Pulling out its stopper, he put the jar to his mouth, let the cool milk flow down his throat, tasted its sweetness. His throat worked on the milk. His swallow was long. Settling the jar between his knees, he bowed his head and said his thanks to God for the gift of the milk and for the person who had left it for him.

He hadn't been in Strath long when the people there had learnt of his trouble with his wife, and although they were afraid of him because they did not understand him, they understood need when they saw it. Their kindness surprised him and warmed him. At various places on his journeys he began to find jugs of milk, lumps of meat, chunks of cheese, jars of ale. He never knew who left these things. They simply appeared and, if his journey took him away for days, there was more waiting for him on the way back. When they had nothing to eat, he had nothing to eat. but when they had he had, and plenty. It was through these acts that the Minister came to know that there was another side to the people of Strath. It took time to get to know them. And time showed him a people childlike in their eagerness to learn the Scriptures, and in their willingness to understand them. He was not stupid enough, nor arrogant enough, to think that what the previous Church had spent centuries imbuing he could change right away. Nor maybe in his lifetime. But he could make a start. With God before him, and beside him, he'd yet turn the stinking place into something sweet. And that was his strength. His God and time and patience. He could also say that with a willingness to learn on his own part, he was beginning to gain a little insight into the soul of these people who, while smilingly embracing the teachings of their Church, still held fast to their old ways, their prejudices and their superstitions. These were still as strong as ever they'd been. That hadn't altered. But beneath the superstition there was something deeper. And he saw it. A soul, clinging for its life to something beyond itself, bigger than itself. They had no notion what this thing was. They did not even have a name for it. But they depended on it for their existence. They were frightened of it yet they were powerless to resist it. Their need was so great that they allowed themselves to be drawn towards it. And it was this, together with what the other Church had done, that the Minister had to work with. He had to probe a psyche beyond understanding.

In the beginning he had no help but he had been younger, fresher, so that although his burden had been heavy he had felt up to it and the walking did not tire him. The hardest part of his work had been in getting them to trust him. Why should they? He was not known among them, and he represented an alien class. Even his tongue was not theirs, but a form of it. And they had grown used to their Bishops. Now he had two readers who shared the work with him, both able men with firm speaking voices who were glad to undertake any of the journeying out into the wider and wilder country. But not this time. This time was the Minister's. He was away again to visit MacIver.

MacIver was a forester who worked the woods belonging to the Earl of Ross. His house was up at the northeastern edge of the wood that Strath people called the Blackwater Forest. For the Minister this meant a round trip of more than forty miles, as the threat from wild animals stopped him from cutting through the wood.

   This visit up to MacIver's was no new venture. The Minister had been trying for a long time to locate the man in the hope of bringing him to redemption. In previous times, when MacIver saw the Minister coming he had turned his back on him and had walked away. So the Minister was trying again today and with renewed hope. Something was telling him that this was the day that he was at last going to meet MacIver. The Minister rolled onto his knees in the heather and asked God to help him to find the correct words to say when he met with MacIver. He stayed there a long time, feeling the sun's heat on his shoulders, feeling peace settling inside him. Finally, his hands knuckling the ground, he manoeuvered himself back into his sitting position against the rock. He bowed his head again and closed his eyes, letting his sharp chin sink against his chest. His hands lay loosely, palms up in the heather. In the warm silence he slept. A swallow came down to look at him, resting for a while on the rock before flying in a wide arc. Some black beetles crawled about him and underneath him, busy at their work while he slept. The Minister dreamt of Arabella, his wife. In his dream she came to tempt him. In his dream she was warm with him, to him. She fed him the most delicious of foods from her own hands. Wild geese, salmon, the flesh of deer, all dripping with the sweetest juices his mind could make. She popped rowan and juniper berries into his mouth and into her own. And there was no end to the abundance. Plates heaped up to heaven. One minute he was devouring the delights of Arabella's table, the next Arabella herself lay spread before him, with her mouth and her hair tasting of the fruits of the earth, sweet with promise. In his dream his soul cried out and it was freed.

She danced before him, her hair a golden web spun to smother him, and her breasts drew him on. And he thought not of God. The devil called out to him and he followed. He felt no pain, there was none. Neither anguish nor sorrow nor sadness. Only her. Everywhere. Even yet.

While he slept the sky darkened. Clouds gathered and came in to cover the sun, cooling the rock and the earth. The breeze stiffened in the trees, calling him from his slumber. Reaching out for the jar he drank off the last of the milk before returning it to its nest. He looked up into the sky. Darkness was falling fast. With God's grace he'd yet make MacIver's before night. His hand tightening on the knob of his stick, his knuckles sharp through the thin skin, he was up on his feet. All trace of his dream had vanished at his waking.

As he ploughed on through the day it felt as if the miles were getting longer. Now the sky did not seem to be so far away. In its dourness it seemed nearer, as if it had lowered right down on him and wrapped around him. After every mile or so he stopped and asked God to keep him for the next stretch, and the next, asked that his legs might take him to where he was going. Once he reached MacIver's he'd be all right. Once there he could rest, maybe until morning. He walked on, into the half-light.

He heard MacIver a good time before he saw him. A sound came out from the trees, through the stillness of the evening, a sound which he recognised as the sharp crack of an axe on wood. The Minister stopped to listen, his ears picked up the axe's rhythm. He left the track and made for the trees. A further half hour's walk took him to a cleared spot. The trees had been cut and only their jagged stumps remained, torn wooden teeth sticking up from them. There was a house in the clearing and a broken barn. No smoke came from the house, nor the smell of anything burning. Near to it a man was stooped over one of the stumps, splitting wood. Lumps of tree lay all around him. Easily, like a knife going into flesh, the axe's head fell through the blocks. His was a one-armed action. First, by burying the axe's head in a log on the ground he'd hook it up onto the stump. Then he'd rip the head free of the log and raise his right arm. The arm's sinews tightened, its muscles bulged. The black hair which covered every visible part of him lay flattened against his skin with sweat. The axe clawed the air, as if for breath, before being embedded once again in the wood.

His wrist was strong and supple. By the most economical of movements he chopped around the block on the stump, round and round, decreasing the circle until only the centre of the tree, the tree in its beginning, remained. He let the axe fall on this part, slicing it in two before scooping the pieces onto the ground with the axe's head. Then he reached for the next block and started chopping again. All this without stopping to take a breath or to straighten up, working the axe, his right arm and the muscles across his back.

MacIver was a bear of a man, his back was wide. He looked to be about as strong as the trees he worked and he was a good way as tall. It was said that one of the Bishops was MacIver's father. That would likely be true enough, the Bishops weren't slow to spread their seed. It was also said that he would lie with anything. That too would likely be true. It was the way of the people of the place.

The Minister moved in closer to MacIver, one arm lifted across his face to shield him from the twin explosions of the axe and the flying wood. The big arm kept on swinging and chopping, the axe whirring and birling through the air before it smashed through the blocks.

The Minister moved from the spot where he stood and edged around to MacIver's right side, being careful to keep clear of any danger. Still no sign of recognition. He moved around to the front and stood there, facing him, shaking on the end of his stick. When he was ready, MacIver looked up from the block. Gradually the swinging arm slowed until with a final swing he anchored the axe's head in the stump's belly. Wiping the sweat from his eyes with the back of his hand, he looked straight at the Minister.

The Minister looked back at MacIver, looked at MacIver's sweat. It poured from his head and down over his eyes, blinding him. He kept flicking it away with a thick forefinger. He had a heavy face and his chin was buried in his beard. Pushed in behind fleshy folds two black chips for eyes glinted. He stood upright at the stump, his heavy belly hanging over his belt, his belt buckle digging into its soft fleshiness, looking over and down onto the Minister, waiting for him to say something.

'G-good evening,' the Minister said and gripped harder on the knob of his stick.

'You're a long way from anywhere, whoever you are,' MacIver said, and he pulled the axe free of the stump, hooked into another block and resumed his chopping.

'Yes,' the Minister said, the word lost in the crack from the axe.

MacIver looked through him and carried on.

The Minister tried again. Now his own sweat was beginning to run. 'I'm here on a mission,' he said. 'I've come before but you were always away.'

'Is that right?' MacIver said, no interest in what he was asking.

The Minister swallowed his spittle and straightened his back. 'Yes,' he continued. 'I'm here on a mission to you a-and to others.' His hands were white-knuckled on the stick and faintness was tugging at him, asking him to lie down.

MacIver squinted through the evening light to him. 'And what mission would this be then?' Still no interest, only words shaping a question. 'After something, are you?'

'Oh,' the Minister said, 'it's not what I want from you, it's what I can give to you.' He spoke quickly to beat the axe.

MacIver had split his last block. He anchored the axe in the belly of the stump for good this time and, leaning forward, placed his hands either side of it. 'And what,' he asked, 'would someone like you be giving to someone like me? Eh?' The black chips bounced off the axe head before coming to rest on the Minister's face.

MacIver had the kind of face that would make anyone take two steps back. The Minister licked his dry lips and took a step backwards. His knuckles looked like they would break through their skin covering. He forgot what he was going to say. Then he remembered. He had been going to say 'God'. It was what he always said. But he judged that it would be unwise to say that here. He foresaw the fellow's ridicule.

While MacIver stared at him and waited for him to speak, the Minister doubled back on himself. He spread a papery hand in front of MacIver, curved his mouth into a half-smile. 'Well,' he said. 'Actually, I'm lost,' and his words sounded poor even to himself.

For a while MacIver said nothing, just continued to stare at him. What was this man looking for? Help? The Minister wondered if MacIver had heard. He opened his mouth to repeat what he had said, but MacIver beat him to it.

The Minister had never in his life heard anyone laughing the way MacIver laughed. If MacIver's laugh was something that he might imagine, he'd imagine it to be like MacIver himself. A loud bellow, coarse, full-bodied. Maybe a rumbling of thunder laugh. Deep, like the fellow's speaking voice. MacIver's laugh was none of those. As the Minister stood on the other side of the stump and looked at MacIver's blubbering mouth, saw his long, strong teeth, he was robbed of thought. MacIver's laugh came out from him on a long thread, a high thin falsetto of sound. His arms were wrapped around his full middle and his heavy body shook with his mirth. He danced under it, staggered under it, his boots pounding the earth like the bear he was. The Minister put a hand to his assaulted ear and his mouth fell open at what he was hearing.

As suddenly as it had started the laughing stopped. The prancing stopped and the screech stayed back in MacIver's throat. MacIver shovelled tears from his eyes with both hands.

'I'll say this for you, traveller, you picked a place to be lost in.' The words came from him dry and hard.

'I see that I amuse you.'

Words fell from MacIver's mouth, but the Minister could make no sense of them. The sound he made was like a horse whinnying. Then he shook his head a few times, like a dog shaking itself free of water.

'For that, traveller, you deserve a drink. You know,' he pointed a finger at the Minister, 'you're the best laugh I've had the day.'

MacIver rolled to the back of his house leaving the Minister hanging on his stick. There was nothing he could say, the man had taken his words from him.

While the Minister was trying to gather his wits MacIver rolled back with a large jar. Tearing the axe from the stump he heaved himself up onto it, his heavy legs spread wide, thighs bulging in their breeches. With his teeth he ripped the stopper from the jar, and put his head back. One-handed, he tipped it to his lips. The Minister watched MacIver's throat working, watched as the colourless liquid trickled from the corners of his mouth and down his chin, fading into his beard. He watched MacIver's lips roll over on each other before parting. 'Take some,' MacIver said and he held out the jar to the Minister.

The Minister let go of his stick and walked up to MacIver. He accepted the jar with both hands. He looked into it before lifting it to his mouth. His sip was timid and it left him supping air. He raised the jar higher, opened the angle and put his head back. The drink was cool to his mouth, pleasant in its taste. He took its taste, then let it run down his throat. He had drunk many brews. Some good, some very good. And some were very bad. Whatever MacIver had given him, it was horrific. Nothing that he had ever put into his mouth had tasted like MacIver's brew. It was ferocious, it felt as if the skin was being stripped from the back of his throat. Its fire took his breath from him, his free hand clawed at his neck as his lungs screamed for air. Tears came in his eyes, he felt his knees and his ankles beginning to buckle under him. Through unseeing eyes he could hear MacIver laughing, the high pitch now offensive where before it had been merely unbelievable. Blindly, he pushed the jar at MacIver.

'Take another drop,' MacIver said, his paw waving the jar back to him.

On rubber legs the Minister shook his head and tried to smile. 'Fierce stuff,' he said through tears.

'Come on. Swallow it. The first drop always gets you that way. Take more, man.' MacIver's voice was booming in the Minister's head.

The Minister let himself be persuaded. If that's what the man wanted. But this time he knew the fire in the jar and his sip was small. 'Good,' he smiled, this time barely wetting his lips. 'Very good,' and the jar went back to MacIver.

When it was MacIver's turn he emptied what was left in one long drink. 'You'll not have tasted stuff like that before,' he said to the Minister, his lips dripping whisky. He whisked his tongue around his mouth, missing none.

'No,' the Minister said. 'No, I have not. I feel faint from it,' and his head spun somewhere high above his shoulders.

With his senses adrift he could hear MacIver laughing again, quieter this time. He lifted his head, gave it a quick shake, making his hat slip to the side of his head, half covering one eye. He did his best to focus. His eyes settled again on the buckle of MacIver's belt. Again he watched MacIver's belly bouncing on the buckle, sometimes swamping it as he shook with laughing. Bending down, the Minister groped on the ground for his stick, and found it. He waited for the laughter to disappear down its own thin reed.

'Come into the house,' MacIver was saying. The Minister didn't want to go into MacIver's house, but his feet were taking him there. His stick shaking before him, he negotiated a rotting heap lying in the doorway and lesser heaps on the way in.

It was dark inside MacIver's house. Despite wood lying everywhere, no fire burned to lessen the darkness.

'Sit some place,' MacIver's voice rumbled.

With the help of his stick, the Minister remained standing. In time his eyes became used to the lack of light and he could see MacIver half-lying, half-sitting with his back to a wall, an arm hugging another jar which was balancing on his belly.

The Minister prodded his way over to him, his stick and his

shoes finding the soft liquid lumps he'd rather have missed.
He sat down near MacIver, glad that the darkness hid what
his face was saying.

MacIver lifted the jar and held it out for him. The Minister
reached for the jar and pretended to drink from it, tipping
his head back and making swallowing sounds before pushing
it back to MacIver.

'Tell me, traveller,' MacIver said, the words coming from his
mouth sounding as if they were rolled in blankets, 'what-what
kind of place are you from?' and if there had been light in
the place, the Minister might have detected the sharp edge
to MacIver's question from the way his lids came down on
his eyes.

'From the place they call Strath.' The Minister's hand
covered his mouth, making his own words sound as indistinct
as MacIver's.

'From Strath,' MacIver said. 'I know that place. Hellish
place for anyone to come from,' and the jar went up.

'Yes,' the Minister said.

'I don't come from this place, from this place here. Hellish
place for anyone to come from.' The jar went back down.

The Minister said nothing. He sat on MacIver's floor, both
hands gripping the head of his stick, and he tried to ignore the
stench. He let MacIver carry the conversation.

'I came up to here,' MacIver went on. 'Work. Bloody trees.
I'm sick of looking at them.'

The Minister's ear caught the sound of the liquid slopping
in the jar on its way to MacIver's mouth. 'What took yourself
up to here? To Strath, I'm meaning?'

'My work,' the Minister said. 'Just like yourself.'

'And what kind of work is it that a man like you does? No
my kind of work, eh?' And the laugh, pickled in whisky, was
there beside MacIver's words. The Minister found it every bit
as bad as the fellow's house.

'No, I don't cut down trees. My work is the Church. I work
for God.' Directness rarely worked with the MacIvers he came
up against. Well it was out now. No going back.

MacIver was quiet for a good time. Even the jar was quiet.

The Minister wondered if he should have said what he did. He hadn't meant it to be so direct. He looked across at MacIver. He could see his head jumping up and down on his left shoulder.

'Ay, well,' he said, 'you'll have some job here. The people are hellish heathen here.' He was spacing the last three words. 'What are you saying to that, church man?' And again the laugh came on fumes of whisky.

'I have brought one or two to redemption,' the Minister said. In the darkness MacIver's loose lips tried to form a round 'O'.

'Oh. One or two eh? One or two to redemption. Is that all?'

'Well, maybe more. Maybe more than that. I – I don't quite know. Yes. Maybe.'

'You don't know? You're sitting there and you're telling me you don't know? It's a good job you're no working in the wood. You'd have to know there. What good would you be if you didn't know how many trees you cut? No one would employ you, man.'

The Minister said nothing.

'Who knows?' MacIver was shouting. 'Who knows then, that's what I would like to know? Who, eh?' The jar danced a jig on MacIver's belly.

'God,' the Minister said, his hand tightening on his stick. 'God knows.'

'Only God? What God? Whose God?' The blankets had fallen from the words.

The Minister shrank inside his clothes. This wasn't how it was meant to go. Things were running ahead of him.

'God knows,' now MacIver was making his voice, the Minister's voice. 'What God?' he growled. 'Where is it that the great God of yours is living? The great God that can do anything? Eh? Can He rip up trees? For I sure as hell could do with Him.'

For a time MacIver's mouth was still. The jar was forgotten. In MacIver's house two men were breathing. The Minister's breath came shallow, down through his pinched nose, MacIver's rattled from his heavy, hanging mouth.

'Is your God living in Strath? Eh? Is that what you're saying?'

The Minister knew now why he hadn't wanted to go to MacIver's house. He knew he was in the wrong place. His hand let go of the grip on the stick. Bringing both hands together under his nose, he made a steeple with his fingers. He stared out over the steeple into the darkness and let the words grow in him.

'Well,' he said at last, 'sometimes I have thought that He does indeed live in Strath, but then, I know that He does not.'

MacIver was enjoying himself. He sounded like a crying sheep. His drinking seemed to have awakened his brain. 'Why is it that you don't know where your God's living? You said you're from Strath, don't you know who's living there and who's no?'

The Minister raked around and tried to find words which would say what he meant and which would satisfy MacIver. 'It's not that easy,' he said at last. 'I don't have answers to everything that's asked of me.'

'How? How no? You're God's man aren't you?'

'But, look, I just don't, that's all.'

'How?'

'Because, that's why. That's all.'

'No, it's no. It's no all though, is it?' And there was iron now in MacIver's voice. 'There's more to it than what you're saying.' He paused now as he waited for words to grow in his head. 'A man tried long ago, tried to sell me on that one. And he didn't know any more than you. How can you tell people what you yourself doesn't know?'

The Minister took a long slow breath and bit on the stench. He wasn't prepared for this, a heathen who thought. And he hadn't fooled him. Not for a second. He needed time. He gave it to himself.

'You work in the wood,' he said. 'Your work is cutting down trees. How do you think the trees got there? Who made them grow?' He spoke as to a child.

'The trees spread, they spread from one another and that's

the way they grow. A bairn knows that much. The spirit is in the trees. They spread.'

'What spirit? Whose spirit?'

'What spirit? Whose spirit? How the hell do I know what spirit or whose spirit? The spirit, that's all. The tree's spirit.'

'The birds then. What about the birds? Who made them?'

'All of the birds.'

The Minister forgot about the smell and he leaned towards MacIver. 'All of the birds,' his voice quickened.

'Ach, away. What are you asking me? You'll have to do better than that. I don't know who made all the birds but I know where some of them came from.'

The Minister waited.

MacIver set it before him. 'The ones that I know about come out of eggs because I've watched them. In the wood. I know where that ones come from all right.'

'Yes, that's true. The ones you have seen do indeed come that way. But who is it that made the eggs?'

'The birds man. Isn't that what I'm trying to tell you? You know that as much as me.'

'And what I'm asking you, again, is who made the birds?'

'Ach, away to hell with you and let me be drinking in peace. Who made the birds, who made the eggs. How would I know? That's your job.'

'The animals then. Where did all the animals come from?' He flung his arms wide. 'The horses that you have working for you, the goats and the sheep that the people keep, the cattle, the wolf, the wildcat, the mouse. The little mouse?' He flicked the last question across the dividing space.

Before the Minister was finished asking his question MacIver was laughing. The Minister's mouth tightened into a line.

'I know where my horses come from, that I do know. Donald with the red hair sold them to me for too much. But I'm onto him. I'll get him yet. And doesn't a man like yourself that's always about know where lambs and calves come from? You should open up your eyes, man. Don't we come the same way ourselves? The exact same way.'

The Minister took MacIver's reasoning and weighed it, quiet

in it. The laughter was dead, it had only been a short burst. In the darkness they looked at one another, seeing only the shadows of people.

'The mountains,' the Minister whispered, words so soft they were hardly words. 'Lift up your eyes to the mountains and tell me who made them and who put them where they are.'

There was in the Minister's words something which MacIver couldn't catch, maybe it was tears. Even in the dark he yanked his head away from it. 'Uh,' he grunted, refusing to accept the question. 'How am I supposed to know that? Things that have always been there where they are?' The tone was truculent and the jar was gurgling.

'That's true. They have always been there. But how? Who put them there?'

'How do I know?' The words covered in drink cannoned out of MacIver. 'Are you expecting me, that's just a woodcutter, to know everything? Everything that even yourself doesn't?'

'No,' the Minister said. 'No, I don't expect you to know. I'm only asking you to think. A tree grows up from the earth, a bird comes from an egg, animals and humans from the female womb. That we know and acknowledge as truth. The rivers and the mountains have been in it since time was in its beginning. That too we know. But how did they get there in the first place? In the first place? That's what I'm asking you. Who made the first tree? The first tree seed for a tree to grow and for all the other trees to grow from? Who made the egg for the first eagle to be born from? The first hare, the first man? The first man? That's what I'm asking you.' The Minister sat back and let his breath come through his mouth as he tried to calm himself.

'Ach,' MacIver's shoulders were up around his ears. 'Birds, trees, mountains and men. Don't be bothering me with your talk, man,' and he stretched himself flat on his floor and shut his mouth on it, leaving the Minister to the sound of his heavy breathing.

With the help of his stick, the Minister heaved himself to his feet and struggled to unlock his knees. He cast around for his bearings and stumbled to where he thought the door might be. On the way his feet missed nothing.

'Traveller,' MacIver's voice told him that more than yards separated them.

'I have to be getting back,' the Minister said without turning. 'I thank you for your hospitality,' and his stick negotiated his way for him.

A strange mix of words ripped from MacIver's tongue. Among them the word 'hospitality', or an approximation of it. But the Minister could make no sense of the rest. He chanced another step forward.

'Can your God shut the wolf's mouth?' The Minister heard clear enough. 'If you're wanting a bed there's the barn.' And still the underlying snigger.

The Minister was undecided. He was uncomfortable around MacIver. He'd be happier this night with miles between them. Better, maybe, to take his chance with the wolf.

'A good bed in the barn,' he heard amid snortings. 'Plenty heather.'

But the Minister was tired. He wasn't looking forward to walking through the night. How far would he get anyway? God may have shut the lion's mouth but could He shut the wolf's? Would He want to? For him?

'I thank you,' he said and he stooped for the door.

Outside the moon brightened the night, showing the Minister the way. Although half of MacIver's barn was missing, leaving the rest of it open to the weather, there was one sound wall and as the man said indeed a good floor of heather. He could make a bed in the corner of the whole wall and the broken one.

The Minister woke with the new light. He had not expected to sleep. His encounter with MacIver had set his nerves singing and when he lay down in the heather his head had been full of him and his infernal laughter. But the journey and socialising had tired him and he slept soundly. No one, no thing came to trouble him in his sleep and he woke feeling surprisingly fresh.

Emerging from MacIver's barn he smelled the fire before he saw its smoke drifting up through the house roof. He stood and looked about him, watched the smoke going up in a straight line. The sign of another good day from God. He ventured into MacIver's house. It had looked better in the dark. MacIver had no furniture, not even a stool to sit down on. A few dirty and ripped blankets were lying heaped against the wall. He tried not to look at what he had walked in the night before.

MacIver himself was nowhere in the house. A bundle of rags squatted before the fire and blew peat ash into its face as it tried to make the flames grow around one of MacIver's blocks. The only part of the creature which wasn't black was the whites of its eyes. Hearing the Minister startled her, making her bones leap about inside the rags. The white eyes gaped at him. Seeing the Minister sent her darting, doubled over, for the blankets. Rags covered in more rags.

The Minister opened his mouth on a question but, looking at the shape beneath the blankets, he closed it and kept his words. He left MacIver's woman under her woollen sanctuary and went looking for MacIver.

MacIver was standing in an open place behind his house, squirting the contents of his bladder high above a whin bush. The Minister bowed his head and waited for him.

'This you off then, traveller?' he said when he turned. 'It's a good enough day for it anyway,' and he wiped his face with the hand which had been helping him take aim. He rearranged the front of his clothes and padded closer to the Minister. The bundle of rags darted from the house, and still bent double, ran straight for the whins, and kept on running.

'Yes, I'll be on my way,' the Minister said. 'My wife, you know, I don't want to cause her to worry.' He turned his head away on the last words, as he felt them dying on him.

'Yourself has a wife? What kind of a wife have you got?' And the black chips squinted against the early sun.

'A – a very nice, a good woman,' the Minister was inching backwards.

'Nice, eh? But is she warm? Eh?' And the laugh which

had been just bearable last night was intolerable with the morning.

The Minister said nothing. His eyes looked away to the mountains, caught the sun's flame on them.

'Warmer than that thing?' MacIver jerked a thumb at the rags fighting against the whins. 'Expects to be fed for nothing. Well, not from this man, not from this man here.' His thumb was prodding his chest. 'What I don't get I take,' and the hand plunged for his groin. The Minister looked at MacIver, at the veins on his neck bunched and throbbing, at the big head flooded crimson, like the sun on the hills. Soon, what had been mounting inside the woodman ebbed, his hand relaxed and fell open and fell away from him. He put his head back, making pleats in the flesh at the back of his neck and opened his mouth on a growl at what he saw written on the Minister's face. Then he too dived for the whins, tearing them apart with his hands as he opened up a path, taking the Minister's voice into the whins with him.

The Minister looked after MacIver. MacIver was a back and a head floating out on a golden sea.

The further MacIver walked from the Minister the better the Minister felt. With distance between them his voice came back to him. 'Will you be coming to the Church on the Sabbath?' he called after the back.

MacIver kept quiet and kept on walking. But the laugh was there, walking among the thorns with him.

'There's a pair of boots in it. For you. Good boots. Strong for working in,' the Minister's mouth worked hard on the words. The words stopped MacIver. He turned to face the Minister from far out on his sea.

The Minister watched the mouth in MacIver's head. He saw it open, strained to catch what was coming from it. 'A pair of boots,' it said. 'You'd give a pair of boots to me? Why? Is that what's going to take me into church? Is it boots that's to save my immortal soul? Eh?'

The Minister stood strong in the opening day and waited for the mouth to say more.

'Why, church man?' it said.

The Minister didn't know what to say. He didn't know why. It was just something he said. And he'd get boots, from somewhere. MacIver's head was waiting for him. He watched the mouth again, saw it forming words to fire at him across the sea. 'If it's boots that's going to save me I'd as soon go barefoot,' it said. 'Barefoot in Hell,' and the laugh exploded from him with the words. 'How's that for hot, traveller? Is it boots that will carry me up to Paradise? Eh? Boots, eh?' He howled away to himself as he kept on walking.

Chapter Three

'You're sure now that the fire's out?' Bell Ross cradled her baking bowl against her chest as she walked.

'You're an awful one, Mother.' Her youngest daughter Anna's own arm was stretched and aching under the weight of the water-jar. 'Every year you say the same thing. The fire is out. You saw Daniel yourself, putting his boot through it.'

'Yes, indeed.' Anna's mother stopped on the road to catch her breath.

The Ross family consisted of seven people. The father and the mother and their four daughters and one son. Ishbel the eldest, Anna the youngest, Flora and Peggy in between. And Daniel the sole male, born ahead of Anna.

Along with the rest of Strath they were making for the track through the heather, which would take them to the foot of the hill. Their houses lay behind them, asleep in alien stillness. The people had left, taking with them some of their stock animals and their dogs. At their backs their hearths lay dead and cold, the only day in the year they would do so. A bride took the living fire with her from her mother's house and her mother took it from her mother before her and so on back down the line. She would be a poor housewife the day she let her fire die on her. Every night before she went to her bed the last thing she would do was build up her fire. She stocked it with peats and peat dross, patted it well down and let it sit and snooze away until morning. In the morning she breathed new life into it from her own lungs.

'My feet's that sore,' Bell Ross said. 'It's me that'll be glad to

sit. Is that our Peggy that I'm hearing?' A high-pitched skirling
cut through the noise of clattering people and animals.

'Need you ask?' Ishbel said as she waited for her mother to
move on. Her sister Peggy trailed somewhere behind with Flora
and the bag of flour. Ahead of her she could see her father and
her brother Daniel walking with the other men.

The men were out in front with the stock animals. The dogs
were everywhere, getting in the way. The children mostly hung
around their mothers, some of the older boys walking with the
men, considering themselves men. Little babies were bundled
up inside their mothers' shawls, strapped to fronts and backs,
leaving the mothers' hands free to carry other things.

The women carried the makings of the bread and a bowl if
they had one. The men were in charge of the drink and of the
wood for the fires. They would light two on the summit of
the hill. Daniel and his father carried bundles of brushwood
on their shoulders.

'Do you think we've enough wood?' His father was small
beside him, stooped with age against his son's straightness.

'Plenty.' Daniel's leg was beginning to drag. It did that
when he was tired. 'We gathered enough yesterday after we
built the fires.'

'You're sure now?'

'Ay, I'm sure.'

'Well, all right then.'

They walked on.

The exodus was a disorderly and ragged tribe strung across
the field of purple heather. Their brown clothes hung on them,
the men's kilts and the women's frocks. The length of the kilt
depended on age. The young men flashed their thighs while
the older men wore theirs longer. Also the young men wore no
shirts, preferring to show off their muscular arms and chests.

The track had taken them away from their home environ-
ment and now it followed the river. Ahead of them was the
hill. It would take them all that they had for the climb.

Two of the men in front were having trouble with a horse.
The horse didn't want to follow them and kept pulling at its
rope to get away. The bigger man of the two kept jerking

the rope, tearing at the horse's mouth. The horse was fighting back, throwing its head back, pulling the man on the rope off his feet. The other man, about the same age and height but thinner, was putting all of his weight against the horse as he thrust at it from the rear. The horse was dancing, its hind hoofs kicking out at the man's legs.

'Look at that pair.' Daniel's father put his hand on Daniel's arm. 'Look at what they're doing on the horse. Go up and say something to them before they'll hurt the beast.'

'I'm no going. If you're wanting to say something you can go.'

'But they'll choke it. The rope's too tight,' his father's concern babbled from his blue lips.

'Look, my leg's sore. And I'm no wanting flattened by one of them or by the two of them. You do it.'

'I don't know what to be saying. I'm not that able.'

'Ach, be quiet man. What are you getting so troubled over a horse for?' And he walked away from his father and fell in with another man.

The straggling line followed the river to its narrowest place and flooded across to the other side. The dogs nosed the strange territory, finding and inspecting interesting places amid delirious tail-wagging. The children were beginning to feel the pace. They grew tired and irritable. Even their mothers' soothings were no use to them. And there were mothers and fathers too who would be glad when they reached the foot of the hill.

They had walked a long way and the things they were carrying was beginning to tell on them. Legs which had stepped out with surety were beginning to slow down. The hill looked as far away as ever. They pressed on, still through the heathery moorland. Arms hung lower, heads drooped, the women's bare feet took shorter strides. The men stayed in front. Although the babies' crying increased, the mothers did not stop for them. Time enough for feeding when they reached the bottom of the hill. Older little ones had given up on walking under their own steam and clutched at their mothers' frocks and were pulled along with them.

At the foot of the hill one old man had to be helped. He couldn't straighten, even with his load off. He stood among them. looking round about and seeing nothing above the level of his chest. His stick was the only thing which kept him from toppling over onto the ground. Two women made the old man lie down and another one took her shawl off and spread it on top of him. A man put a jar to the old man's lips. His thin old hands caught the jar and he took a long drink. The older men looked the tiredest. The old women seemed to fare better. Their tough old legs seemed as if they could walk forever. Many were as slamp as women half their age.

Not all of Strath was there. The infirm weren't, nor were those who had put aside such beliefs. If the latter should have reason to call on anything or anyone, they'd call on their own God, in the Church, in front of those there, and that's all anyone had to know. What they did away from the Church was their concern and no one else's. But among them were the old and the very old. Age would not stop them while they could walk.

The Wise One wasn't there. He was the Wise Man of the tribe and what people did up on the tops of hills was nothing to him. He was beyond that kind of thing. He knew what he knew and he saw what he saw. Climbing hills to sun worship wouldn't add to that.

The lazy weren't there, nor the uninterested. But there weren't many of these. MacIver wasn't there. His main interest, only real interest, was what he could pour down his throat. He hadn't tasted anything to beat his own stuff. So, why waste good time, stravaiging over half the country with that crew?

They sat where they came to rest, their belongings at rest beside them, their animals loosed to graze. Someone, a man, started to sing. The rest joined in. Sitting at the foot of the hill they had breath enough for singing. And the suckling babies took their mothers' milk and were quiet.

There was no harshness in their singing for there was none in their speaking voices. Even in anger their voices were soft. The words came from them and they came from the place. A place of great beauty. And the place was built into them in the way they spoke. Hardy, courageous people, with the gentlest of tongues. They might slip a knife into you, but they'd smile and be quiet while they did it.

They wouldn't have called what they were singing a hymn. It was a song, filled with praise. They sang for help in their times of trouble, for protection against whatever might come their way, for courage to bear that which was theirs alone to bear. Late into the last afternoon in April they sang for the strength in their legs which would carry them up the hill. It was their song of thanks, that they were still in it and able to see this good day.

Who or what they were singing to they would not have thought of as holy, but in their hearts there was the sincerest feeling of reverence and respect.

They sang a slow air, a low air, rising and falling like the moaning in the wind. The wind caught the tune and carried it up to the high places, placing it among the corries and the crags where the eagles found it. The eagles lifted it up higher and released it into the circle which is time, where it would remain as beauty forever. The last note had faded away. Only then did the first man lift up his bundle and set his foot to the hill. And the rest followed.

Speaking broke out among them again but the babies stayed quiet, soothed by the singing and feeding. And Peggy was at her skirling again.

'I know why Peggy's laughing,' her younger sister Anna shouted to Daniel, whose head had turned round at the racket going on. 'It's because she'll see Donald Munro.'

'More like because he'll see her,' Daniel said. 'The fool.' And he shook his head to try to rid his ears of Peggy's shrieking.

Daniel was back with his father. His father smiled under his load but didn't speak.

'And you can just be quiet,' Peggy said, scouring the ground for something she could throw at her brother. She found the correct size of stone and aimed it for her brother's back. Her aim was off. It hit the wood and bounced to the ground, harmless.

He saw it though. 'You can quit that,' he bawled at Peggy. 'It's hard enough going,' and he hitched his bundle higher.

Their mother watched them. She was a short, heavy woman and her weight was telling against her. She looked at Peggy and shook her head at her but didn't speak.

'Well,' Peggy said, and there were tears in her voice, 'I don't even know Donald Munro. I only ever spoke to him the once.'

'Never you mind, Peggy,' an old woman said, one of the slamp old ones with the tough legs. 'Donald Munro would be a fine man for you. Did you see the teeth on him?' The old woman poked Peggy with her sharp elbow and laughed like a hen, cackling in Peggy's face.

The laughing had gone from Peggy. Her full bottom lip shook.

'Don't you be listening to them,' the old one said. 'Anyway, here's your father and your brother waiting for you. We'll go up with them.'

On the slope the people fanned out and climbed as families, in twos and threes. Men waited for their womenfolk, brothers fell in with sisters. It was less the ordered procession that had walked out of the village and through the heather.

'Daniel was just telling me that Donald Munro is back home safe from that war he went away to,' Daniel's father said on meeting them. 'It was the first I heard. Do you know?' he turned back to Daniel. His father's hands were quivering on the rope. 'Did the other men come back?'

'Some of them,' the words had to fight their way past Daniel's lips. 'I just found out that young James Munro didn't and Duncan Ross didn't. That's the only two I heard about. There'll be others.'

'I don't know what to be saying,' his father said. 'Does everyone know? You'll have to tell them. I don't know.' His father's head was bent. He spoke to his chest. 'That's James Munro's mother without a man about the place.'

Ishbel saw her own mother's hands gripping on the bowl, as if it would save her. She saw her mother's body as it tried to move without the power and support of its legs. She reached

37

to put a hand under her mother's arm. 'Take her other arm,' she said to Peggy. 'Quick.'

Bell Ross was glad of her daughters' help. If she hadn't had the bowl to hold onto where would she be? The mothers of the boys who hadn't come back had been girls with her. Now, their own beautiful sons gone. If that had been her own son, if that had been Daniel, what would she do? With him lying dead in that faraway place. How would her heart take it? Only another mother would know how thankful she was that he was standing there in front of her. If it hadn't been for his leg he'd have been away too. And her tears wouldn't have kept him from it.

She pulled herself free of Peggy and Ishbel and forced her legs to move. Daniel didn't know what was happening behind him, the wood blocked his view. His eyes could only see ahead to the hill and the sky over it. She put out her hand and touched him. He felt her hand and he stopped. He looked down, saw her hand against his arm, swollen and worn. She hadn't touched him since a long time. She wasn't that kind of woman and he wasn't that kind of man. His eyes shifted to his mother's face, he saw what was in her eyes. His own eyes creased, he curved his mouth into a soft smile. He lowered the hand which had been on the rope holding the wood and covered hers. He heard her breath breaking in her. They stood there for a short time, beholding one another. They had no words but they didn't need any. It was as if the crowd on the hill that day had disappeared, leaving them alone where they stood. Then she pulled her hand from below his and took a step. And he took a step. And they moved forward with the rest.

Once, on the climb, they thought they heard a wolf. And, as a body, they tasted fear. Their hearts and their footsteps stumbled then. But they didn't stop. And in time the fear abated, their hearts and their feet found their natural rhythms once more. They were brave again. They were going up to their own special place to welcome and give thanks to the great life-giving sun. Nearer the summit, they drifted in, closer to one another, and moved to the top as one.

As the moon climbed over the summit, spreading its light on

them, they huddled under their blankets for warmth in small groups now. Some had blankets pulled up over their heads to try to keep the night cold from their bones and themselves safe from whatever evil was about.

Since their arrival the men had been kept busy rebuilding the two fires, adding more wood to them, reshaping them, making them tighter. The women had made the dough. It sat on large stones around the fires, shaped and waiting for the heat. For the children it was a night of strangeness, of freedom, of curiosity, and they loved it. There was nothing new on top of a hill for them, just to be there was enough. They made their own fun. They ran about like wild things while the old ones kept half an eye on them, and warned them against straying to the far side and let the younger women get on with their work. The animals alone were quiet. Glad of the rest, they cropped and chewed and grazed.

With no more work to be done on the fires, Daniel had left his own family and went looking for the parents of the dead men. Peggy was wandering about, looking at the people. Some others – a man, his wife and their two children – came over to sit with the Rosses. The crowd was singing again. Soft and low, the sound floated down on to the pinewood and their empty homes. Under the blankets shy faces were fond and hearts were warm. They'd sing until there was no more singing in them, they'd sing that old sun into the sky. No sleeping tonight. Time enough for sleeping when Beltane was past. This night for reverence and for watching. And for enjoyment.

As Daniel searched among the crowd, it struck him that he was suddenly seeing a lot of that queer woman. From being unable to remember when he had last seen her, it seemed now that everywhere he turned she was there. Always on her own. Even at a time like this. Away from the rest of the people he could see her, leaping and weaving about, like the wind blowing through the corn.

He stopped for a while to look at her. She was tall for a woman, there was no other woman as tall. Nearly his own height he would say. But she moved like a dancer, as graceful as any he had seen, man or woman, girl or boy. He liked what he was looking on, she was holding him, her tall body bending and arching like the branches of a tree in a storm. A voice called out his name and he went to join it, stepping over a man with straggly fair hair and a lean dog the same. But his mind was still with her.

He knew her, or to be correct, he had always known of her. He'd heard about her in his own house. His mother and father had been talking about her mother and the then Minister. He had been a boy at the time. The Beatons had come out of MacLeod country when she, the queer one, was a small girl and since her parents' death, she had scraped some kind of living. She did for the sick what the Old Wife could not. She knew about plants. It was his mother who had said she was queer, wanting nothing to do with other people, content to live with birds and animals. Seeing her like that had brought it all back to him. Once he had wandered quite far from his home, he had gone as far as the burn and she was there hacking away at some kind of roots with her bare hands. She chased him from the burn, warning him away from the water and from the eagle. She was a big girl then when he was small.

Peggy was looking for Donald Munro but he found her. From his place in the circle, lit by the moon's pale yellow light, he saw her wandering about like someone lost, bending low every now and then to peer at the faces of the men who had black hair. He watched Peggy coming his way. He pulled his plaid up over his head and covered the lower half of his face in it, tightening his grip on it until only his eyes and his brows were visible. Peggy was scanning the face of the man next to him. He watched her straighten, saw by the moon's light how her teeth bit into her bottom lip. He watched her take a strand of hair and curl it around one of her fingers before putting the end of the hair into her mouth. She chewed slowly on the hair. With his eyes still on her, Donald's hand snaked along the ground towards her ankle. His fingers felt the dew on her skin. As soon as he touched her she leapt in the air squealing and dancing like a scalded cat. His hand held her. In the circle, even shy faces laughed aloud to one another, features losing their form in the moonlight. Heads were thrown back, with plaids hanging from them like the hair of time.

Donald Munro pushed back his plaid and lifted his head. 'Well now,' he said, 'I'm hearing that you're looking for me,' and his eyes and his mouth asked her to deny this.

'I am not,' Peggy was too loud as she jerked at her leg to free herself.

He held on to her, his eyes holding hers. Brown locked on black, black on brown. His hair was as long and as black as her own, flattened to his head with grease. He looked dangerous. And he was quicker than she was. Before she realised what was happening the vice on her ankle opened and flew for one of her hands. 'I'd say you found me,' he said and she was down on top of him.

Peggy made a sound like strangled bagpipes. And she was strong. She had breath enough to screech and pummel at his chest with both fists. Her bare legs were everywhere, flashing and thrashing about like wild water. He held her as if she were nothing or maybe just a feather. She thought she was going to die and the hairs on his legs were rubbing against the hairs on hers. He smelt of man.

She struggled against him some more, to make it look good. But her heart wasn't in it. And she wasn't fooling anyone, certainly not herself. She stopped fighting and sagged against him.

'Give her a kiss,' a wrecked woman of middle years shouted. The woman's face was a web of lines. There was a wart hanging from her left eyelid, blurring the sight of that eye.

'I'd say it's more than a kiss she's needing,' a young fellow who bared himself in a short kilt said. Spittle trickled from the corners of his mouth. 'Send her to me if you're no wanting her.' He threw off his blanket and scrambled to his feet. His feet were dancing. 'Come on.' His big hands were reaching for Peggy.

'Sit down, man,' Donald Munro's arms were wrapped tightly around Peggy's chest, pulling her against him. His legs were folded over hers, pinning her. 'She's for me,' and his mouth swooped on her neck. 'I know you,' he mumbled.

'You're the sister of him that has the twisted foot,' he spoke between mouthfuls of neck. 'What are you doing, going about looking for strange men?'

Peggy struck him on the chest with her elbow. 'There's nothing wrong with his foot,' she twisted her head around to yell at him. 'It's his leg that's short. That's all,' and she tried to pull away again. She needn't have bothered. Her strength was useless against his easy strength. With only her forearms free, her hands flapped about like a couple of broken birds as she fought to straighten her clothes and cover her pale limbs. 'And, anyway,' she kept her head down so that she wouldn't see their open enjoyment and they wouldn't see hers. 'If it's strange men you're talking about, yourself is the strangest that's in it,' she felt bold enough to say.

Donald Munro looked around those in his circle. His eyes widened, he raised his black brows. They became a straight line. 'So that's the way, is it?' He was looking at the others but his words were for Peggy.

Now there was silence. Their laughing had stopped. Peggy's hands stopped flapping. Something sharp hung in the air along with the silence. Peggy sensed it and twisted in his lap to face him. Her top lip this time was between her teeth, her eyes swallowing her face, telling him all he wanted to know. The circle waited and watched them. This was good. Someone made a noise like a horse. Someone else followed. Then they were all at it, grimy faces cracked under the moon, mouths split wide, eyes squeezed shut.

The moon beamed down.

'Well?' he said.

'Well yourself.'

'Is it the truth, what I'm hearing?'

'I don't know. What is it that you're hearing?'

'I'm hearing that you're wanting me.' His arms and his hands loosened their hold on her, let her go. She stood up and stepped aside from him. Then he stood up. They stood looking at one another. He was no taller than Peggy and Peggy wasn't tall. Now her own arms were folded across her chest.

She dipped her head and spoke. 'I might be,' she said quietly as if she was telling herself.

'Come on then,' she heard him saying and she felt before she saw his hand gripping hers. This time she didn't try to stop him. She lifted her head and looked at him. What she saw in his eyes made the bubbles gather in her throat. She opened her mouth to let them out. The scream that came with them was wild. The faces in the circle nodded, first to themselves then to one another. It was good. The slavery fellow in the short kilt smiled. Time for himself to be stretching his legs and going looking. This was the night and it was all there for the taking.

There were many screams that night, and not only among the young and the free. It was the one night in the year when married people felt they could ignore their marriage vows. This night was bigger than promises made. Many did, sometimes in sheltered places, sometimes in the open with their children near by. Retribution could come later.

Patiently they waited. They sang this time to put the night in, to keep warm. There was quietness, interrupted by whooping and calling from revellers. None but the youngest slept. The moon stayed with them. She alone was witness to the ongoings. In time the sun moved in and the moon rolled from her place. They cheered the sun. Even after the singing, they found strength from what they believed in to do that. They shook off their blankets and rose on cramped legs and stiffened joints from the cold damp ground, knees creaking and hands clapped to sore backs. Now for the fires. Now they would see some heat. Between themselves the men had picked out two groups, about nine in each. They lined up in two rows, one behind the other. The rest of the crowd stood back to give them room. Four logs were lying in the grass, two large ones with holes gouged in their centres and two small ones. The first man sat in the grass before each big log and hauled the log between his knees. He stood the smaller log in the hole and spun it between both hands. Their hands rubbed the log, until it was dizzy in the hole. And when those two had done their stint they moved aside and the next two jumped in. Soon the sparks came and the crowd was delighted. A shout went up and fists punched the air, bonnets were thrown high, aprons dabbed eyes and the shoulders of the two creating the sparks were nearly broken with fists full of congratulations.

Two other men came, with torches made out of dried heather and put their torches to the sparks. The men on the ground kept birling the sticks, the torchmen turned away from the chill of the very early morning, one hand holding their torches against their chests while the other hand shielded the glowing heather. They blew onto them until they had a flame going. And when the flame came they turned and twisted the torches until the fire spread.

Some came running from the bushes in various states of undress to see the flames dancing. And everyone danced along with them. Torches were taken from both fires. The fires' brilliance bathed them in a harsher light than the moon had done, sharpening their faces, making them look hungrier.

The feet of the torch-men wove dancing patterns in the grass as the red torches threaded glowing patterns through the air. People followed the dancers, still dancing. Men and women and children. Laughing, happy people, the harshness of reality temporarily forgotten. Babies felt safe, tied up in their mother's shawls, bouncing against their mothers' breasts.

Only when the fire had had its first burning and had died down did the dancers begin to slow down. It was this that they danced for. For the time when the fires would be low enough for them to jump through. Men argued to see who would be first through the flames, pushing and tugging at each other in the scramble to be first. And they argued with women. And women argued with men. The children wouldn't dare. They knew what they would get if they started and in any case it was a sacred thing and they had to take their place. A heavy woman jumped first, her child, a little girl, clinging with her small arms to her mother's neck. The woman was heavy, not made for jumping, and the weight of the child didn't help. A flame caught at the hem of the mother's skirt and had the crowd screaming their fear for her. Two other women rushed up to take the baby while three of the men pulled the woman out of the fire, rolled her over in the grass and stamped on her to put her out. Quite a few women took their children through the flames but no one else was burnt. The bigger children held onto their mothers' hands and jumped through with them. The men were good jumpers and their kilts were short, much shorter than the women's frocks. And they had boots on their feet. There were competitions among the men to see who could make the longest, highest jump. And the cleanest. The men took long runs up before launching themselves. One fellow stood calming himself. You could see him trying to get his breathing right before he took off, his chest going out and in like his cheeks. The people in the crowd chanted as they charted his progress on the run up, the noise they made like a flock of wild geese. As he soared up and over the burning wood the geese calling changed to the battle cry of his chief. Mostly the women made small jumps through the fire. Except one. Skirts tucked up about her waist, bare legs glowing, she raced up to the jump-off spot and launched herself into the air, climbing high above the red embers, as high as any of the men. And when their time came, the young ones weren't nearly as daring as the older ones or their talk beforehand would make one believe. They bounced through and hit the ground running on the other side, the girls making more noise than the boys.

There was all sorts of bawling from the frightened animals. Men led them through. Animals are naturally terrified of fire and to see what they were made to do dampened the celebrations. The horses tugged at their ropes and clawed the air but their owners held them. The distress of the animals didn't seem to affect some owners. Tonight was for purification and everything else was shut out. The faces of everyone there were washed in a strange kind of light. It was more than the light from the fire and the rising sun. Neither did the singeing smells of hair and wool bother them. The sheep were whisked through before they knew it. In their case ignorance was indeed bliss.

When the purification ceremony was over the men passed

around their jars, faces leering like hellhounds in unearthly light. Someone's father, someone's brother, someone's son, but not on this night. This night they were neither their own nor anyone else's. It was the bigger thing, the greater power which had control over them.

The women had the bread ready, spread out on the stones around the fire. The bread wasn't for eating, but for appeasing. 'This is for you, Spirit of Life,' a woman, who looked as if she needed the bread more than the fire did, closed her eyes and chanted. 'Watch over our horse. And our cows, our goat and the crop and our home and the whole place,' and the piece of bread went flying into the fire. Another woman threw bread to appease the wild animals. 'This is for you, o eagle. Spare our lambs.' And, 'This is for you, o wolf, spare our cows.' They all had their turn of breaking off a piece of bread and throwing it into the fire but the men seemed to do it best, aiming the bread right into the fire's heart. The women were better with the words. Most men mumbled, they could be saying anything. The crowd was silent during this part of the ceremony, even the youngest of them. Only the one involved spoke. The dogs were ignored. And the drink flowed fast, making the blood run wild and the heart pump. In the new light drink ran into their mouths and it ran out. It trickled down throats and down fronts, between lips and between fingers as they tried to scoop up and suck up every drop. The women as well as the men were good drinkers. But they wouldn't give any to the children.

A man and a woman held a hoop of blazing straw between them. Two others, again a man and a woman, walked up to it holding a little baby. The woman passed the baby through the hoop to the man who was waiting on the other side. The woman's hands didn't want to let go of her baby and kept hold of it while the man was trying to take it. The baby was crying.

During the afternoon and evening of the previous day there had been a mood of patient and relaxed waiting. Now, on Beltane, it had changed. Something bigger than themselves was up on this hill and they all felt it. They didn't know how to cope with what they were in touch with. It frightened them. So they covered their fear in drinking and dancing and loud talking, in loving, and told themselves they were having a good time.

And when the fires were black and exhausted, when they themselves were exhausted, when the drink was done, they straggled down from the hill, a long broken line of ones and twos. That was it, until the next time. And their minds and hearts did feel light though their steps might be heavy.

Men carried torches, lit from the ashes of the bonfires, to rekindle their house fires. The housefires had had their rest, time for them to burn for another year. There was work in it for everyone. The women and the girls bound together bundles of twigs of rowan, of elder and of juniper. They made up crosses for putting above the doors. And the bigger boys had the job of carrying a burning peat inside a pot around the boundary of their land. That was the purifications complete. Their houses were safe, all that was theirs was safe and the whole community was sealed off from any kind of evil.

Chapter Four

Arabella Hutcheon was seventeen years in 1637, the year she married the Reverend Gilbert Kennedy, an out-of-work Minister of the Presbyterian Church in Scotland. He had been forty-two, a friend and contemporary of her father, Baillie Hector Hutcheon of Dingwall in the county of Ross and Cromarty. The Baillie had hired his redundant friend as tutor to his daughters Catherine and Arabella. They were without a teacher since their previous one was forced to retire through ill-health. Arabella was eighteen when she left the modest house provided for them by her father and travelled north to the place called Strath, up near the Sutherland border. In her eleven years in Strath she had not once returned to Dingwall, even to visit, and only twice had anyone come to visit her, Catherine and Catherine's husband James. James was a clerk to the land-owning Munro family of the Foulis Estate in Easter Ross and Cromarty and was also a friend of her husband.

As she scattered the corn and called to the hens and the geese to come to her, Arabella knew that her husband was watching her. Up on the small hill behind the house. She didn't have to look, she could feel his presence. The weight of it hung over her like a lowered sky. He'd lie there until he'd lain long enough, until he decided it was time to come down. It was what he always did when he had been away. No matter the weather, he'd lie up there, preparing himself for meeting her. 'Chicky, chicky,' she called. 'Here, chicky chick,' and she emptied the bowl on to the ground and went back into the house.

The Minister's house was a bare house, built of stone with

a wooden roof and floor. As austere inside as it was on the outside. Once it had been fine but that fineness had long disappeared. Neglect covered its colours. The rich hues of the rugs and the upholstery had turned brown through years of being uncared for. The shine was missing from the dresser and the wooden chairs, curtains faded to grey like Arabella's beauty. But through the neglect the fineness still shone, all the braver for it. The furniture had come from the Baillie along with his daughter, shipped north on a cargo boat from Cromarty pier. No family portraits hung on the walls of the house and no flame flickered life and colour in the fireplace. The inside of the Minister's house looked like a place no one lived in, it looked less welcoming than the houses of the poor people. Its stout walls kept out the sun so that even on a warm day it was cold inside. Arabella either suffered this or had grown used to it.

Arabella sat on one of the faded chairs beside the small south-facing window and worked on a piece of cloth. With fierce, quick movements she jabbed the needle into a piece of cream cotton and pulled a length of green thread through it. Her malnourished body was hunched on the chair, her head bent close to the cloth, wisps of her thin pale hair had escaped its combs and was hanging about her face and getting in the way of her eyes. She worked through the hair, narrowing her eyes and holding the piece of cloth up close to them. In with the needle, through with the thread, in from the other side, back through with the thread. Her stitches were small and neat like the hand that made them. In and out, in and out. Don't let him come, please not yet. I need more threads, the pedlar will come soon. In and out, I'll be needing a bowl. In and out, don't let him come in here.

Her mind distracted, she felt the sharp sting of the needle as it punctured the tip of a finger. She closed her eyes and bit down on the heat of the pain. A red spot, ragged at the edges, spread through the cream cloth. She put her finger into her mouth and sucked the blood from it, tasted its saltiness. Tears filled her eyes and she was a small child. She wished her mother would take her hand and lead her through the days.

She couldn't manage by them by herself, she couldn't, she couldn't. She didn't know the way. If only she could cancel the years in between. If only Catherine were close beside her. And James MacKenzie. And Mother and Father. Oh, if only. If only it could be the way it was then. Before.

To begin with Gilbert Kennedy had been patient with her, kind even. He understood her youth, the sickness she felt at being so far away from her home and her family. But in time her granite-faced indifference to anything he said or did made him stop trying.

They lived side by side in the same house with little communion of any kind, certainly none of the mind. His work had always been his life and he found that he could live quite well apart from her. Food and comfort could always be found.

Her parents had visited regularly when they had lived in the house in Dingwall. But not once since the move north. And Arabella didn't mind. The pain she had felt at being given to Gilbert Kennedy had damaged and changed her. She had been afraid of him at fourteen, she had been afraid of him at seventeen, at eighteen, and longer than that. But not now. Now she was indifferent to him. And to pain.

The first time her sister Catherine and her husband had travelled to stay with them, Catherine had been shocked at Arabella's cold and colourless life. Arabella who had been raised among luxury and comfort, a maid to dress her, a groom to teach her to ride. How could she live like this? In all the time they had been there not once was there a fire lit in any room in the house, although the visit had taken place during the cold days of spring. The food offered had been poor and meagre. Mutton and hen that had been impossible to chew on. One course, nothing else. She surely could get a woman for the cooking? And Catherine didn't know what they had drunk. No place set for the Minister. It had been an altogether uncomfortable stay, and although he would never show it, she could sense her husband's unease and concern for his friend. Catherine's concern had been for Arabella. She barely recognised her as her sister, would not have had she met her some place else. An emotionless thing moving among them. Dull-eyed and dull-haired, apple cheeks that had been pared away leaving harsh hollows. Gaunt and lifeless. At twenty-eight.

Her mind often did this, wandered off into remembering. It was how she got through the days.

She remembered how he was in the beginning. Or rather she didn't. Not much anyway. He had been father's friend, Father's age. A quiet man. A pleasant man. Her and Catherine's teacher. A good teacher, Father said. He had given her books to read and told her she could keep them. And that was all. Mother seemed taken. But he didn't make them laugh, the way Mr Thompson, their previous tutor, had. She hadn't been afraid of Mr Thompson. Mr Thompson had been Catherine's tutor first and hers since she was four.

Gilbert Kennedy was a tall man who walked without surety, stooped slightly even then. Soberly clad always, no colours flashed from his clothes, no buckles twinkled from his shoes. She thought then that Father didn't pay him very well.

The sewing forgotten, her punctured finger forgotten, she looked through the unshuttered window and saw some more of how it was. She could still hear the whispering of Mother and Catherine and Father. She would not believe that James Mackenzie had anything to do with the conspiracy to marry her off to such an old man. She didn't think it then and she did not think it now. She saw how he had looked when their engagement was announced. His face white, as if he was going to be sick.

She saw the way it was like the mountains. Something huge and sharp-peaked which leapt out at her. The quietness which elbowed the laughter from her Father's house. The wedding of Catherine and James and the house as it used to be, filled with fun. But Father with too much wine in him? She ground her teeth together and swallowed as she tried to shake away the way she felt when Father pulled her onto his lap and said, through sickly sweet-smelling breath, 'You're next.' He wasn't like Father. And she was scared of something she did not yet understand. And three months after Catherine married James MacKenzie, she was married to Gilbert Kennedy.

She didn't know him, how could she understand him? She couldn't carry a conversation with him. He was an old man, he smelt of oldness and books. His face was white, his eyes were almost white and she was afraid of what was in him and what was expected of her.

Through the window, away far to the mountains, she saw the girl she used to be. She knew from looking at that girl that it was her, but she didn't know that girl, had no feelings about her. And how could that girl be among mountains, that girl would never be among mountains.

James MacKenzie wearing his sick face, like a dog that had been kicked too many times. The smiles had slipped from it and stayed hidden somewhere around his boots when she had married Gilbert.

'That's what marriage is,' Catherine had said. 'You'll get used to it. Do you know nothing?' Catherine over-controlled in ice.

He didn't do these things now but it didn't matter. It was too late anyway. She jabbed the needle at the cotton and continued in a green arc and waited for the house door to open. She kept her eyes and her head down.

He stood in the doorway, the way he always did before coming in. Hesitant still, one hand holding his hat.

'The day was fine,' he said. 'It kept dry,' and he ducked his head from the lintel. His hair had thinned over the years. He still wore it long about his coat's collar but it was more straggly now. Arabella made a twin arc in the cotton.

He stood before the barren fireplace, his back turned to it. 'It's turning cold again,' he said through his thin lips, chafing his hands together. 'I think it may rain again.' Arabella said nothing.

'I think I'll go to my study. I have work I must do.'

Arabella kept her head down.

In the small room which he used as his study the Minister sat down at the plain wooden table, leaned forward and put his elbows on it and put his face into his cold hands. 'God, my God,' he said. 'Help me to bear it.' Daily he implored the Almighty, nightly lying beside her. He stayed before God for a long time. The study was cold, like the rest of the house. It had no heat and, when it was dark, no light. She wouldn't have it. And he didn't want to upset her any more than he could help. She had been a child, a child. What kind of man had he been, what kind of man was he?

It was her. Something in her had caught him and kept him ensnared. So pure, so pure. He had tried to resist her, he could have if it hadn't been for her mother. How he wished to God, that in the changes in the Church back then, that he hadn't lost his pulpit. It was what drove him temporarily into teaching. He had to earn a living. And if he had to teach, why them? Her? And why, when the call came to a new church, had it to be only after he had married her? Oh God, what insanity had been driving him then? He should have remained strong. He should have concentrated on rejoining the church. That would have been truth, not what he became. That wasn't truth. The way he was now. He put his fist to his mouth and bit down hard on his knuckles, until he winced from the pain. He would have pushed his fist down his throat if it would have stopped him wanting her. But there would never be an end to that. He'd want her from the grave.

He'd been old even then, he'd been born old. He knew that. Youth had never sat lightly on him. His life had always been one of books and study and it suited him to be that way. He looked for no more. Women had always frightened him, their otherness. But he liked children, once they were past babyhood. He couldn't make much of crying babies. But once they had gained their intelligence, it gave him great pleasure to help them to use that intelligence, to think and to read. First through the scriptures and later in tutoring. Boys and girls, they were all one to him then. All that he had come across anyway had been delightful. And they seemed to like him. But Arabella Hutcheon had been different. How? He didn't know. And if he did would things have been any different? He didn't know. All he knew was that from the start he was drawn to her.

And, not wanting to show special favour, he had given most of his time to her sister. But after her sister married things had changed. Arabella's mother had a way with her. One look from her had Gilbert Kennedy trembling in his shoes. He, who had not had dealings with any kind of woman, had no idea of how to combat a woman like Mistress Hutcheon. It started with requests to take Arabella for walks in the garden when the weather was fine. And when the Baillie was away from home she'd insist that they were left alone, so that they should get to know one another, as she put it. Alone with her, without Catherine, he watched her grow to a woman. He knew long before she herself did that the child had gone.

When her mother began to talk marriage (there was no shame in the woman) he was petrified. He had not been thinking in that way, he never would. He was too timid. To enjoy being near her, to enjoy her loveliness was all that he asked. His thinking hadn't once gone beyond that. Until the evening of his birthday.

He had let slip earlier on that day that he was another year older, he was ancient, he'd soon start crumbling. Arabella laughed out loud to him. But nothing would do but Mistress Hutcheon would hold a small celebration for him, her husband's friend and who knew, maybe her son by law. He was embarrassed, he hated fuss. He wished he'd kept his mouth shut.

Through his unease there was Arabella, her hair piled high, giving her extra inches. He found it hard to drag his eyes from her, from her neck, her ears. She had handed him a small package. 'I made it myself.' She smiled her girl's smile at him. Her mother made her kiss him. Her mouth on his mouth. Then there was noise, laughing and hand clapping and tongues flapping. He didn't know where he was, his head was spinning, or was it the room that was going round. There was music, someone was at the spinnet and James MacKenzie was looking as if he would like to murder the lot of them.

He didn't know what to do with what came to crawl about inside him, to gnaw at his gut. It was a new feeling, this not knowing. He'd not experienced it before. He, who had seen himself as strong, shook like straw in the wind. She filled his head, he could do nothing. Work? What was his work? He was a fool. What had come on him had left him stranded. She was still a child.

He frightened her that first night despite trying to be gentle with her. Alone together in the house given to them by her father. It was all she knew in that house, pain of one kind or another. Was this what a man was? An uncontrolled thing, driven by the primal forces inside him? He hadn't known, he did not know now.

The Minister raised his head and reached for the large red-covered ledger lying across the table from him. He pulled it towards him and began to read what he had written in it. His right hand cupped his forehead as he read the minutes of the previous meeting, its thumb and long fingers rubbing his temples. He was having difficulty in understanding what the minutes said. His tiredness showed in his writing. Indecipherable scrapings covering the page. He was going to have to find someone who could do this for him. He couldn't do everything.

Chapter Five

They hadn't been back in their homes long when it was time to move out again, time to gather together their stock and take them up to the summer grazings. Throughout the long winter they had watched the animals growing ever more emaciated as they tried to scratch food and minerals from the poor thin ground. The cattle were the worst, nothing more than sacks of bones, chewing on whins which had been burnt brown from the frosts and the harsh north-east winds. Many of them hadn't the strength to stand, let alone walk or climb. These beasts had to be lifted up to the high ground. The people called this time of their year the lifting time. As a rule it was the man of the house who performed this task. And where there was no man, there were always plenty who offered. There were some hardy women who exerted their independence by lifting their cows themselves.

Whereas at Beltane they were away from their homes for the one night, at the lifting time preparations had to be made for a much longer stay. Two houses had to be run – the women and the girls up on the slopes, the men down in Strath. The men helped with the transport of supplies and herded the cows, the sheep and the horses. They usually left one or two of the older boys up on the hill to watch over the animals at night and to herd them during the day.

Much work had piled up over the winter. Roofs had to be replaced due to storm damage and through being used to feed the cattle. Walls needed to be plugged and strengthened. And if a house was in a bad enough state, a man might have to start from scratch and rebuild on a site beside his old house.

The peats had to be cut and heaped for drying, then carted home and stacked. Enough to see them through the year. And it was the time for sowing the corn, that is, if any seed survived winter's famine.

Strath throbbed to the sounds of people and animals. Sheep calling for their lambs, lambs crying for their mothers. There was the lonesome sound of bleating goats and the distressed bawling of cattle. And cutting through the different sounds there were the shouts of the men, the wild waving of arms and sticks, and flappings of bits of blanket as they tried to get the animals to go where they wanted them to go, and not to go splintering off all over the place. Some of the dogs didn't know they were meant to be working dogs, petted and spoiled as they were by the women and children. When it came to rounding up the sheep and the cattle, the men could make nothing of them. All the shouting and waving and flapping couldn't turn them from running around in slouch-backed circles, getting in the way of the proper working dogs. The air above Strath was very often a bluey colour when a man had to work with a dog like these.

The women travelled fairly light. They didn't have much of anything to take with them. Daniel's mother and sisters carried a bowl, the ingredients for making bread and what blankets the home could spare them. And that left the house bare enough. Daniel carried a spade, his family being better off than some. Some of the men carried heavy ropes slung across their chests, bent under the weight. They staggered their way up. Long winters had taken their toll of all but the strongest. Hungry people, they hadn't the heart nor the will, for much. The euphoria of Beltane was in the past. It was as if Beltane had taken place a year ago instead of just a few weeks ago.

Their noise danced ahead of them, floating high above them, bouncing off the hills before coming back to them, surrounding them and enveloping them in their own hope.

Those with sick cows had the hardest time. One woman, herself as gaunt and ghastly looking as her cows, her face all eyes and cheekbones, covered most of the journey on her knees as she tried to push the cow from behind. With what little strength she had she tried to lift the poor beast from where it had sunk onto the ground, but she could make nothing of it. She bent over it and her fleshless hands, stuck on the end of arms like weathered wood, pulled at the cow's loose skin. Getting nowhere, she went back onto her knees and pulled the cow's head onto her chest. She stayed that way a long time, looking about her, useless, with the cow's head lying on her. She didn't know what to do next. People walked past her, they had offered help and she had refused, and in any case they had their own work in hand. And everyone knew how thrawn she could be. In the end she knew she was going nowhere, not with that cow. She let go, looking down onto the head rolling away from her. The cow sank down further and the woman went with it, letting herself collapse on top of it. The two of them stayed there, sharp angled heaps of rattling bones.

Those cows that could walk, walked as if from memory. They could smell the grass, it was in their nostrils, the smell was tearing at their gut, but their legs wouldn't carry them to it. Some cows, whose spirit was greater than their physical strength, broke into an awkward shamble of a run, but then the memory failed and they, one after the other, buckled onto the ground. But they'd get up and try again, and again, as the sweet juice called.

Once up on the slopes it did not take them long to get settled in. Wood was gathered, fires were lit and bread was baked. The animals were let loose to graze where they would. They accepted their new surroundings with quiet dignity, as if they had known nothing but plenty.

One of the men who went straight back down was Daniel's father. He didn't wait long, there was plenty work to be done on the Strath house and below waited on him. And Donald Munro didn't wait. His going put a scowl on Peggy's face that served ill for the cow's teats. Daniel stayed up. He had work to do on his mother's hut. Some men stayed, the younger ones. When work on the huts was done, most of them would drift back down.

Higher up the weather was very wild. The pelting rain had ice in it which sliced them to the bone, making them round their shoulders and bow their heads beneath its weight. The wind tore into them whichever direction they turned. It tried to stop them from walking, from standing. It sharpened itself in the rain, it battered against them and it stole the heat from their bodies. It tried its best to steal the clothes from them. Only the weight of the rain helped to keep them covered.

Mairead hacked at heather with her father's broken spade. The spade had been abandoned for too long, it would be useless even for cutting butter. Her anger was wilder than the wind and the rain. She threw the spade from her and went down on her hands and knees. It was how she worked best. With her two hands gripping the heather, she sat back on her heels and ripped as hard as she could.

Daniel stopped working on his mother's roof to watch her. It surprised him to see her among people. He'd have thought she'd have gone some place on her own. Was she here last year and before? If she had been, he hadn't seen her. He reached for a turf and wedged it into the gap, thumping it down with his fist, making it fit. She was shouting at the heather, in between tugging and grunting. Anyone would think there were pigs up on the hill.

'What's wrong with her?' he asked a man digging near him.

'Her? That one's wrong in the head,' the man said and kept on digging.

Daniel let go of his spade and walked past three smiling girls who turned to look at him. He stopped beside an old wife who was sitting on a stone, puffing smoke from a wooden pipe.

'What's wrong with her over there?' he asked the old one.

'Ach.' The old one fluttered a withered hand and went on puffing.

'What are you trying to do?' he asked Mairead's back. If she heard him she paid no heed. Still the grunting coming from her, rough big hands tearing at the heather. He stood watching her. She'd rip out a lump and almost collapse on top of it, breath racketing out of her. With her mouth hanging open she'd rest back on her heels for a while and huff and puff away, the rain washing her, flattening her hair to her head, plastering her clothes against her body. Then she'd make a lunge at another bunch.

He crouched down beside her and watched her hands. They were good hands, strong looking, made for work. He felt sorry for the heather, the way she was pulling at it. He saw the long, surprisingly slender fingers open, saw the quietness in her hands. She knew he was there. Her head was still hanging and she didn't look round and he hadn't moved, but she knew he was there.

He kept looking at the shape of her head with its clamped hair hanging straight and covering most of her face, at one ear, exposed by a parting of the hair. Her ear was small. This too surprised him. He'd have thought that her ears would have matched the rest of her, if he'd imagined her ears. He wiped the rain from his eyes and looked at her hair. He wondered what it would be like to touch.

Still he crouched. She became a cornered hind. He watched her head come up. The movement was slow. He knew that behind the wet curtain she was watching him, her ears were listening for him. He saw the head begin to turn. Her eyes were brown. They caught his. The head snapped away again, snapped back down. Her hands were at the heather again, ripping it, riving it, gaining nothing.

'I'll do that for you.' He spoke to her ear. He wiped the rain from his eyes again. 'I'll do that.' This time his words were louder, stronger. He hoped to reach through her fear, through her fury. 'Let me help.' He saw she was shaking and he wondered if it came from the weather or from someplace else. In time words came from her but he couldn't make them out. In her distress her actions became more frantic. Words gathered inside her, words on top of words until they burst past her lips. Kneeling beside her in the heather in the wind and in the rain, he waited. He saw her body sagging, saw her rhythm slacken, give way to sporadic lunges now. Still he waited until at last she settled. The words were done. Now, only the odd grunt, which came from a place in her that only herself would know.

As the storm lashed the two of them he went on waiting until the storm inside her was completely still.

'I'll help you.' His words were softer now, they spoke directly to whatever was frightening her.

Still she wouldn't look at him, then her head swung round, but swung away as quickly.

'That spade's no use,' he said. 'It'll do nothing. I'll do that for you.'

She lifted her head until it was level with his own. She shook the hair from her rain-washed face. This time, her eyes, although shielded by her lowered eyelids, stayed with him, as he dripped rain beside her.

Then she spoke. The sound that came out of her was, like her ears, so unexpected that he lost what she was saying to him. He would have expected her words to be harsh, ugly even. He felt the hot flush of shame for what he had been thinking.

He tried to follow her words. A fairy song, they tinkled from her mouth. She caught him staring at her mouth, saw what was on his face. She jumped to her feet.

'Please.' He jumped with her. He reached out a hand to her. 'Please, don't run.' His own words stumbled from him. 'I'm sorry. It was just . . . I did not know.' He raked about in his head for good words. 'I did not think you would speak like that.' The words flattened out. He dropped them along with his outstretched hand. He pulled the soaking bonnet from his head. 'I'm sorry,' his pale eyes said through the rain.

She stood and looked at him and he back at her. He felt her intensity, it was as if she was trying to penetrate what lay beyond what her eyes were telling her. 'Yes,' she said after a while. 'Yes.'

'Right,' he said, and he raised his shoulders and made himself stand as straight as he could. But he made no move towards her. 'What you're pulling at there's no use for the roof. Overby, there's the right stuff.'

'Yes.' She appeared to think on what he was telling her, he saw her forehead pucker and her hand go up to it. 'Yes. That will be good.'

They were awkward with each other. She was afraid and he was walking blind.

'Right, then. Ay, right,' and the reassurance was for himself as much as for her.

'Yes,' she said, her head nodding. 'That will be good.'

She watched the helpful man as he walked away through the slanting rain. She knew who he was, she had chased him from the burn when he was small. The boy had grown into a beautiful-looking man. She knew, by sight, his family, his father and his mother and all of his sisters. She knew his crippled leg. Watching the back of him she also knew that his leg took nothing from the beauty or the strength of him. His two legs were good and strong, his back was wide.

She laughed, but into herself. With the straightness of him and that red hair he was better to look at than she herself was. A small laugh tore at her throat and she strangled it. Up on the hill, with no one to see her, she hid her hands in the folds of her frock and buried her feet in the heather. On her own she knew who she was. Among people, she was afraid that she would lose that knowledge.

Chapter Six

The Minister's eyes clouded as he gazed on the two moons which swelled from the top of Mary's frock. Mary thrust herself against him. He put his jug down on the rude table and tightened his arms about her.

'Come on.' Mary's closeness nearly smothered him. 'Drink that like the good man you are.'

Her arm lay dead and heavy around his neck.

'Landlord, this man's wanting more,' she called through the blue of the peat smoke.

The Minister said nothing. The front of his coat was stained and stiffened with the food and drink his mouth had missed. His thinning hair stuck to his head in sweaty clumps. His hat was nowhere to be seen.

Mary ground herself against him. It felt good. She heard him sucking in his breath.

There was about an even number of men and women in the alehouse. They sprawled on the floor, over the roughly made tables, lolled about on benches. The atmosphere was thick with the fire's reek and the smell of damp clothes, drink and people.

'You're the quiet one. No words.' Mary's mouth made soft words.

The Minister made a half-smile. Sweat ran from his hair-line and gathered in beads about his brows. It sat on his upper lip.

'You like Mary, now,' her mouth made.

He looked at her, at her roundness, at her dirtiness. She likely carried disease on her. He looked through that, to her youth and to her promises. He thought she was about the age his wife had been when he had married her.

'That's from me.' In spite of having only one eye the cobbler managed a watery wink at him as he handed him a jugful. Mary was his daughter.

The Minister took the jug, raised it to the cobbler by way of acknowledgement and thanks. He put his mouth to it. Mary put her mouth to his throat.

In the beginning he had kept clear of the Marys and their enticements. It was true that his life with Arabella had tried him, but he believed in God and in the beginning that had been enough. In God he had been strong.

But time passed, time passed. Arabella didn't change. She was still a stranger to him. And he lived with the knowledge of what he had created. He would take that to his grave with him. God knew best the price he was paying. And it was his price to pay, only his. But it was she who bore the greater pain. And he knew that too.

Then change came upon him. Sudden change. Doubt replaced certainty and threw him into a sea of wild confusion, showing him just how frail he was.

He was not a proud man, he had no great ideas about how good or how able he was. But he did believe in himself as God-made and in control. Through what happened with Arabella that control had held. Until now. He may not have felt good about the situation, but neither did he feel that the solid rock which was holding him had turned to shifting sand. He felt that now.

Doubt he had known. All his life, plenty of it. It made trouble for him when he was a young man, but as he grew he was able to argue against these doubts. Does doubt enter a closed mind? he asked himself more than once. No. Can anything enter into anything that's closed? It is into the open and questioning mind that doubt will creep. So, he asked himself, what would YOU rather take to God? He knew the answer. Take me and use me most mighty God. Here am I, all that I am able to be in you, a closed mind. No! No! A thousand times no! For him the nondoubter, the nonquestioning would be the suspect one.

He realised, of course, that there were many of his calling who did not think as he did. So be it. He kept his mouth closed around those men.

This doubt in him now, he felt it harder to understand. Quite simply it was that he wasn't who he thought he was. 'I didn't think I was like this,' were the words which were never far from him.

From as far back in his life as he would care to go he had been sure of where he had stood in God. It wasn't that he believed in God, God was his reason for being. In God he existed, without Him nothing.

God was constant, so where was the lack? Sore to look on, sorer still to acknowledge. In himself. It was himself who was lacking in strength, in will and in courage. Oh yes, above all in courage.

The Minister drank a mouthful of the cobbler's ale and with his mind he ravished the cobbler's daughter.

There had always been women who promised. Before Arabella he wouldn't have seen, he wouldn't have been looking. But since Arabella he knew. Looking back, her mother. He had been blind.

Strath, he supposed, was no different to any other place. Only, among the Strath people the loose morals, which were the basis of their lives, were there to be seen. In Arabella's mother, and women like her, from a tidier side of life, a fine veneer overlaid their approach to living. Strip away what they covered themselves in and they weren't so very different to the Marys, from Strath or from any other place. If the time was right they were ready.

A part of him envied MacIver and his like. Mostly he envied that man's hard denial that there was anything wrong in what he was doing. 'How can what's natural be bad?' was roughly MacIver's reply to any challenge to his morals. 'It's no bad for me.'

He was forced to admit that MacIver, untouched by the teaching of any church, had a strength and a surety that he, the Minister, did not. How could that be?

He opened his mouth to Mary's, and all resistance went at the touch of her hands.

He did not come easily to this side of life. The first time, which will always be what the memory retains, was ugly. The woman had been old and hard. Her empty breasts flapped about her waist and her stench was unbearable. After nearly a decade he still shuddered at the thought of that coupling and the wretched thing's energy.

That first time had showed him how far he'd fallen. It frightened him into walking a straight line for a long time afterwards. He had been walking straight for about two years when a girl came to him, a girl with the scent of summer in her hair and on her skin. She was the one he should have remembered.

He walked in guilt. And as he aged he found the load harder to carry. So he tried to drown his guilt in drinking.

Taking his hand in hers Mary led him out of the ale-house. He stumbled after her, past the drinkers (her father was still there). The men wanted Mary, the sly women wanted what the Minister could give them. Pennies for their purse. The status of belonging, even momentarily, to someone of a higher standing than those they lived among.

She led him out into an evening in early summer, where the thick sweet smell of growing grass and the smoke from peat fires filled the air. It was darkening, full night had not yet descended. The village was empty of people, the houses seeming to cluster closer for night. Those who were not in the ale-house were home in their beds, their children rolled safely beside them, safe from whatever might come in the night. Dogs lay sleeping before the dampened fires or against their recumbent owners.

Mary took the Minister past the sleeping houses, skirting the middens and the sleeping dogs. His hand was still holding hers. He walked like a man in a fog, unsure of where to put his feet. On through the common grazing, shared by the cattle, the horses and the sheep. The sheep spread out, grazing, the cattle and the horses gathered together in standing groups at opposing ends of the enclosure. On past the burial ground to the place of the ancient stones. Beside the trees there she pulled him down on her.

It was not the first time with Mary. She was worth the penny or two which he gave her, and which her mother would take from her, to put into a small bag which she hid beneath the mattress.

He was a shy man who had little understanding of himself. His work occupied all of him. And what he had become worked against him, making him feel even more locked in on himself. With Mary he came as near as he ever would come to freeing himself from the things that bound him.

As he lay beside her beneath the quivering leaves of an aspen, he reached over a hand to touch her face. 'Mary.' Her name was a whisper, like the leaves.

She put her finger to his mouth, held her name there.

Chapter Seven

Late summer found the Strath men gearing up for the big cattle market in Dingwall. This was held on Marymas, around the middle of August.

Dingwall, Thing Voller the Norseman who settled the place had named it, meaning Assembly Place. And to this assembly place men came with cattle from all over the north of Scotland. As well as being the main cattle sale, it was also a day out for the people of the surrounding districts. It was a meeting-up place. People bought and people sold, some found a bargain, others lost. Whatever, Marymas was a good time to be in Dingwall, for whoever journeyed there.

Drovers and cattle poured out of Caithness, joined by men from the Orkneys who had crossed the Pentland Firth in open boats with their beasts. Over the Ord of Caithness with its cliffs falling to the sea they came, pushing on through the trees to Helmsdale and down by Brora. Men and beasts came out of the glens of East Sutherland, from the straths called Halladale and Naver.

These men were joined by others from the hilly country of the far north-west, from Assynt and from Reay. All making for where the river narrowed, just south of Strath.

By the time the tip of the black ribbon reached the narrows the Strath men were already there with their beasts. Some were in boats, trying to tow cows through the black water. The small boats were being tossed about like fallen leaves by the thrashing cows. Some men were trying to get their beasts to go into the water by prodding them with long sticks. Under the incoming swell of hoofs and droppings the bank was a churning mess of porridge.

The bank was no place for the human voice. It could never be heard above the bawling bulls and heifers and stirks and the Strath men's sheep. The big stick did the talking that day. And the drover's dogs. The drovers had good dogs, they swam like fish in the water. Their one problem was the sheep. Not used to working sheep, the drover's dogs kept running among them and nipping them no matter how many times they were chased.

The river boiled under so much traffic, and the great numbers sparked off the frightened beasts even more. And their frenzy spread and multiplied.

The drovers weren't shy with their sticks. One of them, an Orkney man, had been drunk crossing the Pentland Firth. Crossing the Black Water he was ten times drunk. The way he laid into the beasts left more than one of them bashed and bloody. The poor beasts just stood and took the beatings, too afraid to cry.

The drovers had the heaviest work to do. They'd been doing it for more than a week. The river crossing was but the next step for them. And they were the experts. The Strath men had fewer animals to put across but they hadn't the skill of the drover men. The drover men had hundreds, some of them thousands, of beasts, gathered from the big landowners.

Daniel and his father had already taken their horses across. His father stayed with them while Daniel made his way back to start on the cows. He was swimming one of the horses back, up to the waist in river water, his hands holding on to the horse's mane. They'd arrived first, before the rest of the Strath men. Word had come into Strath the previous night that the drovers had reached Lairg and were camping out there for the night. The two of them managed to get the horses across in the quietness of the early morning.

From his horse's back Daniel looked across to the north bank. Black cattle kept on coming, pouring out of the trees like a thick stream of molasses, heads down, running to water.

Up river a boat holding four Strath men was sitting low, water sapping its gunwales. The men had the end of ropes looped around a cow's horns. This cow was the leader of a string of eight or nine, which were standing at the water's edge. Two men were hard at the oars, he could see the strain in the curve of their backs and the muscles bulging in their arms. The other two were on their knees in the stern of the boat, heaving on the ropes. They pulled the first cow into the water and the others followed. It was the best way to manage the awkward ones.

Back at the bank a horse was standing on a rock with ropes about it. A small group of men were up on the rock with the horse. From a distance it looked as if they were performing a kind of war dance with the horse joining in, kicking up its hoofs, making the men kick up their heels as they jumped out of the way. The horse was having the best of them, its head was back and the ropes were dangling loose while the men performed their fancy steps and their hands came away with air. They jockeyed for their place on the rock, getting thrown from their positions by the weight and the size and the strength of the horse. One man tumbled into the river, losing his hat to the current. He lunged for it but the river was too fast. He slapped at the water, drowning his hair and face. Those left put their shoulders against the horse's rear and that way they managed to push it into the water. The horse landed on its knees, drenching the men with spraying foam. The men leapt after it and again through thrashing water they trawled for ropes. A waiting boat rowed in close. The men in it caught up the ropes and held on to them. There were six men in that boat, two rowing, four for the ropes, these were on their knees, two on each side of the boat, a rope each. The oarsmen pulled and the boat started to move. The rope men heaved, taking the horse with them.

Another man had been stupid. He was in the middle of the river on his own wrestling with a cow. Both were out of their depth. The cow went down first. Daniel watched the man's head breaking the water and the white bubbles coming up. The man's mouth was wide but whatever he was shouting was lost in the bawling cattle sound. Even with his cow pulling him under the man was still holding on to it. The other arm flopped like a broken wing on the water. Daniel screamed. And his scream was more distressing than anything that came from the throat of a cow or a horse.

It took the best part of two days for the drovers and themselves to get everything across. Men and beasts were both cold and exhausted beyond endurance by the time they made camp on the other side. Having taken the best from them, the river appeared to flow stronger.

Some of the cattle hung about in silent groups in the trees, they hadn't strength left for grazing. Some stood in rows down by the rocks at the water's edge and looked at the river. Their calling could be heard echoing up through the pines, bouncing from silent hill to silent hill. The dogs lay as if dead on the muddy ground and in hollows among the rocks. Around the camp-fires it was the voices of the drovers that carried the loudest. All the hard work plus jugs of whisky did little to quieten them.

Daniel left his own fire and walked down to the river. From the leather pouch hanging from the belt at his waist he tipped a handful of meal into his palm. Scooping some water onto the meal he made a mix. It was poor food but he was glad he had it. He walked back up to the fire, circled round, and stopped before one of the men who had lost a son to the regiment. He offered him some. The man, who had nothing, took a little in his fingers. Daniel stood looking down at the man. He knew the drive and the river would be heavy enough on those like himself. How much more then on men like this.

'Take more,' he told the man. 'I'm not that hungry.'

The man shook his head. He was thinking of his wife and young family. Since his son's death the man had grown afraid. It was as if one day he would waken and they all would be gone.

'Do you think they'll be safe Daniel?' he asked. 'I'm only thinking I should have stayed. Like your own father. He went back.'

Daniel bent his head and put his hand to his mouth. 'Ach, don't be thinking that way. My father has me to see to the beasts. Look, you're here and they're there. Home in Strath.

Safe. Ach, they'll be fine,' he said, licking the porridge from his palm.

'Are you sure Daniel? Is that what you're thinking?'

'Ay,' Daniel shivered, feeling the cold creep about him. 'They'll be fine, now. It's yourself you should be thinking of. We'll be needing the beasts' heat the night to keep warm.'

The ground they lay on was a quagmire of mud and animal droppings and no amount of drinking could make it anything else. River water could be wrung from them, and as the night temperature dipped they lay against the cows in their wet heavy clothes and through the long night hours they longed for morning when they would be on the move again.

The dogs slept. They found holes in the rocks, they burrowed in the undergrowth between trees.

One of the drovers' dogs was back roaming among the sheep, looking for trouble. He found it when he strayed among the cows. He tackled one, trying to sink his teeth in a cow's leg. The cow put its horns under the dog and threw it up into the air. The dog came back down, landing four square in the middle of the herd. The drovers' dogs were rough, but they were also tough.

As soon as the day broke they were ready to move. It was dry and that was a bonus. There was not much getting ready to do. They only had to come to their feet. The dregs of jars were swallowed and the jars left lying. With the river behind them they could expect to make good time, hoping for ten miles in the day with the horses; six with the cows was the best they could hope for.

The horses went first, followed by the cows. The sheep were last. The shepherd's work was built on infinite patience, as nothing would hurry his sheep. They grazed en route, they kept doubling back on him and going in circles, taking the shepherd with them. The shepherd walked more miles in a day than any man, his progress was very slow. Shepherds were usually quiet and uncomplaining men.

Most of the men were kind to the animals but there were one or two on the drive who were like the Orkneyman. Having little understanding of cows and therefore no patience with them, their sticks were never at rest.

But for men like Daniel and the other Strath men this was a good time of year. If the going was hard they did not take too much notice. Life was hard on them anyway, but they were abreast of it.

As they walked behind their cows or at the head of their horses they marvelled at this other country which lay beyond Strath. The forests they travelled through covered the whole of the world. Could that be their own hills reaching up into the sky? Who ever saw a flower with colour like that on it? This was it, this was life, being among other men, enjoying the company and the talk. They were easy with themselves and with others. Like this, the men from the straths and the glens would march forever. They had great admiration for the drovers, with their sure knowledge of the easiest way through untamed country. On long drives like this the Strath man also came into his own. This was home to him, out in the open, under the sky, his stamina and strength tested, driving his cows and his horses. Not for him the lot of the slow-moving shepherd, with his slow-moving flock.

It took them a week to reach Dingwall. They walked in the day and camped out overnight, their stock corralled in holding pens along the way. They took turns to stay with the animals at night. Some men never slept the entire time they were away. For these men the march became a stagger. At one stopping place up on the hill called Struie a man and two of the shepherd boys were lost to wolves that came looking for sheep in the night. They were buried up there.

The came down through the forests at Ardross on a day that was dry and fine, through land that belonged to the Munro of Foulis, then on into Dingwall itself.

The place was teeming with people and all sorts of animals, most of them cows. The drive down had been hard, especially on the animals which had travelled farthest. What the good summer grazing had added to them, the long drive had taken off. Some of the Caithness beasts had that lean, undernourished look about them and those which had come across from the Orkneys were particularly poor. Their ribs were showing.

The animals had become so accustomed to walking that they didn't know how to stop. They piled up behind one another, bumping to a halt. Then there was the job of turning them, and putting them into pens, the cows going in colliding with cows coming out. The horses were led off first, to be corralled at the far end of the field away from the cows. The confined space and too many people milling about frightened them, sending them up on their back legs again, performing their own particular aerial dance with their front legs, heads back and flanks rippling, ripping the rope that tethered them from the hands of the man or boy leading them. And as hands leapt for the rope hoofs smashed against hands and wrists. Daring boys were trampled in the muck as they tried to show how brave they were. Flying hoofs could split a head like a stone cracking a hazelnut.

Turning the cows was difficult. It took skill and time. In their panic they tried jumping over one another's backs to escape. Daniel had to push a foolish man out of the way of some. The man was wandering about with his back to the cattle, deaf to their clamour as they ran towards him.

In the pens, too many animals were crammed into too small a space. It would be hard to drop a leaf between them the way they were packed. All trampling on top of each other, no air for them to breathe. More shouting and cursing and wielding of big sticks.

And here, at the Marymas fair in Dingwall, young boys from the glens and the straths got their education into just how coarse men could be. Boys who had been proud of what had been asked of them, able to task, crying at what they saw happening to the animals. One of Strath's boys, unable to make his horse go into the pen, and with his father lost somewhere in the crowd, caught at Daniel as a short man with a sagging bottom lip lifted his stick to the small horse's back.

Daniel saw what the man was at. He went up to him and grabbed the hand using the stick. 'Lay that stick on that horse and I'll break it over your back,' he said.

The man wrestled with Daniel, then with himself. His fleshy fingers slackened, the stick was in the mud, the man's power lying with it.

Once he got his own horses settled, Daniel set out to have a look around. He joined the crowd watching the cock fight. The crowd was divided, some calling for the black bird, some for the white one. The cocks' owners were taking bets. Men in the crowd were throwing pennies into a wooden plate. The white cock's owner was a long yard of starvation, the other's coat buttons were bursting as they strained to contain his round belly. They squatted on their heels and coaxed their birds one minute, threatened them with murder the next. Saliva ran from the corner of the long one's mouth, ran down his grizzled chin and disappeared into a knot of grey rag at his throat. The man was waving his arms and shrieking his excitement to the gathered crowd. His bird was having the best of the fight. It was smaller but it was hammering the black one, pecking at it until it drew blood from its head. Feathers flew, white and black and there was a mixture of cheering and groaning from the crowd.

Next to the crates of fowls brought in by country wives, the bagpiper was playing, his cheeks going in and out like bellows, his upper arm was working the bag. He was playing too close to the horses and his reeds had to fight against their whinnying sounds. A juggler, a strange looking fellow, his clothes and his face brightly coloured, was keeping four small round leather balls in the air. Daniel tried to follow the speed of his hands and the balls but he could not. He blinked and shook his head to clear his vision, but it made no difference. The juggler was still too fast.

Stray dogs with their heads down, tails erect ran everywhere, nosing everything, mostly the rears of other dogs. It was a good day for a dog to be in Dingwall.

Buyers from all over Scotland were there, from the south as well as the north. Hard businessmen who knew the value of a penny. They poked at the cattle with their sticks and kicked their forelegs. And those interested in horses were as bad. A number of the horses were left in the care of young boys who were paid a penny by the drovers so that the drovers could return to the serious business of drinking which they had begun at the start of the drive. The boys knew nothing of such men and their ways. They were frightened by the things they were witnessing, the cruelty, the drunkenness, but they didn't know what to do.

Country people also brought their round drums of cheese and eggs packed tightly in baskets. Cheese so strong smelling that it stopped the dogs sniffing each other's rears and had them barking at it. The stalls of the cloth-sellers were grouped together, the unrolled bolts fanning out to make manufactured rainbows. Cloth dyed crimson from the roots of the crottle, yellow cloth from the roots of the bog-myrtle, green from the dark shaded heather, blue from the blaeberry and cloth dyed black from the bark on the oak. Tinkers filled every corner with jugs and bowls and pots. Shoemakers from the Black Isle had a stance next to the sheep. Brogues and cheap leather boots were what they were offering. One shoemaker was a woman with one eye. The skin of her face looked as tough and as brown as the boots she was selling.

There were barrels of salted fish and herring from the East Coast villages, trundled in on barrows, coopers with wooden tubs and pails and spoons and spirtles. Fisherwives wandered about bent double under creels of whelks and dulce and tangle and begged people to buy. And there were pedlars selling literature to anyone who could read.

Showmen filled the corners that the tinkers did not. Tumblers came tumbling, fire-eaters swallowed flames, men put swords into their mouths and pushed them down their throats and into their insides. A young fiddler with black curls played as if he had a demon inside him, his head and feet dancing like his music.

Whatever had been poached from the hill was laid out on tables. Deer, hares, wild fowl as well as domestic. All black, with at least two weeks' death on them. Beside the game, and indeed half-covering it, furs and skins were spread, stiffened and curling around the edges. There were wooden work implements – spades, hand ploughs, mallets. Side stalls were sagging under painted pottery and wooden dishes for the home.

Although Daniel had been coming every year since he was a young boy, every year was like the first time. The people, the noise, the smells, the colour. The excitement. Everything that anyone would ever need was here in this place. And plenty things which would never be used. He felt reborn in the exhilaration generated by the showmen – strange people to his world. Men and women drunk on emotion as well as spirits were falling over themselves and anyone, or anything else that moved. Or didn't. Coming to this from Strath, Daniel couldn't think or see fast enough to take it all in.

Caught up on this atmosphere, he collided with a girl. He thought in his dazed state she was Peggy. Her looks and build were Peggy's. The girl squealed and he put out a hand to steady her. He was reminded of Donald Munro. He had to be dealt with. Their paths hadn't crossed yet, but they would. The runt, he was here somewhere. He noticed that Munro's two young brothers were left holding the horses. That meant the Munro would be filling himself up on bad whisky and worse women. Well, Daniel could wait. He had to come back sometime.

Up to his ankles in mud and muck he walked back to his own horses, this time his eyes on where he was going. A man from the south wearing a torn blue coat was there, walking among them, cracking them on the forelegs with a stick.

'Sad-looking lot,' the man said in his southern tongue.

Daniel said nothing, keeping his mouth shut on ownership. His horses weren't the best-looking there, but neither were they the worst. Some rattled where they stood. If the man from the south was interested in paying the best price he'd be among the best horses, not wandering among lesser stock like his own.

The man lifted his stick. For the second time that day Daniel put an end to someone's cruelty. 'If you hurt them, I'll hurt you,' he said. The words were soft, but the eyes were like flint. 'They have had it hard enough, they don't need more from you. State your price or leave them be.'

The man straightened, his body stiffened. Daniel looked at his puffed-up face, at the challenge blazing in his half-closed eyes. The face grew tighter, the eyes bolder as he tried to pull his arm free. In time the eyes slid downward, then the arm as Daniel opened his fingers and released his hand. The man stumbled backwards, his challenge lying in the mud. Then sucking in his cheeks he turned and shouldered his way past the horses and through the crowd, muttering to himself in his southern accent. Daniel clapped the head of the nearest horse, stroked its nose, and told it a story in a voice which would calm them all. Then he went back to check his cows.

On the way he stopped by a cooper's stall. A small crowd, mostly women, were examining the cooper's goods. If he took a good enough price for the cows he'd take a pail home to his mother, she was needing one. Maybe a good-sized spoon.

He listened to the cooper at his work. The words came from him in one long rapping word. There were words in the cooper's word that he had never heard spoken. The cooper's voice was like the river, rumbling on, rising and falling, singing the story of the spoons and the spirtles.

Warm-looking blankets drew him over to the weaver from Strath. So many colours he wouldn't know which he would take. In his mind he saw Mairead, up on the hill, wrapped in a bright blanket as she sat milking her cow. A blanket like one of these would keep her warm. Remembering his father put a stop to his thinking. His father would say something about his spendthrift ways. His father would know.

Even with their baskets discarded, the fisherwives wouldn't straighten their backs. The smell of the sea from them was strange to him. The smell of the earth, the smell of the animals, was on everyone he knew. He was born among it, slept in it, from the first walked among it. It was nothing to him. He noticed it only when it wasn't there.

The girls and women from the coast he would have picked out anywhere. It wasn't only the way they wore their skirts, kilted up to their thighs for easy walking. The salt sat on them, laying pearls on their skin. Their skin was paler than that of the country or hill women. Those women had the earth and the things that grew on it on them, in them. The coast women had a sea-washed cleanness about them. A young girl with tangles in her fair hair stopped before him. She was about his sister Anna's age. Her cheeks glowed, her short white legs looked firm and strong, the toes on her small broad feet took a strong grip of the earth.

'Buy my dulce.' She smiled her shy child smile at him.

Seeing Anna in her he smiled back. 'I haven't money,' he told her. 'I'm here to sell my horses and the cows.'

The smile slid from her face and her face closed on her. Then she reached over her shoulder to the basket on her back. 'Take it,' she said, and the smile was back. The man had a kind face. His face was like her brother Andrew's. She put a piece of seaweed into his hand. It hadn't travelled well and was dry and brown, beginning to harden.

Daniel looked at what he was holding. It looked raggy and felt slippery in his fingers. The girl laughed at what she saw written on his face. He looked as if he thought the dulce was going to eat him.

'Put it in your mouth.' Her straight white teeth bit into a piece and she chomped at it like a horse.

Daniel peered at her mouth to see what would happen to her, watched her even more closely when he saw that she had swallowed the stuff.

'Good.' She fed another piece into her mouth. 'Eat,' she said.

Daniel's face went into knots at the thought. He thrust the dulce back at her. 'I could not,' he said. 'I could not eat that. Although you are very kind.'

The girl from the shore was delighted at the strange man's antics. Dimples came on her cheeks. 'You're not afraid of what grows on the rocks, surely?' She refused to take the dulce from him.

'It's the smell. It would choke me.'

'No more than the smell of horses and cows and sheep will choke me.' Her laugh had the sound of soft waves washing over pebbles on the shore.

Daniel had no answer to give her, and she made no move to take the seaweed back from him. It flapped between them like a gossip's tongue.

'Eat,' the fisherman's girl nodded her head.

Under her gaze, Daniel closed his eyes and opened his mouth. He bit into the salty weed. It was like biting on leather. Its taste and its texture made him want to spew. But a bonnie young girl was looking up at him, so he bit down on his rising bile. He made himself chew, squeezing his eyes tight so that he wouldn't see himself doing it. To swallow the stuff was about the hardest thing he had done in his life, that he was sure of. He'd swallowed plenty of what was strange before now. Hungry, he'd eat almost anything. He'd even eaten grass. His eyes had water in them, but he was still standing. For the girl, because she was beautiful, he crammed the remainder into his mouth. His eyes overflowed. Water trickled down his face. The girl clapped her hands. 'More,' she sang, her hand reaching to her basket.

Daniel put out a hand. 'No,' the word was a squeak. 'No,' he said it again, afraid that his voice was going to fail him. 'But it's good,' he told her, in between coughing and swallowing. 'Not like what I expected.' His eyes crinkled at her, for her kindness and her young ways. 'Good,' he said, his feet already moving away from her. He was still telling her, or was it himself, how good the seaweed tasted when he walked into the Orkneyman.

The Orkneyman was blind with drink. His path swayed from side to side as he tried to walk on it. Daniel went to step one way, the Orkneyman stepped with him.

'Out of my way,' the Orkneyman bellowed through the fumes, trying to belly Daniel out of the way. 'If you had two good legs you'd maybe manage to keep from bumping into folk.'

Shock robbed Daniel of a quick answer. He stood where he was and allowed the Orkneyman to walk right through him. In Strath, where he had been born and had lived all his life, no one spoke to him that way. Some may have thought it, but they were too well-bred for the words to come from their mouths. In Strath the strong did their best to protect the less strong, the old and the young, the women and girls and those who weren't so able. Strath was the cover they drew around themselves for protection. That's what the strongest were for. A couple of times before, away from Strath, he had been spoken to like this and always by men. But by no one from his own country. The one who did speak would think deeply on the price he would have to pay, before he opened his mouth.

The Orkneyman's words hurt him. It took from him the sunshine the girl had put there. He felt the taste of bitterness in his mouth and the rising heat of anger.

A day did not pass, not an hour of a day, when he forgot for one second that he had one leg that was two inches shorter than the other one. Two inches. Say it fast and it seems nothing much. A small enough measurement. Take two inches from, say, the top of a tree. What remained would still be a tree.

Maybe the tree would know what was missing, but no person or no thing would and the tree would still flourish in its glory. Take two inches from a piece of land – what would be the difference? Stunt a horse, or a cow by the same. Still no great concern. But take two inches from the leg of a man, from the earth's hunter, what then? In his blackest times he wished that he had no leg at all, or worse, that he had never been born.

His father and his mother never talked about his leg. Either between themselves or to him. With them it was as if there was nothing to talk about. Was that how they saw what he carried? As nothing? To them he might have two good legs. But he didn't have two good legs. He'd never known two good legs.

He couldn't remember his father ever looking at his leg. He'd always find a reason to look away. Daniel used to wonder at the way his father always kept his head turned away from him, even when they were out on the hill. He soon got used to looking at the back or the top of his father's head. His mother's look never left him. He wished it would. She drowned him in her looking. Was it pity? Or was it guilt? There was a time when he swilled as much whisky as the Orkneyman, and more. Twenty times in a day he could be drunk. A pity it did such hellish things inside him. He could use it now. Being crippled was bad, but being crippled and permanently drunk was worse than bad.

His sisters helped him. Lying out on the hill with Peggy,

tracking the deer. His leg no impediment to his mobility as he grew. And Peggy would never let him look at himself for long. She'd stand under his nose and make a mouth at him and say to anyone who was near, 'Will you look at that face? Poor Daniel,' and she'd cross her black eyes and look along the line of her nose until he had to laugh at her. How could anyone be sad for long with Peggy? And Anna, twelve years and always at him to be doing something. With Anna it was always, 'Daniel,' the syllables of his name strung out in her baby voice. 'Daniel, will you take me too? Will you take me to the hill? Down to the river to find the big fish? To the pool in the dark night and will you show me how to catch the moon in my two hands and will you show me how to hold it so that it doesn't slip through my fingers back into the black water and drown?'

Although less than two years lay between himself and Ishbel, it was Ishbel he looked to, she mothered him from the start, petted him and dogged his toddling footsteps. His sister Flora was different. With her brisk ways she didn't take time for him. Flora was so robust she'd work the whole of Strath single-handed if she had to. There was always plenty for Flora to do. She lifted the water from the burn, baked the bread and she was always in someone's house helping. And her strong attitude stretched to the protection of her brother. The four of them wrapped him up in the blanket of their warmth. And if the blanket felt a little tight in one or two places, well, he was strong, he could pull.

Head down, he took himself and his punctured spirit back to the horses. There'd be no rejection from them. The man from the south was back, trying his tricks again but Daniel couldn't be bothered. He'd learnt that the best way to deal with men like these was to adopt a take-it or leave-it attitude. His disinterest finally got the better of the buyer and in the end he paid the asking price. Daniel put the silver coins into a small leather purse and stuffed it down the front of his shirt. No point in tempting the pickpockets. He'd go along to the cooper for his mother's spoon. Her pail would have to wait. He'd see how the cows went. Then there was the man he needed to see.

It would be as well to be now. Thanks to the Orkneyman he was feeling in the right kind of form for Donald Munro.

Donald Munro was rolling among his own kind at the bar, next to the cow pens at the southern end of the field. Any concern that he might have felt for his young brothers left holding the horses had long since evaporated. No concern there for anything but his own excesses.

'Rossach,' his grinning face greeted Daniel as Munro bounced off a long-faced man, whose kilt had come loose and was trailing in the mud. The partially unclothed man skipped aside, stood on his kilt, tripped and ended up face down in the mud. Munro made a grab at Daniel's front.

It surprised Daniel that Donald Munro could tell who he was speaking to. He looked like a man who had been shot from the inside. His eyeballs were crimson. Daniel flung his sagging weight off. 'Ach,' he said, 'you're rotting, man. But you'll keep. Get back to your beasts. They're not going to stand and wait for you. And you might look to your brothers. The pair of them are shaking. There's a lot here that's frightening them.'

Still grasping a bunch of Daniel's shirt, Munro hung slackly before him, swaying like a sapling in a gale. Then he turned to look for the man in the trailing kilt and, failing to locate him, screwed up his face at Daniel. He tried to turn the rest of his body, but he couldn't make his feet move. 'Are you hearing that?' He sprayed toxic saliva in Daniel's face. With locked knees he walked up to the man, tried to bend down to touch him, overdid the angle and ended up on top of him. Then, 'Come on,' he dribbled at Daniel, from a relatively comfortable seat on Loose Kilt's back. 'Come on you miserable long-faced apology. Hell, there's happier looking grave-stones.' He bobbed up from his drinking friend and fell against Daniel again and put both arms around him. Daniel stood like a rock. 'You're my friend,' Munro slobbered against him. Again Daniel pushed him away. 'I'm no friend of yours, Munro. One day you'll know that.'

'Oh,' Donald Munro's mouth made an O and he tried to wag a finger at Daniel but failed. His face was blotchy and red, matching his eyes. 'You're scaring me,' and he collapsed in on himself, laughing at his own cleverness.

'Ay, be scared. You might be too far gone to bite your own thumb just now. But one day,' and Daniel left Munro to sink back down in his own heap.

The way back was quicker. The drovers weren't with them so the band was thinner. Practically all of the stock had been sold and there was silver clinking in their purses. Spirits were strong and their hearts were glad. They straggled back over the hill they called Struie with their dogs, most bellies filled with drink if nothing else. The men from the straths and the glens missed the camaraderie of the drovers, felt the cold draught of uncertainty without them.

Shambling home at the far end of the line, Donald Munro was in a filthy way. Half of his ponies were going back with him and they felt the stick because of this. The road felt the stick for being a road and just for being there. It was the same with the rocks, with the heather and the weather. He moaned about everything. Nothing was right when himself was wrong. His two brothers kept well clear of him, as did everyone else. To listen to Munro, if his brothers had had the sense that they were born with, he wouldn't be taking sacks of bones home to be fed.

Two days of hard walking took them in sight of their houses. As they filtered down out of the trees to see the smoke rising from their house fires, they found from somewhere the energy to run the last stretch. All except Donald Munro with his clanking ponies. His step, his expression remained the same.

Daniel came on his mother going from the peat stack, her back bent over an armful of peats. She heard them coming and, lifting her head, turned to look. Her face was smiling for him. It was a long time since she had looked on his face. Ishbel was sitting among feathers at the door of the house, a half-plucked white hen between her bent knees. She looked up and smiled as he came closer.

'I took you a spoon,' Daniel said to his mother, his hand going into the front of his shirt.

His mother laid down the peats, took the spoon in her worn hands. For a time she looked at it, she hadn't words. She held the spoon, caressing the grain in the wood with her thumb, her thumb hesitating in the spoon's bowl.

'Oh,' she said to him, shy now, her eyes almost closed, though still smiling, still looking at the spoon. 'Oh.' And, 'It's a fine spoon, a fine spoon. I never thought to have a spoon like this.' Her hands loved the spoon.

'Well,' Daniel didn't know she'd be like this over a spoon. 'It's good you like it, anyway. I didn't get your pail. Where's my father?'

'He's over looking to the cows.'

'I saw Donald Munro but he was filled to the neck. How's Peggy?'

'Peggy's fine. Nothing in Peggy's head but that black fellow. She took Anna up to the pool. You know what the pair of them are like for the pool.'

Daniel could have done without what was waiting for him. He'd sold the best of their cows in Dingwall. The condition of those left had not improved any in the time he was away. Even from a distance there was no disguising the state of them. Part of the herd was by now on the ground, their bellies ballooned, legs sticking out straight. His father was there in the group of men, standing discussing what might be done.

'I don't know what we're going to do,' were his father's first words to him as he walked up.

'Ay.' Daniel stood with his hands on his hips and surveyed the herd. 'Not very bonnie.' He was counting the number left standing of his own cattle.

'All but six we lost since you went,' his father said in a sing-song voice. 'Some have lost the lot. I don't know what we're going to do about the rent, I don't know.'

'Well, that's the best I could get,' Daniel handed the purse to his father. And as his father went to tuck it into his own shirt, 'Aren't you going to count it?'

'Ach,' his father said, looking at the leather purse. 'I'm through other with thinking. I don't know where I am.

Did they take a good price?' Too much of life had dulled his father's eyes.

'Good enough. Fair I would say, seeing the state that some of the cows were in. The horses went best. I sold them to a man from the south,' he plucked the purse back from his father. 'Reach out your hand,' he told him, and he poured the coins into his father's outstretched palm. Thirty pounds. Twenty-four of that for the horses. Not much. It's the best I could get.'

His father's fingers folded over the coins. He felt their weight. 'You got a good price,' he said handing the coins back. 'Take it home and put it by. We'll have to guard it well.' Seeing the money did nothing to lift the old man's spirit. 'I'm just no knowing. Someone's angry at us. Why that? We have never been slack with our offerings. Myself poured out milk on the hill we didn't have just last evening. What do you say? Why do you think it is that they're not hearing us?'

'Who can say?' Daniel wasn't listening to his father's babble. Him and his spirits. He'd never change. Daniel's eyes were still on the cattle. 'But I'd like to know. That's for sure.'

'I don't know is it anger or is it spite? Eh?'

'Well, we're not the only ones suffering.'

'But you'd think they would hear us. That's the thing. We've done nothing. Do you think someone put the eye on the cows? Would that be it?' and he caught Daniel's sleeve, shaking his arm in agitation.

'Be quiet, man. Don't be talking that way here. Someone could hear.' His eyes measured distance, his ears were keen and listening but everyone seemed occupied with the disaster they had before them.

'I don't know,' his father said again, still in his singing voice. 'I'm that afraid,' and whatever his eyes were seeing, it wasn't sick cattle.

'Come on,' Daniel said. 'We'll see to the dead ones. Did you make a start on any?'

'No, no, I never did. I was waiting for yourself. Did you see about the Munro fellow?' They began to walk over to the cows, to search through the stench for their own.

'I found him. Overflowing as usual.'

'When was that boy any different? When was his family any different?'

'Ay, well, there's a day coming on him.'

'It's just that Peggy – her belly's growing. He'll have to take her or we'll have the church on to us. I just don't know. What's coming next?'

'He'll take her,' Daniel clipped the words from his tongue. His mind was with his cattle. 'Leave them,' he put the toe of his boot into a buckled cow's ribs. 'They'll live or they'll die. Maybe we'll get lucky and some of the Gunns will come down in the night and take them. What about that one over there?'

There were about forty young cows lying dead among the dying. The dogs were tearing at the carcases which were blown up with gas. Flies buzzed about the broken-angled heads, swarmed in eye sockets. Daniel and his father put their knives into a cow's belly to hurry along the escaping gas. The other men followed. They covered their noses and mouths with their free hands, the explosive stench threatening to choke them as they tackled the rest. Their economy was built mainly on their cattle, their horses were supplementary. Losing cows meant that the coming year would be even harder. They had to take what they could from them. Some return had to be made, every part made to work for them. Meat from the freshly dead would be salted and stored for winter. Their lives were geared towards winter. Living was easier the farther away from winter the year rolled. The hides would be sold. It was a rich man who could afford to keep his own hides. The men's knives would turn the horns into spoons, into drinking horns or gun-powder horns, buttons and brooches. The fat, melted down, would be used to make candles. Again those would be laid by for winter.

Daniel and his father and the rest of the men worked on the rotting cattle until the work was finished. Gas popped from everywhere as their blades cut and carved flesh, sinew and muscle away from the bones.

The legs were the first to come off, then the heads. The skin was peeled away like a coat. Even although they were skilled butchers, the work was hard. When they were done, what lay on the ground was a jigsaw of a cow.

Chapter Eight

It was too quiet. Daniel felt uneasy. He strained his ears still harder. Only silence filled them. Keeping low to the ground, creeping from the shelter of the trees, he struck out for the horses, his knife in his right hand. Moving for the cover of the herd he circled it. The horses remained unconcerned. It was long into the night and they were standing together in their corner. From somewhere away to the West an owl hooted to the moon.

'Did you hear anything?' he asked a youth who had two eagle feathers twisted in his pale hair.

'No, nothing,' the boy said, his round face white and drawn under the moon's light. 'Only the owl.'

'You're sure? Nothing?'

'Ay,' a cloud sailed across the moon and took the boy's face away. 'Did you?' he said out of the darkness.

Daniel's head moved fractionally to the right, to the left. 'No,' he said. 'And that's what's worrying me.'

'You're thinking they're going to come?' a quiver of excitement ran through the boy's words as the cloud crawled past the moon.

The boy was fourteen years, straight limbed and clean to look at, as tall as Daniel, but without the breadth. His blood was up, and dancing, as the man inside him struggled to be free. The moon had turned his hair to silver. Daniel looked at the boy, at the expectation on his smooth-skinned face, saw himself there. The boy was talking about their old enemies to the North, the MacKays. Of course the MacKays would come. They always came. The surprising thing was that they hadn't put in their appearance when the Strath men had been taking the cattle to Dingwall. They hadn't been long back when word had reached them. An itinerant woodcutter, down from MacKay country for work in the woods around Strath, had brought the news. The MacKays had lost their entire herd to some disease. Every night since then Strath had put a watch on their own depleted herd and waited.

The boy withstood the silence, his only sign of nervousness the way his hand kept going to the back of his head, smoothing his hair.

The boy was proud of his hair and wore it long, past his shoulders. Unlike the other males in the village the boy wore nothing on his head. He felt this would detract from his natural beauty. He wore the eagle feathers in his hair instead, hanging down over his right ear, tangled there by threads. He saw himself in some way like the eagle. One day he too was going to fly away. He had a bow slung behind him and in his hand he carried one arrow. Beneath his hair and the feathers his ears too were sharp and listening.

'Do you think they're going to come?' he asked again.

'I can't be sure,' Daniel's voice was a rumble from low in his throat. 'But we can be ready.'

The boy's ears heard the 'we', fastened on to it. He stood straighter.

'There's something not right about tonight,' Daniel continued. 'I can feel it, I can hear it. Go for the others. And be quick.'

The light in the boy's face died, his shoulders sank. Unmoving, he stood before Daniel. If there was a fight the boy wanted it. He was ready. His father died fighting.

'Go,' Daniel barked, making him jump. 'Now.'

The man in the boy died. His face was all eyes like the face of a startled deer.

The boy flew, his bow bumping against the back of his legs, his arrow swishing through the night. He hadn't gone more than a dozen yards when his gangling lack of co-ordination brought him full length down on the ground, his bow string biting into his mouth and nose, his kilt flying up around his waist.

The thud as he hit the ground followed by his suppressed groans reached Daniel, hidden from him by the horses. He rolled his eyes to the moon as he wondered at the lack in some people. Even with two good legs there were those who couldn't run, or walk, straight.

The boy stayed where he was for a moment. The face in the moon looked down, wondering at the strange moon looking back. A moon from another country maybe?

When his breath had returned the boy sat up, straightened his bow, his fingers feeling his arrow for damage. It remained whole although he'd held onto it through his fall. His hands went up to his hair, felt for his feathers. Ensuring that they were still securely in place, he scrambled to his feet, lengthened his back, lifted his chin and threw a look half-defiant, half careless, to where he imagined Daniel was standing watching him. Then he spun round and raced off into the night.

Daniel walked softly among the horses, speaking soft words of comfort to them, patting their sides, clapping and stroking their long noses. The horses snorted their recognition, the clouds of steam blown from their nostrils rising white against the darkness of the night. He knew the MacKays were out there. He didn't have to see one to know that, nor to hear one. He could feel them in his bones. A MacKay could be smelt for miles. There was no end to them. His clan's story was filled with them and the trouble they caused.

His hand halting on a horse's neck, he leant his forehead against its flank as his ears picked up the loud crack of rock smashing against rock. He rested there, himself a rock, and waited for it to come again. Nothing. He kept moving, using the horses to shield him, his every sinew straining for the sound of MacKays.

The MacKays had been giving the Rosses trouble for too long. Centuries. They stole, they burnt, they murdered. And the reasons were twofold. In the first place geography, they were neighbours. Secondly Clan Ross had what Clan Mackay didn't, good fertile lands. And these fertile lands bred what

MacKay's rocky ground didn't – good cattle. Barring disease or famine. And the Highland way at the time being a case of what's yours is mine, the sons of Iye (Aodh) very often came calling on the sons of Ross. This was the pattern of the clans in seventeenth-century Scotland.

The MacKays were of their time. No better. Some might say worse. And Clan Ross, although not going in for border-raiding to the same extent as Clan MacKay, weren't exactly blameless either.

Daniel lifted his head again. The boy had done his work well. He reappeared out of the trees with about a dozen men carrying the wasted look of middle age about them, the best of those left in the village. The young men were away from home, some off fighting another country's wars, some closer to home, in the regiment of their chief. Their chief was a distant figure to all but those who served under him, residing forty miles to the south of Strath. So not only had many never seen him, they would not expect to do so. This distance gave him an exalted place in their minds. To them he was almost God-like, and they trusted him the way a child would trust a father. It would not occur to them to think disloyally of him or to question his ways. And young boys, once they had reached a certain age, were impatient to enlist in his army.

The boy had also brought with him a handful of boys of about his own age, one or two maybe younger. The boy wasn't afraid of anyone, not of MacKays and not of him out there. Especially not of him. And especially at a distance.

The band drew quietly near to stand in a huddle beside the horses. Some of the men had knives, some sticks. And there were plenty of rocks lying at their feet.

'You,' Daniel walked up to the boy. 'Take them.' He jerked his thumb towards the boy's own cohort. 'And stay out of the way.' And he turned to walk towards the men.

The boy moved to block him. 'You'd treat me like a lassie,' his voice was climbing, his face bright red under his hair. 'I'm good enough to run errands. Is that it? I'm as good as anyone,' his voice cracked on the heat of his last words. 'I know how to use this.' He pumped the arrow up and down in front of Daniel's face.

Daniel's hand smacked the arrow-head away from his face. 'Look, I can't be watching out for you,' he ground his words from between his teeth.

'Let me stay.' The boy's face began to crumble, and his new-found bravado with it. 'I'll stand with you.'

'No.' Daniel didn't even try to keep his voice down. 'No. Do what you're told. Take them and stay in the trees. You'll be safe there. I'm not wanting your deaths hanging on me.'

'I'm staying.' Nothing in the boy moved, in his face or in his body. His voice was controlled, even. The bunched fist holding the arrow was the only evidence of the fight going on inside him.

'Look,' the word had to force itself through Daniel's lips. 'I haven't the time. Go and try your manhood some place else. Men have work to do.'

The boy stood as straight as a young tree. He opened his mouth, but the words wouldn't come from it. He closed his mouth on the unsaid words, bit down on the sob which was ripping at his guts, then fled for the trees, his arrow hanging and useless in his hand. The other boys, who had been content to stand back, didn't argue. They followed him meekly enough. At a distance.

The men closed around Daniel. 'Shouldn't someone be with the cattle? It's the cattle they'll be after,' one said.

'Ay, shouldn't someone be with the cattle?' a parrot at his shoulder said.

They stood and discussed the cattle. Daniel let them. When he'd heard enough, he spoke. 'Everyone knows it's the cattle they're after. But they're not going to touch them once they've had a look at them. Even in this light a blind MacKay'd be able to see the state they're in. And then they're going to go for the horses. You know that. They're not going to go away with nothing. That's why we're here.'

'I still say someone should be with the cattle,' the first man said.

The men muttered among themselves and nodded their heads.

'You go then.' Daniel wasn't about to waste himself arguing. They were always the same.

'No, no, I didn't mean me. I just mean someone.' The man's ground was shifting under him.

'Ay, well, you're someone.'

'No, no, it's all right. I'll stay here. Right enough, no one in their right senses would take cows like ours.'

A smaller rebellion this time, and easily extinguished.

'Right,' Daniel said. 'You all know what to do.'

Even quieter than when they came, the men filtered back into the night. Some took the trees, elbowing the boys from their front-row places, forcing them to move further in. Others crawled away to rocks and bushes. The rest made room for themselves among the horses. Daniel was with them.

The owl hooted, nearer this time. Fists reassured themselves on wood and steel.

The MacKays came out of the darkness on all sides. From the rocks at the back they rained down like massive prey birds, with skirts flying and knife-blades glinting, teeth bared, their screaming scattering the wits of the boys in the trees, turning their hot blood to ice, making them clutch at one another for safe-keeping.

There were more of them. Maybe twice as many, although it was difficult to know because it was night. They were everywhere.

The horses didn't know which way to run. Some ran one way, doubled back and ran into those following, knocking the watching men to the ground.

The Strath men screamed back at the MacKays. Familiar faces wearing the faces of cornered wolves. Men out to kill men. Foam seeped from the mouths of the hurtling horses as the battle was fought on their piece of ground.

The moon played games with the night, one minute lighting up the tangled, tortured shapes, the next plunging their contortions and snarlings into darkness.

*   *   *

The boy with the eagle feathers in his hair could hold back no longer. He slipped out from the trees, into the open moonlit square. Slowly he lifted his bow over his head, taking care not to flatten or dislodge the feathers in his hair. Bending his head, he threaded his arrow along the bow's string. He raised his head and looked into the face of a huge MacKay. The boy felt no fear at the MacKay's appearance, at the blood on his face and shirt, at his hanging right arm. He raised his bow, his own right arm strong as he pulled back at the bow. It didn't shake. He watched the MacKay closing the distance between them. A backward sweep of MacKay's good arm knocked the boy's bow with the arrow away. Still the boy was brave. He didn't look to the ground for his bow. The eyes he kept on the giant didn't blink. The giant twisted his face into a snarl, lifted his knife hand, took the boy's life from him. The boy lay on the ground for the second time that night and the moon in her sorrow did not come from behind the cloud.

The fighting was over. It took as long as it would take to eat a bowl of meal. The MacKays who could stand ran for the river, taking their wounds with them into the cooling water. The Rosses who could stand ran after them, and chased them with stones. The other MacKays made for the hills, dragging their injured over rocks and through bushes. The horses stayed where they were.

Of the Strath men, although almost all had blood on them, only the boy was dead. The MacKays lost two men.

Sagging from the fight, but still intact, the Strath men formed a circle around their boy and sober-faced stood looking down on him. Daniel crouched beside him and turned him over, onto his back, so that the moon could see his face. Then he closed the boy's eyes to her sorrow.

'He was in an awful hurry to die.' Daniel's face had collapsed on him. There was blood on one side of his face and on his nose. He fingers shook as they straightened the eagle's feathers. Then he straightened the boy himself, arranged his clothes about him.

The long-faced men stood in their red satin stains, huge-eyed in their pain and looked at the boy's hair. His death had taken their words from them and made them feel a hundred times old.

Daniel stayed down with the boy. He brushed his hair away from his face, his hand hesitating against the boy's cheek. The boy felt warm.

After a few minutes he stood up and spoke to them.

'He came from brave people,' he said, not knowing what he was going to say. 'Every bit as brave as the people ourselves have come from. He got his hair from the men who came across the ocean in their fighting ships. A long time ago these men came here to our country. They were strong, these long ago men. And brave. And so we will honour him, and the blood that runs through him, that made him twice as brave. Come, we'll carry him home to his grandfather.'

His last words were barely words. They came from him, but he did not shape them, his was not the effort which formed them, spoke them. 'Someone'll have to see to that other men,' he said. 'I don't expect they'll be back for them the night.'

One arm under the boy's neck, the other arm under his knees, Daniel lifted the boy, cradling the broken breast to his own. The boy's hair hung down, covering Daniel's arm. The men hobbled before him and behind him, making sure the way was safe for their young kinsmen. And the frightened boys came crying from the trees.

The boy was wrapped up in a blanket and put into the ground, beside the rest of his people. Only in memory would his golden hair run with the sun. And the old stones that watched over him seemed to stand less tall.

Chapter Nine

The wood where MacIver worked was owned by the Earl of Ross and covered around fifteen hundred acres. Stretching out to the West, it had as its natural boundary two rivers, the Carron and the Black Water. MacIver had about twenty men working for him.

Most of the wood being cleared was used to fire the furnaces of the iron-smelters employed in making cannons.

The best pines, the tallest and the straightest, went for ships' masts, the less than straight for ships' planks. The oak was used for making barrels, its bark to tan leather.

The woods were big business in the middle of the seventeenth century, giving work to many men. Not many of these men worked for themselves. The greater number were hired on the spot, by men like MacIver. Itinerant workers, they'd travel the country in search of a big job. MacIver had been cutting near Strath for two months.

Where Ross met Sutherland, where the two rivers became one, the big axes whirred, the long saws sang.

MacIver cursed as he tried to take a firm grip on the handle of his axe. More rain! What a way to make a living.

It fell from the branches in heavy lumps, battering him on the head and the back, pouring down his neck, plastering his clothes to his skin. It trickled between his shoulder blades and disappeared somewhere below his belt. It ran into and out of every crease that he had. It was washing his oxters and the backs of his knees.

He wiped water from his eyes and rubbed his wet palm on his trouser leg, making his hand wetter.

Taking a fresh hold on the axe handle he tried to re-establish his footing. When he moved his feet rainwater oozed from his deerskin boots. Wherever he put his feet they slid on wet bracken, on the greasy bark of old wet wood. He cursed afresh as his leg disappeared up to the knee in a hole, his foot twisting back against itself, sending pain shooting up its full length when he pulled it free.

MacIver continued to swear. A lifetime working with trees had left parts of him useless. His ankle joints and his knees had taken so much punishment they would never be right, his axe hand was finished. Too many years of gripping the axe meant that his fingers would no longer work for him. He couldn't hold it for any length of time. Add the rain and who knew where the axe might land. In winter no blood flowed through his fingers, leaving them white and dead.

MacIver was fighting himself as much as the trees and the weather. He flung the axe away, not caring where it landed, and hobbled through the wet to find his drink. The thick undergrowth tugged at his legs, trying to hinder him.

He flung himself down, his back to a tree, and lifted the jar to his mouth. After two or three mouthfuls the pain from his ankle eased a little. He drank some more. The whack of the axes threaded through the trees to where he was sitting. Pushing the wooden plug into the neck of the jar, he rose to his feet and fought his way back to where he thought his axe might be. Kicking his way through chopped branches he scoured about until he found it and started hacking at his tree again.

Shouting voices of the men farther in carried quite clearly to him. The separate world which was the wood's heart rang out with noise. Axes smacking, trees cracking, saws singing, men shouting, dogs barking. Any animal that poked its head out for a look pulled it back in quicker when the workers were there. Some were forced to clear out, their homes being destroyed while they were sitting tenants. In the early morning, before anyone was about, the forest animals wandered freely, foxes, red squirrels, pine martins, songbirds. When the tree-cutters were there the only animal they were likely to see was the squirrel, whose home had gone crashing to the ground.

MacIver worked alone. He liked it that way. He worked better that way. Kicking loose branches from his path he weighed up the next tree. He stood back from it and looked up at it to measure its height and its girth, calculating the line along which it had to fall. He walked up to the tree, caught the axe's handle in his two hands and began swinging. The first swipe broke the red skin of the tree and bit into its pale flesh. The tree cried out but only other trees heard it. The tree stood tall, it looked as strong, but inside it was dying. Soon it would be as dead as the snedded trees lying straight on the ground.

MacIver wrenched the axe out and swung again, making another mark above the first. He chopped away within the two marks, shaping a wedge. The tree folded in on itself and trembled.

MacIver was a machine. Sweat poured out of him and ran with the rain, his arms and his legs screamed. The hairs on his arms were flattened by the rain, clotted in the tree's juice. MacIver was powered by a brain which blocked out everything but the desire to beat that which was bigger than he was, that which was stronger.

He forgot the rain, he forgot pain. His rhythm held and he had finished one side. He started on the other side. Another mound of pink chippings grew around his feet. His axe was on target to meet at the trunk's core.

'Tree,' he shouted, and he threw his weight against the tree and tried to move it from its plinth. The tree resisted and MacIver swore. But the tree was not offended, it had heard nothing. The tall pine still stood tall, still straight, but changed. The breath had been cut from it. A tree which had been, its belly gouged out.

MacIver tried pushing with his shoulder, his boots sliding as they tried to find grip. A crack as the wood splintered, and flesh lifted from bones.

'Tree,' MacIver bawled.

But the tree didn't fall. It broke from its base and hung at an angle, its branches caught in the branches of another tree.

MacIver cursed. And the rain. He'd had enough. He needed drink. He put his arms around the tree, embraced it. He wrestled with it against his belly, his feet tapping the ground where he was standing. The bark was slimy in his hands, against him. His hands kept slipping. His heart felt as it if were going to burst red hot as he tried to move the tree. And he couldn't see. He staggered away from the tree and sank to his knees. It was only a tree. It wouldn't beat him. On his knees in the wet MacIver hung there and looked at the hanging tree.

'You.' What was meant to be a shout came out a raw, painful whisper. 'Get the horse.' Pain had melted his fleshy face into a misshapen grey lump. The words came from his mouth with coats on.

The man near him carried on working. He had heard nothing. MacIver struggled upright, stumbling as he tried to level his shoulders, unlock his back and unlock his knees.

'Get the horse.' This time hearing the shout, the man stopped cutting. Anchoring his axe in his tree, he turned his head towards MacIver. An empty face with a gaping mouth silently asked for the words to be repeated.

'The horse, man, the horse,' MacIver said, rolling over to where his jar was lying. Human screaming reached them from farther in. MacIver wiped at his wet face with the edge of his dripping shirt and hoped it wasn't one of his men. He wasn't in the form to go looking for someone else.

'Never mind the horse. I'll get him myself. Go and tell me who it is this time,' he called to the man's back.

The day felt like two days. The man needed no encouragement. Unlike MacIver, he hated working on his own. He was supposed to have someone with him but he hadn't turned up. He loped off through the wood, his expression already brightening.

'C'm here boy,' MacIver lifted a heavy coiled rope from the garron's wooden yoke and coiled one end around the tree, tied the other end to the yoke. Then he brought his heavy hand down on the horse's rump. 'Pull.' There was as much strain in his one word as there was in the horse's shoulders. 'Come on, come on.' The big vein running down the side of his neck stood out like a hawser.

The small, thickset horse was bred for heavy work. Head

down, shoulders straining against the rope, it pulled with every ounce of strength it possessed. At its third try the tree came, crashing down through the holding branches to lie in the tree graveyard.

The earth juddered and moaned beneath the tree's weight. The pines close by shook. MacIver waddled over to the tree, bent down and loosened the rope, tossed it aside. He was straightening up when he saw his neighbour hurrying back. He waited for him, then waited a while longer for the man to speak.

'One of the MacCullochs,' the man had trouble saying the words. He had burst himself in his hurry. 'The little red-haired fellow,' he panted. 'Him on the saw.' MacIver nodded. He wasn't surprised. 'Take him back,' he nodded to the garron. 'I'm sick of speaking to that MacCullochs about their drinking. What can you expect? Coming in here filled to the neck with drink and no looking where they're going. And where am I meant to get another man? There's wood to go out.' The man had no answer for MacIver's logic. He whistled to the horse to follow him. MacIver went searching for his jug.

To hell and back again with all the MacCullochs. More trouble than they were worth. The lot of them put together weren't worth one damn. It wouldn't make him sorry, to see the lot of them lying under the biggest tree that was in it. There'd be peace then. Well, they needn't expect him to go running through the trees to them. Let them sort out their own mess.

The axes birled and danced, the saws kept on singing, the men worked like horses and the horses would work till they dropped. The woodmen's sleek wet dogs, used to coming to the woods, nosed everywhere and barked at everything, even when that was nothing.

All the men worked with horses, it would be impossible to shift the fallen trees without them. Once down, the trees were dragged out to the edge of the wood where the men could roll them and stack them.

It took two, sometimes three horses to pull the biggest of

the trees. Handling the large stuff wasn't easy, moving it less so. Sixty, seventy, sometimes eighty feet of tree had to be removed from among growing wood. The more wood they cut, the easier this became as space opened up. Once the required quota had been cut and the branches taken from them, the horses took over. From the edge of the wood they pulled the trees down to the riverbank where the men roped them together to make rafts and floated the rafts downriver. Again, this was dangerous work. The men were fighting the weight of the wood as well as the weight and the mood of the river. Crushings were common and drownings, especially when the rafts were launched. Men who had worked the wood for years without even being bashed by a branch had died once they tangled with the river.

They controlled their rafts from the bank, again by ropes, steering them down to where the river joined the sea. And that was the worst part of the woodman's work done. With help from the ships' crews, they loaded the wood on to the flat-bottomed barges which sailed away with it to the shipyards and the smelting works in the South. The woodcutter could then straighten his back. Until the next day.

He straightened his back in one of the many drinking dens where, because there was heather growing everywhere, drink was cheap. Woodcutters worked hard so it made sense to drink every bit as hard. And when a job was finished it was their habit to do this drinking together, by way of a celebration.

MacIver had hit form and he was dispensing advice on matters romantic to a soft-mouthed youth, a new recruit to his work squad. 'Look,' he was explaining to the youth, through whisky fumes and the blue reek of peat smoke, 'if you're no going to manage her sober you better get some of that into you,' and he nodded to the jar the youth had been sitting gazing into.

The youth's pink face closed in embarrassment. His mouth tried to tighten but it failed. Behind the floppy wedge of dark hair his eyes watered. Squirming on the rough bench he looked everywhere but across at MacIver.

'Come on. You worked for it. Shove it back. How old did you say you were?'

'Nearly sixteen years.'

'Nearly sixteen years! Then is it no time you were doing something about doing something? Eh?' and MacIver rattled a tattoo on the table as he shouted the youth's virgin state to the whole place. Through the smoke faces could be seen, turning to stare at MacIver's table, but no one said anything.

Leaning forward, MacIver put his mouth to the youth's ear. Redness swelled from the youth's throat, inflaming his face. The smell of his own sweat was rising up and choking him. MacIver's laugh erupted from his belly and splattered the rafters. The Minister heard it where he was sitting at a table with one of the Marys, another young one. A man sitting at MacIver's table made a noise like a horse, displaying a row of teeth a horse would be proud of.

'What's that you're saying, traveller?' MacIver, missing nothing, turned and sprayed the question at the Minister. The Minister, if he heard, ignored him. He was busy with Mary.

'Here, landlord, here,' MacIver was burbling with good humour and better whisky. 'This young fellow's needing some. Bring another jar over.'

The youth had given up trying to resist. He was too young anyway, too unformed. He let himself go with the flood. Head back, his mouth opened wide with bravado, he lifted his jug. He was a man, wasn't he? Doing a man's work. Real work he was talking, not woman's work that some fellows called work. Growing corn, watching over a puckle of cows. Anyone could do that. Lassies could do that. But let a woman try to take down a seventy-foot tree. Let one of them work out the angle it would fall along, let them take the branches from the tree and take it out. Hard, ay it was hard. And at still fifteen it made him hard. He waved the jug under the noses of those with him, dipped his head to it, acknowledging them and himself.

MacIver's steaming company howled and barked and cheered. Their feet pounded the packed earth of the floor, their fists drummed on the landlord's tables. MacIver shouted the loudest. The man who had whinnied was slavering through his long teeth.

The youth drank much too fast. Water poured from his eyes and his throat had twisted against him. His face was a beacon. He thumped his chest and opened his mouth, but nothing came out. The cheering and the calling grew louder, shaking the veil.

'Finish it,' he could hear MacIver saying. 'Come on.'

'Ay, ay.' The youth tried a smile through the tears. 'Man, that's fierce stuff,' he barely squeaked.

'Finish it,' MacIver said. 'The first one always gets you that way. The more you'll take the better it'll taste. Am I right?' he leaned toward his equine friend, whose sharp elbows were spearing the wood of the table while his hands were holding together his splitting head.

As if jerked by a piece of string the man's head went down and up. What he had agreed to he had no idea, never would have. MacIver, on the other hand, was able to drink vast amounts without it making any noticeable difference to how alert he remained.

The youth was ready to try again. With his new-found knowledge he prepared himself. He spread his hands on the table, one on each side of his jug. Straightening his back he thrust his chest out, pulled his chin in and stared at it, fought his own battle with the contents. He put his hand out but quickly withdrew it. He reached out again, his fingers closed around the jug. As if from a long way off he heard his workmates calling. This time he would allow no weakness, no face twisting, no sitting and shaking like leaves in a wind. He'd show them how much of a man he was. He'd be so good they'd think he was taking milk.

He turned his head and looked at them, waited for their reaction. He was not disappointed. MacIver, pressed lips together, nodded to him, was impressed; his horse-face friend whinnied his amazement. The youth, his face now flushed from the effort to remain calm, towered above them all.

The Minister disentangled himself from Mary and, using the

table for support, pushed himself up onto his feet. Something had freed his tongue. He flung his arms up towards the roof. The company carried on with what they were doing. If they heard him, none gave any sign. Mary was finishing off the remains of the Minister's jug. 'It is not in our nature,' he began, 'to love God.' His arms a V shape, his voice was strong, and unhesitating. It cut through the smoke and the smells and the noise. 'For it is not in us to love God.' His spindly legs were shaking but he drove on. 'In our arrogance we will not hear Him when He speaks to us. We will not hear Him, when He speaks to us. The Lord's day has been turned into a day for all kinds of wickedness and the Holy Scriptures fill us with disinterest, and weariness. Hear me when I say to you that desolation will come on the face of Scotland, of this country, for that which is wanting cannot be numbered. The day is coming, and it is coming soon, when there will be a weeping and a wailing and a gnashing of teeth. Rachel is crying for her children. You reject your God and you put nothing in His place. From what you have sown, you will surely reap death.' His words tailed off, leaving him confused. His arms, which had been gradually bending, shot down by his side. His head felt light, his legs were shaking. He looked about as if unsure of where he was. Bubbles of foam had gathered in the corners of his mouth.

'Here, traveller, here,' MacIver waved him over but the Minister didn't hear him. Sitting down on his seat he let his head droop down onto the table. Mary's arms reached for him but he pushed the arms away.

'Here, traveller, here,' MacIver's was the only voice in the place. 'Send her over here. There's a young fellow here.'

The Minister stayed as he was and Mary sniggered.

'Are you hearing me? Traveller! Here!' his beckoning hand was now for Mary. Mary got up and left the Minister. Sparks of excitement glimmered in MacIver's eyes.

The youth nearly choked on his drink when he saw what was moving his way. She looked strong. She was as broad across the shoulders as any man. Her arms were as thick as her legs. She'd be good for taking trees out. One look at her and his bravado drained out of him. She was big and he was getting out of this place. He'd need an awful lot of drink in him for her to look any better. She was speaking to him but he didn't hear her. He couldn't move his eyes away from her breasts. He was going to die. They were making him forget to breathe. He'd seen breasts before, every mother had them for bairns. But mothers didn't have breasts like hers. They were up under her chin, and hard looking. How did they stay up there, like that? He opened his mouth, then he closed it, then opened it again. He was staring so hard he was blind. He looked higher. Knotted red hair tumbled about her shoulders. He reckoned her to be about his own age but twice as wide. Her mouth smiled as if it knew him.

He pushed away the thought of what her mouth would do and forced his eyes from hers. They fell on her breasts again.

The Minister's head had crashed onto the table and it lay there on its side, his thin white hair trailing in spilt drink. His arms hung loosely down to the floor.

MacIver looked up at the woman. 'He can pay,' he told her. Lust dribbled from the corners of his fleshy mouth, he felt it surging in his groin.

Mary placed herself on the youth's lap, her weight flattening him, her breadth almost covering him. She was crushing him to death and he couldn't think clearly. He didn't know what to do with his hands. He'd touch her wherever he put them.

'Don't be shy,' Mary said.

His hands felt huge, and heavy, like trees. He strained his neck to look past her, as if a shower of drunks at the next table were intensely interesting. His eyes weren't strong enough to stay away from her. They came back to her mouth, hanging so close to his own. 'Don't be shy,' he watched it say and he felt her hands in his hair. His spine had turned to water. She had strange eyes, they were less than blue, a milky colour. Even when they were looking into his, he couldn't believe that eyes like that could see.

She started to kiss his mouth. He tried to keep his back straight, his hands clear of her. MacIver and Horse Laugh were quiet. They charted his progress, and her progress, mouths open, awash in their own excitement and the stench of the wet wool drying on them.

As in a dream he became aware of himself responding, of his hands touching her, of his mouth working. A tight wire of understanding stretched between MacIver and Horse Laugh. They winked at one another.

The room and everyone in it ceased to exist for the youth. Everything except what she was doing to him.

Chapter Ten

'Munro!' Daniel's shout shattered the walls of the houses in the village before it darted off the slopes and came back to him. 'Come out of there and stop hiding behind your mother.'

No one, no thing answered him.

'Come out man, or are you wanting me to come in and get you?'

Still nothing.

As he closed on the doorway of the house a wasted woman ducked through it and ran past him. When she had put distance between them she turned to face him, her breath pumping from her. With one hand she tugged at the neck of her frock, with the other made folds in its skirt.

'Is Donald Munro in your house?' Daniel shouted at the mother.

The mother stood looking at him, dumb as a cow, and shaking, her hands jumping to the tremors.

He tried again. 'Your son, Donald,' he said. He tried to speak kindly to her, to remove some of the rock from his jaw. 'Is he in the house?'

Her face remained blank, overstitched in deep lines. In between the lines the skin had a puckered appearance, as if the thread through it had been pulled too tight.

He gave her a longer look, which she ran into the next house to get away from, before dropping to his knees and crawling into her house. A quick look told him his quarry wasn't there. A tiny girl, tied up in a blanket, played before the fire, a squad of cats crawling over her while she stuffed a dirty hand into her mouth. One cat kept leaping at the edge of the blanket. He scooped the little girl up, and still bent, moved her against the wall of the house, away from the fire, trailing cats behind him.

Back outside he found the mother creeping home from the other house. She wouldn't go far from her child. 'Where is he?' he barked at her, not caring now how he sounded to her.

Slowly, as if it carried a weight on the end of it, the woman's arm came up and she pointed. Still no words from her. But he did not need words. He knew where she meant. 'Have you anything to eat? Any meal?'

'Our bellies have nothing in them.' Neither had her eyes.

Her other hand left the neck of her frock and reached out to him, hung in the air between them. 'Nothing.' The word broke on its emptiness.

Daniel backed away from her hand, and from her eyes. Turning, he headed west out of the village.

About three miles out on the hill he found Donald Munro coming back. Even at a distance he knew it was him. No one else had that shape, his backside scraping the heather and his knees getting in the way of each other. He was bent under the weight of the young hind he was dragging through the heather on a rope. Anyone else would have hoisted the beast on to his shoulders, taken it home that way. Anyone with sense. But Munro had decided to spread the beast's scent everywhere for the gamekeeper's dogs to pick up on. He was lucky that he'd made it this far.

Daniel stopped and watched him coming. As yet he didn't think Donald Munro had spotted him. Not with his head down. He came slowly, a painful step at a time. There wasn't much strength in him. Every few yards he had to stop, to yank at the rope. As if sensing him, Munro lifted his head and looked across the space separating them.

'Munro,' Daniel shouted. 'I'm after you, Munro.'

Ignoring the threat, the Munro put his head down again and ankle-deep in heather ploughed on. He knew that Daniel would come looking for him. It was only a matter of when. But he wasn't worried.

They closed on one another.

'You're mine, Munro.' Daniel hardly had to open his mouth to say it.

Donald Munro, if he heard, still took no notice. Still he came on, his shoulders rounded, his body leaning forward, his calf muscles straining, as he pulled the rope. Daniel eased back on himself and let him come. When he drew level, Daniel stepped across to block him.

'Get out of my way.' Donald Munro's mouth was gagging on the words. Without looking, he tried to push his way through Daniel. Daniel held his ground.

'We have words to be speaking.' His words were unhurried, even.

'Move from my way.' Donald Munro's eyes stayed on the ground. There was a hole in his hat and a clump of black hair sprouted through it.

'I'm moving nowhere,' Daniel said.

Donald Munro tried to go round him but the hind's weight stopped him. He pulled as hard as he could but the rope bit his fingers and into his bare shoulder. 'And neither are you.' Daniel's mouth was grinning at Munro's unease.

Donald Munro was beat. He was beat from hunger, he was beat from lying out on the hill for three days and four nights and he was beat from dragging the beast. And he was utterly exhausted from the fear of one of the keepers finding him.

Without looking up, he let go of the rope and hung there, his breath coming thick and fast through his open mouth.

'Now,' Daniel whispered, 'Peggy.' His eyes flashed as dangerously as the blade of his knife as it rested against the soft hollow at the base of Munro's throat. In the heavy quietness the far-off sounds of the woodcutters boomed in on them.

Munro squirmed under the dagger's threat. His black eyes crossed each other as they worked hard to find the blade's tip. Donald Munro was a good head shorter than Daniel. He was the one who had to look up, stretching his throat against the sharp steel. 'W-watch what you're doing with that thing.' His dry tongue went round his lips, tried to soften them. 'My-my family hasn't food.'

'Don't come that,' Daniel said, moving closer until he

was looking down on Munro. 'All you've ever been is torment to them. Peggy,' again her name came soft through clenched teeth.

'P-Peggy! Wh-what about her?' The blade's point sent Munro's voice soaring up with the eagles.

'You know,' Daniel's voice still soft, almost friendly. His knife hand was steady like a rock.

'No, no. I don't know nothing. Go easy with that blade, man. Watch what you're doing.' One hand was flapping the air at his side, like a gull that had forgotten how to fly.

He stumbled backwards, Daniel went with him. Both came up against the hind. As one they danced around it, joined together at throat and hand by the shiny blade.

'Peggy,' he breathed her name into his face.

'Take that knife away. How can I speak with that at me?' Bubbles of white spittle formed on his loose bottom lip.

'I'm waiting, Munro. Speak before my blade ends up tickling the back of your throat.' Before Donald Munro could utter the first syllable his knife was under Munro's ribs. 'Speak about Peggy.'

'Oh, ay, Peggy. She's your sister,' Munro's tongue, free to move, moved smartly.

'And.'

'What and? How do I know? Nothing. Nothing and that's all. That's all I know.' Two men under a bright sky. One bent almost double to release the pressure of the knife as he leaned toward the other.

'You know more.'

'No, no, I don't. Not me. What would I know?'

'Tell me.'

'Look,' Munro was like a fish on dry ground. Maybe that was best. If he'd been in water he'd be drowning. 'What would I know? Peggy's your sister. And that's it. That's all I know. You can believe me or you can no believe me.'

'Peggy's belly. It's growing.'

'Oh. Is that right?'

'Ay, oh, it is right. Peggy told her mother that you put the bairn into her.'

'Me? Me? How could it be me? I'm only back from Germany.'

'Look, Munro, I'm starting to lose my patience. If you don't tell me right, do you know what I'm going to do?' He put his mouth to Munro's ear. 'I'm going to take the skin off every part of you.' The promise was the other side of a caress. The blade twinkled before Munro's petrification and grabbing him by the hair, Daniel almost yanked his head backwards from his shoulders.

'Don't kill me, don't kill me.' Donald Munro was squealing like a trapped pig. 'I'll do anything. Honest, I will.'

'Then I'm going to slice off that thing that's hanging between your legs, that thing you use to spread your poison through clean women.'

'Don't kill me.'

'But don't worry. I'll no kill you. Yourself'll do that.'

'No, no. Please man, please. Don't, don't. It was me. Honest, it was me.' Munro's body was folding on him and the big bastard was trying to stop it by pulling his scalp from his head.

Daniel let go his grip on Munro's hair and he dropped like a stone on to his hands and knees into the heather.

'Right?' Daniel stood over him, his breath coming from his nostrils in short snorts.

'That's it. Me and Peggy. You know.'

'No, I don't know. That's why I've walked over the whole of the country looking for you.' He slipped his knife back into his belt.

Donald Munro went stupid with relief.

'Ach, man,' his mouth began galloping on him. 'She was all over me. I thought she would eat me. Are you hearing me?'

'Shut up your mouth.' Daniel used his boot on him, sending him sprawling. 'That's my sister. Shut your mouth.'

Donald Munro crawled from further kickings. 'Honest man, I'm speaking the truth to you.' His mouth was filled with heather, his knees under his chin.

Daniel leapt at Donald Munro. Munro's arms went up to protect his head. 'You and the truth have never met.' He had

Donald Munro's hair again. His hat was lying beside the hind. 'So you would know the truth? Or honesty?' He threw the battered heap from him. Its head darted off the ground. The hind looked more alive than Donald Munro did, and in better shape.

But Donald Munro could not stop. 'Ach, you don't believe me,' he blubbered.

'No, I don't believe you. I don't believe one word of you. The only thing that's saving you is Peggy. And if you're what Peggy wants, then you she's going to get.'

Donald Munro hadn't the sense to know when he was beaten. He opened his mouth again. But the heat coming from the eyes of the man watching him melted his words down before they could be said. 'Remember,' Daniel said, 'I'm watching you.'

Donald Munro kept quiet now. He knew how men repayed other men who played dirty with their women. He himself, although only nineteen years, had paid back. More than once.

Daniel knelt down on one knee, his back to the hind and hoisted it on to his shoulders.

'If you gave Peggy a present from Germany, I'm coming back for you,' he said. 'And that's a promise.'

'I don't know what you're speaking about,' Donald Munro, stretched flat in the heather, called out to Daniel's back.

'You know.' Daniel didn't turn. His step was light despite the weight of the hind.

'I'm clean. Honest.'

Daniel kept walking.

'And that's my hind you're taking.'

Daniel kept walking.

High up an eagle circled, looking for food.

Chapter Eleven

Late summer, and the days still lay long on the land of the people of Strath. The disease in the cattle had passed, taking with it around two-thirds of their young herd. Because of this they were slavish in their praise of those surviving. They told them, and each other, how beautiful they were looking, how shiny their coats, how round their bellies, how straight their backs.

Knocking hard on these good thoughts, however, came the thought of fearful winter and of how soon it would be on them. They knew their cattle wouldn't look good then. To see what spring and summer had added to them being lost was hard for them to bear.

For the state of their land they'd blame anyone but themselves. Top of the tree, again, were the MacKays. The MacKays did burn whatever lay before them. So they were right enough there. But it also suffered from the people of Strath themselves, for they were not kind to it. They loved their land, but theirs was a jealous kind of love. They didn't believe in draining, that meant losing a few feet of grass; they didn't go in for planting, that would disturb the undergrowth; and they did nothing about the weeds. To their minds weeds were nourishment for the soil. So they did nothing to help or encourage the ground, yet they expected the best from it. All this unkindness, this neglect, which they looked on as the opposite, left them with poor, sour ground, lacking in minerals. And the condition of the cattle, which this land had to support for six months of the year, suffered because of this and couldn't be expected to fetch a price at market.

*   *   *

Daniel took his time as he walked about in the cornfield, now and then stooping to pull at ears of corn, rubbing the husks between his palms and popping the seeds into his mouth. The sight of the crop did little to lift him. They were all waiting for him to tell them things weren't as bad as they looked. There were times when he wished they would look to themselves instead. No broad sweep of gold here for them. The crop looked what it was, something that had struggled out of the ground, and had been struggling ever since, choked with bindweed. Ears clustered on stunted stalks, dirty in colour, greyish like the clouds. There were large blank patches where only weeds and flowers grew. It would never yield enough to take them through the winter. He put a seed into his mouth, chewed it between his front teeth, and stood looking at what lay before him. A pity they couldn't eat stones. He walked back to them, his leg buckling on the round stones.

The men and women were standing together. The men carried blades. There was an expectant look on the faces they turned to him. The women didn't seem so keyed up as the men. They kept chattering and laughing as if they were out for a picnic. One was shouting at some children, who were running with a dog in the crop and flattening it.

'We'll cut,' Daniel told the men as he came near. 'It's dry enough. Hand me my cutter,' and a man standing on the edge of the group came forward and put the long blade into his hand.

The men went first, fanning out, leading the field. The women waited. When there was something for them to work on they would split into twos, threes or fours and work behind them. It didn't take long before their feet were punctured by stubble, streaked in blood and harvest dust. Bending down, they gathered together bundles of corn, and holding the corn against their legs they bound the bundles with strands which they had knotted into lengths.

Peggy's baby was growing in her, making it hard for her to bend. Some of the old men, slower than the others, worked with the women. The children didn't work, all but one or two keen girls who liked to help their mothers. The rest ran with the dogs, sometimes getting in the way of the cutters, sometimes running in circles around their gleaning mothers. The field reverberated to the noise coming from them.

Peggy put her hand to her back as she straightened from her work and looked along the length of the field. Her back was aching and she tried to ease away the pain by rubbing at it with both hands. Ahead of her she could see him, bent to his blade, swinging it like a soldier. Peggy forgot her back and her feet. She liked what she was seeing, so black and so bonnie. She was never going to think otherwise. Her smile held her secret as her arms instinctively enfolded her belly. In the field there was only herself and him.

It was going to be all right, everything would be all right. Daniel had spoken to him and he was going to take her.

She could hear some of the women singing. The tune came in on her and she joined in, singing it for him and what was growing in her belly.

The tune floated away from the women, down the field to the men. One or two came in at first, at the back of the women. They took the tune, strengthened it, gave it substance. The women gave it life. The old ones were the best singers, they had been singing for longer, they were easy in it. The old ones also worked with an ease which the younger ones had not yet found. They were easy with themselves, with the earth, even with the hills at their back. And that day the hills, if not the sun, seemed to be with them.

Their lives were harsh. Like the crop they were harvesting, they struggled to be born and they daily struggled to live. But maybe their fiercest struggle was to die. None went easy to their graves.

Theirs was a constant battle to take something, to make something out of a little or nothing. Always coming from behind and hoping that one day, while they lived, they would break even. And always the quiet patience. If only they could have another day. And the singing. They couldn't have lived if they didn't sing. It held them together, carried them through. It shaped the pattern of their life.

They did not think of themselves as being any worse off,

nor any better off, than other people. Most of them didn't know other people, only themselves and their own lives. And the men who'd been away with the regiment, what they saw was enough to make them wish they'd never again have to leave Strath.

So they lived out their lives that way, looking in different places for the strength their living required. They offered up their sacrifices to one God or another, and always they expected things to get better.

They knew their crop was poor, they couldn't not know, it was there before them. And when they couldn't fathom out why, they were like children, wondering what it was that they had done, what it was they were being punished for. So they sang themselves past it. They existed collectively.

'Never mind that fellow. Get on with your work,' said Peggy's sister Ishbel, gathering beside her.

'But don't you think he's lovely?'

Ishbel stood up, her fingers busy knotting blades of corn together. Her hair was dirty fair, like the colour of the corn. Strands of it clung about her face, she felt it heavy on the back of her neck. She shook her head, drawing her forearm across her forehead, then her mouth. With Peggy she stood looking at the object of her sister's desire.

'Him?' she said. 'Lovely? You're surely not seeing what I'm seeing.' She took a step, then turned to Peggy. 'Get back to your work.'

Ishbel looked nothing like Peggy. She was smaller built, shorter, narrower. And the Norsemen's blood had somehow been passed to her. Peggy was black-haired and black-eyed, and the summer sun had warmed the colour of her skin. Everything about Ishbel was pale. Scrape the dirt from her and she'd be like marble. Her eyes were paler than the palest day.

'Well,' Peggy's eyes were still down the field, 'I think he's lovely. Look at his legs and his arms. Look at his hair. I never saw hair that black. It's as black as the blackest night.'

'Ay, and so's his face. And his heart for all you know.' Ishbel's hands were throttling the bundles of corn she was gathering.

Some of the colour went from Peggy's face. The whole of her sagged. Her back was hurting again. 'Don't say anything kind, whatever you do,' she said, her head hanging down.

Ishbel knew she had been hard, but sometimes, just sometimes . . . one day she was going to say something. She was just so tired of always being the strong one. 'I'm sorry.' Her hard dry hand caught Peggy's. 'I'm sorry,' she said again and she put her arms around her younger sister. 'You love him and so he is bonnie looking and strong and I'm a bad sister,' and they stood together, the larger girl leaning on the slighter one.

'You're not bad,' Peggy said. 'Ever.'

'It's just that if he'll be bad to you . . .' and Peggy knew the steel in Ishbel's voice, the marble in her face.

'He'll not,' Peggy said. 'He'll not,' and to break the tension she rubbed her forehead against her sister's. 'I'm that happy I could dance,' and she caught up her skirt and birled away from Ishbel, featherlight and balanced despite her growing size and torn feet. The comforting resonance of the cutters and the gleaners gathered them into its web of secure maternal sound.

'Ishbel,' Peggy came laughing and skipping back, 'It's you that's needing a man. You do, you know fine you do,' as Ishbel's eyes, naked-looking ringed in fair lashes, dared her to say more. 'Rory MacCulloch's back home!'

Changing shadows like the sun moving across the hills chased across Ishbel's face. 'Rory MacCulloch? For me?' Her hollow laugh cracked in the middle.

'He's back from the fighting in Germany.'

'And I don't suppose that one came alone. Well he's not spreading anything on me,' the words rushed out of her. 'They're all the same. They join the regiment, and they go off some place and if they live they carry the diseases from that place back to us,' Ishbel's voice dropped, leaving her words ringing in the air between them. 'I'm telling you Peggy. He just better keep clear of me.'

'But you're surely not saying that Donald has the disease on him? He hasn't, I know he hasn't.' Peggy felt fingers pressing on her heart and a sob gathered in her throat.

'How would you know?' The heat in Ishbel's voice had given way to lumps of ice.

'I know. I'm telling you. I just know. He is laughing always.' Peggy had forgotten the pain in her back. She stood twisting the fingers of her left hand.

Ishbel had no answer to that. 'Anyway,' she said, 'they all drink forever, until they're so stupid they can't stand up. Of course it's easy in this place.'

Peggy's hands had stopped playing. Her laughter peeled out of her. 'The things you say. What else would men do? Isn't there plenty in it? If we could live on it we'd never be hungry. That and peats.'

'Everybody does not drink. Everybody doesn't need to. What about our father and Daniel?'

'Daniel!' Peggy squealed. 'You and your darling Daniel! That's all that you know. And father only because it makes his guts bad. What about mother? What about our mother then?'

'Oh, don't be daft. Mother only takes some now and again when she's feeling bad.'

'Now and often you mean. She must be feeling bad a lot of the time, that's all I can say.'

'Oh, you,' Ishbel ground out before bending back to her work.

'Oh, you,' Peggy echoed her, before doing the same.

'I don't need anyone,' Ishbel spoke to the ground, but Peggy heard her. 'Certainly not a MacCulloch,' and she gave a violent tug to tighten the string bands binding her sheaves.

'Well, I don't know who's going to take you then,' Peggy was gathering with one hand. 'It's not as if there's anyone in it. And you're getting very old.'

Ishbel let that pass. 'I don't need anybody,' she said.

'Then it's me that's sad for you.'

'Don't be sad for me. Be sad for yourself.'

'You're funny, you know that,' Peggy had stopped gathering and was stooping with her hands clasping her knees. 'I thought I was supposed to be the queer one. But I am sad. Not because you don't need anyone, though that's a sad enough way for anyone to be. Just like the old wife. But because you think you don't. That's an awful way to be.'

'What are you speaking about?' Ishbel's hands were still. She swayed her head around to look at Peggy. 'You know I can't make you out.'

High up a hawk was going in circles, looking for a homeless hare. A bank of black cloud blotted out the sun, taking the heat from their backs, from the land they worked.

Their land. Did they come from it, or did it grow out of them? They didn't know. It was more than their home, it was their mother, it was their father, it was themselves. One couldn't breathe without the other. One complete energy, one soul. Chip away at a part of their land, at what lived on it, at themselves, and everyone and everything became less, felt dimmed.

They came from the land and they went back into it. Their blood and their bones fed it. They knew, because they had been told, that from far, far back, to a time beyond which their eyes could see, that other people, who had been their people, had also been put into the earth.

Yet the land remained, with the sky stretched like a blanket over it, their shelter. There were two lights in the sky, the same lights that the old ones were told about knew. One made day, and gave life to the trees, it ripened their corn, and kept them alive. The old night light kept them safe when they were out, it showed them where to put their feet.

One body, one soul, one heart beating. They were like lost children away from it, it lay weeping without the least one of them.

When the stone cracked against Daniel's ankle everyone heard him shouting, but no one lifted their head.

'Who threw that stone?' he shouted again, his face as bright as his hair. From a standing position he scanned the field. Every back was bent, every arm kept up its industrious rhythm. Too industrious. The children were romping with the dogs. Working on her own, Mairead Beaton worked like a man.

'Was it you that did that?' he shouted at the cutter on his

left, a narrow-chested fellow of about his own age who'd got his hairstyle wrong. On the right side of his head his hair reached his jaw, on the other it skimmed his left ear in an upward curl.

'Who? Me? What?' the man was an idiot in his innocence.

'Don't you come your innocent face here. Someone threw that rock. Look at my ankle, it's in bits.'

The man put his blade down and walked over to Daniel.

'I suppose what you're telling me is that you haven't a good leg to stand on.' The man's face was straight, even if his hair wasn't, his tone light and easy. He looked past Daniel's right shoulder to the hills, as if he was seeing something to interest him there.

'Ay, I'm bursting myself laughing at you. But that stone didn't fly by itself.'

'You'd better watch you'll not put the field on fire with a face like that,' he said. 'It was likely one of the young ones. You know what way they are when they're together,' and he sauntered back to his blade.

'Ay,' Daniel said, giving him and the field a long look.

They worked in bursts, with singing. When working they worked well enough. But, too easy, boredom began to creep in on them. Then the singing would tail off, the pace slacken and devilment would find a place to surface.

Two men, who had wives and children in the field, rolled on top of each other in the dirt, their skirts up around their waists, their naked behinds scratched by stubble. The field stopped and closed into to watch.

'Run to the Wise Man.' A mother with a young baby tied up in a shawl on her back cornered two big boys who were pushing to get past for a front row view. People called these boys The Runners.

The Runners had been running all of their lives. Some said that they came into the world running. It was their speed that took them past childhood when they could be expected to die. They were too fast for any disease to sit on them or accident to catch them.

As small boys they ran to the peat cutting and, with small baskets on their backs, they ran home. They ran up hills, passing hares, and they ran even faster coming down. As children they ran away from their mothers, too fast for their fathers to catch them. They ran to church, but as they grew they ran slower. They still ran home fast. Around seventeen years, the Runners had not yet encountered girls in that special way. The village waited to see what way they would run when they did, and how fast.

Although they had always gone about together since their cradle days, the Runners were not brothers, neither were they related in any way that anyone knew of, and anyone knew everything, always. One was a Ross, the other fellow a Denoon. They looked alike, at least at a distance, both being long and gangly and black-haired. But the Ross's face was a moon, where Denoon's was like a spade.

The Runners found the Wise One sitting at the edge of the field, listening to the wind making music in the long grass and thinking long thoughts. The Wise One never did work, no one expected him to, it was enough that he was wise. He was one of the fair-haired Rosses, his hair reached in knots to well below his shoulders and his blue eyes were always looking to a place beyond Strath. The Strath people didn't know about his eyes, what they saw, they only knew what his name told them. He was young for his wisdom, around twenty-six years they thought. He inherited his wisdom from his father, they said, who had been killed by a stone. A MacKay had been holding it. No one knew what happened to the MacKay. All them men of the Fair Rosses were quite wise, but the oldest son of each generation seemed to inherit the Pure Wisdom. The Wise One wore no boots, preferring to go barefoot. This, he felt, showed how wise he was.

'What are you two wanting?' his twisted mouth girned at the panting Runners. He didn't appreciate being pulled from his thinking.

The Runners slowed for him as they went back to the fight, the Wise One didn't run.

'What is it now?' he barked to the crowd as they moved

aside to let him through. With his hands on his hips the Wise One stood looking down on what was before him.

'This two's going to murder someone,' said the women who'd sent the Runners for him.

'We tried to make them stop,' breathed an old man who'd been working too hard. His dying breath wouldn't be shallower.

'The Wise One's here.' A young woman with a firm shape, wife to the man on top, pulled at his hair and tried to haul him off. He gave her his arm in the chest for her trouble, but that didn't stop her. She held on to his hair, pulling at it so hard she nearly took his scalp off.

The Wise One put a foot on the face of the man underneath.

'Clear off,' he told the woman and she did.

'What's going on here?' he asked the two men.

His words and his foot were enough to make the man on top let go. He scrambled to his feet and pulled his skirt down. His wife was back and she gave him a hard look from the corner of her eye. Then the other stood up and the accusations started. The one who'd been stamped on was short and square, a block. The other fellow was big. And he looked hard.

'Someone should teach him how to use a blade,' the short one whined.

'He's cutting all wrong with it. He's throwing straw into my face all the time. I'm near blinded with him.' Despite the Wise One's presence, he was ready to swing at the Big Hard Man. The crowd was with the Big Hard Man, cheering him, winged arms urging him on. Not his wife, glassy-eyed and with an edge to her face like an axe; she looked like she would murder him as she rested her folded arms across her chest.

The Big Hard Man refused to be threatened. Ignoring his wife, he looked down at the Short One and said a swear. 'That man is mad,' he said. 'What I cut I keep. Someone may be throwing straw at him but it's not me.' Big Hard Man's wife cheered. She was the only one who did.

The Wise One made ground between them and watched his feet. He was taller than the Short One, nearly as tall as the Big

Hard Man, and slimmer than either of them. His kilted skirt hung in folds from his narrow hips to his knees.

Placing an open hand against each man's chest he held them.

'You say that someone,' (he stressed the someone) 'you say that someone is throwing straw into your eyes?' he said to the Short One.

The Short One nodded, not trusting himself with words. Too many were boiling up inside him. The crowd stood by and in silence waited. The children and the dogs forgot to run.

The Wise One turned to the Big Hard Man. 'And you? You're saying it's no you?'

The Big Man was also a composed man. His heavy head nodded in a clipped sort of way.

The Wise One said nothing, he was thinking. His eyes swung between the pair of them. They marvelled again at how blue they were. Wise eyes. Then, 'Could it be,' he asked the Big Hard Man, 'that maybe, we'll just say maybe, one or two speckles of dust are flying from your blade and into the face of this man here?' and he inclined his head toward the Short One, his long hair falling away from his face like a sheet of golden rain.

Short One put his shoulders back, straightened his short spine. Big Hard Man looked like he would lose his composure. His face began to boil. 'I have been watching you,' the Wise One soothed and curled his toes. 'You're a good worker.' The Big Hard Man believed him. The Wise One could see far. The Big Hard Man's composure settled.

The Wise One spoke to the Short One. 'And yourself,' he said. 'What if I was tell you that you're nowhere near to being blinded, except by your own rage,' and here the Wise One knew that he was walking on thin stony ground. He could feel the stones hurting his feet. 'Supposing,' he swivelled his slim hips, balanced himself more evenly, 'supposing one or two specks of chaff or stoor drifted your way, carried along in the gentle wind, and fastened themselves to an eyelid. What then?'

The Short One thought about that as he stood in the middle

of the still silent crowd. He didn't know there was a wind in it. Surely he would have felt it. But if the Wise One said there was there must be. The heat drained from his face and sunk itself somewhere below his boots.

'Now do you see?' The Wise One's smile as well as his eyes reached beyond Strath. 'Only the wind.'

It hadn't occurred to the wrestlers to think of the wind. Their expressions lightened, their eyes widened. Of course it was the wind. What then? The Wise One was wise and they were foolish. Never once would they be wise.

'It's me that's sorry,' the Short One told the Big Hard Man and he reached out his hand. The crowd cheered and his wife's face was soft once more.

'And me too,' the Big Hard Man said, and he took the hand in his large one. 'I'm sorry for your trouble and for your eyes,' and he lifted the Short One's blade and handed it to him. The crowd and the wife laughed and were glad.

'We're sorry,' the Short One told the Wise One.

'And you're wise.' The Big Hard Man was a straight-talking man.

Then the Wise One said something very kind to the Big Man. 'One day you will be,' he said and he walked back to the edge of the field, tall and slim and very wise.

'That man there is very wise,' the Big Man marvelled.

'I don't know how people get to be wise,' the Short One said. 'I'm not wise.'

'No, you're not wise. But he is. It is said he doesn't sleep. Would that be it, do you think?'

They both thought on that and agreed it was probably that way. They themselves slept a lot, too much. They would never get wise like that. They decided to sleep less. Sleep was only practising for death they decided, and that would come quick enough.

'I hope that wind drops,' the Big Man said, and he bent to his blade and the crowd dispersed, refreshed and ready to get on with their work.

Mairead felt his presence before she saw him. It was his boots she saw first. They stopped where her hands were gathering, making her feel hot and confused inside. She held her breath and drew back on herself. Her fingers refused to make knots in her straw and the chanting started bubbling from her lips. It was unintelligible, it could have been anything. Only she knew what it meant. The babbling quickened, became one long word. Tears were near.

She wanted the boots to go away, she wanted her words to make the boots go away. The straw had beaten her. She threw it away from her and sinking to her knees, put her hand to her mouth to try to stop the word. But the word came through her fingers. And the boots stayed.

He didn't know why he had stopped. It was Donald Munro he was looking for. Further down the field he could see him working, or what Munro would call working. That fellow only had one pace and he never worked beyond it. A swipe of the blade, a rest. Then another rest before the next swipe. He had the usual crowd of women gathered about him, all laughing and dancing at his beauty and intelligence and wit.

He stood looking down on her, aware of her upset. Saw her impatience with the sheaf. She didn't believe in making things easy for herself. He waited for her to lift her head. When she did not, he gathered up what she had scattered and, with a few quick turns, bound the sheaves together. He dropped it in front of her. It stopped her chanting but still she did not look up.

'That should do it,' he said. His voice was easy where she had no voice. She recognised kindness in him, she wanted to say something but she didn't know how. She could hear the people singing and above the singing a louder, harsh voice which had no song in it.

'That man must have awful holy knees.' He was looking to where the Minister was kneeling in the stubble. 'He's never off them. He'll be down there till the sun goes.'

The Minister had come to help with the harvest and had stayed to pray. They had heard his prayer, or a variation of it, many times. It was loud. He told Heaven how wicked they were from the top of his voice. He told Heaven nothing about how poor their harvest was. No wonder some of them turned to the old ways.

The Minister's voice made her lift her head to look at him. 'That man,' she said forcing her words to come out. 'I'm frightened of him. He is too near to me.' She spoke with spaces between her words.

'What's to be frightened of there? He's only a man. Full of wind. Like a pig's belly.'

'My – my mother,' she said, turning her head and looking up at him. 'My mother, my father.'

'Will you not go over to my own mother and my sisters?' he asked her, and he put his hand out to her. She took his hand and he lifted her to her feet. She came easy, her weight seemed like nothing to him.

'Go over to them,' he was standing very close to her, holding on to her hand.

She pulled her hand away and turned her back on him. The chanting was back. She smacked the heel of her hand hard against her forehead to try to stop it, but she couldn't break the word.

He moved around to the front of her. He saw the closed eyes, her mouth quivering, the way her hand darted off her brow.

'Don't,' the word burst from him. He caught her hand, stopped its assault. 'Don't be hurting yourself like that.' His words, his mouth were soft. He didn't know what else to say, he didn't know what was inside her. So he just kept holding her hand. For the second time she opened her eyes to his. Her eyes were level with his own, the iris almost as black as the enlarged pupil. She was his height. And as he stood looking at her he saw through the curtain that she wrapped herself in. It fell away and he was standing gazing at someone who didn't know what to do with what she was feeling.

'Go over to them,' he said it again, taking his hand away. 'I have to see about a house for my sister Peggy.' His eyes dropped first, he looked at the ground. 'I must go,' and he was backing away from her.

*　　*　　*

Mairead had lived by herself, with herself and had not thought of herself as lonely. Every day that came brought thoughts of her father and her mother. Was that loneliness? Or was that loss? Was there a difference? She didn't know. What she did know was that she never wanted the feeling which these memories evoked to leave her.

The way she missed her father was different to the way she missed her mother. She saw her father's hands, the way they gripped the cutter, laughter, sometimes tears, in his brown eyes. A song in his mouth. She didn't miss her mother in pictured places like her father. There was quite simply a large hole somewhere in her, and only her mother could fill it. She missed her father, but she wanted her mother. This want haunted her through the days, it came into her sleep so that she couldn't sleep.

But loneliness was different. Lonely was a cold place to be. It wasn't cold in the places she met her father and her mother. These were warm tight places. Tight, tight, inside her. It wasn't cold among the animals and with Master. But it was cold now. As she watched him walking away from her it came on her. Such emptiness. Was that lonely? One day she might die from it.

She had felt warmth up at the sheilings, that good place to be, up on the hopeful hill with the sweet grass growing and the wind biting at her bones. She wouldn't allow it then but, oh yes, it had been there.

This thing that had come on her was so large that it pushed the Minister from her mind. But in a different way, it was every bit as frightening. What was she going to do with it? If only her mother was with her. Bending down, she went back to her work.

After her mother died, people had come to her with kind and open hearts, eager to help, but she didn't repay their visits and in time they stopped coming. Now she only went near those the old wife couldn't cure. Everyone recognised she had healing in her.

Stone by stone, rock upon rock, she built a wall around herself and stayed behind it. There she was safe. And if no one could get past then no one could harm her. And after all this time, this careful time, he had walked straight through her wall as if it were made of smoke. She didn't know how. By doing nothing he'd torn down everything she'd built up. Not by stopping and speaking, but by walking away from her today, he had shown her how she was. And if he could get through, who else?

Maybe he didn't want to be near her. Maybe no one did. Why would they? But then he had been kind to her, had spoken kind words to her. He'd helped her with the roof. He didn't seem to be afraid of the Minister. He hadn't been unkind about the Minister, just not afraid. Should she think this way? She couldn't. She was frightened. She battered her forehead. Why didn't it all go away, why didn't it all go away? She'd lived with too much swirling like fog inside her for as long as she could remember. She wasn't suddenly going to feel free, supposing she knew what free felt like, because of the way someone else was. Someone with eyes blue-green like the sea she sailed on to come here. She'd try to hold on to safe thoughts. Master. And the animals, the birds. She'd go from this work, leave it and go home to them. The animals knew when time was right, their instinct told them, not mangled, jangled thoughts and feelings. She'd go home and let the squirrel and the hare and the birds be her teacher.

But his words had been sound, his eyes kind when they looked at her. She had wanted to say something. She should have said something but nothing would come. She had not thanked him for tying the sheaf. Her face was hot with the shame she felt at herself. She had forgotten how to be with people. For a second a vision of the Minister scythed in on her. She thought about his knees and her mouth opened and laughing fell out. Then she jammed her fist into her mouth to stop the laughing and looked around to see if anyone had heard, if the Minister had heard. But there was no break in the loud monotone.

On and off they took four days to cut their corn. They left it out to dry for longer than that, then gathered it into the barn ready for threshing.

Chapter Twelve

After the harvest they built a house for Peggy and an old man died. The man had lived for a long time, he was one of the oldest in the village, but it did not lessen the shock and the sense of fear which losing someone always gave them.

First the cows, then their crop. And now the man. And so the seeds of suspicion were sown.

Daniel heard it in his own house as they were sitting around the fire. 'I wondered about the cows,' his father was saying. 'Do you remember?' he looked at Daniel sitting beside him. 'Everything we have done, always. What have we not done?' his voice tailed off, became a thread which coiled on the floor. 'And now this man.'

'The man was old,' Daniel said.

The women said nothing.

'I'm thinking that someone's doing something on us.'

'That's stupidness talking,' Daniel said.

'This sort of thing used to happen.'

'What sort of thing? An old man and if you'd work the ground you might grow some decent crops.'

'What about Mairead Beaton?' Daniel's mother and his sisters were sitting across the fire from him and his father. His mother's voice was strong and accusing. 'I heard her at the harvest. You're no saying anything to that.'

'No, and I don't think you should either,' he told her, his knife's blade caressing a piece of stag's horn.

'Why ever not?' Ishbel's face was red from the fire. 'That's a queer one. And what were you doing with her?'

'Mairead Beaton's not anything but frightened of living.'

His own voice was quiet. 'And I wasn't doing anything. I spoke, that was all.'

'Well, that's not the way it looked to me.'

'You'd do better looking to yourself. You can't go speaking about people because you don't like the way they are.'

Her brother's tongue stung her, her pale eyes flashed back at him but she held her tongue.

He had never spoken to Ishbel that way, it surprised him that he did now.

'Daniel's right in what he's saying,' their father said. 'No word will be breathed from this house. Her father and her mother were good people. There is nothing to say the daughter is any less.'

No one challenged him. And so it was.

But the thought remained. And if it had been expressed inside one house, it would be foolish to think it would not be expressed inside others.

Chapter Thirteen

A fire had been burning in the Minister's house for the past two weeks, ever since Arabella had received the letter telling her that her sister Catherine and Catherine's husband were coming to visit.

The sight of flames in the cold fireplace comforted the Minister somewhat, gave colour and warmth to the days he spent at home. Fire, however, brought neither colour nor comfort to his wife. Lighting it was an extra chore, done only to prevent her sister's nagging tongue.

The letter had been vague as to when they would arrive, so every day since she'd received it Arabella left her house in the middle of the morning to wait for them. Taking the track through the trees, heedless of whatever animals were roaming about, she'd walk the several miles through the open country before her, until she reached the jutting-out rock. There she'd sit on its flat top and wait until dark.

She had done what she could with the house, and with herself. On dry days, she had hauled the bedding outside and spread it on the whins, Catherine's words in her head as she was doing it. Daily she cooked food, by evening the geese and the hens ate it. Her husband ate away from home most of the time. There was always food somewhere for the Minister. Arabella herself did not eat much. Most of the time she forgot to eat. They weren't short of food the way the poor people were. In that the Minister's friends kept them well supplied.

The Minister showed little interest at the prospect of guests, but then he didn't seem to be interested in anything that took place within his own home.

He would have been at one time. James and Catherine were his friends as well as Arabella's family. 'That will be nice for you,' was all he said when she showed him Catherine's letter. He hadn't said anything since. No mention of being there to receive them when they came. He showed no inclination to walk down the track with her. She'd asked him once but if he heard her he'd made no reply. He'd gone into the room where he kept his books and closed the door.

'That will be nice for you.' Strange words for him to say. Why should it concern him whether things were nice for her or not? At one time he had been to kind to her, in a fatherly kind of way. Then it had been, was she warm enough, shouldn't she be wearing heavier clothes and was she eating enough, she'd feel better if she did. 'No,' she silently screamed. She did not want confusion. Just let things go on the way they had been, let things assume the same order, then she'd be all right. She didn't want or need change. Of any kind.

Waiting for them was hard. What made it so hard? A year ago, six months, three, it wouldn't have been hard because she wouldn't have cared. But now some small thing inside her was claiming its right to life. No! Ignore it, forget it, and it will not live. But she couldn't, no more than she could forget to breathe in and out. I am powerless, she acknowledged, as she walked along the road.

She cried over the bolster. And the mattress. Both were filled with rocks and however hard she shook them she could make them no softer. Catherine would be bound to say something. She couldn't get the hang of the fire, she forgot to feed it and so it kept going out, and her hands and the front of her dress were covered in its dirt. How would Catherine see her, Catherine who could see right into her?

She'd cleaned herself as best she could and tied a ribbon in her hair. In a wooden chest she found a dress, put there in the days prior to leaving Dingwall, and she put it on. It mocked her. It was a girl's dress and much too fine. How much better to be wearing the rough brown like the other women here. Wasn't that right for her? Wasn't that what she was now? Wasn't it?

'Who am I?' her soul whimpered as her hardened hands caught on the skirt's smoothness.

She wandered back to the room with the fire. She felt the fire's intrusion. It too mocked her, encroached on her solitude, the crackling flames jarring on her nerves. She couldn't bear it, she didn't want its smiling warmth. Going back through to the room where she slept, she pulled a blanket from the bed and draped it around her shoulders. Two pillows had been placed lengthways down the centre of the bed to separate her from her husband. Once she thought of walking into the loch to get away from him. Later it didn't matter. And neither did it seem to bother her husband the way things were. He accepted change without comment.

Outside there was no sun in the sky, its warmth and its light keeping away from Strath and its people. The wind which had been soft early in the day was beginning to stiffen. Arabella drew the blanket tighter about her as she walked away from the house. Already the leaves on the trees were turning from their greens to pale green to yellow, to russet and gold.

She wasn't afraid to walk on the road on her own. When she first came to live in Strath, Gilbert was adamant she must never stray from the house. 'It's not only the four-legged animals you have to watch out for,' he'd said. Fear had stopped her then from disobeying him. But she wasn't afraid now.

When she had covered about one mile she decided she would stop for a rest. Maybe she would just stay here by the edge of the track and not bother about going as far as the rock. From here she could sit and watch the sky changing as the wind blew the clouds across it. She could still see her house, small and white in the distance.

The Minister's house sat in a high place, clear of and looking down on Strath and its people. Long and low, it had two windows which looked south. Between the windows was the door, tall enough for a man to walk upright.

Sitting on the cold ground, with her back straight and her legs drawn up in front of her, Arabella strained her ears to catch any strange sounds but all that she could hear was village sounds of dogs barking and people's voices calling, behind them the fractured notes of a bagpiper.

That particular evening wasn't the first time she'd thought that she couldn't live in the place any more. She'd known it from the beginning, every day she knew it. This place didn't belong anywhere in the world. Neither did its people.

She knew mountains, she had grown up knowing them. But they had been distant mountains, the kind she could look away to from the garden, through the windows. They weren't something you had to constantly feel and think about. They were only there when you remembered to look up. Mostly she didn't. But here they came down to your feet and stood on you, they squeezed the breath out of your lungs and strangled you, they sat on your shoulders and pressed you down into the earth. Their shadow obliterated your shadow.

I can't live in this place. But she did.

When first she had caught sight of Strath's people she had been glad of the safety of the coach. She remembered how they appeared from behind the trees along the way. Sometimes singly, others in groups, staring dirty faces swallowed by eyes. She felt threatened by their sudden appearance, by their empty expressions, by their otherness. Women mostly, with small children. Brown-skinned, ragged, ill-nourished. All bundled up in the same coarse brown cloth. Hair which didn't look like hair, more like knotted ropes, as if it had just sprung out from their heads. All black-haired except for one. A small child. Male, female, she couldn't tell, but it had pale hair, whiter even than her own. Seeing that child had somehow offended her. Where had it come from, so different, to be among them? With hair like hers.

The arms and the chests of the men she saw were naked and muscular. Some wore breeches, some their kilt type of garment, a length of the brown cloth wrapped around their lower bodies, the other end going over a shoulder, toga fashion.

The children had the same closed faces as their elders. All looking at her from behind the trees, through the veil of their ignorance. At a distance but nevertheless unnerving. Later, when she attended church, there were those who would venture closer, and would reach out a hand and touch her, to see if she was real. And when she turned to look at them they scampered away like frightened squirrels. They brought their smells with them into the church. Why didn't they go and wash? There was a stream running past their village. And a river near it.

Who knew what, if anything, went on inside them. Gilbert was convinced he saw something. She saw nothing. Those who did come to church huddled together, even there, as if it was the only way they could exist. And Gilbert emptied himself on these people. People who despite their church attendance, dwelt in another world with their magics and their superstitions, their fear and their distrust. It would be easier for him to reach and to teach the wild animals.

Now hearing only the wind, oblivious to the clouds, Arabella sat at the edge of the track for a long time and thought of nothing. It was easier that way.

They came out of the fading light, four horses, Catherine and James MacKenzie and a man who guided them leading a pack-horse which carried the bags.

'For goodness sake, Arabella. What are you doing outside in the dark? Alone. Where's Gilbert?' were Catherine's first words. It might have been only a day since they had last been together instead of some years.

There was too much to say so Arabella said nothing. She stood and looked at her sister and James Mackenzie, her back erect, her chin level.

'Oh, I don't know what to say. Help me down some-one. You, man, get me down,' Catherine shouted ahead to the guide.

'It's all right, I'll do it.' James MacKenzie, having him-self dismounted, forestalled the man and went to help his wife.

'Hullo Catherine, hullo James,' Arabella said when Catherine's feet were on the ground.

James MacKenzie had grown fat, he had gained a chin and his buttons were struggling to close his coat. But his eyes were the same. 'Hullo, Arabella, it is good to see you.' He took her hand between his two. 'How are you?'

'I'm well, thank you.' She allowed her hand to remain within his and they stood that way for a few seconds.

'Well, James, don't just stand there, let's go up to the house,' Catherine said. 'We'll walk. I'm not getting back up on that thing. Such a journey. Really,' she was tugging at her skirt, brushing it down with a gloved hand. 'Arabella, I couldn't begin to tell you,' she re-set her hat to what she judged was the correct angle, 'I really did think we were heading for the end of the world. Didn't I, James? Didn't I say just that?'

'My dear, you did. Many times.'

'Come then, don't let us stand here. I'm beginning to freeze over. Is it always this cold here? I remember last time. Rained the whole time,' and Catherine led the way, the guide following her with the horses.

'Gilbert not about?' James MacKenzie asked Arabella as they fell in behind.

'No,' Arabella was looking straight ahead of her at the bulging muscles in the flank of one of the horses.

'Oh, my aching bones. I need a comfortable place to sit,' Catherine's voice floated back to them.

'Is Gilbert not at home?' James MacKenzie said it again as he stood with his back to the fire.

'His work takes him from home.' Arabella sat on the edge of a chair, trying to relax in a room where she had never felt at home.

'Does it not worry him, leaving you alone in this place?' Catherine's voice sailed through to them. Having rid herself of her hat, her coat and her shoes she had gone to examine the bed she would be sleeping in.

Arabella opened her mouth to reply, but it was Catherine's words which filled the space. 'I hope this bed's well aired. If it's not I'm not sleeping in it. And I must say this bolster feels very lumpy. What's in it? Rocks?' She was still complaining as she flopped down on the sofa, dark coils of hair bouncing about her shoulders.

Her husband gave her a long look which she caught and held, in the widening of her eyes. James MacKenzie turned to Arabella again, curved his mouth into a smile.

'Well,' he said, 'You're looking well, Arabella.'

'I know how I look,' Arabella thought, but the thought remained unsaid.

'She looks awful,' Catherine said. 'Are you going to keep your hair like that? I must say Arabella, you could pass quite easily for one of your wild women. What does Gilbert say? Or is he too busy telling these people about God to notice?' And Catherine laughed. It was the first time Arabella had heard laughter in her husband's house. She felt as alien within it as she did among the people of Strath.

There was no unkindness in Catherine's words, nor in her attitude. Catherine was bossy, she always had been. Arabella's first memory of Catherine's domineering attitude centred around her dolls. When they were children they both had wooden dolls. Where they had come from, Arabella had no idea, they had just been there. Arabella played with her doll, and Catherine played with hers. Until the day Catherine decided she'd have Arabella's. 'This one's face is squint,' Catherine had said thrusting her doll at Arabella. 'You can have it. I want yours. Her face is much nicer,' and she had pulled Arabella's doll from her.

'I don't know what the fuss is about,' their mother had said. 'If Catherine's happy and you're happy.'

Arabella had said nothing and she soon came to love the squint-faced doll.

In the dim light of the flickering candles she looked at Catherine, at Catherine's hair, at her dress, at her shoes lying on the floor beside her. Catherine would always be beautiful. That dark blue colour had always looked well on her. It would be the finest fashion of course, Catherine would wear nothing else.

Catherine's loveliness made Arabella even more consious of her own appearance. Where once it had fitted, her girl's dress now hung on her. She knew how Catherine saw her. And James. It was how she saw herself.

'Will you eat now?' she said. 'You must be hungry. Come through will you?'

'Was it all right?' she asked after they'd pushed their plates away.

'More than all right.' James MacKenzie drank the last of his wine. 'The venison was as tender and as juicy as new grass.'

'James has not lost his ability to flatter, Arabella, but yes, you've learned much.' Catherine was touching the corners of her mouth with a scrap of the finest lace. 'I don't know how you do it. Live as you do, I mean. Surely Gilbert could have got you a woman.'

'I want no one,' Arabella said, rising from the table. 'I do what I have to. I manage.'

The first time she had visited, Catherine had been deeply angry at the state in which she had found her sister. Arabella, how could she bear to live in such a way? And still she wondered how Arabella had come to this. And Gilbert. What about him?

Back in the main room, while his wife chattered on and her sister gave little or no response, James MacKenzie leaned back in his chair beside the fire and studied them both. Poor Arabella. What in heaven's name was Gilbert Kennedy thinking of? He knew from the start it had been wrong, she had been a child. He also knew he should have spoken, but he hadn't. Catherine was to be his wife, it wasn't for him to cause trouble in her family. He knew where that would lead him – away from Catherine. One did not cross Catherine's mother. And the Baillie was no use. No point in saying anything to him, he did what his wife told him to do. And anyway it wasn't as if it was any of his, James's, business. Still, poor Arabella. What an utterly drab life she had. She used to be lovely, there was the faint trace there, her mouth still full and soft. But her dress was hanging from her, as if from the body of a girl yet to develop.

He'd thought about Arabella quite often since she left to live in Strath. Not in any romantic way but about the way her life had gone. In the intervening years he'd come to understand why she couldn't bear to have her parents spoken about. Their betrayal had destroyed her, had robbed her of the strength she needed to fight her other battles.

He saw her mouth curve at something Catherine had said to her. Poor Arabella, she was in there somewhere he supposed, but who was going to find her?

He remembered that time her mother had touched him on the thigh, when he had been seated beside her at the table. It had startled him. He hadn't spoken of it to Catherine, but he contrived afterwards to sit at a safe distance from Mistress Hutcheon.

The mother had been a warm woman and his wife was like her mother. His fortune. He wondered about Arabella though, living the way she did.

'He doesn't touch her,' Catherine had said after the first visit. 'If she didn't take with child before she's not going to now. Poor Gilbert, to be rejected like that. Still, I suppose he finds his comfort somewhere.'

James came from his musings to the sound of his wife still speaking. 'Isn't there anyone in this place who could sew a dress for you? That thing you're wearing is horrid. Isn't it horrid, James? That dress?' Shrugging his shoulders he looked at Catherine and said nothing.

'Who do you imagine cares what I wear? I don't.' There was heat in Arabella's words.

'You don't mean that. You can't. Come on, come with me.' Catherine leapt to her feet. 'I have something you'll like. In my bag. Come on.'

'Close your eyes,' she said when they were standing in the room Arabella had prepared for their stay. 'Go on,' when Arabella looked as if she would refuse. 'Do as your sister tells you.'

From the leather bag Catherine took a dress made from the palest silk. As pale as the sun's light. She shook it loose on the bed.

'Open them,' she said.

Arabella opened her eyes, then her mouth.

'Now, don't say it,' Catherine said running a hand down

the folds in the skirt. 'Isn't it beautiful? Isn't it? Say you love it.'

Arabella said nothing, but continued to stare open-mouthed at the dress.

'I'm giving it to you. We used to be the same size before you got to be so thin. Still, we can make it fit you. You do remember how to sew don't you? Well, what do you think? Say something.'

Still Arabella said nothing. Slowly she put out a hand. She wanted to touch the silk, but she was afraid to. She made her hand move. Her breath caught in her throat at the feel of it.

'Oh Cath.' A single tear rolled down one cheek. 'Oh, Cath.'

'Sh now, sh,' Catherine turned and put her arms around her sister. Holding Arabella was like embracing a statue. She stood there, head down, unmoving. Catherine was alarmed at Arabella's thinness. Under her dress she was nothing but bones. Her poor dear sister.

'I'm sorry.' Arabella lifted her head but still she didn't look at Catherine. 'I'm sorry,' and tears ran from both eyes now. 'That's the kindest thing anyone's ever done for me.'

'You do talk nonsense, Arabella, I must say.' Catherine was back at the dress, straightening it, fingering its buttons. 'People were always kind to you, and still would be if you'd let them.'

Arabella remained silent. She didn't know what to say, what to do. Unkindness she could deal with. Kindness was different. 'I'm sorry,' she said again. 'It is a most beautiful dress. And I do thank you. I have to go now,' and pulling away from Catherine she made for the door.

'Aren't you going to say goodnight to James?'

'No, no. Not like this. You say it for me,' and she hurried to the door, pulled it open.

'What about this?' Catherine's words made her turn. 'It is yours,' and she held out the dress for her.

Arabella took the dress, looked at it, then crushed it to her. 'Yes,' she tried to smile, but her face wouldn't work. 'Yes. Thank you. Goodnight,' and head down, she ran from the room.

*　　*　　*

Lying in her bed, the dress lying in Gilbert's place, Arabella sobbed through a mouthful of pillow for most of the night. The dress had touched what she had been. Before Catherine's arrival she would have said that nothing ever would. And she'd have been proud of that.

On her own she had grown strong. She wasn't afraid any more. Not of Gilbert, not of the place she lived in, not of its people.

She would never like the place, a place like this could never be her home. But her young girl's nervousness had gone. Just as the girl had gone. So, too, had her desperate grip on a past she on the one hand rejected and, on the other hand, needed to cling to, to remember how to survive. The past had fallen away from her and she found she could still stand. On her own she could stand. But she was fragile. But that too was all right. She had thought that as long as nothing touched her she could tell herself she was strong and she would be strong. But just let one thing touch her, just one thing. What then? Well, one thing had and she didn't die. She was crying but she wasn't dying. Her tears were dissolving and washing away her pain.

Chapter Fourteen

The Minister thawed before James and Catherine, and for James the stay turned out better than he had thought it would. It was with reluctance that he had allowed Catherine to persuade him to go with her. But he knew that behind Catherine's brisk manner she worried about her sister, and so he had said yes.

'Tell me, Gilbert,' he asked the Minister one day as they walked not far from the house, 'what are you doing here? I mean,' he gave a short laugh, 'the people here, they're little more than wild animals surely? A waste of your time, wouldn't you say?'

The Minister stopped walking and pointed with his stick. 'Look down there,' he said. 'What do you see?'

'Mud huts. People living among filth. Not even people. Not what you and I would term people. And certainly not living. Existing.'

'Ah, but they are people, James. Oh, their ways may be savage to the likes of us, but that's because they know no better. The Bishops had them for how many years? Too many. And taught them nothing.'

'I should think that would be because of the impossibility of such a task. I mean, how on earth can one know what they're thinking? Do they think?'

'Imprisoned souls, James, imprisoned souls. It suited Rome to keep them that way.'

'But Gilbert, I mean, they're not even civilised. How can you teach that?'

'What's civilised, James?' the Minister's voice became angry.

'You? Me? What's happening to our church, to our country? Who's the uncivilised there James?'

'Oho,' James MacKenzie raised his hands to ward off the Minister's words. 'You're much too deep for me. Always were, mind. And I commend you,' he nodded his head. 'But here? This place?'

'Where else would I be?' The heat had gone out of his voice, a bleak note edged in. His face hung in tired folds. They walked on in silence. They hadn't gone far when the Minister stopped again.

'Do you know what it was like when I first came? I saw then what you're seeing now. I had doubts, grave doubts. And I was frightened of what was before me.'

'You? Frightened?'

'Oh yes. I was like Jeremiah. You know, why me Lord? It took me a long time and a lot of work to get past their shyness and their very natural distrust of anyone coming in from the outside world. Do you know,' he leaned on his stick, 'it was the children who came to me first. I hadn't been here long when one or two began to follow me. At a distance. And as soon as I'd stop and turn round to look at them they'd scatter. But one day one didn't. Scatter I mean. He stood looking at me and I stood looking at him. Neither of us moved, it would have been wrong of me to. Soon others were standing beside him and myself still looking. Aren't little children wonderful, James? Don't you think?'

James MacKenzie smiled and nodded. The look on the Minister's face robbed him of his ready words. 'Then one day a boy walked out from the group and came up to me. Stood right in front of me. Toe to toe nearly. He didn't open his mouth, not a word, just looking. Such a poor little thing. But in him I saw, I saw James, all the very best, all the beauty that God could make was in that boy.' The Minister shook his head, gave a half laugh. 'It's in all of them.'

James MacKenzie looked away from the sheen in his friend's eyes. 'Hm, well, yes, as I've said, you go too deep for me. Remember I have a hatch of these little beauties as you would have them. Vile little beasts.'

'There's this fellow,' the Minister had resumed walking, his shoulders rounded as he leaned on his stick, 'a forester. A coarse brute I was warned.'

'And is he?'

'Oh, yes. And more. In every way.'

'And?'

'I had been up to see him a dozen times but he was never about. But at last I got him.'

'And?'

'I don't know James, I just don't know. The man's not as stupid as he pretends to be. Thoroughly godless, absolutely no morals – well, most of them are like that. Filthy habits, the usual. But I don't know. There's more to him than he lets on. He laughed the minute I opened my mouth and he was still laughing when I left him.'

This time it was James MacKenzie who stopped. 'Don't you ever get tired of it all? There must be easier ways to live. Easier parishes to serve. You know, you're not so young any more.'

'And you're not so slim, James old friend. But no, this is where I must be. Let others go to the other places.' He paused. 'There are still plenty of them tied to the old ways. Magic, superstitions, it's all here. But some listen, some listen. Of course I don't delude myself that even the listeners have put it all away. But maybe one day, maybe one day. To the Lord a thousand years is but a day. Why would I be in a hurry?'

'You're a man of great faith, Gilbert. Even this place doesn't seem to have diminished it.'

The Minister smiled as he lifted his head and sniffed the clear air. 'Oh, I can see the way it will be. The sweetest scented garden of all,' his eyes glittered, 'Eden. It's hard on Arabella though. Poor Arabella. A sojourner by Babel's streams.'

James MacKenzie had often seen that look on Gilbert Kennedy's face. The Minister had left him, had entered some far-off realm. Silently James thanked God that his destiny lay in architecture, in other houses. For a split second his eyes grew bleak. My God, Arabella. Imagine if that was Catherine.

They walked on together through the long afternoon of the day, without speaking. James Mackenzie felt more comfortable in the silence than he had listening to his friend talking about sweet scented gardens and Babel's streams. There had always been a zealous streak in Gilbert.

'The rumour has it in Dingwall,' he now said, hoping to stay on safer ground, 'that Montrose is in Denmark, trying to raise an army there.'

'Montrose, huh,' the Minister said. 'Now there's a man to take the wide path. No straight and narrow for our great marquis.'

'Yes, but have Strachan's Convenanters anything to fear from him?'

'I think not, James,' the Minister said. 'I think not.'

Chapter Fifteen

The Minister sat at the head of a square table in the room which held his books. Ranged to the left of him sat three men, his Church Elders. An open ledger lay before him, papers and rolled-up documents by his right hand, an inkstand in front of him. He dipped his pen into the inkpot and wrote something in the ledger. The Elders waited on in silence, all gazing at the top of the Minister's head. From the whitened wall at the Minister's back two candles in brackets fluttered.

The Minister looked up. 'Kenneth Bain,' he read from the ledger. 'What about him?'

An Elder spoke. His face was closed, tight. Slits for eyes that barely opened, pinched nostrils that barely breathed, pursed mouth that barely moved. Whichever power had fashioned this man had wasted no time on the materials of his face. A quick cut with a sharp knife would have achieved the same effect.

'Kenneth Bain's ears are deaf,' the Elder said. 'What's he caring about the Church for? The man's a heathen.'

The Minister groaned. Kenneth Bain was only the first. Was this going to be the way of it again?

'I despair of that man. Well, I'm not going to waste time on him. The matter'll have to go before Presbytery,' and he scraped something into the book. 'Let them deal with it.' He replaced his pen in the inkpot and slid a sheet of paper from under his book.

'I have here,' he said, reading the sheet, 'a report from the Moderator. Bain, it states, has admitted to fathering Kate MacRae's two children and he offers to donate money to the Poor Fund. But he has said he will not stand. I see that Kate MacRae has come before the Session twice. Is that right?'

He looked to the three Elders for confirmation.

Three heads, as one head, nodded.

'Seven merks against Bain then. We'll move on,' and he scraped his pen across the page.

'John Ross is asking the Session about that bit of ground to the west of the church. His father's lying there and he's wanting to be buried beside him,' the young Elder said.

'Do any of you know of anyone who has a prior claim on that ground?' the Minister asked.

Closed Face shook his head for all three.

'Then let it be granted to him,' and the pen scraped it into the book. 'Next.'

'Long Peter, him with the fair hair, was seen carrying a pole through the whole of the village on the Sabbath,' said the Elder who hadn't spoken. His words rolled slow and thick from his tongue.

'He will stand on the stool and be rebuked before the congregation.' The Minister noted it. 'I see that John Tulloch hasn't brought his child forward for baptism yet. Three days in sackcloth outside the church door for him.'

'I spoke to him three times about it,' the young Elder said. 'He says he hasn't money.'

'Nevertheless three days. Next.'

'Peggy Ross was seen fornicating up on the Sheep's Hill with Donald Munro last April. You should see her,' the quickening voice of the Closed Face said. 'There's a bairn in her all right,' and his hands were jumping.

Pen scraped paper. The Minister did not look up. 'Next,' he said.

'The widow MacRae says Mairead Beaton's stopping her cow from giving milk.'

'Next.' The Minister's voice was as quiet as the candle's flame.

'Isa Denoon. Fornicating with a forester they call MacIver.'

The Minister noted MacIver's misdemeanour and took a break from writing. 'What prevents Alexander Ross from registering his child?' he asked them. Perspiration covered his face, giving it a waxy look in the light from the candles.

'Death,' the Quiet Elder said. 'His death.'

'Whose death?'

'Alexander Ross's own death.'

The pen made a heavy black mark on the page.

The three Elders had eased themselves into the meeting. Now they leaned back in their chairs and loosened their tongues.

'Donald Ross was seen rolling drunk on the Sabbath with Mary Tulloch. Half of her clothes were missing.'

'Duncan Denoon went into his own house on the Sabbath with another man. The other man was carrying a bundle on his back. Although he was at home in time for the church sermon he didn't attend.'

'When I went along to Alexander Bain's for to get his goods to pay off his church debts, his wife started battering me over the head with a lump of wood and split my head open,' the young Elder said.

'Rory Munro and John Red Ross were round at the widow John Munro's house dressed in women's clothes and near frightened the old cailleach to death.'

The Elders kept the stories coming and the Minister kept on writing. He'd write for a spell then he'd take a break and enquire without much interest into the whys and wherefores of the alleged misdeeds. The misdeeds were always the same, people were always the same.

'Peter Ross was seen by many people chasing his cattle beasts from the corn field on the Sabbath.'

'You baptised Matthew Ross's bairn when he was still under the scandal of fornication,' Closed Face said.

The Minister's pen stopped its scraping, rested on the paper. 'Why did I not know this?' he looked at Closed Face.

'You did know it. We told you. Twice.' Closed Face's lips were clamped so tight they might have been stitched together.

'Ay, we told you, twice.' The young Elder said.

'Twice.' The Quiet Elder nodded.

The Minister made a note of Matthew Ross's aberration. 'Next.'

'It was Duncan Munro that put the church on fire.' Closed Face had that one. His throat almost closed in the telling. The other two wrung their hands and shuffled their feet on the wooden floor. They could feel their sweat washing their armpits.

The Minister's right hand hesitated again on the page for a second, then wrote on. The damage to the church pained him, more than anything else. It wasn't the first time the church had suffered. Not long after he'd come to Strath, the tribe from across the border had burnt it to the ground, to spite their Ross neighbours.

'Hector Ross was up at the Blackwater with a rod on the Sabbath.'

The Minister wrote down Hector Ross's misdeed and returned his pen to the inkpot. 'It has come to my notice,' he said, squeezing the bridge of his nose between his thumb and forefinger, 'that a Helen Denoon, with child, has left for another Parish. I'll write to the Minister of that Parish to make sure that she and the child are well. Also a James Tulloch has come into our Parish looking for work. I haven't had his papers. Someone see to that.' His picked up the pen. 'Next.'

'Janet Ross and Agnes Ross were seen selling on the Sabbath.'

'John Ross and his brothers were seen travelling across the country with horses on the Sabbath.'

'Alexander Bain and James Munro left the church in the middle of singing the psalms.'

'There's altogether too much of baking bread and lifting water on the Sabbath going on.'

'Ishbel Ross, drunk as usual, went into Alasdair Ross's house and started laying into his wife, battering her until the blood came and covering the woman in bruises. On the Lord's Day at that.'

The Minister's pen kept writing and the Elders drew breath.

'Now we come to Any Other Business,' he said. 'I'm going to leave the church till last. I have before me,' he shuffled among his papers until he found what he was looking for, 'I have here a bill of slander from a Donald Munro. He cites Daniel Ross. The two will appear before the Session at a date and time I will give you. Is there anything any of you want to say?'

The three Elders mumbled and shuffled in the negative. In time they would say plenty. The Minister made a short note in the book and put the pen back in the inkpot.

'Does anyone know of anyone who can help me with this? My workload is heavy, it's too much for me,' he said.

The Elders looked at each other. Then they looked at the Minister. Then back to one another.

When it looked as if no one was going to say anything, Closed Face opened or half-opened his mouth. 'I've been told that one of the Weavers has a book.'

'Can he write?'

'Write? Oh, I don't know about that. No one told me.'

'Find out, and if he can, get him. I can't be expected to do everything.'

Closed Face spoke again. 'There's people coming to the church that are still carrying their old ways. If they drank as much milk as they pour on the hills they might look better. And charms. For everything. I was told about a man who fornicates with horses.'

Closed Face nearly burst himself on that one.

'Names, man, names,' the Minister said to him while the other two sniggered into their hands. By now sweat was soaking more than their armpits.

'Of every one of them,' triumph flowed from the mouth of God's holy helper.

He rattled out a string of names, his face growing pinker with every name uttered. The Minister put the names down in his book.

'I want one of you to go about in the time of service and find out who's not coming to church.' he said.

The Quiet Elder raised his hand. He was for that.

'Also those leaving the church in the time of the service are to pay a fine and they'll be rebuked in front of the public. And if anyone can't pay, other means will have to be sought.'

All agreed, many times, by a drumming of hands on the table.

'Now,' the Minister straightened in his chair, rested his elbows on the chair arms and made a steeple of his fingers. He looked at them over his fingertips. 'I mentioned earlier a man coming here to work and we don't have his papers of identification. It's come to my notice that there are likely to be others. Find out and also get them to hand in their papers and report back.'

They made their noise again.

'One of you, you,' he pointed to the Young Elder. 'Go through the Parish on the Lord's day. Anyone who is to be found carrying out profane acts is to be severely rebuked. This vicious custom must stop. And we're going to have to put an end to people sleeping in church.'

The Young Elder put his shoulders back. Wasn't this what he came into the church for? His legs were strong, they'd take him wherever he had to go.

'There isn't enough coming in to help the poor. Somehow it will have to be increased. What say any of you?'

'There's too many of them,' the Young Elder said. 'They're too big a drain on what we're getting.'

'What you say is right, of course, but if we ask those who have I believe they will give more. We must ask. Too many of the people have nothing and their harvest was hardly worth gathering. Winter'll be on them soon.'

He peered at a sheet of paper which he'd picked up. 'Rory Ross, the smith's son,' he said. 'He was seen out with a rope on the Sabbath. I had his father up to see me, pleading for his son. It seems the boy is becoming increasingly difficult for his father to discipline as he grows. In view of the boy's tender years a rebuke before Session should suffice I think. What do you say?'

They agreed, variously.

The Quiet Elder thought that the Minister's suggestion was about right. Closed Face thought that if he was his son he'd give him rope. The Young Elder was convinced the Minister was getting soft. And old.

'The bagpiper struggled with the smith's wife for her stool and pushed the woman down onto the ground. He'll stand before the congregation. This sort of thing is getting to be a habit with him. He'll pay twenty merks. And that goes for anyone fighting for seats and making noises in God's house.'

The Minister's tone was short. He drew two lines under the bagpiper's doings. Under cover of the table the Young Elder rubbed his hands and reversed his earlier opinion of the Minister. The bagpiper'd be skirling like his chanter. The other two nodded.

'Mary Munro and Samuel Denoon have handfasted for the required year and they find they are not suitable. The child of the union will remain in its father's keeping. Mary Munro, I believe, has returned to her own home.'

That was good news for the Young Elder. Mary Munro was nice.

'There's only one birth and baptism before us. Donald, lawful son of Donald Black Ross. William and John Ross to be the witnesses. No marriages. Now,' he said. 'We come to the question of the church.'

The three sat up and waited. The place was freezing, their sweat had dried on them. You'd think the Minister would have a little comfort about him. There was more warmth in their own places. They'd be as well to be in the open, better maybe.

'I'm not going to waste time on who did it. He will be found and dealt with. It is a bad thing that one of our own would do such a thing. I propose to set up a church fund. Those who can must give. I don't expect it'll be much. I have already sent a letter to the Bishop asking for his help. I'm going to need volunteers.'

'I know a man who can gather some others for to build a pulpit and put in new rafters,' the Quiet Elder said. He had worked in the wood once. He had contacts.

'That's good,' the Minister nodded. 'The Earl will supply the timber.'

The Elders nodded, ferociously, their acknowledgement becoming garbled.

'And get together some people to take away the burnt wood. The roof'll have to be on before the winter. It's already getting too cold for people to be standing in the open.' He leaned forward, put his clasped hands on the table. 'They haven't the clothes,' he said.

'What about the stools?' Closed Face asked. 'There's not one left whole.'

'Never mind stools. Those who have can bring their own. The rest can sit where they stand. The earth's the Lord's. If we can get the rafters built, it would be a start.'

'Ay, ay,' the Elders agreed. That was true enough.

'Well, that concludes matters for this Session. Is there anything we have overlooked?'

The Quiet Elder shook his head. I don't think so, he thought.

The Young Elder shook his head. I need heat, he thought.

'You know all of them that have to appear before the congregation and all that,' Closed Face said. 'What about all that when we haven't a church? I mean, you canna stand on a stool in the open. You'd tumble off.'

'They're in the book,' the Minister said. 'And our church will be rebuilt,' and he scraped back his chair and stood up, rested his hands on the table. The Elders rose with him. He bowed his head and mumbled a short prayer. The Elders mumbled Amen. Then they bolted from the Minister's house.

Chapter Sixteen

Peggy sat on the bank of the Blackwater and cried. The river flowed on, unaware of her misery, taking her tears to the sea.

She forced herself to place her hand on her belly. It was swollen and hard. Her mother had said there was a bairn in there. Peggy didn't believe her mother then. Her mother was a daft old woman. What did she know? Her mother had used the witch word about Mairead Beaton after their father had spoken. Her mother's words had enraged Daniel. Still, her mother had said. Peggy wasn't quite so believing now. But she didn't know how a bairn got to be inside her guts. She hadn't done anything bad. She was good. Was she being punished for always laughing?

She forced herself past her fear and let her hand lie for a while. Gathering her strength she pressed down on her belly. Her belly still felt hard. The hard thing moved about inside her sometimes. She was afraid that her guts would burst and spill on to her feet. She was afraid of every step she took. If it wasn't for her mother's tongue she would have stayed lying down in her bed. She snatched her hand away and made it rest beside her and pluck at the grass. She must be awful bad. Why else would God put a bairn in her? Or was it the spirits? Why not Ishbel? And how would this bairn get out of her? It would rip her guts. It would, it would.

She wished that Donald Munro would come back to her. But Donald was going back to his regiment. He told her there was work to do. There was word of an army for the King being got ready to take on an army of the

Covenant. Peggy didn't understand about fighting and soldiering.

Mairead had come down to the riverbank to gather and from a distance she saw the girl sitting there. Something about the girl's bent back and bowed head made Mairead stop what she was doing to look at her. As she looked at the girl, she recognised something of her own loneliness. She went to turn her back but the girl, unknowing, had broken in on her. The girl was wounded. Mairead went to her. Time for gathering later.

She stood before the girl, one hand clutching the skirt of her frock. She looked to her left and to her right as she spoke. The eyes would be watching her.

'What's hurting you?' she asked the dark sobbing head.

The girl made no answer, did not look up or around.

'You're Daniel Ross's sister,' she raced on before she would stop altogether. 'They call you Peggy,' and she bunched her skirt tighter.

At the mention of her name the girl's head came up. She knew this woman. It was Mairead Beaton. Mairead Beaton was standing as tall as a tree, looking down on her. When their father was out of the house their mother had said the witch word about Mairead Beaton and Daniel went wild. On seeing her standing there, Peggy forgot to cry.

'How do you know my name?' she sniffed. Her tears had cleared a channel down her caked cheeks.

'I know,' the flat face gave a half-smile.

'Are you a witch?' Peggy asked.

Mairead's mouth held her smile, but it slipped away from her eyes. Now wariness replaced warmth.

Peggy saw this and she was sad for what she had done, sad for putting the cloud between them.

'Why do you ask me that, if I'm a witch?'

'I don't know. Nothing,' Peggy put her head down again and screwed a hole into the ground with her forefinger. For a while all that could be heard was the hushed sound of the river as it continued its way south.

'I mend what's broken,' a melody of words floated in the air above Peggy's head.

For a while Peggy stayed as she was. And Mairead. Then, 'What? What can you mend?' and Peggy twisted round to look up at Mairead Beaton.

'Birds,' light and air were back in her words. 'I mend birds,' and she lowered herself to the ground. 'I find them, poor things, with their wings all broken and I take them and mend them and keep them till they're ready to fly away in the sky again,' and she made wings with her hands and laughed as she showed Peggy the way her birds would fly. Her laughing sounded good. It burst out from deep in her. It made Peggy want to laugh when she knew it was the last thing she should be doing. And her speaking. She spoke quickly, as if she would run out of words before she had finished telling the things she had to tell. Words as fast as the wind. And no matter how hard you chased the wind, it could not be caught. Peggy had tried. And Daniel. He was sure he was the one who was going to do it. But he hadn't. The wind was still out there. Every one of them tried at one time or another. Peggy never told but there were still times when she tried to catch it, when the mood was on her. But she'd never catch it now. Everywhere she went, they'd be watching her, waiting to catch this baby.

'Can you catch the wind?' she asked Mairead.

Mairead's laughter tinkled on the air before dropping down into the river, to be carried along like Peggy's tears, to the sea.

Peggy looked at the face. It didn't look like a witch face. She expected to be frightened of a witch face. A witch face would be black. Hers wasn't. With laughter in it, it was bright, light came from inside it, like the way the sun came through the pale leaves on the trees when the summer was going.

'No,' she said. 'I don't know anyone who can do that.'

'Did you ever try?' Peggy sounded urgent.

'I always try. I tried three times today.'

'And you didn't get it?' Peggy's disappointment dripped between them.

'I couldn't,' Mairead shrugged her shoulders. 'I always

think I will.' The fist still gripping her skirt beat on her thigh.

'Our father says that Angus Glic, the Wise One, told him that no one in the whole of the world has ever caught the wind. The Wise One said that if someone once did, all sorts of bad things would happen. Do you think that's true?'

'Well, my own father told me, when I was a small girl, that the oldest living man on the island told him that many years before that someone did. When that old man was a young boy there was a young man who went out one wild night when everyone was afraid to fall asleep, that's how wild it was. The wind was so angry, picking up anything it could find and throwing it to where it would never be found. The people were so afraid they nearly stopped breathing. Their houses were broken, their cows and their horses taken clean away, never to be seen. And some of the people too. This young man kept his eyes open and watched everything that was happening before him and he could stand it no longer. He put on his clothes and stuck a good knife in his belt and threw a sack over his shoulder. 'Right' he said, 'who'll go out with me? I'm away to catch that wind.' All were agreed that he should go, that he was brave indeed to think of saving them, and all that was theirs. Indeed, they said, there would never be braver. But not one man went out with him.'

'Not one?'

Mairead shook her head. 'I'd have gone,' she threw back her head. The words were strong, her tone scornful. 'He was my own kinsman.'

'Did he go?' Peggy wasn't interested in Mairead Beaton's family.

'He went out,' the river ran along with her words. 'No one knew where to. All had opinions. But all through the night the wind kept up its battering. Such strength in it. And the poor people cried inside what was left of their houses and were afraid to go out into the open in case they would be snatched up and carried to where the wild wind lived. Then, when their spirits could stand no more, when their tears wouldn't come, as the daylight came the wind stopped its carry-on. Just like that.' She smacked her thigh. 'The people were dazed. It was many days before they could stand up straight. But they knew, without being told, that Angus Beaton had caught the wind. He'd be sorry, they said, that he couldn't do it sooner, but didn't he need the day's light for to see the wicked thing.'

Sitting by the river, watching it burble past, the two women were quiet. Mairead didn't know she had so many words in her mouth.

'They never found again what was taken from them. But more was given. Only a gentle breeze ever came to disturb that place on the island they lived in. And it didn't really disturb them. They looked with happy hearts for it, were at peace when it came. For, they argued, they wouldn't like to be in a place that never saw the wind. For didn't they see it from the split second they were born.'

'And your kinsman? Was he a hero?'

'Indeed he was. But he was never to know it. No one ever saw Angus Beaton again. They found his sack laying beside the Big Pool. The people thought that when he finally caught the wind it was so strong and it struggled so violently against him, that as Angus Beaton went to drown it the wind pulled him down to the bottom of the pool. They looked inside the sack but the wind wasn't in there. No, Angus Beaton caught it and drowned it in the pool they said. But he never came home.'

'But you said no one can catch the wind?' Peggy said.

'That is what I said. But the people of those days thought in different ways. And that was the way the people on my father's island thought. And so we must allow people to be how they are and to think how they think.'

'I don't know what your words mean,' said Peggy.

'My words mean that our thinking is our own. My own father taught that to me. Though it's been hard to hold on to.'

Peggy's attention had wandered. She began to tear out handfuls of grass. What was the woman on about? Peggy wanted more story. The Wise One of their tribe had told her father that the man was never born that could catch the wind. And that was that. Words and thinking. Peggy shook it from her, grateful that she wasn't made that way.

The story told, Mairead had grown shy again. She didn't know what else to say. Her skirt still bunched in her hand, she scrambled to her feet and stood looking down on Peggy, her lids half-shielding her eyes. A blind had come down on her face. 'I can mend what's broken and hurting,' she said. Peggy didn't let on that she heard, but continued to tug at blades of grass. Mairead Beaton turned away to retrace the path she had taken. The eyes would be everywhere.

With the strange woman gone, Peggy sat on in her sorrow and her solitude. Maybe she should have told Mairead Beaton of her trouble. If it was true what was being spoken and she was a witch, then she could take away the swelling from her belly, send this baby some place else. Witches were stronger than fairies, they said. Oh, she didn't know.

She wished Donald would stay with her. It was warm in the house with Donald.

Chapter Seventeen

Inside MacIver a storm was gathering. He had walked across fifteen sodden miles, through freezing fog, to answer charges laid against him by the Church Session, that court of good and holy men whose lives were spent spying on people.

MacIver lived far out on his own, miles away from anywhere. He had thought that there he could live his life as he chose to live it, according to his own set of morals. He had thought wrong. The flying disciple had travelled to the middle of the wood to find him.

The Minister sat at the head of his table. His three cronies sat to his right and wouldn't look at MacIver, standing among them. MacIver faced them. He was drenched and his legs were in bits and he'd never stood in such a cold hole in his life. Give him the wood in the worst of weather any day. He needed a drink.

'Take your hat off when you stand before the Minister,' a weasel of a man with a face as tight as a full night shouted at him.

MacIver wanted to smack the weasel, to flatten him with one fist. He pulled the wringing woollen rag from his head and, raking a swollen hand through his hair, stood dripping onto the Minister's floor. It wasn't the first time he had faced these men. He knew that it wouldn't be his last.

'James MacIver,' the Minister said. 'You are charged that on the fourteenth day of last month you did perform an act of fornication with a Janet Tulloch. How do you answer this charge?'

'It's a bloody lie,' MacIver's fist made the Minister's table dance on its four fine feet. 'Bloody liars every one of you,' and the sodden bonnet bounced up and down on the table-top and sprayed raindrops into the eyes of the Weasel and over the pages of the Minister's big book.

'Do you mean to say that you weren't fornicating with Janet Tulloch?' the Weasel said. His voice trembled over the word 'fornicating'. He paused before it and after it. The word stood alone. 'Do you deny this charge?'

'I do deny it, I do deny it,' MacIver shouted, shaking his hat at them to underline it.

'You were seen,' a soft-looking pap said. MacIver knew what he'd do to that if he had it for one day in the wood.

'And who saw me? Who saw me? Answer me that!' MacIver, although angry, was trying to hold on to his dignity. It was hard, the mess and the pain he was in. He pinned the pap to the back wall with his own uncertainty.

'Never mind who saw you. We know you,' the Weasel came back in. MacIver was going to smash that runt into a hundred pieces. He wanted to slap the words, sideways, right out of the twisted tight mouth. The Weasel snickered and the other two joined him.

MacIver erupted. If his twisted foot was taking the breath from him, he never even noticed.

'You know nothing,' he bellied the table against the Elders' chests, imprisoning them in their chairs. The Minister's two papery hands grabbed for the inkpot. 'Nothing, do you hear that? You shower of bitches. I was not fornicating with Janet Tulloch. Mind you, it wasn't for trying,' he threw across the faces of the three trapped mice and the big noise at the head of the table.

'Janet Tulloch wouldn't look at me, far less lie down for me. Tell your spies to get it right,' he blasted at the Minister. 'It was Janet Denoon,' and he had enough breath left to roar at their dumb faces.

The Minister alone remained calm. He straightened the table, released the prisoners, collected together his scattered papers. The ink was safe. 'James MacIver . . .' he said.

The minute the Minister opened his mouth MacIver opened

his, prepared to start on him, but with the same strength he needed to cut down trees he held back.

The Weasel dived in. 'Then you were seen fornicating. With Janet Denoon. Answer, man. Fornicating,' he was testing the word. 'You do know the meaning of the word?'

'Fornicating,' MacIver broke the word into syllables, repeated it, 'fornicating. No. I never heard of that one. What does it mean? What was it that you and your spies saw? Eh?' The small black eyes glinted like the raindrops on his hair.

The three smirked at him down their noses. Then across to one another. The Minister kept out of it, his head down, as he sorted through his papers. This was the fellow he'd once promised boots to.

'Come on,' MacIver shouted. 'If you're accusing me of something I'd like to know what it is. Tell me. You,' he put his hands on the table and leaned towards the Weasel, 'you're saying plenty, say more, dog vomit.'

The Weasel sucked in his breath and tightened his entire body. 'You were seen with the woman known as Janet Denoon, sprawling about in the open near your house.'

'And?' MacIver pushed, 'And? Am I not allowed to be seen with anyone. Is that it? I could be "seen" here with you. Would we be "fornicators" then? Eh?' his face asked each of the three before it wheeled on the Minister. The Minister's head was now in his book.

The Weasel swallowed and struggled with his tongue and lost. 'Heathen. Fornicator of the devil,' the third one said. The Weasel was up on his feet, his pointing finger jabbing at MacIver. His mouth moved but words didn't come. Froth bubbled on his lips. He wiped it away with his sleeve.

'Can we move on?' The Minister sounded tired. His face was bleak, without any colour. It told nothing.

The Weasel was back in his chair. 'I'm just waiting to hear what it is I'm supposed to have done.' Now it was MacIver's mouth that mocked.

'Look, can we get on?' the Minister said. 'There's others to see.'

The Weasel had regained his composure. He straightened

his back and turned to face the Pap, gave him a half-nod. 'You think you're clever . . .' the Weasel began but he was stopped once more.

'No,' MacIver said. 'It's you shower that thinks you're clever. Well, you're no. Ach,' the flapping hat dismissed them, disgust filled his mouth. 'Don't expect me to play your game. I'll fornicate every day of the year if I'm wanting to. And every other day. If it walks it'll do for me. And even if it doesn't,' the veins at his temples bulged. 'What in hell's name has it to do with any one of you? Eh? They can't get enough of it. Nor can I. So where's the harm? Or is it maybe the thought of all that warmth that's no wrapping itself around any of you that's bothering you? Is that the way? Hm? You're just . . . jealous. No good, no holy, no nothing. Just a shower of jealous bitches. And you,' the Minister's hand had stayed on the page, he was looking up at MacIver. 'You're every bit as good a fornicator as I am. Better for all that I know!'

The Minister's cold gaze held the heat of MacIver's bubbling wrath.

'What charges do you lay before yourself, Minister? Hm? Shower of whoring hypocrites the lot of you,' he wiped his face with his hat. MacIver had spent himself, leaving the walls of the house vibrating.

MacIver's eyes continued to hold the Minister's, to burn in to him. In the Minister's expression he thought he caught something. What the thing was MacIver would never know. But the Minister knew that what he read in MacIver's eyes was reflected in his own. It was a momentary recognition of souls.

The Minister pulled his eyes away and scraped something into his book.

'James MacIver,' he said, 'this Session has decided. You will stand for four Sabbaths outside the church door. You will be informed when.'

'I'm standing outside no church door.' MacIver was shouting again. 'No, nor inside it either. Nor anywhere near it. And if you're wanting wood for your church don't look to me nor any of my men to cut it for you.' His hat was jabbing the air again. The pain in his leg was crippling him and the beads on his face were more like rain. 'Anyway, do you think a church with a roof is going to impress your God? He made the sky. Why would he be impressed by a wood roof?' and without waiting for the Minister's dismissal he blundered his uneven way outside, his left leg dragging.

The Weasel, the Pap and the One Without Words had never heard such blasphemy. The Satan. And the Minister let him go without saying a word.

Daniel and Donald Munro were next. They stood as far from each other as it was possible to stand inside the small room and still face the church's court. The Minister read the charge. 'Daniel Ross, you are here before this Session to answer to charges of making slanderous remarks concerning Donald Munro. And you, Donald Munro, cite that Daniel Ross did defame and threaten to kill you. Is that correct?' The Minister looked to both of them for an answer. He sounded bored, no inflection in his voice, it was dead.

'That is correct,' Donald Munro jumped in. Donald Munro had about him the makings of an Elder.

'How do you say, Daniel Ross?'

Daniel stood in MacIver's pool, gripping his bonnet in both hands. He looked directly at the Minister. 'That is correct,' he conceded. 'But I was pushed into it.'

The Minister turned back to Munro. 'Is there anything else?'

Munro opened his mouth, turned from the Minister to address the Elders.

'Ask him,' he squealed. 'Ask him what names he called me? A lump of cow's dung, that's what. A shower of sheep's droppings, a weasel and a snot. And worse. I'm not going to say all he said in front of men like yourselves.'

Daniel held himself for as long as he was going to. 'Lucky for you it was only my tongue you got, you snivelling little disease.'

'Are you hearing that, are you hearing that?' Munro's voice was as high as heaven as he threw himself at Daniel, his face like a torn bannock.

The Minister let them go at it. The Elders waited. They could kill one another for all any of them cared. Two less was two less.

'You say you were provoked?' the Minister said to Daniel when peace had settled. 'I have here before me the reason for the provocation,' he leafed backwards through his book. 'What do you say?' he asked the Munro.

Donald Munro looked at his boots. He wished he'd kept his mouth hinged on the slander thing. They hadn't started on him yet. But the big red tink had got to him.

'Do you both swear,' the Minister droned, 'on oath before this Session, to show just remorse for your behaviour to one another?' the Minister's pen hand hovered over the page.

'I so swear that I'm sorry for how I behaved to . . . him,' Daniel's tongue had difficulty in finding a final word.

'I swear on oath too,' Donald Munro mumbled.

'Then the pair of you are commanded to make public your signs of repentence, by order of this Session. You can go,' he nodded to Daniel. 'And don't come before me again. Stay,' he told Munro. 'Is Peggy Ross here?'

The Young Elder followed Daniel from the house to fetch Peggy in.

Peggy was shaking like a falling leaf outside the door of the Minister's house. The men had come to her house and shouted at her that she better be there if she knew what was good for her. And that went for everyone in the house. What would they do to her? It was all because of this baby. Did the others waiting with her feel this way?

Peggy looked at them from the corner of her eye. Men and women, one young boy. The boy looked frightened, the rest as if they hadn't a care. Making jokes and laughing, the men and women together. Only herself and the boy stood out on their own. She wished she could laugh. She wished that herself and Donald could be together, in their house, in the warm.

When the bull came to the cows and gave them calves no one said that the cows were bad. They were nursed and fed and looked after. No men to put the fear of death into the cows. Peggy wished she was a cow. To be nursed and fed and warm and free.

She almost leapt from her skin when the Minister's door opened on a long slow scraping sound, banging her foot on a sharp stone. But she felt no pain, immobilised as she was inside her fear.

Her brother Daniel came through the door. She searched his face for some clue to tell her what had gone on inside, but she could find nothing. He looked easy, for Daniel cocky even. One of the men had followed him to the door. Daniel did not look at her as he walked past her, his head held high, his bonnet swinging from his hand.

The man in the doorway looked along his long nose at those waiting. It was easy to read from that what his cruel face said. He didn't look much older than herself.

'Which one of you is Peggy Ross?' he asked them.

Peggy slowly approached the doorway. He stood in it and blocked it. Peggy didn't know what to do. She stood before him, her eyes resting on the man's shoes. Behind her the others were still speaking and laughing. At length the man stood aside and with a snap of the head beckoned her inside. Peggy stepped through the door, past the men. But where to go next? She had never been inside a house like this. The man kneed her from behind. 'Move,' he snarled. 'Along there. Who do you think you are to keep the Elders and the Minister waiting?'

Peggy shuffled along a narrow passage until she came to an open door. It was dark in the Minister's house.

'Inside,' and the man pushed her into a room.

As she went through the door Peggy had an impression of dark clothing and white faces. A table. Some light. After that momentary glimpse, nothing. She was afraid to lift her head. She sensed Donald standing over in the corner but she did not look at him.

'Come forward,' said a voice that sounded heavy and tired.

'Look at the Minister when he's speaking,' said the man who had come for her. She knew his voice.

Peggy raised her chin. One foot sought comfort against the

other. Her eyes flew to Donald. He stood where he was, not looking at her but down at his hands.

Another man spoke. 'Peggy Ross, this Session accuses you of fornicating with that man there. What do you have to say to that?' His voice was like a knife's blade.

Peggy's head went down again. Beneath the dirt her face was the colour of milk.

'Filthy bitch,' the man who fetched her said it softly.

'Answer,' the man whose tongue was a knife said.

But Peggy couldn't speak.

'Don't be afraid, girl,' the tired voice was accompanied by a kind of scraping sound.

'Hurry up,' the man who fetched her said.

Peggy tried. She lifted her head and nodded. She nodded many times, she was frightened her head wouldn't stop.

'So,' the sharp voiced man said, 'You did perform an act of fornication with that man there.'

'More like acts,' the other man said.

Peggy nodded in her blanket.

'So,' six eyes said.

'Filthy bitch,' and his hands made fists of the table.

'Quite,' the sharp voice said. 'Now,' it oiled itself forward, around her, 'Where was it that these, uh, acts took place?'

Peggy muttered something into her blanket.

'Speak clearly,' there was an impatient edge to the sharp voice.

Peggy wasn't MacIver. She had no weapons. From the folds of her blanket the sobs came.

'She's guilty,' the man who fetched her shouted, bringing his fist down on the table. 'She can deny nothing. She was seen on seven separate occasions. Once she was up on the Sheep's Hill, two times in the long grass down at the river and another time in the cornfield. She needn't deny it.'

Peggy was beaten. She could do nothing.

'There's a bairn in her,' he was ranting. 'Just look at her,' he was bawling it out for them.

'We'll have to satisfy ourselves,' the other man said.

'Ay,' the man who fetched her laughed from his crimson face and wiped his mouth with his hand.

The men stood up. Peggy screamed. Donald didn't look at her. The Minister was writing in his book. His Elders could deal with these matters. That's why they were Elders, not to hand out sympathy. He was tired.

Peggy's eyes mutely sought Donald's help.

'You needn't bother looking to him,' the man who fetched her said. 'This is nothing to do with him,' and he walked up to her.

In the room where the Minister kept his books, Peggy's wails grew louder, her chin bouncing off her chest.

'Take your clothes off,' he said. 'Or are you wanting me to take them off?'

'She wasn't always so shy,' the sharp voice said.

'You?' he said, 'Or me?' as his hand reached for the neck of her frock. In an outburst of hysteria Peggy sank her strong teeth into the fleshy part of his hand.

His reaction was not immediate, but as the message reached his brain he boiled over.

'Rotten, filthy bitch,' he used his other fist on Peggy, smashing her about the head, the chest and the belly. And when he'd finished, he tore her frock from her. Peggy stood before the church's Session with her swollen belly and a blanket covering her head and shoulders, her frock on the floor at her feet.

'There you see her,' he screamed. The other two said nothing, just looked. Peggy bent for her clothes but he kicked them from her. The Minister's eyes were closed and Donald didn't look at her.

'By God,' the man's voice throbbed.

Using her arms, Peggy tried to cover herself but they made her stand up straight.

The other man closed his eyes and swallowed. The Young Elder's senses swam. The bitch was bewitching him.

Peggy never had much to fight with. Now the little she had had been drained away. They could kill her, she didn't care. She could do nothing to stop them.

'Donald,' she whimpered. Her head hurt from the Elder's fist and her eyes wouldn't work. Donald was far away, in the corner.

'Don't look to him,' he wrenched her face back to look at them.

Peggy stood before them, a rattling wreck, while they all looked at her.

'Put your clothes on,' the tired voice said. 'Give her her clothes.' He still sat as if in sleep.

No one handed Peggy her frock. On her knees she scrambled across the floor to retrieve it. The three walked back to their chairs and sat down.

'Peggy Ross, is there anything you want to say to the Session?' the Minister had come awake, his pen was back in his hand.

Peggy shook her head.

'And you Donald Munro. Do you have anything to say?'

'Myself and Peggy Ross have handfasted since after the corn harvest. We have a house and some beasts.' Donald Munro's face was the colour of the paper the Minister was writing on.

'Fornication is a most evil act. The Church cannot and will not stand for it. We will do our utmost to stamp it out. Do the pair of you swear on oath before God and this Session that never again will you disport yourselves in such an obscene and unholy manner?'

'I swear on oath,' Donald Munro's voice shook. He coughed to clear it before going on. 'Before God and this Session.'

They waited for Peggy to speak. Her voice was so low and thin it was barely a voice at all.

'Peggy Ross, you will spend six Sabbaths from the date I will give you on the stool of repentence before the church.'

Peggy nodded.

'The stool's broken in bits,' the sharp voice said.

'When since?'

'Since before the church was put on fire. They can't leave the stools in peace. Some of the men jump up and down on it until it's wrecked. That's the fourth stool this year already.'

'I see. Well, we'll have to get another.'

The tight-faced weasel with the sharp voice shrugged.

'Peggy Ross, you will stand outside the church door. For six Sabbaths. You will be told when,' and he scraped it into the book.

'Donald Munro, do you have any money?'

'A little.' Moisture beaded his upper lip.

'This Session fines you seventeen merks to be paid forthwith.'

Donald Munro swallowed his spittle and nodded. His adam's apple bobbed up and down.

'You can both go,' he didn't look up at them.

Head down, Peggy dragged herself to the door. Once outside she ran for her house. Donald didn't try to catch her.

The Weaver stood with his son. The boy looked scared, not so his father. The Weaver had something the three crows at the table did not. The boy did not open his mouth, his father spoke for him. Couldn't they see the lad was simple-minded? More to be pitied than pilloried. And himself and his wife for the heartache they suffered. But the Weaver wasn't looking to the church for help or kindness or understanding. Himself and his wife could see to their own. And he was mortally sorry that his poor witless son should be seen up at the river with a rod on the Sabbath. But it would never happen again, not while he had breath. Before God, no.

'You have a book in your possession,' they said.

'I have two,' the Weaver said.

'Can you read?' they said.

The Weaver smiled. 'I can do more than that,' he said.

'Can you write?' they rapped.

'I can write,' the Weaver said.

'Then,' they smiled, 'you can write for us and ease the Minister's burden. The church has need of men like you.'

'But my work,' the Weaver protested. 'Who will help me?'

'Your work doesn't matter,' they said. 'Only God's work.'
'But I don't believe in such as you.'
'And we will deal leniently with your son,' they smiled.
And so it was.

Chapter Eighteen

Peggy stood to her waist in the river and watched the lumps of red satin flow from her. No tears, no more tears, but a tune on her lips.

She scooped up a handful of the bright water and peered into it. Slowly she opened her fingers to let the rubies in the river fall free. Come with me, said the river, come with me, and it tugged at her legs and pulled at her feet and washed the stains of her sin from her.

Later, lying in the house in her wet clothes, she tried to remember Donald's face. She looked and she looked for him but he wasn't in the corner.

Chapter Nineteen

'I'm hungry,' the children's cry went up from nearly every house in Strath. They lay curled with the dogs, too tired to play.

'I have nothing to give you,' the mother's hearts said, as pain at their children's plight tightened their faces and made their arms reach for them.

'I would take it from my own mouth and put it in yours if I had it.' Daniel's mother sat on the stool before the fire and cradled Anna on her lap, staring past Anna's head to the bubbles in the pot. The boiling pot with nothing but water in it.

Their communal style of living worked for them and it worked against them. And a poor harvest set them against each other.

'There's them that's getting more than their share and only two of them in the house,' a woman with a complexion like porridge and half a dozen children tugging at her skirts shouted from the centre of the village one day, demanding for her family what her man would not. The woman's voice was loud and raw, frightening the children, making them clutch at her legs and bury their faces in the folds of her frock. Soon, other women came running from their houses to join her, their children trailing behind them. The presence of these women added to the first woman's strength, pushed her further. 'Them that have plenty left should share it with the ones who have nothing. It is not right to see bairns hungry.' The woman's voice was harsher than any man's could be.

'We all got our share.' A hard-mouthed man with no living

children walked up to her. 'That's the way it is,' and he turned his back on her, to return to his house and the smell of baking bread.

'If they'll not give what we need we'll take it,' the woman said to those with her. She stood tall and strong-boned. Broad across the back, strong arms that a man would be proud of folded across her breast. She stood up to her ankles in cold mud and wondered at herself, where this that was raging inside her had come from.

A skeletal man, her man, walked up to her and apologised for her behaviour. He laid a hand on his wife's arm, as if he would lead her home. She pulled herself free and turned her angry face on him. 'It's not right,' she said, her head level with his. 'Who's going to help us?'

There were women who were prepared to stand with her, and one or two men, but what could they do? Nothing. Always, they could do nothing. So they too bowed their heads and went back to their homes, leaving her with her children and her thin husband, standing alone in the village square.

In their homes the whispers started. Why, they asked for the thousandth time, did the crop fail? Didn't they do everything right? The ground they had was good ground. Look at how the weeds grew. And they didn't pull up the weeds, they left them where they were so the ground could be at peace, fed by the good weeds. And there was nothing wrong with the way they sowed the seed. And wasn't there more weeds than ever this year? Surely that was good?

So, they watched their corn grow. And it was poor. They gathered it in and put it into the barn. They winnowed it and they shared it. As always. And the straw went to feed the cows and thatch their houses. What had they done that was wrong? Could someone tell them? There was some bad thing at work among them.

'I don't know what we're going to do,' Daniel's mother said as she stirred the poor pot.

'We'll get by,' Daniel said. 'If we go easy. The winter'll pass and we'll get the seed corn planted,' and she didn't dare to tell them that it was the seed corn that was keeping them living.

'You go for Peggy,' she told him. 'Tell her, tell her to come.'

'I'll go, but you know Peggy . . .' His head bent as he laced up his boots.

'Try again, maital, try.' She was useless for them. What kind of woman was she, with nothing in the house and her daughter lying sick and far away from her? Everything was past. The year would soon be done and everything was starving, people and animals. The poor cows eating the whins. And her own Peggy but a shade of herself.

She looked at the other three under the blankets. She hoped their father would come back with something in his hand. In her mind she saw him coming through the door with a big hare. But she had to stop herself thinking that way. In that strange human way she knew she could face disappointment easier than she could face joy.

Daniel found Peggy curled on the floor before the fire. If there was only a little life in the fire, in Peggy there seemed to be less.

Struggling to raise her head, her eyes fastened on him as soon as he came through the door. That much she recognised, that someone had come into the house. But there was no recognition for who he was.

'It's me Peggy, it's Daniel.' He knelt beside her, but there was nothing there. He took her face between his hands, looked into her eyes. 'Peggy, it's Daniel.' Still nothing.

'Come on Peggy, come with me,' and his arms went out to lift her from the floor. 'We'll go home,' he said and this was one time she didn't fight him.

'Can you stand?' He picked up her blanket from the floor and wrapped it around her, covering her head. 'Hold it there now, like that,' he said, taking her hand and making it grip the blanket beneath her chin.

'Right,' he said as he stamped on the already cold fire, 'that's that,' and he put Peggy through the door ahead of him.

Outside there was no colour. Greyness. Grey sky, grey earth, grey trees. A pale moon, older than the hills, already in the sky. A grey gauze over it. The grey houses, inside them spirits in shrouds.

He took it slow. Peggy would walk a few yards, he would carry her the next stretch.

'Daniel,' she said, her first word making him stop.

'Daniel,' and she looked up at him.

'Ay,' he said and his mouth and his eyes were kind.

'Daniel,' and her eyes made him catch his breath, made the tears come in his own eyes. He tightened his arms around her and walked on. And he made a promise with every step that the ones who did this to her were going to pay.

'You shouldn't have left us,' he said after a while, 'we would have looked after you.' His arms around her were shaking, through not from her weight. There was no weight in her.

'I am ashamed,' he heard, and his legs buckled under him, making him stagger as he kept hold of Peggy.

Apart from his name, it was the first words she had spoken since the Session. He stopped and set Peggy down. She sagged against him. Putting his hand beneath her chin, he lifted her face up. There was no flesh left on her face, he could feel the sharp bone of her jaw. 'Tell me,' he said, and he led her over to the old stones and set her down with her back to one of them, arranged her blanket around her. 'Tell me now,' he said looking into her face, 'before we are home.'

For a long time she said nothing, her eyes were transfixed by the golden hairs on her brother's forearms. There was too much inside her. It was buried too deep for her to reach. Too much of everything and she didn't know anything.

'My m – mother told me I ha – had a b-b-bairn in, in my belly,' she spoke as if she had forgotten how to make words. 'I-I never never had a b-bairn in my belly.' Against the greyness of the stone her face was the colour of the cream on the milk, her hand a small broken claw holding the blanket.

He said nothing. He knew that if he were to interrupt her that would be it. She'd never free herself. He nudged her with his knee to tell her he understood even when he knew he didn't.

'The man – the man,' her hand beat her breast, 'the man

hurt me,' and he saw teardrops splashing on her knuckles. He gathered her against him and rocked her backwards and forth. He had no voice.

'Blood,' she was crying against him. 'Blood. From me,' and her hands made fists which battered his chest. He didn't know about this. He held her tighter and they sat a long time that way, beside the old stones with no words coming from either.

Then she said, 'Donald left me,' and he pressed his cheek against hers. 'He went – he went – he went to the regiment,' so broken that even the dead would feel it.

'Peggy,' he pushed her back from him. 'Peggy,' the words had to force themselves from his mouth. 'He's a dead man. Believe me. I'm telling you Peggy. I just have to see him, once. That's the truth. And the other one,' and he shook her by the shoulders to make her hear.

'Daniel,' she groped as someone blind for him.

'Shsht now. Shsht. It'll be all right. It'll be all right. Don't be crying now.'

'Mairead Beaton.' More words rolled out on a whimper.

'What's that you're saying?' He put his ear to her mouth.

'Mairead Beaton.'

'What about Mairead Beaton, Peggy? Look up at me. Now tell me.'

Peggy lifted her head, took a deep breath. He could hear it rattling out of her. 'Mairead Beaton said,' she tried to make herself calm, 'she can mend what's broken.'

He waited for the rest.

'Mairead Beaton told me at the river. She said, I can mend what's broken, what's hurting. I'll go to Mairead Beaton.'

'Can you walk all that way?'

'I can walk all that way.' She reached out a hand for him to help her up.

'We'd better go then.' His arm was already around her. 'Are you sure now?'

She nodded, her hand reaching for him.

'I hope we find her somewhere for it's a long enough road the way you are,' and he led her to the track away from their father's house. 'They'll make themselves ill with the worry till I come home,' and his face said they could, there was nothing he could do about it. Their progress was very slow. Peggy, already weakened by her terrible ordeal, was doubly weakened through lack of food. Her body was getting nothing to repair it.

Many times he had to rest with her, many times he would have turned for home but she wouldn't hear of it. He took comfort of a sort from the fact that from somewhere his sister had found the strength to oppose him. They pressed on. But her will was not robust. When he had to carry her there was no protest.

They stumbled on through the colourless day. All hung still in and around Strath. As they left the village behind them and struck east for Mairead's house the little light that was left was going from the day. The trees, like leviathans, leapt from the roadside to block their path. Daniel was beginning to feel her weight on him, his leg was beginning to drag. There were so many things frightening Peggy, they fought for space inside her. The blood, the man, the other men, her mother saying there was a baby in her, Donald, the dark, the fairies, the wild animals who might hurt her. They were all claiming her sanity.

Mairead was squatting in front of her fire, stirring up her pot with a stick, Master's eyes monitoring her movements. There was more in Mairead's pot than in the pots in most of the houses. She scrambled to her feet when she saw who was coming through the door. A wide smile, which showed a mouthful of strong straight teeth, chased the severity from her face. 'I knew you would come,' she told Peggy and Daniel, and she rubbed her hands together. 'Come to the fire. You are cold. You poor things, you're all cold,' and she hopped aside so that they might have the fire. At their entry Master put his ears back and raced for the far wall, crouching low against it.

They sat on the floor and reached for the heat. Mairead scrabbled about in the half darkness behind them and returned with a skin for Peggy's shoulders. She scurried away again and came back with an armful of peats which she dropped onto the floor beside the fire.

'Mind yourselves.' She hooked her pot from the fire with her stick and set it down away from them, then piled peats onto the fire.

'This is good,' she said, sitting down across the fire from them, her smile splitting her face. For a time no one spoke. They looked into the fire, and at each other, and eased themselves into each other's company. The big cat came crawling around Mairead, lying down beside her. Its eyes never left her.

The house was filled with animals, outlines and shining eyes spelling their presence in the dark interior.

After her warm greeting Mairead had run out of words. She looked from beneath her brows at the two who had come into her house, then shifted her focus back to the fire. Under the animal skins tremors shook Peggy's body. She looked at her brother. He was staring into the fire. Now that he was here he didn't know what he was supposed to say.

'There were women arguing about food when I came through the village,' he said for the sake of saying something.

'There was no harvest to speak of,' Mairead sounded indignant. 'What do you expect when they won't pull up the weeds?' She jabbed at the fire with her stick. 'Don't they understand?' He thought she was going to start crying. 'The weeds choke the corn,' but the tears stayed in her voice.

'Who told you that?' he asked her.

'My father,' she said. 'He tried to tell them here when he came, but no one would listen.'

He looked to her for more.

'My father's own father knew about plants. He taught my father about the healing that's in some plants. And he taught him which plants were bad. I have remembered some of what my father told me. And I try some things myself. That plants there,' she nodded to the pot. 'I will throw the plants to the birds. What's left will help you, mo cridhe,' she smiled across to Peggy.

'Do your plants have names?' he asked her.

'Only the names I give to them. They wouldn't make sense to anyone else. But I know where to find them.'

'Bl-blood,' Peggy said and she put her fists to her mouth.

'She's troubled,' he said. 'She asked me to take her to you.'

'You did the right thing,' and they looked at each other across the fire. And they did not look away.

'Go to your father and mother and tell them. I'll see to Peggy. No, don't be worrying.' She raised a hand when he would speak. 'When Peggy's whole she'll come back to you.'

He rose, and from his stooping position he looked down on Peggy. He worried about leaving her. He wanted to say something but he was no use with words. He turned to look at them before he left. 'She will be all right with me,' her words firm, sure. 'Go now, before it gets right dark,' and he left them.

He had time to think on the way home. Mairead Beaton. She wasn't at all the way they'd said she was. In ways, she was like himself, he felt that. He felt the easier for Peggy being in her keeping. The people in the village shouting for food, the woman who seemed to be their leader was his own mother's sister. He thought of his knife sinking into the softness of Donald Munro. But he didn't dwell on the thought. It was dark enough to be seeing where he was going without that red mist blinding him.

Mairead Beaton. Her knowledge and her kind way. 'I knew you would come.' Did she mean Peggy or himself? She was like the Wise One. And when he had to go he wanted to stay, and not only for Peggy.

Peggy, with the laughing gone from her. That was Peggy dead back there. He should have finished the Munro when he had the chance. Gralloched him, like that stag he had carried on his back.

His mother's sister was a fierce woman. He wouldn't want to be the one that tangled with her. A face on her like a grave and arms that could throttle a bull.

His thought grew no easier as he walked with the moon. Winter would clean out the old and the young in any case. The corn situation only meant that they'd die quicker. The

Old Wife flew past him but she didn't speak. Neither did he. She was either seeing someone out of the world that she'd brought in or she was bringing someone into the world she'd likely enough see out. The Old Wife was always there. She rode above disease and famine, untouched by either, touching all of their lives. There was a spurt on her tonight, her fast old legs were leaping over the ground.

'She didn't come?' his mother's face peered through the smoke to look past him as he came through the door.

'No, she didn't come,' and he took the stool by the fire. His mother put her face into her lap and started to cry. His sisters' blank faces watched him and waited. Then Anna left the other two and crawled over to her mother. His mother caught hold of Anna as if she were a rock that would save her from drowning.

'If you'll stop wailing I'll tell you,' he said. He was too tired to be soft with her. From when the day started he didn't know where he was, what way to think. So much going around inside of him. He thought his head would burst. It was hard sometimes, living in a house filled with women.

His mother moaned on for a long time and he wasn't going to speak with her like that. He glared at the fire and ignored them all. He didn't open his mouth until she wiped her eyes and put Anna from her and straightened herself.

'Peggy didn't come with me but she is some place,' he said to her, but his words were for all of them.

'Where Daniel? Oh where?'

He couldn't look at his mother, at how she looked. Always a strong capable woman who worked hard for all of them, she'd become less with each day that brought no sign of Peggy. Her lumpy face was often washed in tears.

'Peggy asked if I would take her up to Mairead Beaton.' He heard the grunt in her throat, felt his sisters' eyes on him.

'I don't believe that of Peggy,' her voice went wild, screaming in the small house, shocking him, shocking them all. 'What would you be taking Peggy to that one for? Are you hearing what's been said about her?'

Daniel's laugh held no mirth. 'I might have known this is how you'd be,' and a boot shot out to kick the fire.

His mother looked at her fire and then at him. 'You might have known nothing,' she spat at him. 'I asked you to bring Peggy home to me and instead you took her to that black witch.'

'I'm not sitting here to listen to your tongue.' He was up on his feet. 'You're never going to hear anything I have to say, whatever.'

His mother was up with him. 'I'm not wanting you to tell me anything.' There was no trace of tears now. 'I'm wanting my own daughter back here with me, in her own home where she should be.'

'I'm not staying in this house and listening to your spite.' They were both boiling and their heat had nothing to do with the fire.

'Then you'll go,' Her voice put him in two.

'Yes,' he said. 'I'll go.'

Outside he wondered how he'd got there. He'd thought he'd done things right. But with her he'd always do things wrong. As he walked away from his home in the dark of the night he thought he heard her calling his name. But that would never be. Anna likely, or Flora. It wouldn't be Ishbel. Ishbel was like herself. Well, she could end up in Hell for all that he would care. It'd be different if he'd two good legs. You'd never catch him in Strath with a shower of clacking women. But he'd be all right. He'd find some hollow to lie in. It was her who was the witch, a spiteful old witch. What would his father be saying to it all when he returned home? What a mess. As if they hadn't enough coming on them.

Chapter Twenty

It was wet again. Daniel lay on the hill, oblivious to the sleeting ice slicing him to the bone. Beyond cold, beyond hunger, almost beyond reason. Water ran from his head into his eyes, made rivers down his face. It trickled around his neck, running down his back, across his front, over his belly. It soaked his boots and everything he was wearing. Rolling onto his side he squeezed it in handfuls from the hem of his kilt before pulling the heavy plaid up over his head, looking out at the world from beneath its dripping canopy.

He moved with difficulty, his body locked into its cramped position. Every muscle screamed and begged for release. Out on the hill, in the drenching rain, he moved like an old man, drunk from tiredness and lack of food, his hands, his face and his knees purple from the cold.

He'd been tracking the herd for two days, covering miles. Walking, crawling, running. Sometimes over the same ground. And each time he'd got close the swirling wind had changed and they'd caught his scent and were off. Twice he'd lain for long hours, watching a clump of trees, certain they were in there, only to find they'd gone by the time he'd closed in.

Up on the hill he used what he could for cover. Hollows, rocks, the trees, the colour of his clothes. He kept low to the ground, sometimes crawling on his belly, his elbows and his knees his propellers.

His face in the heather, Daniel watched the stag. Less than a hundred yards separated them. He was a big beast, fully grown. Daniel counted the points on his antlers. Twelve.

'You beauty,' his lips formed the words although his tongue

stayed silent. 'What did you find to chew on to make you that size?' His teeth rattled in his mouth.

He was still looking when he saw the head come up, saw it turning to look along the line he was lying. He put his hand over his mouth to muffle the sound of his chattering teeth. He noted the perfection of the beast, the proud erect head, sitting atop the long neck, the straight back. He could feel the sob swelling in his chest, making him bite down on his bitterness as he saw the head go back, and the stag float over the ridge of the hill, lost to him yet again.

No part of him would work. He could not rise. For a long time he lay in a heap in the rain, seeing nothing, feeling nothing, thinking nothing. A man suspended. Neither hunger nor cold to trouble him.

In time he used his elbows to roll on to his back, lying with his face to the rain. The big drops battered him. His mouth drank them in. Gradually he came to his feet and pushed the plaid back from his head. His ears at least were working. In them he could hear his heart pounding as if it were getting ready to burst. He wanted the stag. And the wanting was in every heartbeat. Still stooped and stiff, his kilt sticking to his thighs as he walked, he set off back up the hill, this time cutting away to the east. With the river on one side of him, and a belt of trees on the other, his boundary and shelter, he trekked through a drowned world. Something he couldn't name, something outside of himself was pushing him on, quickening his senses, keeping him attuned to any sign of the Earl's gamekeepers. There could be no excuse for being caught this far up, even supposing he was capable of thought. The end of a rope in Dornoch jail would be his end.

The deflation he'd felt at losing the stag yet again brought his hunger back, forcing its pain up into his chest, his head. He couldn't remember food. He thought Mairead had given him something to eat but he couldn't be sure. Maybe he just dreamed she had. The herd would be back in the trees, waiting, this time watching for him. Coming across an overhanging bank he rolled into it to wait on his strength returning. There was no urgency now.

Out there he was fighting a battle with himself, continually doubting himself. What was he doing lying out in the rain? If it weren't for his mother he wouldn't have been there, not then. It was her tongue that drove him to it. For huge chunks of time he had no idea where the stag was. All he could do was go on. He didn't know how to turn back. How he was going to get the beast home was something that he didn't dwell on. He'd do it because he had to. The village was starving and beyond that there was nothing to think of.

He didn't know how long he'd lain curled there, there was nothing to tell him time. No sun, no light of any kind in the day. All grey, all wet. Bent almost double, he surged for some trees. Inside the wood it was no less dry, and very dark. He stood listening but heard only silence. He inched through the trees, using his hands to tell him the way. As he walked he tried to regulate his breathing. Sometimes he stopped breathing altogether as he listened for the sounds of anyone or anything near him – a hoof striking a stone, a branch snapping under a human foot, the yelping of the keeper's dogs. Like a stag, he lifted his head, his nostrils flaring and sniffing for any strange scent.

He zig-zagged deeper into the wood, then cut to the east again.

The dark was getting darker as the third day was beginning to close. On all fours Daniel crawled up an uneven slope. Rough ground, stones and bits of broken branches tore and bit into his knees and hands. From the top of the slope he could see a clearing. There was a pool in the clearing and his stag was there on its own, drinking from the pool. Seeing it so unexpected he didn't know what to feel. He was useless to do anything but lie like a log and look, eyes unblinking, brain unthinking. And as he was looking at the stag he saw his people before him, their filled bellies and satisfied mouths with juice dripping from their chins.

He slithered on his front, feet first, slowly back down the slope. At the bottom he didn't straighten, but crouching as low as he could, crept through the trees and edged west. He had him! He had him! His thudding heart was telling his feet to fly. But he wouldn't. His left hand tightened on his knife as, by taking mouthfuls of air, he forced his heart to go slower.

He knew the path he was on now. It was a path little known by the keepers but well used by the poachers who risked their lives to feed their families from the Earl's natural larder.

But familiarity with the place did not make him careless. In common with the other boys from his village, Daniel's father had taken him to hunt stags when he was twelve years old. His father had taught his son well. Where a boy hadn't a father, someone else's father took care of him. It was part of a boy's development and part of his family's livelihood, the difference between living or dying. Being lame could not be allowed to interfere with that.

The stag was lying on his own, still separated from the herd. No old hind to keep watch for the men who were coming after them.

Daniel could feel the excitement clamouring through him. His tongue was sticking to the roof of his mouth. His heart was galloping on him again. The mist had cleared from his head and his eyes. Now he was moving faster through the trees, surer with every step. His right leg sang in tune with the left doing whatever he asked of it. Now he was behind the stag, looking directly down on it. So close he could almost feel it in his hands. He crawled higher to get the correct angle for descent. His eyes were watering and his breath was being forced through his nostrils as his clamped teeth stopped it escaping through his mouth. His knife was ready, his hand could feel again. He flexed his fingers on the handle. As he opened his mouth, his surety flooded from it, his lips peeled back showing his teeth. He was the hunter of his tribe. There was nothing he could not do. He could march across the whole of the earth, strong and straight. He was so powerful he could take on every MacKay who ever lived and beat the lot of them. He could do it with one hand and still stand.

In his crouching position he rocked back and forth on the balls of his feet, felt the spring in his legs, the strength in his thigh and calf muscles. The minute his feet left the ground the stag was a dead stag. He fell like an arrow straight on to it, his knife finding its throat at the first thrust, his hand feeling the last jerking movement of the stag's life, He pulled his knife out and the stag toppled sideways, taking him with it.

The blood from the stag's throat ran sticky on his hands, it clotted his legs, a thick pool of it spilled onto the ground. Scraping together branches, leaves, earth, rocks, whatever he could find, Daniel covered the dark red pool.

Getting the stag up on to his shoulders wasn't easy. In death it seemed to weigh twice as much as it had alive. He knelt on one knee with his back to it, and reached out behind him for the hoofs. He pulled. But the stag didn't budge. Taking a long rasping breath he tried again. He wanted to shout at himself, to tell himself to be strong, to shout at the stag but he did not dare risk it. At last he had it up on his back. One knee was off the ground, his ankles straining as he struggled to straighten his legs. He was up. He locked his knees, relaxed his shoulders under the warm weight. He breathed in and out until his breathing was even. His prime threat now was from the wolves or the keepers' dogs. They'd smell the blood and come running. He made his weak leg lead, forcing it forward. The left trailed after it. He rocked where he stood and he could feel the stag slipping lower on his back. Bending over, he hoisted it back up. His leg wasn't going to make it. He begged the good one to work for the two. An inch at a time he pushed his left leg forward. He asked the right to follow. His right leg obeyed, his foot dragging sideways along the ground. He took another step but then he staggered back. His whole body was shaking, lashing him in sweat and he could feel his hands losing their grip on the legs. Readjusting his grip he bent over again to haul the beast higher. Strength came back to his wrists, he could feel it in his arms. The stag moved easier that time. He straightened his back. He could feel his strength.

Between the wolf and keepers, it was a long dangerous journey through the trees. The lower the stag slipped, the heavier it seemed to weigh. It was black in the wood and the stag was forcing his head forward. To look ahead, to negotiate his path, he had to force his head back against the stag and let his feet feel the way. He rested often. Wherever he saw a bit of cover he'd make for it and throw the stag down. Then it'd be time to move again and there was the job of getting it back up on to his shoulders.

The stag sagged on him, its heat warmed him and he was glad of it. Being warm was the only good thing that day. As he fought against everything he felt sorry for the stag. All its majesty gone from it. Lying down in the dirt or across his back, with its dignity dead.

Its antlers kept bumping against trees, knocking the stag and consequently himself sideways, slowing his progress even more. His shoulders felt as if they were being crushed to dust and when he could carry it no further he let it go where he stood and gave no thought to who might be prowling. Then he'd looked at it, the big antlered head lying at a broken angle and he'd find himself bending before it. And that way he took the stag home to the village.

He reached the village just as the church was emptying. Dogs mooching around outside saw him first, and ran to meet him, tails up and teeth ready. Bearded in their saliva they wound around his legs and leapt at his back, going mad for the stag. He ploughed on through them, not having the strength to kick them out of his way. Tearing after the dogs, the big boys came, the fastest one way out in front, leading that pack. He kept on walking. If he stopped he'd crumple to the ground. The Minister and his three cronies were standing at the church door, looking at him. Let them look. That'd be him up before the Session again. So what? Just don't let any of that mob come looking for something to eat. The boys ran and ran, their bare feet running to salvation. And so did the people in the houses. For them something to eat won over a Minister standing at a church door.

The church grown-ups were not so free in their hurry to get to him. They wanted to be, it was there inside them, but their belief in the Sabbath held them back, made them walk when they wanted to fly. But hands did clutch breasts, and shielded their eyes from the new day and the dazzling brightness of what he was bringing to them. In the dull-eyed, sharply etched faces, hope was reborn. Shuddering breaths trembled on the threshold of hope. Weakened, buckling, legs carried them out to meet their saviour.

Unlike the children, the adults did not close in on him, they could not show what their heart was feeling. This far but no further. So they kept to a respectable distance and despite the Minister's presence fell in behind him. But at a distance.

He had made it. He was home, and he could walk the last stretch blindfold. His back became straighter, his shoulders levelled, the stag lay easy on him and he felt as if he was walking on two good legs. He walked into the village like someone out for an early morning stroll. His boots had wings. They were lifting him clear of the ground.

By now everyone in the place was out, and gathered about him. He opened his hands and the stag slipped off him. The children squealed as it fell and ran away clear. The dogs scattered a short distance before rejoining the party. The stag was seeing nothing, feeling nothing, knowing nothing of its forest, its river, its hills, its glens. His face twisted in agony, Daniel spread his hands on his thighs, and drew painful air into his burning lungs. He couldn't straighten, the stag's weight was still on him, pressing him down.

He sank on to his knees in front of them. Now he'd stopped he couldn't go another yard. With his back arched and his head hanging, he saw none of them. Just in time, he reached for the ground, to stop himself from toppling over in a heap. Like the stag.

'Leave it to us.' As if from far off he heard a man saying, 'You've done enough.' Someone speaking, someone with his father's voice said, 'You did well,' and he felt a hand touching him on the arm.

'You'll be needing this.' The strong woman who'd been shouting about the grain when he'd left put a jug down on the ground beside his hand. She'd gone round the houses until she found something to give him to drink. One of the boys came running back with the axe he'd been sent for.

Daniel couldn't look at the stag, nor at the butchers. He sat on the ground, drinking the woman's ale. Silently, swiftly they worked. First they opened its belly and tore its guts out, scattering them for the dogs and splattering blood over whoever was in the way. If Daniel had gralloched the stag where he had killed it, there was every chance the keepers' dogs would have found the waste and then him. Inside the dogs, no one was going to trace anything. Next the head. Daniel put the jug to his lips and let the cooling liquid run slowly down his throat. They broke the antlers off. These would make spoons, buttons, powder horns or drinking horns to sell at the fair. Brooches maybe to hold a shawl.

In time the stag ceased to exist. Like the cows, a jigsaw, its flesh torn into pieces and thrown to whoever could catch it. So hungry they couldn't wait for the hanging or the cooking, they sank their teeth into the fresh flesh. A small girl, sitting in the dirt, had a piece. Her small hand packed it into her mouth, her baby mouth sucking at it, blood covering her face and trickling down her front. The people were as bad as the dogs. Every piece the butchers cut was fought over, people pulling at one another to take what the other had. What couldn't be eaten would be set aside to be used for something. The stag's coat would be someone else's coat. And what they couldn't use they would bury. Nothing must remain to show that one of the Earl's beasts had been taken. They fought their way through him, some getting more where others got less, some getting little where others got none. Their strong teeth ate him where they stood, choking on him, grunting over him, gasping for him. And never enough, there could never be enough.

Daniel was feeling slightly better, having finished off the contents of the jar. He got up and went across to the butchers. Without words a man handed him a lump of venison. Without words he took it, then lifted the stag's coat from the ground. Draping it around his shoulders, he walked away from them.

Chapter Twenty-One

He should have been feeling better. He'd been instrumental in helping Peggy on the road back to health. If he hadn't been there to take her to Mairead's she'd have tried to make it on her own. Then where would she be? Lying dead on the ground and the whole place out looking for her. And if he'd taken her home . . . Where would Peggy be then? A slower death maybe under his mother's misguided coddling. And their father without the sense to know different.

Even the stag didn't make him feel good. He'd put food in their mouths and all he felt was emptiness. There was no speaking with them. Every stag that ever ran could disappear down their throats and they'd still cry for more. Their hunger was something that food would never fill. It came from far back in themselves. It was there since before any of them were born. It would still be there, in the place, long after they were all dead.

One stag. And their faces devouring the little they received. Glazed eyes fastening on the flesh. Mouths feeding on their fear. As if it were their last. It could be. And never enough, just enough to know they were needing more. Mouths hanging and seeking more, like a bairn at the breast, when the milk was swallowed and gone and all that they were left with was air. Not knowing how to be, what to do with the emptiness before them.

He tramped on, the stag's coat his coat, the lump of venison tucked into the front of his shirt, wetting it, wetting him, warmed by his warmth. All that he could see before him had once been the stag's to run across. Hills, trees, and glens. The stag had been part of something freer than he, Daniel, was. The stag moved with the herd, he enjoyed the young hinds. Now he was inside people's bellies, and he, a man, was wearing his coat. The poor stag. It wasn't much of a trade he got.

He moved the skin from where it rubbed at the back of his neck and shook his head as if he would shake his depressing thoughts from him. He was as hungry as the rest of them but he couldn't look at the stag's flesh. He was finding it hard to walk. The stag's weight was gone but not the heavier weight which pulled at him. His legs were gone and his feet didn't know which direction they were meant to take. Too much of everything was telling against him. As he ploughed on all that kept him going was what was living inside him. Whatever it was, it forced him on, making him walk when he didn't know how to, kept him living when he didn't know how to.

The short winter day was closing and it was still a fair way to Mairead's house. Something was happening in his head, making his eyes blur. As he trekked over the rough and rocky ground the pain in his legs and his back had reached his head, blinding him, begging him to stop. But he couldn't listen. He knew that once he stopped, once he lay down, he'd never get up, and it's himself who would be lying dead on the ground. More than once as he waded through whin bushes or became knotted in the hanging branches of a tree he cursed Mairead Beaton and the awkwardness that made her live miles away from anyone, in the middle of nowhere. Why couldn't she live among people?

In time, instinct more than vision or direction brought him to her house. It was this same instinct that drew him down the slope, made him stand before it, hesitating to go inside now that he was there.

As he crawled in through the doorway the red glow from her fire lit the darkness. An animal came crawling about him, smelling the stag on him, seeking its meat.

'Are you wakened?' He spoke softly in the darkness. 'Peggy, it's Daniel.'

Someone moved to the left of him, a rustling sound out of

the gloom. 'Don't waken her,' Mairead's voice whispered. 'I gave her something to take. She'll sleep for long if we'll let her. That way she'll mend, in sleep.'

'I got a beast.' He moved closer to her voice. 'I got its skin for Peggy.'

'Can you see me?' she said from beside him.

'I can't see a thing,' he said, his voice still whispering with hers.

'Hand the skin to me.'

He pulled the skin from his shoulders, and inched nearer. Feeling for her hands, he put the skin into them.

'I'll put it over Peggy. She's here with me. I'm keeping her warm.'

'Is Peggy going to be all right?' He spoke against her maneouverings and heavy breathings. He himself couldn't breathe right with her that near to him.

Busied tucking blankets about Peggy, Mairead did not answer straight away. Then he could feel her breath on his face. 'Peggy's going to be fine,' she said. 'Don't be worrying.'

'Someone's going to pay for Peggy,' he told himself again, as well as her. 'Yourself has been kind to her.'

'Sh,' she said and he could feel her hand touching his face. He jerked his head away as if something had burnt him. 'Sh, now. Come down beside me and we'll all keep warm.'

His hands were shaking as he tried to unbuckle his belt. It was good to get out of his heavy wet clothes. 'I took you a bit of venison,' he said, his other hand reaching inside his shirt.

'Give it to me quick or those ones'll have it.' Her hands were pulling the meat from him. 'They're on the prowl. They're smelling it. I'll put it under the pillow at my head. They'll have to get past me first. We'll eat it,' she said, 'when you've had your rest. Come, now,' and her hand was tugging at his, pulling him down. Wordlessly he went, sliding under the blankets and the skins.

He was glad it was dark. It hid his confusion, his feeling that this wasn't right. Who wasn't right? Him? Her? The situation between them? What situation? His knee touching her naked leg, making him realise that she too had taken her clothes off. He moved to put some distance between them.

'Don't move away,' she said. 'Put your head here beside mine,' and again her hand was there to help him. 'Come to me.'

Looking up at the roof, even though there was nothing he could see, he moved in against her.

'I can see you.' He could hear laughing in her voice.

'How?'

'Can you not see me?'

'No.'

'That's because you're lying there looking at the stars.'

He said nothing.

'Turn your head. Look at me,' and her hand was turning his head for him. 'Can you see me now? Can you see my face?'

'No,' he said.

'I can see your eyes.' His breath caught at the way her voice was, purring like her big cat. He closed his eyes and let her fingers move on his face, and as her fingers touched his mouth he couldn't keep the sob back. 'Sh, now. Sh, now. It's all right. Let Mairead warm you. Roll in close to me.'

Through the night she warmed him and he let her. And on the other side of them Peggy slept, under the stag's skin.

In the morning she rose and boiled the venison, and they took their share, putting a third aside for Peggy to try to eat. He, who had thought he could never put it into his mouth, swallowed it before it could touch his teeth. They didn't speak to one another. He stared into the fire and she looked at him, not in an open way but with shy glances, veiling her eyes in case he should look up and his eyes should catch hers.

But the time came when she did not look away, and he didn't look away. Her eyes, he saw then, mirrored what lay in his own. And it was the same with hers.

Once he rose to go over to Peggy, he bent over her and laid his hand against her cheek. Peggy was warm and peaceful, her breathing was easy. He pulled the blankets up about her shoulders and tucked them around her neck.

Going back to the fire, he reached out his hand to cup the

back of Mairead's head before he went to sit down in his own place, across the peats from her. The flames told him many things and that morning they told him why people fought so hard to live. It was for this unnameable thing which he felt living inside him.

Mairead felt it leaping across to her and, as was her way, she dipped her head before it would eat her. She had known always that what she was feeling now was what life was. Its warmth spread up and down and sideways through every part of her. She had waited so long for it. She didn't know it was missing in her until it came. And the waiting had been so cold. Sometimes she thought she would die from the cold. Sometimes she thought it was warmer clothes she needed, a bigger fire, food inside her. But nothing had cut through the cold. Looking at him, she thought, 'I want to be warm like this always. Forever.'

He was sitting so straight, gazing at her fire, as if he would like to live in it. She wondered what he was thinking. She giggled softly into her hand and busied herself about the pot and stirring the fire.

'Leave it,' he told her. 'Come over here.' She came on all fours, staying on her knees before him, her eyes level with his. 'Mairead Beaton,' he said and she felt his hand shaking against the side of her neck.

They continued to look at one another as if they could never look enough, each liking what they saw in each other's faces. She made small grunting sounds when he touched her and for him that was good. When she moved her mouth to brush his hand, he felt his spine turning to water. He wanted to collapse before her so that she could put her mouth to every part of him.

In their weakened states their energy for each other was wonderful. It was him who rolled away from her.

'I'm going out to take a look at the snares,' he told her as he pulled his belt through its buckle.

She made a mouth, she didn't want him to go. She would have stopped him if she knew how. Long after he'd left, her hands were reaching for him. That way, sitting on the floor, with her head swaying as if she was in a dream, she began to sing her mother's song. She'd sing it to him when he came back. Maybe. Oh, but he'd laugh. Then she wouldn't sing to him. Not one word. But . . . yes, she would. He wouldn't laugh at her, he wouldn't laugh.

He walked like a man intoxicated. He had no idea where he was going or where her snares were. Was he anywhere near where she had set them? He didn't know, he didn't care.

He wanted to shout her name to the hills. Mairead, Mairead, Mairead. She was a song in his mouth, a secret on his lips. His heart beat to it, telling the trees. The wet bog soaking his boots made him stop and look at what was lying all around him. He put his hands to his mouth, made a horn out of them and shouted his secret to the high hills.

Chapter Twenty-Two

A bundle of rags lifted itself from the floor where it had been lying beside two smaller heaps. Rain seeped through the roof in heavy brown drops, turning the floor to mud. Where part of the roof was missing it poured in. Nowhere inside the house was really dry. Old rotting straw and stones packed the holes in the walls and tried to stop the wind blowing rain in through them. The fire had to fight against the wind and the rain to stay alive. Its heart glowed but the wind stole its heat. A constant hissing sound could be heard as the drops landed on the hot stones surrounding it, as they hit the pot, hit the water in the pot.

'Good day to the Minister,' the woman said. She did not look at the Minister but kept her head bowed.

The Minister stood before the fire, his hands reaching to what heat there was. He did not reply to the woman's greeting.

'My man is from home,' she mumbled into her chest. Authority paralysed her. Faced with it, all she could do was wring her hands and chew on her gums. She didn't know the Minister. It was the first time he had come into her house. But she did not forget her manners, nor who she was. 'Something to warm you,' and in her eagerness to hand him the jug she slopped some of its contents onto his hand. She clapped her own hand to her mouth and cried something into it as she drooped beside him.

The Minister said nothing but finished the drink with one gulp. She poured him more.

'Will the Minister sit down?' she asked him. 'Sit on the

stone,' and she showed him to the large flat stone beside her fire. She scuttled away for more peats, made an inverted V of two of them in the fire. 'My man's away from the house,' she said and she stood ill at ease in her own house.

The two small bundles of damp rags half rose from the floor. Four dull black eyes, two small shrivelled faces which looked as if they had been shaped from candle wax looked silently at the man on the stone. The man on the stone paid them no mind. He was almost on top of the fire, trying to get the best from the heat, trying to draw its heat into himself, blocking the heat from the rest of them. The woman left him and went to sit with her children, pulled them against her, doing what she could for them, giving them what little of herself she had left. One of the children (they were both boys) had enough strength to whimper. The other made no sound as he pulled against his mother's breast. The woman looked with her dumb eyes at the Minister. A thread had puckered her lips, had pulled them tight, and flattened them on her gums. The Minister lifted the jug to his lips. The boy went on moaning. The woman's hands hung loose and useless and knotted around her children.

'Some people are eating the seed corn,' the Minister said without looking at her.

The woman said nothing. Her own seed corn had gone.

'What on earth do they expect to live on next winter?' His voice was quite loud. 'Tell me that.'

The woman could tell him nothing. It wasn't her place.

'How can you people expect anything to grow without seed?' he went on. 'Nothing'll grow and you'll all starve.'

The woman just looked at him. And the Minister went quiet. All that could be heard in her house was the moaning boy and the hissing, plopping sound of the rain.

Then the Minister began shouting, as if he was in church. The woman could make nothing of what he was saying. His words deafened her ears. The Minister's hands were smacking his knees, his white head was thrown back. His throat was shaking. The woman was a statue with each arm holding a dying child. She found her breast for the one most living.

Her man had returned to her with nothing in his hand. She pulled more straw from the roof and gave it to the cow. And more rain came in.

Chapter Twenty-Three

'If you'll take more from that roof we'll die from the cold,' her mother called up through the hole in the thatch to Flora.

'What else are you wanting me to do?' Flora's face peered through the hole. 'If we don't give them something they'll die on us. Then where will we be?'

'And if you do we will,' her mother kneaded dough on the big stone. 'What difference is it going to make,' she muttered to herself. 'We can die from the cold or we can die from hunger. Once you're dead you're dead,' and she battered the dough and pulled at it. 'There's nothing after this,' she told Anna who was crouched over the fire beside her.

'I'm not hungry,' Anna said.

Her mother looked at her but said nothing. Flora's actions up on the roof sent bits of straw and stick and stour showering down on to the top of her head and baking.

'Will the two of you watch what you're doing?' She shook the bread free of the stour and the muck. Flora and Ishbel had succeeded in making the hole twice the size that it had been. It did not, however, increase the light coming in.

Flora came with a piece of the roof in her arms. Two cows were lying in their own mess, sharp angled and fleshless as if their bones would break through their skin. The family liked the cows, they liked their company and they liked their warmth. Their smell they could well do without.

The mother turned the bannock with a quick wrist. 'Tell Ishbel I said she's to come down,' she said to Flora. 'That's enough.'

The cows kept them, kept the roof over their heads. Well,

some of it. She knew that, of course she did. They all knew it. It wasn't something to think about. The whole place depended on their cattle and the cattle had to come first. That was the way of it, no questions.

But today she couldn't be bothered thinking about them. One way or the other. She hadn't the energy. The cattle, the rain, hunger, Daniel, Peggy, that black witch. She couldn't be expected to see to everything. And what was keeping her man from his home?

'You can eat that,' with a sharp edged flat piece of wood she divided the baked bread into four on the stone.

'I'm not hungry,' Anna said.

'Tell your father when he comes,' she was knotting her shawl around her shoulders, 'I'm going for to get Peggy.' She unrolled her sleeves, pulled them to her wrists, then wrapped one quarter of the bannock in a piece of white cloth.

They weren't surprised at her going. Ever since Daniel had come back without Peggy and had then left himself they could see the time coming. They were the ones who had to watch it bubbling away inside her. It was never a question of if, only of when. She wasn't one for letting things be, even when things worked for good. They were concerned, however, for her walking all that way by herself.

'I'm coming with you,' Flora with straw in her hair said.

'No. No, you stay. The pair of you look after Anna for me. Try will she eat some bread and keep some for your father.'

'He should never have taken Peggy up to that one,' Ishbel's words burst behind her mother's back as she was on her way out. 'Peggy should be with us.'

'Your brother is nothing to do with me.' She stopped and turned to look at them. 'But what happens to my own daughter is. I'm finished with him.'

'Don't,' Anna cried from her place at the fire. 'Don't be saying that. Don't be saying that. I love Daniel. I miss him. I'm wanting Daniel home,' her head rocked up and down on her sobs.

'Well I don't,' Ishbel said. 'He can stay with the witch.'

'You're only saying that because it's not you he's wanting,'

Anna struggled through her tears. 'You were always at him. You just wouldn't let him be. That's how you're the way you are. You're mad because Daniel's happy with someone that's not you.'

Anna knew by the looks on the three faces that she had said too much. But she hadn't the strength now, without Daniel, to go on pretending. And where was their father? And her head had been feeling sick for a long time. Where had her happy thoughts gone? What made them leave her? And her songs? Where were her songs? The storm was inside her head, wild, wild as winter, battering at her, drowning her. And the calms that came weren't the calms she used to know. These calms left her without any life. Not the calm that was a fine spring day, a warm summer at the pool, the rested time of the falling leaves. Where did all the days go? Now she was tired. She'd never known tiredness like this tiredness. She wanted to sleep, to sleep past everything. Oh, to lie out on the hill in the warm, wrapped in the summer sun.

'Try and get her to eat.' A veil had come down on their mother's face. She, along with everyone else, knew what it was to bury bairns. She'd had fourteen and she thought herself one of the fortunate that five had been left to her. Many weren't so lucky. Her days for having babies were past. What was now was the way it would be. Until death came again for one of them.

'Let me come with you,' Ishbel tried again as their mother stood in the doorway. 'Flora'll watch Anna.'

'No. The two of you stay. Your father'll come soon.'

'I'll be frightened without you.' Strong Flora was chewing on the tails of her hair.

'The pair of you'll be fine. Don't leave the house, any of you. I'll go as quick as I can,' and she left them.

Flora held a handful of rotten straw under the cow's nose. The cow didn't smell the straw, or see it. Neither did it see Flora. She stroked its head and sang in a soft voice to it. 'Poor things, poor things,' she said. She was sitting between the two, trying to comfort both. It was better than sitting in the draughts like Ishbel. She laid her head against the side of one of the cows.

Although the house was small, small enough for Flora to speak to Ishbel without raising her voice, heavy silence hung between them. It was there in every corner, sitting on every stone, wedged between every turf. Flora didn't know what to do to break it. This was a new thing which had come into their house. The inside of their house had always been filled with the sound of people. She didn't know how to be in silence. She thought hard about what she could do to restore the familiar comfort of the old sounds, she looked about for inspiration. But all she could see was broken walls, with Anna lying sick, and Ishbel sitting beside her, like doom itself, and her mind had no answers. She didn't have the words to deal with what should never have been spoken. She didn't know how to make it unsaid. Closing her eyes, she nestled against one of the cows.

Ishbel didn't know what to do about Anna. Anna looked dead. A thin rattling sound coming from her mouth now and again was the only indication that she was alive. She turned from Anna, sought understanding from the fire. The fire warmed her face but the rest of her was ice. She couldn't be colder if she were under the ice. She'd be as well to be there, down in the dark of the pool, as to be without Daniel. Why wasn't he wanting her? Why that black one above her? She, who had always been there for him. Always, and just for him.

It was into her own hands that her mother had put him when he was born. He had been hers ever since. Her, the little mother and he her own little tiny baby. And she made him to her way. His mother fed him, but he was hers. Until he was eleven years.

'Will you stop telling me what to do!' She could still hear him shouting at her when she stood too close, could still see his face saying it. 'You're not me and you're not my father either. Or my mother.'

If the rest of them had lived she'd have had them to go by, she'd have had before her the pattern of a growing boy. But they hadn't and there was only him.

'Leave that boy be,' her father used to say. 'He's right

enough. You'll only turn him against you.' What did her father know about anything?

Her mother gave her no help and no direction. Neither one way or another. Her mother always had the next one in her, the next one growing. She was too worn to notice. She was glad that one at least was off her hands. And Daniel stayed hers after her mother had no more babies.

As he got older his dependence on her became less. What was between them changed. She had thought she could make him hers, he told her she could not. So she moved even closer. When he was out with the other boys she had to be there. Lying on the hill, watching the stars in the night sky, tracking the deer herd, there. Always there. And it was he who paid for it in the teasing he received from the other boys. To them his leg was nothing, never had been. To have her at every turn was the real cruelty.

The time came for him to spread his wings, to find out what far away places were like. Himself and the other boys would stay away from the village for days at a stretch – a cave up in the rocks, a hole in the ground, the fork in a tree. More inviting to him than his home.

Back then she lived in a permanent nervous state. It was only with time that she learned to relax herself a little and the rope she had on him. And that way they both grew. No more battles to see who was strongest. She'd lost part of him, she knew it. His young days were past.

Unlike Flora and Peggy, Ishbel had never had much time for men. She was so focused on Daniel that apart from one man none had showed interest in her. The village was small and her ways were known. On the other hand girls had always smiled at Daniel. And as he grew past boyhood their smiles grew deeper and lasted longer. They never saw his leg, it was his whole self that attracted them. There was more than one small red-haired child running about the village carrying his stamp, whether he knew it or not.

When he was sixteen he rolled home drunk. The whole house was sleeping, except herself. She'd never sleep till he came home. She took him quietly into her own bed. No one knew. And he didn't know. Until the morning. She saw murder in his eyes when he woke and saw where he was. Murder in his mouth when he said, 'You're evil.' After that he only spoke to her when he had to. The years passed and the hunger that only he could satisfy increased. He grew to detest having to see her, the thought of what she had tried with him made him want to vomit. These hateful feelings were only surpassed by the hatred he felt against himself for allowing himself to be her pet dog.

Ishbel harboured no such feelings. To her the way she felt was perfectly natural. She gave no thought to how her ways might affect him. The only feelings which mattered to her were her own. He had always come back to herself before. But with this one there was the fear that he wouldn't. That he wouldn't be wanting her, that he would never want her.

Chapter Twenty-Four

As she put the miles behind her, Bell Ross didn't know what way she was feeling. It was the first time she had gone so far, and the wide openness of the country terrified her. A short stout woman, she covered the ground in a rolling kind of gait, taking the steep ground on all fours. The piece of freshly baked bread nestled between her breasts. She felt very old and the way seemed interminable to her. What if she never reached the place she was going to but kept on walking for the remainder of her days? With the comfort of the village at her back, she was growing more uneasy with every yard she covered. Afraid of the trees she felt were following her, afraid of the hills looking at her, afraid of every bump and rock. She saw no one about. It was winter and everyone stayed indoors while the earth was sleeping. Better by far to sleep through it if the cold and hunger would let them. The snow was lying quite far down on the high hills although it hadn't yet reached the lower ground. Far behind her now the graveyard with the new graves. Oh, Anna. My daughter. She wouldn't think of Anna. She wouldn't think of anything but where she was going. If she started thinking she'd be lost. And where was her man?

She trudged on, keeping the trees to her left, the dark looming hills to her right. A far way round, her eyes seeing nothing but forest, her ears hearing only her own heart beating. She wouldn't let her mind dwell on what might be in the trees, watching her. On over the hard ground, kinder to her feet than the soft ground with sharp stones lying buried in it. The ground climbing then dipping, herself the same. Then resting and resting. On her feet. If once she sat she'd never rise. And no one would find her, lying dead on the stone-hard ground. She passed the pool, lying like pewter plate in the fading day. In her mind she saw Anna at the pool, with Peggy and Daniel. With the pool far behind her she knew she was nearing the end of her journey. She knew where she had to go. The words kept going round in her head. On past the pool, then take the road which goes down into the flat place, follow that road past the old broken houses of the people you don't know and keep to it till you come to the turn-off. Then climb. She wasn't stupid, she wouldn't go wrong.

She saw the house when she was still a good way off. From far up on the hill blue smoke was rising straight up. The house was sitting on the side of the hill, looking as if it might slide down to the bottom. Who on earth would build a house there, away from shelter of any kind? Her breath coming from her in heavy lumps, she took the slope on her hands and knees, grateful for the heather her hands gripped to stop her feet from slipping. She had reached the place where she was coming to. She could stop and rest until her breath returned. Sitting in the wet grass, on the hard ground, she watched the house. She could hear no sound coming from it. But Peggy was inside. What was her mother doing, sitting down? She hadn't walked all that way, frightened out of herself, to sit. She was almost running as she rolled up the trampled path.

'Is there anyone in that house?' she called through the door. She had aimed for a shout but there was no strength to carry it. What came out of her was more a whisper. She was about to try again when a burnt bannock of a face jumped in front of her. Mairead Beaton. The black one. Black face, black hair, black eyes. Black through and through. Bell Ross's heart started to rattle inside her again.

'I'm Peggy Ross's mother and I'm wanting her. Peggy Ross is my daughter and you have her in that house of yours.' She didn't know how she managed to get the words out. Fog was swirling inside her head, blinding her, so that she thought that she was going to fall down at the black one's feet.

The face said nothing, it just kept looking at her as if it

hadn't heard what she said or else it didn't know what she was talking about.

She shook her head to try to chase the fog away. 'I'm Peggy Ross's mother,' She spoke slowly, telling herself as much as the person standing in front of her. 'And I'm wanting her. I came to get her. Now, let her hear that.'

'Peggy's sleeping,' Mairead Beaton said, the whole size of her blocking the door. 'Sleeping's healing.' Her hands were kneading each other under her apron.

'Never you mind any of that, never mind your sleeping's healing. She'll come with me. I'm her mother. Peggy'll come with me.'

Mairead was afraid of the woman at her door, afraid of what she saw in the woman's face. Her eyes were sharp, her mouth too. She knew by looking at her that this woman would fight. She also knew that she didn't have that kind of fight inside her. She didn't know what she should say. Her hands and her head wouldn't keep still. They jumped in rhythm. 'Please,' she said. 'Please, come into my house. Peggy's sleeping.'

She was ready for her, she was ready to say no, she wouldn't go into her house. She had been ready on the long walk there. But when the time came she dipped her head for the door.

'Sit,' Mairead Beaton was telling her before she was right inside. 'Sit,' she said again and pointed to a blanket spread before the fire.

'No, I'll not sit. I don't want to sit. Peggy—' she was making for the heap of blankets and skins against the north wall of the house.

'No, please,' Mairead put out a hand to try to stop her but she pushed past it. 'Peggy's sleeping. Please.'

'Look, if you're thinking I came all this way to sit at your fire, you can think again. I'm here to take Peggy back with me and you'll not stop me,' She thrust the crumbling bread at Mairead. 'For your house,' she said.

Mairead took the bread from her and swallowed what she had been on the point of saying. 'It's dry up in this corner,' she said instead. 'The cow makes it warm.'

'Peggy,' her mother was on her knees beside the bedclothes.

Downward of Peggy lay a cow, oblivious to what was going on around her. 'Peggy, is that you?' she asked of a black head peeping out from the blankets. 'Peggy,' and with both hands she began to shake Peggy through the thickness of the bedding. Peggy did not move, there was no sign that she was awake. Her mother kept shaking her, saying her name with every shake.

At length Peggy stirred, turned her head to the sound of her name. 'It's your mother, Peggy,' she told Peggy's unseeing eyes.

'It's your mother that's in it,' Mairead spoke softly to her.

'You'll come with me now,' She used her squat bulk to push Mairead away from Peggy's bedside. 'This is not your place. Your place is with your own. Come, now,' she tried to pull Peggy from the bed.

Peggy didn't want to go anywhere, but her resistance was poor. And her mother's hands were hurting her. 'No,' she started to cry and to thrash wildly at her mother's grip. 'No. Leave me. I'll not come.'

Peggy fell back onto her pillow, exhausted. Her mother fell with her, smothering her. 'Mairead.' Peggy's hand fluttered. 'Mairead.'

Ignoring the mother, Mairead reached for Peggy's hand, rubbed it between her two.

In the darkened house, three women: one kneeling, one lying and one stooping. The mother the dominant one, Peggy the frail one and Mairead, the strong one.

'Tell her, Mairead. Tell my mother.' Peggy had turned her back on her mother and rolled away from her.

'She'll tell me. She'll tell me. She'll tell me nothing,' Bell Ross straightened herself to shout out all that had gathered inside her since Mairead Beaton had broken in on her life. Peggy, on the bed was a cracked shell before her mother's onslaught. But not Mairead. Mairead stood with her hands under her apron and faced the storm that was coming at her. She did not blink from the names that were being put on her.

Peggy had not the strength to cry. Her crying came out a feeble thin effort which every now and then tailed off into long silences. Her mother softened her stand. 'Why can't she come?'

she asked Mairead. 'I can look after her every bit as good as you can. I didn't walk all this way for to get nothing.'

'Look,' the word shook on Mairead's bottom lip, 'Peggy'll be all right. Already she's stronger than she was when she came here. Every day that's in it she's getting stronger.'

'When can she come home then?'

'Soon. In a few days from now. She'll come to you soon.'

'And what have you been doing to her to make her the way she is?'

'Nothing. Nothing bad. There's a drink I make from plants. I know about plants, do you see. There's nothing bad in anything I use. My father showed me. He showed me the ones to look for. I know about plants.'

'Maybe you do know plants, Mairead Beaton, but I'm here to tell you this. My daughter had better be back in her own house in a few days like you're saying. If anything bad should come on Peggy you'll be the one to pay.'

'Peggy won't weaken from anything I give her. Without it . . .' she looked down at Peggy then back to her mother. She couldn't say the words.

'We'll see.' The flame was still there in Bell Ross's small black eyes.

Mairead had said everything she had to say. 'Sit over at the fire,' she urged her. 'You can't go back tonight.'

'Then I will.' Bell Ross's tone was far from gracious as she shuffled over to the fire. Once on the blanket, her body seemed to fold on her, losing all semblance of strength. She sat hunched over the heat. Now it was she who was wringing her hands.

'This will keep the cold from you.' Mairead put the stag's skin across her shoulders.

'This'll be my son's skin. Where is it that he's hiding himself?'

Mairead felt the cutting edge of his mother's tongue and turned her head from it. 'He's up here with you. Isn't he?'

'I have snares set. Daniel's checking them for me. Peggy's needing to eat.'

That night two women waited for Daniel. Mairead kept the

fire going although she did not sit at it. She stayed with Peggy,
lying beside her to keep her warm. Neither of the women slept.
The fear that had fed generations kept them awake through
the night.

Daniel still had not returned by morning. Mairead rose to
see to the fire and Peggy's mother went over to sit with her, her
mouth chewing on nothing as she looked down at Peggy.

She was slower on the road back, even though for most of
the way it was downhill. Her legs were made of water and she
felt her weight on her like dead weight. There was nothing
left in her. She'd used up everything she was made of. She
felt the sharp wind coming off the hills and she pulled her
shawl about herself and ducked her head into it. She let the
wind blow her home. It blew her the right way, carrying her
upwards, carrying her down. She hardly needed rest at all.
Even although she hadn't slept since she couldn't remember
when, she felt she could have walked forever, to anywhere.
Was this the world she was in? Was this her out walking in
it? Walking to her home? Or was it someone like her walking,
just walking and walking over the same bit of ground and
going nowhere. At one time she thought she saw the Minister
passing her. 'Good day, Mistress,' the Minister said to her and
he lifted his hand. She didn't speak to him, but stepped off
the path so that the Minister could pass. The Minister wasn't
wearing his hat and it was cold. The Old Wife, her bag stuck
to her hand, overtook her. The Old Wife was almost running.
Neither stopped to speak.

It was the furthest she had ever been away from her home.
The longest time she had ever been away from anywhere. Her
home was far from her, separated from her by more than
miles. All that existed now was the track and herself, blind,
walking on it.

Chapter Twenty-Five

It was a long winter. In time no longer than any season by that name, what lengthened it for them was the complete lack of food. Where they lived at all they lived a half-life, battling hunger with already weakened bodies. The disease brought home by the men who had fought abroad had wreaked its havoc. And as their earth was like iron and lay sleeping, they tried to do the same. They squeezed what animals they could into the houses with them and tried that way to sleep past winter. Their livelihood depended on their cows, what price they could get for their beef stock and what food their milk cows could provide. They would rather feed the cattle than themselves; in money terms a cow was worth more than a human. So winter claimed the old and the young, as it always had done, the starving and the sick. And more came to try to fill up the empty places. The newborn were their hope, the hope that they would live past childhood and grow with them and be of help to them.

Inside one of the houses a mother and two of her daughters lay like curled clay, shivering under their coverings. Peggy put pieces of heather from the roof into her mouth. The wind came in from the north-east, scything through the gaps in the walls and the holes in the roof. The fire's smoke was blown into every corner, the fire's heat sucked out through every hole.

Since their father had failed to return, their mother had stopped speaking. Anna had died two days after she had come back from Mairead Beaton's. They did everything for

Anna themselves. They had to, the Old Wife couldn't be everywhere, burdened as she was with so many falling sick. Flora had combed Anna's hair and their mother had washed her and then they wrapped Anna in their warmest blanket. Between them they carried her to the graveyard and, while their mother sat with Anna in her arms, Ishbel and Flora had dug the grave. Now Anna was with the rest.

Arabella lifted the lid of the oak chest and took Jean's dress from it. Holding it against her, her hands smoothed the silk to the lines of her body. Colour heightened the cheekbones of her pale face. The years rolled back. Once more she was the kind of woman who would wear such a dress. One day soon she would wear it. Not this day. But one day. When the time came. Maybe when the winter was past.

The Minister stood in his thin shoes and gazed up at his church. The wind whipped at his clothes and tried to tear them from his back. They'd come through most of the winter without a roof. Soon they'd be into March. March could be the worst month. The Minister was thinking about MacIver. If that man could bear to stop his drinking, the church might have had its roof on by now and there'd be some sort of shelter for the people. Not that they cared. They didn't exactly stir themselves as far as the church was concerned. The Minister despaired of the lot of them. It was always what the church could do for them, never the other way around. He knew what they were up to, despite their protestations to the contrary. And they'd still come looking for the church to bury them. He was up to his armpits in their dead. And it wasn't the first time. He doubted it would be the last. But did it send any more of them in to the church? He'd passed a huddle of them on the way here, women mostly, one or two men. For once no children trailing after their mothers. He knew them and he knew them as non-attenders. He didn't speak. Some looked at him as he walked past but they looked away quicker. Great God, he thought, help this place and the people living in it. Nothing but decay whichever way you looked. Death dancing outside every door. They wouldn't learn, they wouldn't be told, not even when it was for their own good.

His eyes watering in the wind, he looked on what was approaching. A woman, he thought. She could have been any age. A creeping bundle of rags. He knew what was coming before she opened her mouth. 'Please, Minister,' the scabs at the corners of her mouth were cracked and weeping, 'will you come to my house?' He didn't need to ask what for. It was looking at him.

'Yes,' he said, trying to make his mouth kind for her. 'I'll come shortly. You go home.'

He wasn't an unfeeling man, it was just that he didn't know what to do in the face of so much pain. He wished he was more, could do more for them. The woman rattled back the way she had come, her hesitant steps unable to chart a straight line.

There are many bad things and death is one of the worst. Surpassed only by evil. Evil repels, it is shameful and obscene. But death takes away from the whole. Even one death diminishes not only the people and the community it touches but the whole of mankind. The Minister knew this and understood it. And the people of Strath, even if they couldn't shape it into words, felt it.

He could smell it as he approached the village and as he passed the houses its sweet smell came out to meet him. The people were dying the way their cows used to. They went down and that was it, they didn't rise again. The cows seemed to have more resistance in them. He understood that weakened bodies were nothing to fight against death with, but there should have been more. In the name of the God he believed in, there should have been something.

Putting his hand over his mouth and his nostrils he entered the house. Even so the smell almost choked him, made him want to be sick. A girl wearing death's colour was lying on the floor. Her mouth was as pale as the rest of her face. It was hanging open and her eyes stared unblinkingly ahead. The eyes were already dead. Two others, who looked to be a child and another adult, lay beside her. They had nothing covering them, neither flesh nor blankets. Cutting through the bad human smells was the stench of rotting cow.

'Have you anything in the house?' He spoke from behind his hand. 'To give to them?'

The woman shook her head. Eyes like two flat stones looked back at him and saw Hell.

'Have you water? For their mouths?' His hand was still cupping his mouth, warping his words. Hearing only what sounded like a far away mumbling, she said nothing. She thought her ears were done.

'They're not going to be in it long in any case. Have you anyone to go to?'

She looked at his hand covering his mouth and said nothing.

'Can anyone come in to help you with them?'

Again, nothing.

'Go into one of the houses,' he told her. 'See if there's anyone who can come. There's no point in you waiting. The Old Wife has her hands full, she can't be everywhere. Let us now pray.' He dropped down on to his knees beside the girl and waited for the woman to do the same. When she didn't move he looked up at her but didn't say anything. He clasped both hands in front of his face and rattled through his prayer. The woman heard only noise. If ever he had found her, he lost her then. People were dying in her house and the Minister was shouting as if he alone would raise them.

Chapter Twenty-Six

Although no words passed between them, Daniel's mother wasn't openly antagonistic towards him. That would have taken energy she didn't have. And, although he was now living with Mairead, family feeling was still strong in him. He had wanted to be there when Anna was buried, but his mother, speaking to him through Ishbel, could wait no longer for news of his father. He had been away from them for more than a week. He would have to go out that day, themselves could see to Anna. He knew all of his father's haunts, they had often gone out together, to hunt and to trap.

He'd already found his father's inlying snares, still set. The unbroken snow showed him that no one had been near in the last four days. He made for the higher ground; his father could have tried further out first, intending to check his snares on the way back. He tried every place he could think of, even some places that in his heart he knew his father would never have gone to. It was on his way back down that Daniel found him, half-hidden by a blown tree. His clothes were black against the white of the snow, his hand still clasped on his plaid, which he had pulled up around his head and wound around his body. His father's foot, twisted back on itself, told its own story. He must have slipped and twisted his ankle and had found himself unable to walk very far. He had tried to crawl part of the way, trails fanning out from behind the tree showed that, but the cold had beaten him. He had taken shelter behind the tree and must have fallen asleep, a thing he had warned Daniel against from the first time he took him out.

He lifted his father out of the snow and carried him home.

This time it was Daniel who broke open the ground and laid him beside Anna.

Much of what he was came from his father, almost all his learning. Maybe the best part, although he was not yet ready to think that way. He had spent a large part of his life struggling against what he imagined his father expected of him. Now, with his father dead, he was forced to admit that it was himself he had been struggling against, and the things of his own mind. Because of his leg. His leg had always made him feel less. And he had wanted his father to tell him he was not, to tell him in words. To tell him he loved him the way he was. And with his father lying in the graveyard he realised that he had never stopped telling him. His leg hadn't stopped his father taking him out on the hill like the other boys his age. His father was telling him when he showed him how to use a bow, where to find the hazel to make the bow, how to line up his quarry and aim at it. His father was telling him when he showed him how to listen to the wind, to hear what it was saying, how to be more of a deer than the deer itself, how to read his way home from the stars, how to tell what time it was from the sun. His father had taught him how to tune himself to the earth and what lived on it, how to survive out on the hill in a blizzard, how to find his way back home when snow had covered every track and how to tell what disturbance in tops of the distant trees meant. All these ways were his father's words. And many more.

'That's me off now,' he whispered to Peggy as he crouched down beside her.

Peggy caught hold of his hand with her two. 'You'll come back?' She was afraid to ask the question.

'I'll come back. I'll always come back. Don't you be worrying about that.'

'Everyone's dying,' Peggy said.

He looked at their mother. She was sitting over the fire, as grey and worn-looking as one of the old stones that the rain had washed every feature from. 'It's a pity we can't eat peats,' he made the old joke for Peggy, his words dropping on to the floor.

Peggy's doleful expression didn't alter. She looked at him for more.

'Things'll be starting to grow soon,' He squeezed her hand. 'You and Ishbel watch your mother. I'll do what I can.' He turned his head and looked at his mother's rounded back, her head hanging. He wanted to say something to her but the words stayed inside him. Pulling his hand free of Peggy's, he walked past his mother and went out.

He wasn't right through the door when Ishbel found her voice. 'You know whose fault all this is.' Her voice was too loud for the house, for their pain. 'It's that other one. Her and her mixtures.'

Peggy was too tired for Ishbel's onslaught. 'Be quiet, you,' she was slurring her words. 'Your mouth is dangerous. Think of our mother for a change instead of always yourself.'

'It is my mother I'm thinking of,' Ishbel's voice was no less strident. 'Who took her son away from her? Her only son. We haven't a man to help us but she has. As if Daniel would ever look at the likes of her. She has put her spell on him all right.'

'You better hold still that tongue of yours. I'm warning you.'

'Don't warn me. It's not me that's needing warned. Warn the right one. I know what I know. Of course I might expect you to side with her.'

'And I know what I know. I know who the witch is around here. And her name's not Mairead Beaton. Up with her all I was shown was kindness. And a rest from your wickedness.'

'And what's Daniel getting? That's what I would like to know. Answer me that then. There's plenty who think about her the same as I do.'

'You mean you spoke to other people about what's said in this house?'

'No, I haven't spoken to other people about what's been said in this house. Not yet. But my ears hear plenty. I've been hearing what's been said about her in the place. It wouldn't take much to settle her.'

'You're wicked, you know that. Really wicked. Evil. You're frightening me.'

'You frighten easily, sister.' Ishbel closed her sour mouth.

That winter there wasn't much singing left in Strath. The heart was gone from the people, taking their strength with it. The Church did what it could. It wasn't much, the Church didn't have the means. The Poor Fund was practically empty, not enough contributed to it. The best that could be said was that where requested the Church was able to bury the dead decently and with dignity. And Strath's people were a dignified people, despite their many hardships. What they had to face did not detract from them, in a cruel way it added to them. They only had themselves to look to. Any help that might be available would have had to come in from outside and, in winter, with the road impassable, that was not going to happen. And when things were blacker than they themselves knew some looked to the Almighty God and some to their own gods. And there were those for whom their thinking was not that clear; they swung from God to their gods and back to God again. Some prayed to their saints, some to Christ's mother, that she would look kindly on them in their sorrows. They covered their dying in twigs, tied into bundles and shaped into crosses. But nothing worked for them, nothing came to save them. So, then, they looked inward to their own community for the source of their trouble. They turned their attention to the one who was different. It wasn't long before the ears of the Church heard the rumour. Closed Face with his mouth tightly shut and his ears wide open heard it first. He lost no time in flying over the hard ground to the other two. He didn't bother to tell the Weaver. The Weaver wasn't like them, he was a queer sort of fellow. He was apt to come right out with things themselves would never have thought of saying and care nothing for who heard him. The three raced to the Minister, standing like steel rods in front of him in the freezing room. The Minister heard it twice, the Young Elder diving in before Closed Face had finished speaking and telling him louder. So that the Minister would know. The Quiet Elder didn't say anything, it wasn't his time yet. He just stood still, waiting for the other two to tell things their way.

The Minister's reaction shook them. It shook the table he was sitting at when he thumped his fist down on it. 'Enough.' They'd heard him like this before, roaring like a demon, they thought the roof was going to lift. 'Don't come before me with talk of that kind. I don't want to hear it.' Spittle was bubbling in the corners of his mouth. 'This place has had enough.'

The Young Elder's bright red face darkened to crimson, Closed Face sucked in his breath, his mouth was like a tight purse. The Quiet Elder remained much the same, whatever he was thinking he kept to himself.

'Sit down.' Some of the steam had left the Minister. 'Instead of standing there like stranded fish, sit down, sit down,' his waving hands motioned.

The Young Elder ran to his chair, the other two eased themselves on to theirs.

'Has any one of you anything . . . worthwhile to tell me?' For a time it appeared that no one had. Then Closed Face rose to his feet. 'I have,' he said, looking straight at the Minister, his small mouth no impediment to the strength and clarity of what he was about to say. 'I have something to say concerning one called Mairead Beaton. For months now the people of this place have been putting up with things. They haven't said anything before but they're saying something now. She's always all over the place, you never know when you're going to meet her. And she doesn't even live here. She never speaks, just looks at you, always looking. What's she always looking at people for? Casting her eyes over them and their beasts. Everything's going wrong and she's the one that's doing it they're saying. One old one told myself that Mairead Beaton gave her stuff to spread over her sores and in one hour every sore was gone. One hour, mark you. And I got that from the old one's own lips. She hadn't a sore on her that I could see. You can go and look yourself. You'll see her everywhere, pulling up plants and stuff. Even in the night. They say she took Daniel Ross away from his father's house after his father was dead and his mother and his sisters were needing him. He's up there with her now, living with her.'

When he'd finished a heavier silence hung over the room. Most of it hung around Closed Face.

'You say that the village is whispering about this woman?' The Minister was rolling his pen between the palms of his hands, scattering drops of ink on to his white page.

'You show the one who has something good to say about her.' Closed face was ready for the next stretch.

'And where did these rumours start? You can't accuse people without evidence. This church will not stand for such behaviour.' The blots on the page were spreading into one another, forming a pool.

'But the old one's sores. The cattle. Dry as anything. A harvest that wasn't worth gathering.'

'The old one's sores, old one's sores. Old ones will say anything as long as they've got an audience. And when did they last have a good harvest? They expect miracles. Evidence, man, evidence.'

They hadn't any, so no one spoke. They'd come across this in him before, he was like that.

'This village has had more than enough,' he muttered as he scraped something into his book beneath the inky pool. 'Have the . . . what did you say the woman's name is?' He waited for Closed Face to supply it then wrote it in the book. 'And the man concerned? Who did you say?'

'Daniel Ross. Daniel Ross his name is.'

'Daniel Ross then and Mairead Beaton will appear before the Session two days from this day. No later,' and he drew two lines under the last words he wrote.

Closed Face nodded with a clipped lip.

The Young Elder's black face brightened. His chest swelled, blowing his breath down his nose. Yes, they had the witch.

Chapter Twenty-Seven

They had Mairead in first. She stood where Peggy had stood and waited for someone to speak. Her feet were planted wide, her chin level, her hands remained under her apron, but they rested easy. There was no outward sign of nervousness about her.

'Mairead Beaton,' he said, 'do you know why you're here?'

She looked at him, at his mouth, as if she would see the words coming out of it. It was a long time since she had heard his voice, it used to paralyse her. Today it was just a voice, coming from an old man.

'No,' she said.

'Keep a civil tongue when you speak to the Minister,' Closed Face rapped.

Mairead turned her head and looked at Closed Face, saw the emptiness behind the puffed-up pride.

'Do you understand what you're doing here?' the Minister's voice called her back to him. He was nodding to Closed Face. 'Tell her,' he said, 'What you have told me.'

Closed Face was happy to repeat every word, adding, 'Everyone knows it.'

'Now do you understand?' the Minister said. 'What it is you're being accused of?'

'Yes.' Mairead's chin was still level as she spoke to the Minister. 'But it's not the truth.'

'Don't listen to her,' the Young Elder bawled at the Minister. 'How can you expect someone like that to tell the truth? It's lies, all lies,' His chair was rocking on its four fine feet.

The other two looked across him at one another and made

what sounded like growls from deep in their throats.

'Mairead Beaton,' the Minister said, 'accusations have been laid against you by certain people of this parish. It is the duty of the Session to look into these accusations, to find the truth. Who's going to speak?' He looked to the three.

'Me. I will. 'The Quiet Elder moved back his chair and came noiselessly to his feet. 'Is it true that you charmed water before giving it to Daniel Ross to drink and is it true that you used your enticements to get him to leave his own home to go and live with you in yours?' He smiled at Mairead. Mairead wasn't fooled by his smile. She thought it made his bland face look ugly. She took a deep breath. He had said plenty but she had caught it all. 'I did nothing of what you say,' she told him. 'Who's telling such lies?'

'The only one in this room telling lies is you!' The Young Elder's voice was hitting the roof, his own feet dancing every bit as good as his chair's had been. 'He's up there with you, isn't he? Living with you. Deny that.'

Mairead's mouth opened, then closed on nothing.

'Isn't he?' the Quiet Elder persisted.

'Yes, but . . .'

'Yes but nothing,' he said. 'That question's answered,' and he bowed his head to Closed Face.

Closed Face stood up and leaned his hands on the table. 'Has a man ever lain with you, Mairead Beaton. Before Daniel Ross?' His shoulders were hunched around his ears, his head thrust forward.

'No.'

'And why do you think that is?'

'I have never bothered with any men.'

'You have never bothered with any men.' Closed Face was spacing the words. 'Are all of you hearing what she's saying? She's asking the Session to believe that she has never bothered with men. Are you seeing her?'

The Session obviously were. They laughed.

The Minister kept his head down and kept out of it as he wrote something in his book. He was wondering if he was going to be able to rely on the Weaver.

'Say that again. What you said. Say it so that we all can be sure we're hearing right.'

'I have never bothered with any men.'

'And you're bothering now. Is that what you're asking us to believe. Eh?' and the three laughed again. The Minister was still keeping out of it. Mairead kept her head up. 'Is it not the other way about? Isn't the truth that no man has bothered with you. Not one in his right mind anyway?' He looked to the other two for their reaction. The Quiet Elder was chewing his lips while he laughed inwardly, his head rocking on his shoulders. The Young Elder's head went back and he bellowed like a bull from his open throat. When they'd enjoyed their mirth they put their heads together, leaving Mairead not knowing what to do in the middle of the floor. The Minister's eyes were closed, his hand still. She heard their mumbles, words which she couldn't understand running very fast. Among them one black word jumped out at her, its weight making her cower from it. Then the Young Elder was walking over to stand beside her, so close she could see the blackheads clogging the skin on his nose, at last making Mairead look down at her feet.

'Face me when I'm speaking to you!' He was shouting his words.

Mairead wouldn't. She lifted her head and looked past him, at the candles sputtering on the wall at the Minister's back, the melting wax running down the candle's stem and gathering like bunches of milkwhite berries at the base. The Young Elder had no diplomatic strengths to draw on. His face the colour of the setting sun and his eyes bulging like a frog's he tried using noise to threaten Mairead. 'Do what I say!' He had brown uneven teeth and a bad smell came from his mouth. 'Face me!'

In her own time Mairead dragged her eyes away from the candles. Her shawl covered her head, her face was a still pool.

'How old are you anyway?'

'I don't know.'

'You don't know, you don't know?' His voice was mocking hers. 'What are you, stupid as well as old?'

'No, I'm strong.'

'You're old. You're an old woman. What would a man be wanting with an old woman like you when he could have his pick of young flesh?'

'I don't know.' Her eyes challenged his, so he bawled louder. 'This place is full of women, every one of them younger and better to look at than you. Admit that's right.'

'Yes.'

'So, I'll ask you one more time. What would make Daniel Ross go to someone like you? Unless you bewitched him?'

'I don't know.'

'Well, that's it then, isn't it. There you have it.' He flung wide his arms as he turned to the other two. 'You heard what she said. She can't deny it. She doesn't know, she doesn't know. She doesn't know because every word's true. You can't prove different, can you?' He was almost pushing his nose up Mairead's nostrils.

'No,' She was holding her head away from his.

'Are you a witch, then?'

'No.'

The Young Elder hopped back to his chair and flopped down on it, sweat streaming from his hairline to seep across his brow. For a short time they put their heads together again. Now it was up to the Minister.

The Minister stopped writing. He laid his pen aside. 'What do you say, Mairead Beaton?' The tone of his voice said he didn't care one way or the other what she said.

'I don't know.'

'What do you say?' he asked his elders.

Without rising, Closed Face spoke for all three. 'Our feelings tell us that Mairead Beaton is a witch. We'll have to examine her for marks, seeing she'll not admit it.' He was half out of his chair when the Minister's voice sent him crashing back on to it, pinning him there. 'No,' there was no tiredness now. 'There'll be no more examining. Mairead Beaton, go outside and wait there. One of you fetch in Daniel Ross.'

Mairead did not immediately move. She didn't know what to do. Was that it? What she had heard? Was that them done with her? Did he believe her word? He said to wait outside. She let her arms swing by her side and without looking at one of them she lifted her head higher and walked to the door of the room.

Daniel was the one who was strung tight with nerves. He was finding it very hard to keep a lid on his temper. He felt that at any moment he was going to blow up and make a mess of everything. He didn't care. Not for himself. But Mairead. His back was so straight it was beginning to hurt, his shoulders rigid with the strain of showing them that he wasn't bothered by anything. His eyes drilled a spot in the wall high behind the Minister as he strove to shut the room and those in it from his mind. But he felt them, these men whose mouths could do more harm than the sharpest knife. He clamped his mouth on his anger and swallowed his bile.

'Daniel Ross, do you know why you're here?' the Minister asked him.

He took his eyes away from the spot on the wall long enough to look at the Minister, sitting at the head of his table with a rag of a blanket pulled around his shoulders, the stains of past meals decorating what could be seen of his coat, stitched into the folds of the black cloth. His eyes flew back to the safety of the wall, boring deeper, held it. 'Yes,' the word shot from the side of his mouth.

'Then you'll know that such accusations must be investigated. It is the duty of this Session to find out what is true and what is not. Do you understand that?'

'Yes.'

The Minister had said what he had to say. The Quiet Elder stood up. 'Daniel Ross,' his words and his mouth were soft, smiling, 'the Session has been told that Mairead Beaton has put a spell on the water she gave you to drink and that was why you left your father's house to go and live with her in her house. What do you say to that?'

'It's a pile of lies.' He barked at the wall, then shut his mouth before he could say too much.

'So you deny the accusations then?' The bitches would get

nothing out of him, not one word. Let them work for what they were wanting to know.

'Answer when you're being spoken to!' The Young Elder was throbbing with rage.

Still he didn't speak, his eyes on the spot on the wall. He could hear them humphing and mumphing to the left of him. Let them.

The Quiet Elder kept a clear head. It would take a bigger man than this one to unsettle him. Many tried, but he knew all of their tips. 'So you're not living at Mairead Beaton's?' If Daniel had been looking at him he would have seen the smile that slithered across his heavy face. 'Is that what you're telling me?' With his teeth he pared the fingernail on his left index finger, and let his eyes slide to the face of the man standing before them. Oh ay, he'd come across ones like this before. A hard man. At least by his own thinking. A face on him like a cliff face. But he'd have him. Oh ay. In time. He'd open that clamped mouth. The bigger they were the better he liked his job. 'I see,' he acknowledged, his face still wearing its smile. 'You're living in your father's house. I see.'

Daniel still said nothing.

'Let me think now. That would be with your father and your mother and your four sisters, isn't it? Oh, no, that's not right. Your father died, didn't he? Sad, very sad. And one of your sisters too. Well, well. Yes, yes, yes. Now have I got it right. There was no one else was there who died?' The Quiet Elder allowed himself another smile at the face which whipped around to face him. Ay, that got him. The big man wasn't looking so big now. The Quiet Elder took a long shallow breath. Now? No, not yet. Just a little more. Easy, now, easy. 'How's your mother managing without your father? Sad, very sad. Oh yes. Of course he never came to church, of course none of you did. And your young sister. Bad, bad. Of course the Session gave its condolences at the time. Yes. And still does, of course. Your poor mother has her troubles. A pity she wasn't in the habit of attending the church.'

The Quiet Elder's smile had moved to the inside by now. He was indeed getting there. He could always tell by the way their shoulders slumped and their mouths hung open. Oh yes, the signs were here. 'They must be having a sore time of it right enough. Your mother and your remaining sisters. Just as well yourself is in it to see to them. You need someone with you at such times and who better than your own?'

This time Daniel turned his head slowly, the flame which had been burning in him had turned to ice. The dirty fat bastard. So that was his game. He'd like to give him a taste of the knife to see if that would wipe the smile from his self-satisfied face, to see if that would stop his dirty words from falling from his poisonous mouth. 'My family are my concern.' He was looking at the Quiet Elder but he wasn't seeing him. All he could see was what was boiling up inside him.

'But a troublesome family. Yes. A troublesome family. Even yourself has to admit that. Hadn't we your sister standing before the Session not long ago about her doings? Dear, dear, your poor father and mother. Oh, I forgot, your father's dead, isn't he? Dear, dear, dear.'

Daniel was back with the wall. He needed it to survive.

'And what about your other sister? The one that has the fair hair. The living one.'

He wouldn't stop, he wouldn't stop. Daniel was going to murder him and take the rope if he could only stop that mouth. It was inside his head now, battering him down.

'The one who told us,' he dropped his last words like stones into a still pool.

The other two were sitting back on their chairs, both with their arms folded across their chests. Their heads kept nodding to every question their colleague asked. They nodded twice as hard to Daniel's answers or lack of, as they saw them. He had him though. Themselves would have been no use in this case. No, he was the right man here, he had the right touch. Themselves weren't very subtle whatever else they were. No, their strengths and skills lay in different ways. They looked across to the Minister. They never saw a man like him. He was sitting half asleep in his chair, his head drooping to one side, his arms hanging loose. He might as well not have been there. But the Quiet Elder was and he was the kind of man who had more answers than there are questions.

'You lying bitches,' Daniel blazed at them. 'I don't believe one word of it. You lot are nothing but a shower of rotting hypocrites.' The two in the chairs said nothing, but their arms dropped from their chests, they jerked upright on their seats.

'No, not liars. Of any kind,' the smile had disappeared from the Quiet Elder's face, revealing his open animosity. 'You can be sure it's the truth. Your own sister we got it from, your own sister. Go and ask her if you don't believe it.' The Quiet Elder wrapped himself in his smug smile. That had him. That knocked the pride out of him. Soon he'd be squealing like a stuck pig. Where were his fine words now? He looked at the big face. He could see it crumbling. But the Quiet Elder hadn't finished. So far he'd only taken the heat from him. There was more yet. But, so far he was pleased with himself. And the faces of the other two were telling him he was on top form. He didn't bother to look at the Minister. He gave nothing away, no one would would ever know what he was thinking. Not in Session anyway. He was ready to finish this. All pretence at being solicitous fell from his voice. Steel entered it. 'Do you deny what has been put to you? Answer, man, answer.'

Someone was smashing the back of Daniel's head with a heavy hammer. His shoulders felt as if they had sunk to his waist. His leg was hanging off him, making his back scream all the way up to his neck. 'What is it, holy man?' he said. 'What is it that you're wanting me to say? That I took a drink of water from Mairead Beaton because I was thirsty, or that I drank water that my sister's spite said Mairead Beaton put magic in? Now, what will I say?'

'Spite, spite. What spite? There's no spite in it. Why would your own sister spite her brother?'

'How would I know?' Now it was his own booming voice that was filling his head. 'Why don't you go and ask her?'

'Because it's you that I'm asking. And I'll ask it again. If it's not the truth, why should your own sister say what she said about yourself and Mairead Beaton?'

'Because, good and righteous man, she's wanting me all to

herself. She's wanting me in her own bed, right, not in anyone else's. Whichever woman I looked at would be the wrong one where she's concerned. It wouldn't be her and that's all she can see. Now, will that do for you?'

'Are you laying accusations against your own sister?' The Quiet Elder's mouth opened before Daniel had closed his.

'Since it's the truth, I am.' He shut his mouth again. He'd said more than he meant to but it had to be said. He was tired of carrying it, he was starting to feel the weight of it. And they weren't touching Mairead, not one of them and not one finger. And that witch back at home, with his mother.

'Sit down,' The Minister's vice floated through the mist to Daniel, making him think he was speaking for him. He turned to look and saw his hand flapping at the one he'd got to do his dirty work for him. 'This is a bad business.' The Minister was sitting back in his chair, his arms resting along its arms. 'A very bad business. Families setting themselves against one another. Maybe God knows what gets in to you people because I don't. Why is it that you can't live at peace with each other? I don't know,' his hand seemed to be flapping of its own accord. 'Where did all of this ill-feeling between yourself and your sister spring from?'

Daniel looked down at the floor then back up to the Minister, the Minister's look demanding an answer. There wasn't an answer to what he had asked. Had the man heard nothing that he had said?

The Minister put his elbows on the table and leaned forward, clasping his hands. 'The people in this place are dying,' he told Daniel. 'And I am useless to help any of them. They've turned their backs on God and yet they cry about their miserable lives. What do they expect me to do? Go home. And tell Mairead Beaton to go home. And sort out whatever it is that's wrong in your family. And may God help the lot of you. There's nothing to answer here. A waste of the Church's time.'

The elders couldn't believe what they were hearing. 'You're not going to let them go, just like that?' The Young Elder exploded out of his chair, his hands gripping the edge of the table. 'Mairead Beaton has been fingered for a witch. I say we examine her to find out!'

'Keep your seat.' Now it was the Minister who was shouting, louder, his voice cracked ice. 'Remember who it is you're speaking to. Mairead Beaton's no more a witch than anyone else is. She's been blackened by a vengeful woman, that's all. The sister of that man there. Let them mend it. This Church has more to do.'

Daniel had decided to stay with the spot on the wall. It was safer that way, safer for them and safer for himself. Whatever he had expected it wasn't this. Never this. Their voices raged about him as they fought hard to turn the Minister to their way of thinking, their words swirling and skirling and losing their meaning.

'Go home,' he heard through the storm. He nodded to the tired voice and, without looking at any of them, he walked from the room.

Mairead gave a jump when she heard the door opening and when he came through it her heart forgot to beat. She looked at his mouth for his words, but nothing came from it. She felt the hard skin of his hand as it gripped hers, hurting her. 'I need this place at my back.' He was half-running as he pulled her after him. He didn't stop and he didn't speak until he was back with the river. Sitting on the bank, he turned to her and said, 'I can hardly bear this,' and the eyes she was looking at were as dark and as moist as the stones lying in the bottom of the burn, as deep and as lost as the stones under the river.

She had no words either. If she had she would have given them to him. She put her hand over his hand, where it was lying in the grass between them, and brought it up to her breast and with her other hand she squeezed it between her two and tried to give him her strength that way.

'I'll go as far as the stones with you,' he said, not looking at her but at the black peaty water flowing in front of them. 'Then I'm going to go to my mother's house. There's something I have to see to.'

Mairead wished words would come. She was needing them

now. She was needing to know and she didn't know how to ask. Standing outside that room inside the Minister's house and him in there with them was the only time she had been frightened. Not for herself but for him and what he might do. And then she heard the door opening and he came through it. Not a word out of his mouth to tell her what had happened with those men and the Minister. And not a word from him the whole time he was pulling her behind him. And still none, not for her anyway. And she knew there would be none, not this night nor for who knew how many nights. And days. Mornings and wakings. Just herself and whatever madness her mind could make. For a short time it had been good just being herself, free.

Chapter Twenty-Eight

And there were no words from him when he left her at the stones to set off across the hill to his mother's. He saw nothing as he tramped on, blinded by a slow burning anger. If his feet hadn't known the way it wouldn't be his eyes that would tell him. He passed one or two people he knew. They hailed him but he didn't see them. The people took no offence, that was Daniel Ross, hurrying somewhere as usual, too busy to see anyone or anything. Snow, which the icy wind had foretold, was beginning to fall in large flakes, driven against him by the tearing wind. He ducked his head into it and staggered on.

Despite the open roof there was warmth in his mother's house. His mother was keeping a good fire on, piled high with glowing peats. She was on her knees at Ishbel's bedside, trying to spoon something from a watery bowl into Ishbel's mouth.

'She'll take nothing.' His mother's face looked about half the size he remembered it.

'Speak to Ishbel, Daniel.' Peggy was kneeling on the other side of Ishbel's bed. 'Please. She'll listen to you.'

He stood beside his mother in melting snow and looked down on Ishbel. Her eyes were closed, the skin below them black against the wax of her face. Sweatings and wipings had cleaned the dirt from it leaving it shiny clean, like the shell of an egg, had plastered her hair against her forehead. He knelt down beside his mother, the snow turned to beads of water, running down his own face. She had been a wicked bitch, nothing was going to alter that. But anything he wanted to say would have to wait. There were too many of his family lying in the graveyard. And how much was his mother supposed to stand? And what about Peggy? At least Peggy was getting stronger, strong enough to see Ishbel's state and to want to help. Looking down at Ishbel, lying like a doll under the blankets, he felt the anger and the hurt draining away, melting inside him like the snowflakes on his hair. On his feet he prayed out of his confusion to anyone who would hear him. To the almighty God, to the Mother of Christ, even to those his father spent his life pouring milk sacrifices to. For them he had no real names. 'Please,' his silent prayer said, 'please, no more. In any house.'

'Ishbel. Ishbel, it's Daniel.' He saw the pale lashes trembling at the sound of her name but Ishbel didn't open her eyes.

'She'll not know you,' his mother said. 'She doesn't know myself even,' His mother's fingers, freed from the bowl, played with each other. 'Why are our people dying, Daniel? I know we haven't food, but we've been without food before this. We didn't used to die like this.' His mother's face looked like a lump of squashed dough with her weeping.

'Ishbel,' he said again, his mouth against Ishbel's ear. 'I'm going to get someone to help you, someone to make you better. You'll have to try to take something for your strength,' and he looked away from Ishbel to his mother, then back to Ishbel. Did she hear him? He didn't know. 'Keep trying,' he told Peggy. 'I'm going for help.'

'There's no use in you going there.' His mother put a hand on his arm.

'I'm not going for the Old Wife. I'm going somewhere else. I'll be as quick as I can. You two do what you can,' and he was ducking through the doorway into the thickening snow before she could question him further.

He took longer going back than he had in coming from Mairead's. The heavier snow made it difficult to see more than a few yards ahead and his rage, having dissolved, took the wings from his feet. He went up to the house first but Mairead wasn't there. The animals were in residence, her big cat lording it over the rest. He found Mairead down at the burn. Long blades of ice daggered its banks. She was standing past her ankles in the water, her frock kilted up to her thighs. She had her head back and was laughing open-mouthed as she scooped handfuls of icy water over her face, drinking in snowflakes. Every time the water hit she gave a loud gasp as it bit her face and soaked through her frock to her chest. Defeaned by the sounds of her own delight, she was unaware of his approach. He stood back a little from the edge of the bank and watched.

Her laughing like that stopped him, put a knife into him. It was beautiful, as she was beautiful. This was his Mairead, floating free out of her mouth and tumbling over the stones in the burn, making music with the ice. He kept watching as she hopped from one foot to the other, laughing as her feet froze.

'Mairead,' her name came from low in his throat. Despite the distance between them she heard it. Her head whipped round and she stood still, listening through the sound of the running water for it to come again, her feet frozen. He could see the puzzlement on her face as she looked up, the laughter still on her face and in her hair. Then she saw him and from the middle of the burn her hand was reaching for him, waiting for him to come to her. 'You're looking awful wild,' she said, pressing her wet face to his. 'Urgh,' she growled, and she was laughing at her own ferocity and at him.

'I need you,' he told her.

'I know that,' More than laughter was dancing in her eyes as she looked at him.

'No, you don't understand what it is I'm telling you. Come on up out of there,' He was pulling her up onto the bank. Once there she stood facing him, both wrapped around in drifting snow, and waited for him to speak. He looked at her expectant face and his words went. How could he ask her? And yet he had to, there was no other way. Where to start though? She'd never come, never. If he'd been in her place he wouldn't. The thought of his mother terrified her. That alone would keep her from coming. She'd face the Session again before she'd go near his mother. And what about the Session? She'd come away from there still innocent of who had accused her. And he was going to ask her to try to save the one who put her through all that? She mightn't know the web that had been woven around her but he did. How could he do this to her?

Seeing her standing so close to him like that, and waiting, he pulled her against him and put his arms around her. 'I need you to come to my mother's house, Mairead,' the words were rushed out. 'To help Ishbel. She's very sick. We think she's going to die.' He looked away from her to the swirling snow. 'But why would you want to?' His last words were barely spoken, but she heard him.

'Why?'

'You don't know?'

'No. And I won't if you'll not tell me. As usual you start at the finish. All I know is that Ishbel your sister is sick. So, of course, I'll come. Why wouldn't I? I'll do whatever I can.'

'Not when you know, you'll not.'

'Know what? What's frightening you?'

'It was Ishbel that told the Session about you.' By now his hands were gripping her arms, hurting her, making her breath catch. 'That was Ishbel's doing.'

'But why did she say that?' She was flinching under his hands. 'I have never done anything bad on her.'

'By her way you did.' Now his hands were still and he was looking through snowflakes at her. 'By her way you charmed me away from her. She called you a witch.'

'But I'm not. I didn't. I didn't do anything.'

'Oh, ay, you did. You charmed me Mairead Beaton as sure as I'm standing here,' and he put his mouth against hers. 'Witch.' His lips moved softly on her lips.

Mairead took his kiss, she was kissing him back. 'I did nothing.'

'Och, look,' – he was like a fish caught in Ishbel's net – 'you have to try to understand her. She looked after me from when I was born. She was a mother to me. And as I grew she thought that's the way it would stay, just me and her. Some women are like that, you know.' His words tailed off. He hoped she wouldn't ask anything else. Because he didn't know anything else. His excuse had sounded hollow, even to himself.

'That's what she said? That I took you away from her?'

'Ay, something like that.'

'Poor Ishbel.'

'Ay, poor Ishbel. Right enough.'

'I'd be sad if you went away from me.'

'What about what she made you face?'

'That's past. She's needing help. And I have you.' She put her face against his. She could feel his heart, it was racing her own. After a while she said, 'Your mother won't want me.'

'Never you mind my mother. My mother's not herself just now. It'll be all right. Don't be worrying about that.' She could feel the strength in his arms as they tightened around her.

'We'd better go then. There's some things I need to get from my house. I don't know what I can do, but I can try.'

When they reached his mother's house she wouldn't go in. He had to go and get his mother to come out to tell her she was welcome. And even then she made him go in before her. Once inside she was like a wild horse. There were long looks from the corner of her eyes for his mother, she moved away if his mother came too close to her. His mother didn't speak after the initial 'It's good of you to come,' and 'You're welcome in my house.' Neither fear nor pleasure seemed to change his mother's face. It hung on her in its heaviness. Grudgingly, she gave way to Mairead and went to sit over the fire with Peggy, waiting for time to make the change.

'You'll all have to go outside.' Mairead stood up after examining Ishbel. 'Have you water in the house?' she asked.

'There's some,' Peggy answered.

'Go for more,' Daniel told her. His mother did not stir. Picking up the wooden pail, Peggy hurried to the burn.

'You too,' Mairead said to Daniel. 'And your mother.' These last words were silent shapes on her lips. 'Take her with you.'

'Come with me, Mother.' He bent down to put a hand under his mother's elbow, and lift her to her feet. Wordlessly, she allowed him to escort her outside. 'Is there anything else you're needing,' he came back in to say, 'before I go?'

'No, I have what I need.' Her back was to him, she was dropping roots into the pot on the fire. Then, 'Yes, get me some ice from the burn.'

He nodded to her. 'And you'll need more peats in,' he said, before making for the door.

Lifting the pot away from the fire with the hem of her frock, she set it down on the floor next to the bowl with the clean white cloth. The bowl and the cloths were her own, with the roots and the mosses the only tools she used. When the water had cooled she'd strain it through the cloth into the bowl. Another bowl, belonging to the house, was filled with some of the freshly lifted water which Peggy had fetched. Pieces of ice floated in it. Taking that bowl and one of her cloths, she went over to Ishbel and sat down on the floor beside her. Dipping the cloth into the water, she squeezed the excess from it and gently began to dab at Ishbel's face. She did this over and over, dipping the cloth, squeezing it just enough to leave it cold for Ishbel's hot skin. Her actions were unhurried and sure, her touch light as she murmered soft words for Ishbel to hear. Once Ishbel's dry lips moved a fraction but that seemed to be as much as she could manage. No words came but Mairead was pleased. She nodded to herself and rhythmically worked on. She strained the root water and fed drops of the infusion to her from her fingers to begin with, before progressing to the spoon. For long spells, lifting Ishbel from her pillow, she cradled her and sang her mother's songs to her. There was nothing much of Ishbel to hold, no weight, no flesh, only the sharpness of bones. 'Drink,' Mairead would tell the lolling head as she tried to support it with one arm. She worked through that first night getting very little response. Ishbel slept through most of it and Mairead had to labour for the waking times. By morning Ishbel was sipping strongly from the spoon and Mairead made sure the drops went into her and not onto her.

Although only a few years separated Ishbel and Mairead, even in health Ishbel had looked much older. Now she was as an old woman. Gently lowering her onto the pillow, Mairead withdrew her supporting arm and pulled the blankets up around her before returning to her spongeings. In between times she kept going over to the fire to rebuild it. And at other times she sat looking at Ishbel, this woman who did not want Daniel to be with her, Mairead. She looked closely, as if by looking hard enough she could see what made Ishbel the way she was. But it was difficult to know anything about Ishbel the way she was. All that was written on Ishbel's face was the story of how near to death she had been, and how near yet. Right now, the real Ishbel wasn't present. So Mairead stopped looking. If Ishbel recovered, there would be time then. If she wanted it. And if he wanted to go back? What then? No, she wouldn't think that way, no use in that. Through the day and the next night of flickering candles into the following day she sat with Ishbel. Outside the muffled silence of deep snow, inside the deathly silence of the grave. She had no idea where Daniel with his mother and sisters went to for shelter. She was grateful for the peats he brought in before he left. Despite snow coming in through the roof she was able to keep the house warm.

She was needing to sleep and yet she thought she could never sleep. Too many pictures kept going around inside her head. And Ishbel needed her awake, so there was no room for sleep. Her eyes stayed open for longer now, but they still were not seeing. At least not what was in front of her. When Mairead said her name, there was no indication from Ishbel that she heard. After two nights the heat had not left her. But by the time the third morning came, change came with it. Ishbel was still hot, but the film had gone from her eyes, leaving them clear. That was enough, it was plenty. Holding Ishbel's small frail hand in her own strong hand, Mairead looked into her eyes. 'You'll be all right now,' she told her, speaking slowly. 'Sleep now, sleep now,' and leaning over her she stroked Ishbel's face with her other hand. 'Sleep, sleep, sleep now,' she sang, feeling sleep creeping over herself as she said the words.

Chapter Twenty-Nine

Daniel stayed on in Strath with his mother and sisters for four weeks. Back in her own house Mairead counted the days he was away from her. They were very long. Every minute without him seemed stuck in time. What then an hour, a day, a night? Even with the weather raging at its worst, with the wind and the sleeting rain making her head ache, she found it impossible to stay in the house. She wandered everywhere, anywhere, to put the day in, thinking that when she returned he'd be there. Days upon days, sitting in the open, her shawl pulled over her head her only covering, sitting to see if he would come. Crying his name into the storm and the storm too full of its own noise to hear her. She abandoned her chores, she largely abandoned her animals. She rarely saw Master these days, he was away from the house as much as she was. Her fire was left to go out. She knew she was a poor housewife, but she hadn't the energy to go gathering plants, much less wood. Even on calm days she did nothing, as if by concentrating her mind on something else meant she might forget him. She was no good for anything, to anything, no use to herself.

Every day and night the same. No sleep, no peace, no rest. Living on bites of bread. In the morning impatient for the day to pass and with the day fading afraid of the approaching night. Sick for want of food, sick for want of sleep, sick mostly for want of him. And yet when he did come, she didn't see him.

She couldn't count the number of days she had walked down the same track to wait for him. Then one day when she was sitting on the cold wet ground she crumpled over into a heap.

What did she care, the storm could take her. He wasn't coming back to her. And she didn't want to be where he wasn't any longer. She lay sprawled out on the muddy earth with the hail battering her when she thought she heard someone calling out her name. She paid no heed to the calling, it was inside her own head. She heard it again, a little louder this time. She shook her head to try to shake the name away but it wouldn't go away. She tried lifting her hand to push it away but her name came on, stronger. Crying loudly, she hauled herself on to her knees, her hands clawing furrows into the ground. 'Daniel,' his name was a wound on her lips. 'Daniel.' She was crawling through the mud to him, her face streaked in it. All that she could see of him were his legs walking towards her. She made for them and lunged at him, wrapping her arms around his ankles. Holding tight to him she kept crying his name as if it was the only word she knew.

'What are you crying like that for?' His face looking down on her was comical in its concern for her. 'And what are you doing out here? I looked everywhere for you.' She clung to his legs and cried louder. 'Come on, come up out of there.' His hands were reaching down to her. 'Are you all right? You're looking in an awful mess.' He was wiping her tears away with his cold hands. 'You're a strange one, right enough. Come on, we'll go home now.'

Grey and red ash was all that was left of her fire. To get away from him she crumbled a peat on to it and stayed on her knees, blowing into it. Busy with the fire she had time to gather herself. What would he be thinking of her? His mother wouldn't let her fire go out. Nor Ishbel. When she saw the smoke rising she crumbled some more peat on. And herself like that, hanging on to him and crying all over him. What way was that to be? She had never been one to cry, she hadn't cried since her father had died. And here she was, herself, Mairead Beaton, crying all over Daniel Ross like that. The thought of it brought fresh tears, making her blow harder into the fire in the effort to keep them inside her and scattering peat ash into her mouth and her crying eyes.

'It'll go now,' he said from his place beside her. 'Have you anything to eat in the house?'

Still keeping her back to him she scampered away to a corner and came back with a piece of bread.

'Have you any for yourself?' He didn't take the bread from her. He was still on the floor, she was standing. The bread hung between them.

'I don't want any,' she told him, looking away from him so that he wouldn't have to see her swollen eyes. 'I'm not feeling right. In my belly.' She rubbed her stomach with her other hand.

'How's that?'

'I don't know. I just don't feel good. My belly is sick feeling. I can't eat.'

'Do you think you have the fever?' Still he didn't take the bread from her.

'I don't think I have the fever. I'm not hot. And I can breathe right. I just feel bad, weak. I can't run.'

'It's no wonder you're weak. Anyone would be weak that doesn't eat. When did you last take something?'

'I don't know. I can't remember.'

'You know what happens to people who don't eat, you've seen enough of it.' His voice was filling her house. 'Take this,' he was tearing the bread in half, 'get it inside you.'

'I can't. I can't eat.'

'Eat it. I'm not going to watch you dying in front of me.'

Taking the bread from him, she sat down beside him. She opened her mouth and bit into it. She was watching him, he was watching her. He watched her mouth, waiting for her to swallow. When he saw that she had, he took a bite of his. Still with his eyes on her he chewed, then swallowed. He waited for her to take the next bite. Eyeing each other, matching each other mouthful for mouthful, they began to eat the bread.

'Now what?' he asked her.

'Nothing.'

'Are you sick?' His eyes were staring at her.

'No, I'm not sick. My belly's fine.'

'That's good then. No more of this not eating. In God's

name, Mairead. People are dying because they have nothing to eat. There's people here trying to live on grass, heather, anything. And you'll not eat when you have it.'

He didn't realise how loud he was shouting until he saw her eyes filling. He looked away from her and concentrated on chewing his bread. For a time neither spoke. The atmosphere between them hung where the bread had been, for each heavy with the presence of the other.

'It's not needing food that's killing people,' she said to break the silence. Her head was down, she wouldn't look at him.

'What then?' His tone said he didn't expect an answer.

'Having nothing to eat makes people weak . . .' she started.

'I know that.'

'And that's how they can't fight the disease.'

'What disease?' She could hear the incredulity in his voice in the sharpness of the question.

'The people in Strath think that I'm stupid. That I can't hear. Well, I'm not stupid. And I can hear.' She was kneading what was left of her bread back into dough.

'Eat that,' he said. 'What things are you hearing?'

'Things.'

'What things?'

'You'll say that I'm stupid too and that I'm bad for saying it.' She had to force herself to swallow the doughy bread. She was feeling sick again. She kept her head down so that he wouldn't know.

'No,' he was telling her. 'I'll not say that you're stupid. Or bad. I could never think that way about you.'

'Well, that time I was at the Minister's house.' She raised her head and turned to look at him. 'I reached there before you came and the Minister's wife said wait inside the house to me. Out of the cold. She was a kind woman. I waited outside that room. And I could hear what the Minister was saying to his men. He was speaking about all the people that are dying and there wasn't coffins for them all, that he would have to use the one without the bottom again. One of the men was bawling right through the wall to me about how stupid the people were. They'd be facing the same next winter because they'd eaten the seed corn. And the Minister said,' she waved her hand at him as it seemed he would hurry her, 'wait now, the Minister was saying to him not to be a fool. That no one ever died that quick from hunger. They might be starving, he said, but it's disease they're dying from. That's what the Minister said. He said what kind of hunger ever created what we are witnessing.' She fell silent, her chest rising and falling to her heavy breathing. He also was silent as he looked into the fire and tried to make sense of what he had just heard.

'Is that what he said?' His words were quiet.

'That is what he said. He said it was them in the regiment. Taking it home from wherever they are. In Germany or some place like Germany. Spreading it everywhere. To people and to the crop.'

'You're not stupid, Mairead. It was what myself was afraid to think.' He was back speaking to the fire. 'You saw Ishbel. Anna the same. Poor Anna. A wee girl. Ishbel's still not right. But the spring'll come, Mairead. The spring'll come. Then we'll get the berries. There'll be nothing on them. Things'll start to get easier then, when the bonnie days come.'

In the fire's face he saw Donald Munro's, saw him coming home dressed up like a peacock, strutting about as if he were the Chief. If ever a man had it coming to him it was Donald Munro. Spreading his disease on women and cattle and crops. 'We're the lucky ones, staying so far from it,' he said.

'I'm not that clear, if someone needs me I'll have to go to them.' She was looking into the flames with him.

'Well, just keep clear of the village as much as you can. Don't go near it unless you're sent for. Watch yourself, whatever you do.'

'And you? What about you? Every time you leave me I think you'll never come back. You're going back to it all.'

'Don't be worrying about me. I'll be fine. I can look out for myself. We'll not be speaking about this any more.' He turned to her. 'We'll look past this time. To the spring. And right now, you're going to eat. Come on in close beside me.' He parted his legs and Mairead sat between them, with her back to him while he put his arms around her.

Chapter Thirty

Daniel lived between his mother's house and Mairead's, doing all that he could for both homes, trying to ensure that neither fell into even more desperate need. Most of his time seemed to be spent out on the hill, traipsing from one place to the other. Flora was still with the family of motherless children she had gone to when things were at their worst in Strath. It was likely that Flora would stay on with that family, and her mother and the rest of them would see her when they went up to the shielings. For Daniel there were two roofs to repair, two sets of walls to mend, food to be found for two families. And Mairead? She learned to cope with half of him.

She was still eating very little of what he brought home, although she was careful to hide this fact from him. It was easy. He hardly took the time to sit down before he was off again. She saw him growing thinner, his clothes becoming more ragged as they hung on him. She didn't know who she had become. She grew listless and slow, she who had never walked where she could run. She cried all the time now, over nothing and everything. She cried when making the fire, when she could light it, when she could not. Most of her old fears were gone, pushed out by the new ones which came to take their place. She hardly thought of the Minister any more. Having stood before him, and having walked away from him whole, showed her some truth. It was as Daniel had told her that time, it seemed a long time ago: the Minister was only a man. What went to make that man was something she didn't know, something she didn't want to. It was her own mind that had turned him into the monster she thought he was.

Now it was doing the same with Daniel. Would he stay with Ishbel? Or would he come back to herself? What if he would die with the disease? What would she do then? She wished that she could put out her hand and that Master would be there, Master who had always been there and who had understood her loneliness. But Master had upped and left one day and hadn't come back. Master was likely dead. Everyone was dead, everything was dead. But, no. She wouldn't think that way. If Daniel knew what way she was thinking he'd be upset. She had to keep herself right for him. She was needing water. Yes, that was it. She'd take her pail and go down to the burn.

As she walked down the hill to the burn she still could not run like she used to. Taking her time she breathed in the sharp clean air, her pail in one hand, the other hand pressed against the small of her back. As she stood in the water, she looked along the banks for the first signs of new plants. The signs were there. Soon the banks would be covered in primroses. She hugged spring's promise to herself along with the promise of what was growing inside her. She looked up into the clear blue of the bright sky. Although very cold, there was colour in the day. Blue in the sky, green blades growing among the strawy grass. There was still snow on the hills but, for now, the wind had left them alone. Spring was coming. She could see it, she could smell it. Daniel was right. Just thinking about it made her feel better. She hopped about in the icy water. No matter how many times she stood in the burn she never got used to the water in winter. She opened her mouth as she felt the pain and the pleasure of it biting her feet. In the burn she played her imagining game. What way will he be when I tell him? She saw his face, the way his mouth would be and her face mirrored her thoughts, her mouth turned down. She imagined again how he would be and she saw his mouth smiling and her mouth smiled. And with his smile she saw worry for her and her arms felt strong for him. What way will I be when I tell him? She hopped about on the stones in the bottom of the burn to try to escape the temperature of the water. I know what way I'll be, she thought.

In that place where no one but herself lived and where no one but Daniel came, the sound of someone approaching carried easily through the stillness. It was him. He was coming to her. Her heart started its racing, she did not expect him to come back so soon. And her with nothing done about the house. Would the fire still be burning for him? Oh, but what she had to tell him. Her heart was singing as she waded out of the water and up the bank, her smile ready for him she looked up. But two men were coming. She saw only him. It was his name she spoke when the Young Elder and Closed Face reached her. She looked past them, looking for him, the pail of water still in her hand.

'Come up out of there or by God I'll come down and drag you out!' The Young Elder's eyes were bulging in his face. Closed Face, overweight in Strath at a time of famine, stood doubled over and panting as he struggled to regain his breath.

Mairead stood looking at them. She didn't understand. Her eyes were looking for Daniel. Her mouth called his name.

'He'll not save you.' The Young Elder was balancing unevenly on the bank, his shoes sinking in the soft mud. 'Don't make me get my feet wet if you know what's good for you.'

As he advanced on her, whatever had been holding Mairead together flew apart. She had been walking the knife-edge of euphoria and despair for too long. And with a baby growing inside her too much had come to change her. Even Daniel. Everything that he was involved in she was also involved in. 'Daniel'. Her scream shattered the air as his shoes hit the water. Letting go of the pail, both of her hands were tearing at his face and his hair as she fought to keep him away from her. She was strong but he was a man. And when she wouldn't, couldn't stop screaming, he put his fist in her face. 'Shut up,' he was screaming louder, 'shut up,' and he was crashing down on top of her into the water.

On the bank Closed Face was looking unhappy. He chewed his lips. This wasn't the way it was meant to go. They were only supposed to be asking the woman about what spells she used. That was all. There was no harm in that. They were only going to give her a fright. When the other fellow had come for him he never thought to say no. If only she would stop her skirling, it was making him mad.

'Go easy, man,' he felt he had to say when he saw what he was doing to her clothes. There was no mention of anything like this, he'd said he was wanting to see the witch's mark. Just that. To satisfy himself. If only she'd shut that mouth of hers he wouldn't have to bash her so hard. All that bawling would make any man mad. It was the Minister's job to sort out this kind of thing, but the man was soft, soft.

The Young Elder forgot his friend on the bank. He forgot everything but what was driving him. His ears were closed to the calling from the bank and the screaming from below him. 'Open your legs!' He used the flat of his hand to make her. 'Open them!'

MacIver found her. It was the middle of the afternoon and he was powering his way to the alehouse. He was about to leap the burn when his eye was caught by something black lying upstream from him. Why, he thought, would anyone dump old clothes in the burn? Still, you never knew. There could be something he could wear. As he came closer he saw two legs, lying naked and white among the rags. Then a woman's head with blood coming from it. Holy Hell. Someone had murdered a woman in the burn. There was only one woman living this far up that he knew of. What now? What now?

Running as fast as his bulk would let him, MacIver closed the distance between himself and the woman. Ay, that was her right enough, her that was always gathering plants and stuff. Bending down, MacIver straightened her clothes, covering the woman's nakedness. Oh dear, dear. The woman might have known what she would get one day. Living away up here, away from any kind of folk. Who knew what travelled this country?

'Please,' she squeezed the word past her burst lips. 'Please.' She was trying to lift her hand to him.

'What happened to you, mistress?' He didn't know what he was meant to do with her hand. He tried to pull her up, but she wouldn't come for him. 'Who did this on you, mistress?' Putting an arm under her shoulders he tried to make her sit up. 'Who was it?' He didn't know what else to say to her.

'I fell.' With his help she was sitting, her legs stretched straight in front of her. Her mouth felt wrong, not like her own mouth. It tasted of salt and was bigger than the whole of her face. She cupped a handful of water up to it. The water burnt her lips. She swallowed it.

MacIver didn't know what he should do. He couldn't leave her like this, the woman was hurt, hurt awful bad for someone who slipped in the burn. And in some queer places. Her face was twice the size it should have been, it looked as if a horse had kicked her. Her mouth was black with caked blood and bruising and she could hardly open it to speak.

'Help me to stand up.' She was putting her hand out to him again.

Stooping over her, he put one arm around her back and gave her his other. She caught that hand between her two. She was shaking from head to feet like a falling leaf. 'My pail,' she said. 'I need water.'

MacIver ran for the pail and, scooping it full of water, he ran back to her. 'I'll take you along to your home, mistress. Yourself is not able.'

Mairead knew that what the man was saying to her was right. Now wasn't the time for arguing. If she was to get back up to her house she was going to need his help. She wouldn't be able to get out of the burn without it, she'd never be able to climb the bank.

MacIver put the pail up first then he almost lifted Mairead up. She was shaking so much she couldn't get her legs to move, nor hold her. Where had her bones gone to? Her legs felt as if they were made from water.

'Lean against me, mistress.' MacIver's thick arm was supporting her. 'It's all right. I have your water here.' He waved the pail in front of her. 'Just go easy, mistress, and we'll get there.'

MacIver put her into her house and sat her down on her mattress, pulling one of the blankets around her. Then he built the fire up for her and stayed until he was sure it was going. He poured some of the water he had brought into her bowl and set it by her. 'Who did it to you?' he asked as he was leaving.

'I slipped,' she said, 'in the water.'

'Well, you'll be all right now you're home. And don't be going wandering about. You don't know what's out there,' and with that he left her.

When he had gone her hand reached for the stag's skin and she pulled it against her. She rocked with the skin, the words which were one word pouring from her. She didn't want Daniel to come, she didn't want Daniel to come. 'Master, come,' she cried into the skin.

He'd been away from her for too long. As he hurried to her, his every thought was of her. When spring came and things were easier for them all, he was going to stay with her. Always, forever. Who'd have thought this could happen to him? He wished he had known her years ago, he was jealous of the time he didn't know her. The wings were back on his boots, making them skim over the ground. His heart was beating to a Mairead beat, his blood was dancing to Mairead tune.

He had never seen the country looking lovelier. Everywhere he turned was the promise of what was coming. Spring in all its beauty thrusting its glorious intent at him. It was there in the grass under his feet, on the trees and the bushes, and above him on the high hills. Over the whole of the place it was bursting to get out. The country was singing for him, only for him. And his heart was singing to the one who put the song in him.

The song faltered when he saw that she wasn't where she'd said she'd be. What a woman, where was she off to now? It lurched to a stop when he found her lying curled in her bed. Ice then his heart. 'Mairead,' he was afraid to whisper. 'What's wrong?' He was on his knees beside her. She lifted her head to look at him and there was nothing in her eyes for him. They might have been two black stones.

'I fell in the burn,' Her head was the only part of her visible, blankets covered the rest. 'I battered my head on the stones and hurt my body.'

'What a fright you gave me. I thought that something bad had happened to you when you weren't there to meet me. 'His fingers were tracing the bruises on her face, the cuts on her head and on her mouth. 'How did you fall? Was there ice?'

'I don't know.' She shrank from his hand. 'I was getting water. And it was so cold, it was like ice. And I was jumping on my feet trying to keep warm, and I was thinking about you and I just fell.' She pulled the blanket over her mouth, she didn't want him looking at her.

'You must have come down awful hard. That's a nasty crack your head took. And I don't think I'm going to be getting any big kisses from that mouth for a while. Your face is in an awful mess. Couldn't you have saved yourself a bit?'

'No, I couldn't save myself a bit,' she was mumbling through the swelling and the blanket. 'Well, anyway, I didn't. And my face is better than it was. My face will be all right. I know what to do about my face.'

'I don't know what to say to you. You look as if a horse kicked you.'

'Don't be wild at me. Please.' He could see her head start its rocking.

He was at a loss. She used to do this when he first knew her. In a minute she'd start her moaning. He hated it when she did that. He didn't know how to break through it. 'Come here,' he said and he was gently pulling her to him. 'Why would I be wild at you?' he said into her hair. 'That's fright you're hearing. just let me hold you for a wee while,' and he was rocking her as he spoke. And as he rocked her, she rocked him. 'I thought at first that someone had done this on you.' He laid his lips against the cut on her cheekbone. They stayed that way for a long time. Her softness was beautiful to him, she who thought she was so tough. Her head was resting against his heart so that his heart became her heart. One heart beating for the two of them. She completed him, made him whole. It was something he had never known.

'There's a baby inside me,' she whispered from her safe

place. The words were hard for her to say but in there she felt she could say them. She must have spoken too quietly for him to hear because nothing about him changed. His arms had neither tightened about her nor pushed her away. No words came from his mouth. His heart was still her heart. 'Daniel,' she whispered louder.

'I heard you.' He was still rocking her. She tried to guess what he was feeling from the way he spoke to her but she could gauge nothing, neither pleasure nor displeasure. She was afraid to look up at his face. She held her breath and waited to see if he would say more.

'Look at me,' he was saying, and she could feel the small leaps one of his arms kept giving. Moving her head, she rubbed her face against its downy hairs. 'Look at me and tell me.' He was waiting for her. She made herself lift her head. His face above hers looked as if it had been shaped from wood. And his eyes? She wouldn't look at his eyes. But she did and his eyes were good, they were smiling. 'A baby,' he was still whispering and it was she who would devour him. 'How do you know?' he asked when he was able to speak.

'I just know,' her mouth was stinging but through its pain she was smiling. 'Women know.'

'Oh, is that right? Women know,' his tone told her he didn't. Taking his hand she laid it on her stomach. 'In there,' she said. 'You made it in me,' and her hand on top of his hand they protected the baby.

'When will it come?' he asked.

'Not for a while. Late in the summer.'

'I was coming to tell you. I'm going to stay with you, Mairead. For always. It was going to be soon. But I can't go back now, how can I leave you like this? Are you sure you didn't hurt it when you fell?'

'No, no, everything's fine.' Her hand tightened over his.

'Anyway, I'm staying with you. My place is here. I'll build us a new house, bigger than this one. Ishbel and Peggy'll have to find themselves someone who can look after my mother. I don't expect Flora'll go back home.'

She lay inside his arms, listening to his heart and his voice telling her all that he was going to do for them. He said that his place was with her and this was her place, beside him. It was where she should be. She'd heal in time. Nature, that had always been there for her, would help her. She wasn't afraid. There was nothing to be afraid of. He was strong enough for both of them. And when he needed her, she'd be strong enough then. The animals didn't complain; who heard the flowers saying anything when people walked over them, or the broken-down trees? No more then would she. And she'd mend just as well. Without complaining. Mairead believed that people had much to learn from the natural world, there was little they could tell it. The earth and what grew and lived on it was the teacher. And wise ones gained knowledge from it. No need to say anything to him about what really happened at the burn. No need to say anything ever.

Chapter Thirty-One

There was nothing to eat in the Minister's house, or rather, nothing that he wanted to eat. He banged about in cupboards looking for something which would take the edge off his hunger.

Winter was always hard on his stomach. When the people had nothing, he had less. Very little extra came his way, nothing left out for him. Resigned, he went back to the mouldy cheese and stale bread and poured himself a beaker of ale. These he took with him to the chair by the dead fire. Lighting it hadn't lasted long. He had no idea where she was, the house had been empty when he returned.

Arabella was shut in the bedroom with the wooden trunk jammed against the door. It had been some time since she had looked at the dress, she was almost afraid to now. She was afraid of what it might do to her, of the way it made her feel. She hadn't been ready before, she needed time to get used to how it felt to be wearing it. She needed to try to understand what her reaction would be.

That day she had risen early, before dawn, grateful that her husband had spent the previous night from home. She hadn't slept. Through the night she had tossed and turned. In her agitation she might have spoken to him if he'd been there.

The dress was spread out on the bed. For the past hour she had been sitting beside it, looking at it, touching it, remembering the way things used to be. There was pain in her remembering. Her fingers played with the lace around its neck, took pleasure in how rich it felt in her hands. They moved across its bodice, caressed its fine smoothness as a lover might. Her hands grew bolder. They traced the small waist, gathered in the beauty of its full skirt. It was a sun dress, golden, glowing, life-giving.

Catherine knew. Catherine knew. Catherine had always known. Out of her harsh no-nonsense manner Catherine above everybody knew how to reach the broken part of her even where she, Arabella, did not. No words of sympathy from Catherine, well, not many, but a cool assessment and understanding of how things were for her. Catherine, whom she had always envied. Catherine with James, Catherine without troubles. And Catherine making the dangerous journey to see her and bringing her salvation. Catherine spare of visible emotion. 'I brought you a dress.' Oh, gracious, gracious Catherine. Arabella wept, but the sharp pain had gone from her tears.

Her crying done she stood up and undid her old dress, tearing it from her in her hurry before kicking it into a corner of the room.

She lifted the sun dress from the bed and held it against her, felt it against her. She put it on. First one arm, then the other. How dirty and roughened her hands were, how brown her skin where it showed. Her hands like brown gloves against white arms.

She was too dirty for a dress like this, her cracked finger nails snagged on the silk. She smoothed it down over her chest, over her waist. She looked down, surprised to see her bosom.

Now that it was on she wanted to wear it forever. She wanted to be this Arabella again, not the peasant woman Arabella. She lifted her head, tilted her chin. 'I am Arabella Hutcheon,' she told herself. Then she spoke the words aloud. She heard her words. Now, all she had to do was to believe them.

She didn't know how long she had been in the room, getting used to herself again. It was growing very cold. Taking the sun dress off, she laid it back on the bed, before fetching her old dress and putting it back on. Standing in the corner of the room she waited to see if the old Arabella would return with the old frock. She stood waiting for her with her head held high. She wasn't afraid of her coming, if she came she was ready to meet her.

But the old Arabella didn't come back with the old dress. In the old brown frock stood Arabella Hutcheon. She said it again, out loud, 'I am Arabella Hutcheon,' stressing the 'am'.

The Minister was still in his chair. A shower of breadcrumbs peppered the front of his coat, the ale jug had joined the beaker and the plate on the floor beside his feet.

'It's a cold day,' he said to her when she walked into the room. He said no more, he didn't ask where she'd been, how she was. She wouldn't have answered if he did and so, long ago, he had stopped asking. There was nothing to mark out this day as any different. Why should it be? He saw no change in her, she looked as she looked.

'I think we should have some heat in this house,' she said to him. 'It is very cold. Don't you think it's very cold?'

The Minister swallowed and struggled to find his voice. His eyes looked as if they would pop from their sockets. When he had imagined her speaking to him, the words he had imagined her saying had certainly nothing to do with anything that might make his life any easier.

'What did you say?' his spittle had gone down the wrong way. He coughed and spluttered through his words.

'It's cold. In this house. We must have heat. This place is so . . . so lacking, don't you think?'

The Minister looked at her, really looked at her this time. She was sitting perched on the edge of the sofa; she always sat on the edge of things. Certainly there was no difference in her that he could see. He looked at her eyes. He looked twice. Yes. Something had changed. Something was living in them. But he didn't know how to talk to her. He had forgotten.

'But you don't want fires, you have never wanted fires,' he said.

'Well, I do now,' she told him. 'And a woman. Two. Look at me. Look at the state I'm in,' and she lifted up the skirt of the brown frock, waving it at him to show him.

He swallowed again. Surely this couldn't be Arabella he was hearing. Where had her timidity gone? She sounded like her sister Catherine. He'd need time to get used to this. He shifted in his chair.

'I am Arabella Hutcheon,' she told him.

'Kennedy, my dear, Arabella Kennedy,' he spoke the way he had spoken to her when he was her tutor. Whatever he had here required delicate handling. He'd have to tread with the utmost care.

'Look at my hands,' she leapt from the sofa and pushed them under his nose. 'Just look at them.'

'Well – uhm – you wouldn't have help, my dear,' he said. 'But,' when he saw she was ready to say more, 'you shall have, you shall have. As much as you need.'

'Tomorrow. When I have thought about it. Tomorrow I shall light the fires. You shall have a fire.'

'Yes,' he said. 'Yes. That will be good. And tomorrow I shall find you some servants. Two, did you say? Only two?'

'Two will do to begin with. There's so much here that requires to be done. I really need an outside woman, don't you think?' and she darted from the room.

He was flabbergasted. Where did it come from? He'd grown used to to the bleak pattern of life. It had become normal for him to go without, to live without, without warmth even in his home. He had sought out the warmth which life needs, if it is to survive as any kind of life, in other places. His life had quite easily assumed a shape, a pattern, he, as a younger man, could never have envisaged. And now that pattern, however harsh, however awful, was about to be changed. And not by him, not by him, but by the one who had forced it on him in the first place. What now would she expect, what now would she demand from him? He would be a blind man again, skating over very thin ice.

She wanted servant women. That wouldn't be a problem,

there were some girls left in the village. That girl Peggy Ross. She had sisters. There were still two living.

She was going to light fires. He never thought he'd live to see this day. He rose from his chair and went to get another jug of ale.

Chapter Thirty-Two

When James Graham, Marquis of Montrose, came marching down through Caithness on his way from the Orkneys on the twelfth of April 1650, to do battle for his king and his country, his glory days were already behind him. By then Scotland had seen the best and the worst of the once great tactician. She had suffered for his victories and had suffered for his defeats.

With him he had twelve hundred men, a mixed bag of Orkney peasants, and Danish and Dutch mercenaries. Gathering next to no support on his drive down from the far North, the Highland lairds having more to occupy them than Montrose and his grand schemes, he marched on until he came to the high ground above Strath, where he set up camp among the pine trees.

In the small town of Tain, about thirty miles to the South, General Strachan was kept well informed of Montrose's moves. With his stronger army he marched north, prepared to make a stand for his God and the National Covenant. They camped out in a small wood, about nine miles to the south of Montrose's men.

The winter was nearly over and Strath was still there. In less than three weeks it would be Beltane again, that time of great hope. It would be time soon for them to be gathering up the old wood for the fires, time for them to be gearing themselves up. The earth was living and themselves were living on it. The song had crept back into their mouths, a soft song maybe, but a good song for all that. Even the children heard it. The bagpiper had found a new tune during the long winter months and flies were starting to bother the cows again. The Wise One could be left in peace to think again instead of being bothered by people coming crying to him. Busy Strath, filled with busy hopeful people.

Mairead had walked far, following the river all the way to where it changed into the burn, looking for new plants. What had happened with the men wouldn't stop her. That would be foolish. The burn was part of herself. Would she then turn from that part? The baby was still inside her and the sickness was gone. She felt strong again. Her eyes had a shine on them like the sun on the river. Her belly was growing heavy. In the late summer when she was up at her summer house the baby would come. She sang one of her mother's songs to the baby as she bent to pick the young plants.

Arabella was also growing, but in a different way. As the days turned, more and more of the old Arabella resurfaced. Peggy Ross and a thin raggedy girl did all the work now, both appearing out of the mist first thing every morning and disappearing into it in the late evenings. There was a fire in the Minister's house every day. It didn't keep the Minister at home but the sight of it pleased Arabella.

Arabella had wandered farther than she had meant to. It was such a special day. After winter's long drag it seemed to her a brighter day than there had ever been, created just for her. Shielding her eyes with her hand she looked about her. Upstream a woman was bending, picking at something which was growing there. Arabella moved on. Her sun dress floated above a sea of purple primroses. She stopped to pick some. She'd take some into the house no matter what Gilbert said.

The Minister was at a loss. He still didn't know what to make of Arabella. She was easier to live with, that was true. A degree less cold toward him, a degree less indifferent. Her appearance had begun to matter to her once more. In that respect she was like the Arabella she used to be. Her voice, when speaking to him, had lost its cold edge. It may not have conveyed warmth, but neither did it freeze him where he stood. Also she gave the impression of listening to what he said to her. But he didn't know what to say to her. Long ago he had stopped saying anything to her other than passing remarks on the weather or the state of the crops. Why the change now? Why? The Minister didn't know. And he could hardly ask her. But enough. It was a good day, the birds were singing in the trees and Mary would be waiting.

Daniel was running to Mairead. On such a day even the burn was singing her name. He took it in one stride, the water spurting from his boots on to the grass as he walked. He'd left Ishbel and his mother. Two silent women in a silent house. Peggy was mostly up at the Minister's and Flora had her new life. He was glad to be out of it. He'd set his foot to another path. There would be no turning from it. What was past was past. His kilt swayed about him with each step, his shoulders were back, he carried his head high, his wrong leg was the equal of his good one. In fact both his legs felt like they had lengthened, making him as tall as the highest hills. Inside he was laughing out loud. He wanted to throw it out for the whole world to catch. He called a greeting to the Old Wife coming his way. The Old Wife smiled her surprise. Someone was happy any way. He was going to Mairead, he was going to stay with her always. Forever. No more partings, no more tears. There was the house to build before the baby came. And he'd get started on a good herd of cattle, a really good herd, good quality, like the cows he saw with the drovers. Himself and Mairead, himself and Mairead.

MacIver was more than browned-off with the Tullochs. What a crew, he couldn't rely on one of them. One day they were there, all fired up and ready for timber, the next who knew where they were. What a shower. It was beyond any of them to turn up two days in a row. MacIver was headed for Strath to find them. The problem with the Tullochs was that not one of them could pass an alehouse, any alehouse. That was their problem. They'd be lying in one now, drunk to the neck.

Why couldn't the Tullochs keep away from drink and stick to women? Damn, now he came to think of it, he could do with a good drink himself with all that thinking about alehouses. But here was the Minister haring up the glen. That old rickety-legs didn't half cover some distance. Better give him a wide berth. The Minister drifted past. Thank God the man never said anything about his church's roof. He looked like a man on a mission to somewhere. MacIver came level with two of the Minister's holy men. He bored right through them, throwing them from the path and leaving behind him two of the dourest, sourest faces he'd seen yet. The rear end of his worst horse looked a sight better. Off to put the fear of blackest hell in to some poor frail unsuspecting soul. Ach, to hell with it. The day was good anyway. Too good for him not to be in the wood. Damn every Tulloch that was ever in it anyway. If they couldn't do the work he'd soon get a squad that could. There was plenty men looking for work and wanting to work.

Arabella stood and watched the woman bending. What must it be to be one such as her, she wondered. She couldn't see the woman's face, she wasn't close enough, but didn't they all look alike? They certainly all dressed alike in their drab brown heavy cloth. Men and women dressed in the same material, and their children. Watching the woman, it shocked Arabella to think that that was what she had been in danger of becoming. She could see that this one's belly was filled with the fruit of some union. Arabella's face soured in distaste. The woman could scarcely bend to pick whatever it was she was picking at. Everything female in this place was always the same, always filled with young. Dropping them everywhere. Anywhere. They had no sooner given birth than another was taking root inside them. You'd think these women would grow tired of burying them if not of having them.

A soft breeze jumped up and played with her hair, blowing loose strands of it across her face making them catch in her mouth. Still, it was a fine day. It would be nice to talk to someone.

*　　*　　*

Mairead watched the golden woman from out of the corner of her eye. She was standing just upstream from her. If a strong wind came it would blow the golden woman away. She looked so frail, so light. She wasn't doing anything, standing so still, looking, looking at her. Mairead resisted the urge to stand up and look back at the woman. She was a little afraid of her. Why would a woman, dressed like this one, be watching her? The sun shone on her hair, making the woman's hair like gold. Her frock was gold. The sun seemed dull beside her. Mairead was afraid that she might come over to her. What would she do if the woman spoke? Even when there was nothing left to gather she stayed where she was, still bending, her fingers picking at the ground. Maybe if she waited long enough the golden woman would go away. Mairead wished she would. She was needing to straighten her back.

They continued to look at each other without openly seeming to do so. Locked up inside their own worlds, both were repelled, as well as attracted, by each other. Afraid too. Their fears may have had different roots but the end was the same. Fear, the name of every negative emotion. Arabella felt threatened by this woman who was of this place, who looked as though she might have grown from the earth she trawled. A woman from her place, in her place. And Mairead? Mairead could still be a little afraid, and especially of someone like this. Like herself, a woman, but so far superior, so far removed from herself.

They knew how to fear superiority in Strath, and they knew how to cling to it. It shaped their lives, yet they had no part of it.

Chapter Thirty-Three

'Are you seeing what I'm seeing?' said the voice that didn't come from Strath.

'Huh, huh, huh,' panted his fat friend, his tongue flapping from his mouth. Both men were wearing what was left of some army's uniform. They carried no visible weapons and their clothes and their hands and faces were splattered with dried blood.

'My friend,' smiled the tallest of the two, who was missing teeth from the side of his top gum, 'this could be a good day for us after all.'

The fat friend sniggered. Toothless sniggered. They sniggered into one another's faces.

The woman from the stream had gone, to pick different kinds of plants Arabella supposed. Arabella was crouching in the sun, picking primroses. The sun felt warm on her head and on her back. Engrossed in her picking she did not hear them coming up behind her until they were a few feet from her. She turned her head. Was it the woman coming to speak to her? When she saw who it was she tried to run before she was standing and her foot caught in the hem of her dress, sending her sprawling on the ground, the primroses spilling around her. They stood watching her, grinning silently at her terror. Still silent, they allowed her to stand up. By now one had gone to stand in front of her while the other covered her back. Her eyes huge in her face, she looked at the one in front of her. He was a dirty man, and torn. A twisted smile simpered on his lips. Heavy lids had come down to shade his eyes. She knew by looking at him that he did not belong to this place.

He was waiting for her to move. Whirling from his leering face she came up against the other one. He was standing so close to her she could smell the sharp stench of the blood on him. She could see the sweat shining at the base of his throat, could almost feel his breath as it pumped out of his mouth. His mouth dominated his face. Hanging open as it was she could see his yellow teeth and his tongue playing about inside it. She watched as one of his hands came up, felt his fingers touching her hair. Her eyes swivelled to follow the hand. She saw her hair, white against its caked brown. She could smell his hand and she put her own hand up to her mouth. She stood with her hand cupping her mouth, watching his hand playing with her hair.

Two hands from behind spun her round. Another hand played the hair game. 'Nice,' that thin-lipped mouth breathed. Now her eyes were on the other hand and the muscles which controlled them were beginning to ache. She watched the hand drop from her hair, saw it moving to her throat. She arched her neck to try to get away from it. The hand stayed on her throat, its thumb with the blackened thumbnail making circles on her skin. 'Nice,' the mouth said again while his other hand, holding a knife, moved towards her. That hand and its knife cut the sun dress away from her and tossed it to the fat friend. The fat friend put it on his head and pranced about, like a ghost man dancing.

Lying below him, she blocked out the world. She knew how to do that. She blocked out how he felt on top of her, what it felt like to be her, lying under him. She blocked out all his smells, what his hair tasted like in her mouth. Her ears blocked out the words that spewed from him as he fed on her. He took his time but she didn't say a word.

'Hurry,' the prancing fool said. He was ready. Watching that would make anyone ready. When he got her she was as if dead. But that didn't stop him. Because he had to wait he enjoyed her many times. 'There's something all the way from Nederland,' he said before he rolled off her, his slavers running over her throat and between her breasts.

*   *   *

Mairead felt she had walked far enough that day, she'd gathered plenty. There were always other days for gathering more. As she walked along, her plants bundled in her apron, her step was light and she felt as if the sun was shining deep inside her. She was singing as she walked. The song stumbled when she rounded the bend in the burn. Two men were hurting the golden woman, like those two had hurt her, one was rolling on top of her and the other one was shouting words that Mairead didn't know. She turned and raced as fast as she could for the bushes, throwing herself behind them, forgetting in her fear about the baby inside her. Sitting on the ground, her heart battering her, her breath choking her, she rocked backwards and forward. What she felt now was not fear, not the kind of fear she had previously known, fear of the Minister, fear of the Church Session, fear even of Daniel's mother. Or like when she thought Daniel wouldn't want to stay with her. What she felt here was a different kind of fear. This was utter terror. Her arms went round her belly. They'd hurt the baby. Not again, please. Daniel, where was Daniel? She couldn't breathe any more. Daniel, come.

She stayed hidden in the whin bushes for what seemed to her a very long time before another kind of clothes found her. She knew this clothes, they were wearing the uniform of Strath's men. She crawled from her refuge for them, and stumbled towards them. But these familiar clothes, if not face, had rough hands. She was a mad woman, she gouged his eyes, ripped handfuls from his hair, tore his face with her fingernails. But he was drunk on something. His mouth only laughed at her. 'Is this one of your women, Munro?' he was shouting to one of the men coming up behind, as he held her away from him with one straightened arm. 'This is what I like,' he told her and above the sound of her rage she could hear him laughing.

'We've no time for that.' The man who had come behind was shouting too. 'If they get back across the Kyle we may as well forget it.'

Mairead's attacker pushed her away from him and followed his leader. She crawled back to the safety of the bushes.

Through their dead branches she could see men. They were everywhere. They came pouring out of the trees in their torn clothing, yelling and waving their arms. All of them seemed to have blood on them somewhere. Strath's men seemed to be the ones doing the chasing. Men running and men screaming, the pursuers and the pursued seemingly no different. It was hard to tell who was doing the screaming or what their screams said. Broken men and torn men, mad men, crying men and frightened men, all intent on killing one another. She could see Donald Munro, the Donald Munro that Daniel said he was going to kill for what he did to Peggy. She didn't recognise anyone else. She didn't know the young Strath men. In the uniform of his regiment Donald Munro didn't look any bigger, nor prettier. But she had never been more grateful to see anyone. 'Oh, thank you,' her lips mouthed. 'Thank you, thank you, thank you.'

The song also died in Daniel when he saw what he was walking into. Where in God's name did they come from? There were thousands of them. What was going on? Diving behind a rock, he flattened himself against it. His clothes were the colour of the earth and had worked for him before, he prayed they would work for him this time. His knife was in his hand, he was ready for anyone. As far as he could tell, those running away seemed to be carrying no large weapons. Some still carried their knives and that was all. One or two of those chasing waved swords, otherwise it was only knives he could see among them. A lot of men had nothing.

It was the end of the road for Montrose. A man who hadn't learned to listen, he had walked straight into Strachan's much stronger army. His mercenaries, the bulk of his force, were useless. Two minutes into the fight and they were heading for the hills, for the river, for any place that would hide them. Of course they flattened Strath first. The houses which had seen so much were as nothing against mad men on maddened horses. They rode clean through them. One rode over the Wise One. He fell to the ground with a cracked head, his long pale hair trampled in blood and clay.

In the time it would take a woman to bake the family's bread or a man to tell a good story, it was all over. Between them the two armies wrecked everything. People, houses, the washing-pot sitting outside on the fire. Clean clothes that had been spread to dry on the whin bushes were dragged through the mud by the horses. What they couldn't destroy they set on fire. A dog, blinded by someone's clothes, was making mud circles in the road outside what was left standing of the Old Wife's house. A small naked boy was standing beside the dog, crying for the dog to stop. A horse came hurtling towards the boy and the dog. The horse missed the dog but caught the boy. The horse's rider, drunk to the teeth on all kinds of evil, laughed as he went riding past. The mother grabbed her child to her breast, her mouth an empty cave, the scream which came from it too late to save her child.

The women couldn't fight like men, but they could fight in their own way. Ishbel and her mother lifted stones and threw them at whoever came near, not looking to see whether it was their own men or the enemy. Some people tore turf from their houses and threw that but it didn't seem to make any difference, seeming only to increase their madness. And when they thought that everything was finished, when they thought they would be left alone, there were those who came circling back to have another go.

The men left in the village could do nothing, there was no strength left in them to fight with and they hadn't a good weapon among them. Their young men were out there, in the middle of it, more intent on upping their score than in looking to their fathers. Some died and some cried and there were those who couldn't even do that. And there was more than Arabella pumped full of foreign seed that day.

From his hiding place behind the rock Daniel watched the black smoke rising above Strath. Should he try to go back or should he keep going? His mother and sisters were in Strath but Mairead was waiting for him. His mother had no one but they would have had to come past Mairead's. She'd be out there someplace, gathering. She could be anywhere. He could make no sense of what he was seeing. He'd seen battles before, plenty of that. The Mackays weren't shy when it came to killings and burnings and neither were themselves. Strath had suffered enough from both in the past. But not like this. This was what came in nightmares. This was nothing to do with them, they who had been trying their hardest to live.

His thinking only took seconds. There really was no question, he knew what he was going to do.

Crawling clear of the rock he stood up straight, blocking the path of the oncoming men. The sun was high in the sky, polishing his hair, turning it to burnished copper. He put his shoulders back, and straightened his back, his tall body hanging long and open. Unafraid. His knife was in his hand and his two legs felt strong. He knew the one in front. 'Munro,' he called to him as he came nearer, and took a step to meet him. 'What's going on here?'

Donald Munro and his small band came stamping on, closing the gap before Munro answered. 'Well,' he shouted, 'If it isn't the cripple. Shouldn't you be back there?' He was jerking his thumb in the direction of the village. 'With the rest of the women.'

'Have you seen Mairead Beaton anywhere? I'm looking for her.' All the fine uniforms ever made wouldn't change Donald Munro from what he was, nor all the blue bonnets.

'Do you think that's all fighting men have to do, look out for your women? Look for her yourself.' Munro's head was level with Daniel's chest as he stood in front of him.

Daniel looked down at Donald Munro. There was no blood on him and he was carrying a good-looking gun, long-barrelled, and he was wearing new boots. His men were also armed with guns and knives. 'Just let me come on you, fine boy, on your own,' he was thinking. 'One day, there'll be you and there'll be me,' he thought.

'What's happening?' he asked him again.

'We've kicked the Montrose to Hell, that's all.' Munro's narrow chest was puffed out and he spoke as if he'd managed the affair single-handed. 'Who knows where the bonnie boy is? He ran. Took to the hills. Headed up Assynt way.' Munro turned his head and shouted at the men at his back to move forward. 'But he's going nowhere,' his head swung back. 'And neither are you, Rossach.'

Daniel couldn't lift his knife hand, he couldn't lift his knife hand. His hand opened and his knife clattered to the ground. His eyes were on Munro's eyes, he saw the change in them the instant the knife went into his guts. Donald Munro had killed him. With what was left of his strength he put his hands on top of Munro's hands and helped him to pull the knife out.

Donald Munro wiped the blade of his knife on the hem of Daniel's kilt. 'You had your chance,' he said to him as he lay on the ground. 'You thought you were so bloody good.' He stuck the knife into his belt and hurried away to catch the others.

Mairead knew he was dead before she found him. She felt the knife going into him, she felt it in her own stomach. The hurting was so bad she thought she was going to die. Her flesh felt the knife sinking into his flesh, tearing at his flesh, as they pulled it out. And her scream tore the whole of the Strath.

She shut her eyes and lay on the ground beside him and covered both of them with his plaid. 'Oh Daniel, my beautiful man. A brother's knife has taken you from me. I will grow old in that house up on the hill. And thinking of your beauty will be the only thing to keep me warm.'

She lay beside him all of that day and through the night. And on the morning she walked into Strath.

Strath was no more. A black ruin of smoking broken houses and broken people. Even the hills wept for Strath that day. The place was filled with the smell of burning animal flesh. Black rain drizzled through the smoke. And the hills in their sorrow wore shrouds.

Mairead looked for Daniel's mother but at first she couldn't find her among the drifting people. Some were wearing blankets over their heads but most stood in their wet clothes.

She walked up to the women, seeing their faces. No one spoke to her, not one word. She kept looking.

She found Ishbel in one of the broken houses, spooning water into an old man. 'Daniel is dead,' she told her.

The spoon tipped sideways spilling the water onto the old man's beard. He opened and closed his mouth on nothing.

'Where is your mother?' Mairead asked.

'She's in the houses.'

'Then I will find her. Daniel's dead.'

His mother was going from a house when Mairead came across her. 'Daniel's dead,' she told her.

'Yes,' his mother said, on an intake of breath, making the word sound like yeth. She had no blanket for the rain. Her thick short body shook in its wet clothes.

'Someone will have to take him home.'

'Yes.'

'Who can go?'

'Leave that to me,' Mairead watched his mother's hand coming up to touch her arm. 'Come,' she said. 'We'll find someone.'

'Daniel's lying dead,' his mother told some men. 'You'll have to go for him.'

'Where's he at?' one of the men asked. All of their eyes were ringed in red and their hands and faces blackened from working among soot.

She told the man where to go. 'We're sorry for you mistress in your trouble,' the man's voice was quiet in its dignity.

'And myself is sorry for you, for all of you, in yours,' she said back to them.

'We'll go for him,' the man said.

'You'll take good care of him,' she touched the man's arm as she had touched Mairead's. 'He's my beautiful son.'

'Please,' Mairead was afraid to speak. It wasn't her place. 'Go easy when you carry him. Please.' She wanted to go with them, but it wasn't her place.

A crowd had gathered. 'You people,' his mother said. 'All of you. There's no good in you standing about waiting for someone to help you. There's work to be done. There's graves needing to be dug, for your own as well as for mine. And houses to be built again. We have to do the best we can. Come now.'

Not one of them moved as much as an eyelash. Blackened beaten faces hung hypnotised. Beyond them the Old Wife, still going her rounds.

'Are we going to stand in the rain or are we going to do something?' the strong-armed woman from the grain incident, her own sister, came over to stand beside Daniel's mother, her eyes raking those in front of her. As one a murmuring came from them. 'Right,' the woman shouted. 'You men, you can start digging graves. You'll need to find out how many dead's in it first. Let them go to their rest.'

Mairead and his mother left them and they went in to what was left of his mother's house to wait for Daniel coming back. The two women took care of him themselves. They worked as one, no words going between them. Only the low moaning of a lament coming from the two of them.

They buried him themselves beside Anna and his father and the little ones. A big chunk of the graveyard was filled up that day.

Afterwards they did what they could with the houses. Everyone helped, even the youngest. Mairead stayed to work with Ishbel and his mother. The young ones carted cut turf. They hurried through their work. In a few days they had to be ready to go up the hill to welcome in the new light.

In the folding day the Minister stood looking at what was left standing of his church. There wasn't much. At least it solved the problem of the roof.

A boy found Montrose's flag among the battle's dead. Another one found his cloak. The boys wrapped themselves in the flag and the cloak and marched like fighting men. Someone carried a sword into the village. The people looked at the sword and went on building their houses.